LAS VEGAS BATeria
"What plays in Vegas, stays in Vegas!"
By: CC Darling
(Based on Actual Events)

Chapter 1 – Anderson Memorial Hospital– Las Vegas

Dr. David Cooper yawned, took a sip of his coffee and looked at his watch. It was 6:00 a.m. As a doctor of 14 years he was hired five years ago as the Director of the Preliminary Disease Immunities Department, Anderson Memorial Hospital in Las Vegas. He was use to his crazy working hours and shifts. He walked down the long corridor to the research lab. His small office in the back was like a closet, but that was of no bother to him. The décor was amateur.

His team of four, Sylvia, Don, Greg and Emily worked the normal hours of 9:00 – 6:00 p.m. Don and Greg, both Disease Biologists in their early 30s, worked well together. They both were on a six-month Cancer project.

His entire work was to concentrate on cell count and a cure for Cancer and Preventive Disease Control. He took his white long coat jacket off the back of the door and put it on. One requirement the hospital had was everyone was to wear the white coat. He sat down and looked at the stack of research files in front of him. The ones that were red were the ones that needed immediate attention. There were three. The files indicated that several tests had been done on the patient but no final analysis was determined on their illness. And their illness was getting worse not better.

Dr. Cooper picked up the first file and studied the charts. Patient, Rose Davis, 27 years old, came into the hospital two days ago with a rash on her abdomen and back. Patient said the rash appeared about one week on her abdomen and then spread to her back. Patient said she took allergy medicine and used an ointment to see it would go away, but it didn't. Patient started to have flu-like symptoms and had a 104 fever, fatigued, with some chest pains. Patient checked in on July 1st.

 Several biopsies were taken on the rash and no clear origin of the rash was determined.   There was no sign of it being contagious. The patient indicated that her best friend, Rebecca O'Connors who spends a lot of time with her does not have the rash. No other individual she had spent time with had the rash to date.

He finished reading the last folder and looked at his watch again. It was 8:45 a.m. He got up and walked down the long corridor to the elevators. Emily ahead walking down the corridor gave him a quick waive. As he passed, he smiled and said "Good morning Emily". Emily smiled back. "Good morning Dr. Cooper." He pushed the elevator button to the 8th floor, which was the Isolated Patient Floor.

There were 10 rooms on one side and 10 rooms on the other side. There were five patients rooming on the floor. He stopped by the front desk. Wanda the receptionist said

2

"Good morning." Dr. Cooper smiled at Wanda and said, "Good morning Wanda." "Do you have Ms. Rose Davis's chart?"

"Yes, here it is." She handed him Rose Davis's chart. He stood there and flipped through the chart, looking at all the notes. The attending doctor on the front of the chart said Dr. Emily Martina. A well-known Disease Physician from Chicago Presbyterian Hospital in Illinois. He asked Wanda if Dr. Emily Martina was in her office. Wanda shook her head. "No, she is out today returning tomorrow." Dr. Cooper smiled and handed her the file chart and said,

"Okay Wanda, thank you." "Have a good day."

Dr. Cooper walked down the hallway to room 810. He lightly knocked on the door and walked in towards Rose's bed. Rose was sitting up on her bed watching TV. "Hi Rose, my name is Dr. Cooper and I am the Director of the Preliminary Disease Immunities Department." He looked into her green eyes and shook her hand. "I am here because I wanted to talk to you a little bit about the rash you have." "May I?" "Sure," Rose said as he lifted her blue hospital gown.

As he lifted her gown he saw the rash on her abdomen. He noticed it was red, raised with a white layer of crust on the top of it. "Can you roll over, Rose, a little please?" Rose winced and rolled over. He also noticed it has spread to her back. He quickly put her gown down and patted her on the knee and said. "We are going to take good care of you, Rose." "I just need to ask you a few questions." "Do you by chance know where you got this rash?" Rose looked

down at her hands in her lap. She knew that, if she were
going to get well, she would have to be truthful. She kept
her head down and twirled her thumbs. Never looking up,
Rose said, "my friend, Rebecca," and I work as *"Ladies of
the Night."*

She looked up at Dr. Cooper. He didn't flinch. He had
seen it all in Las Vegas. Nothing surprised him.

 "How long have you been doing this kind of work?"

"For about two years now," Rose said.

"And where were you last when you noticed the rash?"

Rose looked down and began speaking in a low voice.
"We were at *The Diamond Club Casino*. Rebecca
O'Conner, my best friend and I met two customers on the
sixth floor about two weeks ago. Dr. Cooper moved on
with the next question.

"And when did you notice the rash spreading?" Rose
looked up at Dr. Cooper and then lowered her eyes again.

"It started out as a small rash on the front of my stomach
and then it grew from there. "I tried ointments and allergy
medicines but it wouldn't go away. When it started to
spread, I got a fever of 104 my chest was hurting off and
on, and it still didn't go away, I knew then it was time to go
to the hospital."

4

"Rose, I know these questions will be hard for you, but I need you to answer them truthfully." Rose looked at Dr. Cooper squarely in the eyes. "Sure."

Dr. Cooper continued. "We did not find any alcohol or drugs in your system. You are not HIV positive." Rose looked at him closely with a scared look on her face, she sighed a sigh of relief.

"Do you currently take drugs or drink alcohol?" Rose watched Doctor Cooper taking notes as he circled the hospital bed.

"I casually experimented with some drugs when I was younger. No. I don't do drugs. I am a social drinker." Doctor Cooper continued writing, looking at Rose occasionally to see if she was giving him any hint of any lie.

"Did you see any of your clients with the same type of rash?"

"No," Rose said.

"Have you had any venereal diseases in the past?"

"No." I was checked three months ago and to date I don't have any venereal diseases." Dr. Cooper looked into Rose's eyes to see if she was really telling the truth. He didn't see anything unusual.

"Okay, Rose, I want to keep you here a few more days for observation. Your fever is still high and you have a mild cough. Do you have any chest pains?" Rose looked into Dr. Coopers eyes, studying him again. She looked out the window.

"I have a slight chest pain maybe every now and then."

Dr. Cooper looked at her and moved towards her holding his stethoscope. Rose looked up at him with his instrument in hand. He looked down at her.

 "I'm going to check your heart rate." He put the earpieces in his ears and placed the small disk-shaped resonator against her bare chest and turned his head to the left and listened. He stepped back and looked at her again. "I'll have our lab technicians run a lung test (MRI) so we can make sure there are no fluids in your lungs and your heart is beating correctly."

Dr. Cooper smiled down at Rose and patted the bed railing. "I have a good team Rose that will help you." My staff will check in on you periodically. We need to find an antidote for your rash. Most likely it will be an antifungal antidote." He walked to the doorway and turned. "We need to keep you here for at least a few more days." Dr. Cooper smiled again at Rose. "Rest now Rose. I'll be back to visit you in a day or two."

Rose put her arm on her forehead and closed her eyes. All she could think of was how she was going to pay the medical bills. A tear fell. She lay in the hospital bed her mind wondering. Her mind racing, she wanted to do was get up and run. She had the time now to think. And to feel feelings she did not want to feel. Shame was one of them.

How long was she going to be living this reckless life? She wasn't getting any younger. She was 26 and her body was taking its toll. She wondered how she could get out. Both her parents were estranged from her. She had no brothers or sisters she could call or lean on. Her Grandma, Nana Meme whom she grew up had passed away a year ago. She only had her best friend Rebecca.

Rose dreamed of getting out of the small corn town of New Albin, Iowa, a community of 642. Rebecca, her best friend, who grew up with her had saved up everything they had, a whooping total of $1,500 and drove to Las Vegas two years ago.

After six months of living in a cheap motel and barely getting by, she realized now what a joke that was. Las Vegas was not about getting rich. It was about trying to have a good time and spending as much money as you had in your pocket and credit cards. She thought back when it all started when she and Rebecca first came to Las Vegas. At first it was fun. Staying in a cheap motel, the Lazy View Inn, going to the various casinos and playing different games was exciting.

But after a while their luck was slowly running out. They were down to their last dime. Sitting at the bar at the "Fun Time" casino, Rose put a $10 bill in the Keno game at the bar. The bar tender came over to her and asked her what she wanted to drink. She told him a *Keno Kick Butt Winner Tall*. The bartender laughed. She laughed too and said. "No, I think I'll take a seven-up tall. Thank you." She knew she didn't have tip money and that would be rude.

A guy came to the bar, sat down next to her and put money in the Keno game. "I'll take a tall *Creepy Crawler*," he said. Rose turned and looked at him. He was handsome, she thought. She casually looked at his wedding ring finger and there was no ring and no white lines. He turned and looked at her. "You here on vacation?" he asked. She looked into his eyes timidly. She was sure he saw her pain.

"No, I'm here with my friend Rebecca. We came to Vegas two years ago to see if we can make a go of it." He hit the draw button on the machine and looked at her again.

"And how is that working out for you and your friend?"

Rose pushed the Bet button and then the Draw button on the game again. She won $10. She looked at him and pondered with an answer. Should she tell him the truth or should she make up a lie? She thought for a moment. She would never see him again. What did it matter?

"It's not working out very well, she said. "We are actually down to our last dime." Their eyes locked. His eyes turned to sadness. He looked down at his game.

"Well, I am sorry to hear that."

"My name is Grant Benedict by the way. I actually am a Casino Financial Advisor for some of the hotels in Las Vegas. Rose looked up from her game, "Oh you live here?" Rose asked. Oh great, I hope I don't run into this guy again, Rose thought. Right now, she didn't care. She blurted out, "My name is Rose, Rose Davis." She looked up at him.

"Nice to meet you, Mr. Benedict." Rose reached her hand out while looking into his crystal blue eyes. "Do you live in Las Vegas?"

"No, I don't actually live here," he said. "But I am here for long periods of time."

He immediately liked her. She was pretty with long red hair and green eyes. He knew she was down on her luck. He knew she needed someone to lean on. He didn't even know her. But he felt compelled to help her. But then again, he knew it wasn't the wisest decision. He took the last gulp of his drink and put his glass down. "Well Rose, it was nice meeting you."

He got up and smiled at her. "I hope you and your friend find some kind of work that will help you here in Las Vegas." Then out of impulse, he took out a business card and handed it to her. "Here is my business card and cell phone number. If things don't change for you and your friend, please give me a call." Rose stared at her drink and then stared at the Keno machine. She was down to her last $5 now. She knew things wouldn't change. She smiled up at him.

"Thank you, Mr. Benedict." As he walked away, he turned and smiled.

"Call me Grant."

Rose picked up the side hospital phone near her bed and dialed Rebecca's cell phone. "Hi Rose, tell me it's you,"

9

Rebecca said. "I have been sick worrying about you for the past two days."

"I am sorry, Rebecca. I am actually at the Anderson Memorial Hospital in Las Vegas. I got a rash on my stomach and the back area and got the flu and a high fever of 104." "I have been out of it for the past two days." The doctors are trying to figure out what it is and give me something to get rid of it so I can go home". Rebecca sighed a sigh of relief. She was so worried about her friend.

Rebecca sat down on the bed in the sleazy motel room. She looked around the cheap motel room and tears came to her eyes. Both her and Rose had been living there for almost two years and the future wasn't looking any better. The tears began to fall. "Oh my God, Rose!" Rebecca started to talk fast and then faster. "Do you want me to bring you anything?" "When will you be getting out?" "Can I come see you?" Rose could hear the panic in Rebecca's voice. She whispered into the phone, "No, Rebecca I'm good." You just need to keep working so we can pay the monthly motel rent and buy some food." Rebecca sat with her head hanging down low. Feeling defeated she said, "Yes, I know Rose." Say you'll get better Rose. And please call me when they release you and I will come pick you up." "Okay Rebecca, I'll talk to you soon. Bye now." Rebecca didn't want to tell Rose she had lost her job at the *Rinky Dink Diner* as a part-time waitress. It would be too much of a burden for Rose to handle.

Dr. Cooper walked the long hallway to his office. He yawned and looked at his watch. It was 11:00 a.m. He had sent an email out to his staff for a 1:00 p.m. meeting in his office. He walked into his office. Yep, they were all there. He sighed and then sat down. "How's my geniuses today? I have a new first priority project for my little peeps today." They all stared at him and laughed. Emily looked at him, "Little peeps?"

Dr. Cooper leaned back in his chair. "We need to find a Fungus antidote for a rash. One of our patients is Rose Davis who came into the hospital two days ago with a high fever, slight chest pains and a rash on her abdomen and back with white crusty top. I want to make sure there is a Fungus antidote that works before Rose Davis leaves the hospital." Let's start with the biopsy tests we took this morning. The biopsy sample is in Case A refrigerator with Rose Davis's name on it. I have also requested an MRI to make sure her lungs and heart are clear."

"Dan and Greg, I know you are working another project now, so Emily and Sylvia can you please work on this one for me?   It will be your first priority until we find the remedy. Run as many tests as you can from the blood samples. I have advised Rose Davis to stay a few more days.

"The medical record is in the computer database under Research, Rose Davis for your review. Please read it carefully. "Okay, anybody have any questions?" "No, no, no, no." "I guess all of us "Little Peeps" are all on board," Emily said." Dr. Cooper laughed. "Okay, I think we are all good. "Oh, if you need to visit the patient, Rose Davis is on the 8th floor, room 810. Please let me know as soon as you know what you each have evaluated. Emily and Sylvia looked at each other as they walked out the door. Sylvia smiled at Emily, "This is going to be an interesting day."

Chapter 2 – Rebecca wants to be a Dancer - "Job Hunting"

 Rebecca hung up the phone with Rose went to her bedroom and flopped on her back on the bed. She started crying. All she could think about was how two years ago she thought her best friend Rose had big dreams. They would both make it big in Las Vegas and everything would be great.

Two years later and they were *"Ladies of the Night"* hustling to pay the hotel, keep their car running and eat. Rebecca knew she had to do something. Something different and something now! She thought of her friend Rose and this mysterious rash. She got up and grabbed her purse and car keys and walked across the street to the entertainment ticket booth. The small *Free Entertainment* booklet was staring at her. Grabbing it, she stuffed it in her purse. Across the street, the *Give Me a Break Coffee Bar* was calling her name. The waiter came over and she ordered a glass of water.

Rebecca started quickly flipping through the Entertainment book again. In the back of the book were ads for dancers. She took dance in middle school and high school. She thought she was pretty good. She kept on reading. *Dancers Wanted. Must have dancing talent and be able to work at night from 5:00 p.m. to 1: 00 a.m. Monday through Saturday. Pay is $200 per night, six nights a week paid weekly. Please call 333-333-xxxx.*

Rebecca got her cell phone out and called the number. "Yes, my name is Rebecca O'Connors." "Are you still hiring dancers for your show?" The receptionist said, "Yes, yes we are." "Are you at least 5' 8"?" "Yes", Rebecca said. Once again the receptionist asked, "Are you 120 lbs. or less?" "Yes, Rebecca said. "Can you come in tomorrow at 5:00 p.m.?" "Sure. Sure." "What was your name again?" "Rebecca O'Connors." I'll be there." "Okay the receptionist said, bring an ID. Also be ready to do a dance for seven minutes and look presentable, some make-up, but not caked. The address is 2622 Santa Moon Street, 3rd floor. *The Gala Casino*. We need dancers for a nightly jubilee performance. Rebecca hung up her phone, got up and screamed, yes! "Yes! Yes!" This was it!" she thought.

She walked back to the hotel all the way thinking what she would wear. She wanted to make a big impression. She knew that Rose and she needed this. They needed a real break. She closed her eyes for a second, crossed her fingers and prayed. "Please God if you give me this job, I promise I will try to be good. I will work very hard. I promise. She opened her eyes and skipped and ran all the way back to the hotel.

Chapter 3 – Welcome to *The Diamond Club Casino* - "Los Angeles BFFs Arrive"

Bethany walked to her closet and pulled some dresses out and threw them on the bed. "Yes Dad, I know". Yes, Dad, I will drive carefully. "I am so proud of you Bethany," her Dad said. "You did so well on all your finals and your 21st birthday bash was a hit! I thought you and your friends deserved a break before you started your final year of college. I am so very proud of you".

"Yes, Dad, thank you and I love you too".

 "Okay, have fun and drive carefully!"

"Okay Dad, I will. "Hey, Dad listen one more thing. I am going to tell the girls to only use their cell phones in case of emergency. I don't want to spend this girlfriend time in Las Vegas texting on cell phones only. With that being said, Dad I not trying to be ugly with you, but I want you to know that I will not be calling you on my cell phone and please don't call me." Her Dad started laughing.

"Okay, deal! Love you Dad, need to go!" She hung up and screamed.

"Yes! Yes! Yes!" Bethany grabbed her pillow and a blanket and yelled out, Megan you ready?" She and Megan had been friends since grade school and were now roommates.

Bethany was outgoing and was accepted to the University California San Diego studying medicine. Megan, her roommate of one year had decided she wanted to be a Fashion Designer. Always carrying her sketch pad around with her head bent down wearing black framed reading glasses with a charcoal pencil in her hand. Stephanie, her other BFF, lived with her parents still but was vivacious, daring at times the colorful one. The anything goes girl! But in a good sense, she was a good student and was studying to become a Sports Physical Therapist. Bethany called Stephanie. "Hey Stephanie, Megan and I are on our way. Las Vegas, here we come!" Stephanie, yelled back, "Yes, *The Diamond Club Casino*, 4th of July, here we come!" "Woohoo!"

Stephanie threw her suitcases in. Bethany put her sunglasses back on and hit the road. "Okay girls, the only thing I ask is when we get there "no cell phones! "You can take pictures, but no texting or answering cell phones. So please call your parents and friends now and tell them the rule so they don't freak out when you don't answer your phone 20 times when they call just to see how we are doing. Only in case of emergency! "Got it!" Megan and Stephanie looked at her and then they both looked at each other and winked.

"Got it!"

Six hours later driving and of girl gabbing and 3 bathroom breaks, Bethany spun the BMW around *The Diamond Club Casino* parking lot garage structure. Around, and around, and around the parking garage. "I guess it's going to be the 6th floor girls". The six-hour ride had gone by pretty quickly considering there were three best friends, chit-chatting all the way.

"Wow! I can't believe we are here! I am ready to have fun and party!" Stephanie yelled. "Hey let's go check out the pool when we get checked into the room."

"I am all in on that one!" Megan said, grabbing her luggage out of the trunk. "Okay, let's roll!"

Bethany glanced around the front lobby receptionist area.

"May I help you"?

Yes, my name is Bethany Bishop and we are checking in. "Okay Ms. Bishop, may I have your Driver's License ID and Player's card please the receptionist said." Bethany reached in her purse and handed the receptionist her Driver's License.

"We don't have a player's card yet."

"Okay Ms. Bishop you and your friends can get one at the Rewards Center down the aisle and to the left.

"My Dad, Professor Peter Bishop, made the reservation for us."

"Yes, I see it here in the system." Wow! I actually one of your dad's classes at the University of Berkley" the receptionist said.

"Really?" Bethany said.

"Yes, I was studying medicine and his class was a requirement. It was Preliminary Disease Immunity Prevention.

"Yes, that's my dad", Stephanie said, proudly. Professor Peter Bishop, my dad, the medicine man."

"Oh, I see you in the system. Your Dad has booked a suite for you and has also booked you girls into the *"Relax While You Can Spa"* on the 3rd Floor on the 4th of July at 1:00 p.m." Megan shifted her purse.

"Oh, the spa, how nice of your dad!" Bethany looked at Megan and smiled.

 "That's my dad. I think it's his way of keeping me out of trouble for a few hours." She laughed.

"He has a good heart."

Can you please add Megan Delaney and Stephanie Windsor to the room please with two keys each room card packet. Just in case we lose one." Megan pushed up her glasses and rolled her eyes.

"Sure Ms. Bishop." The receptionist handed them each a room packet with two keys. The receptionist smiled, looking at each one. "Have a good time, Girls!"

The room was a double suite on the 10th floor; the "Cabana Suite." Bethany slid her card in the slot door that turned green. She flung open the door! Stephanie walked past her, "Wow, Bethany!" She threw her duffle bag on one of the queen beds. "Your Dad is the best!" There were two rooms with double beds and a living room and two bathrooms.

 "I've got dibs on the second room," Stephanie said as she pulled the curtains back. It was a huge window 10 feet high and 25 feet wide facing the strip. She turned and laughed. "We are going to have the best time!" Piling their clothes into the drawers, Megan and Bethany grabbed their bathing suits and headed for the bathroom to change. Stephanie went to the other room and flopped on the bed. "Wow!" She yelled out.

 "I can't believe we are really finally here!" She got up and started unpacking. She had the whole second room to herself!   She grabbed her swim suit and headed toward the bathroom.

The pool was packed. Stephanie, Megan and Bethany all looked around for some available chairs. "Look Bethany said; "over there" she pointed. The music was playing and everyone was round the pool or in the pool with a tall drink in a bong looking plastic colored container.

 "Cool," Megan said. "Let's go". They threw their orange towels on the chairs. Stephanie saw the drink girl and motioned her over. "What are we going to have?" Bethany smiled, "a cool, large, margarita with salt sounds great." Megan, said, "I'll have the same." Stephanie pointed to a tall long drink with a long straw in it that someone in the pool was drinking.. "What is that drink over there?"

The waitress turned to look. "Oh! That is a famous 1 1/2 ft. *Yard* drink. It is a frozen drink, such as frozen margarita, frozen strawberry, banana or mango with vodka. Stephanie and Bethany looked at each other. Stephanie took off her sunglasses for a minute. "Yum! I think I will have one of those in strawberry!" Bethany joined in, "Me too!"

The waitress smiled, wrote down the drink order. "Okay then, I'll be back in a few minutes." Stephanie was scouting out the pool scene. There was a small band, two guys, one girl singing and playing music.

"Wow, look at this place"! Stephanie tipped her sunglasses on her nose while scouting out the pool area. She smiled. "I see some fun in the pool". "Don't look, but the guy in the blue swim trunks, dark shades, in the far west corner with his buddies looks really fine."

The drink girl came and then it was Stephanie who made the first move to the pool, cascading down the steps, sliding down in the opposite corner staring at her future prize. Bethany joined her. Both of them, sipping their *Yard* drinks from a long straw.

Megan sat back in her chair, positioned her black framed glasses and got her sketch book out and charcoal pencil. The pool was packed from side to side with all kinds of young and older bodies in bathing suits, some holding long colored plastic bong drinks. She saw some cool bathing suits and thought she'd give it a drawing whirl.

Stephanie made her move closer to the boys in the pool. Closer, to her main target who was wearing the blue bathing-suit in the west corner with his co-conspirators.

Bethany slid in beside her gliding along the pool edge, inch by inch, keeping pace with Stephanie. She told herself, the drink was making the moves. Stephanie flashed one the guys a "let's get to know each other" smile. He smiled back and nodded his head as if to say "What's up pretty girl?" Stephanie made the mouth move, "Hey, how are you guys doing?" Johnny shifted his sun glasses and cocked his head to the left looking at her as if to say, "Hey pretty girl, come on over?" Stephanie took a long sip of her drink. "Hi my name is Stephanie and this is Bethany. "We are staying here at *The Diamond Club Casino* until July 5th Sunday.

Stephanie pointed to Megan sitting in the blue striped lounge chair, "Our other friend Megan is over there lounging." He looked at Stephanie from behind his dark sunglasses. He liked what he saw. "My name is Johnny and this is Brett and Darren. We flew in from Boston, Massachusetts last night." Johnny took off his glasses so he could see her in full view "Where are you from?"

Stephanie took off her glasses so she could see Johnny in full view. She liked what she saw. "We drove from Los Angeles, California, Stephanie said. The music was somewhat loud.

Stephanie relaxed against the side of the pool, trying to keep her cool. All the while thinking "these guys are hot!" "So? What are you guys doing tonight? Bethany asked, making small talk but eyeing Johnny. Brett looked at Stephanie. Then he smiled, looked at Bethany and spoke up. "We plan on going to the club here tonight, *The Canyon Roller Club*." "Sounds like fun!" Bethany took her sun glasses off and smiled at Brett.

The pool waitress walked near and Bret yelled up to her; "hey do you have a pen?" The waitress handed him a pen and he gave it to Bethany. "Write down your cell phone number on my on the top of my hand here." Bethany took the pen and wrote down her cell phone number. She handed back the pen to the waitress. "Thank you." She smiled at Brett.

"Maybe we will see you guys there?" Bret took his shades off and winked at Bethany.

"Sounds like a plan!"

Stephanie took another sip of her drink and said loudly over the music, "So we'll see you maybe tonight at the club? It's called *The Canyon Roller Club*, right? Bethany looked at Brett and winked. "Okay guys we are going, the music is getting too loud to talk." Bethany tugged at Stephanie's arm. Stephanie and Bethany tip-toed in the pool, through the crowd, back to Megan who was sketching away.

Megan took off her sunglasses. Bethany and Stephanie got out of the pool soaking wet with grins flashing. Megan put her sketch pad away, "What's up girls? Have a good time in the pool?" She lifted one eyebrow up and said, "Hey, I got your numbers." Stephanie chimed.

 "Funny you say that Megan, because I did give it to one of the guys, Brett," Bethany said. "I think we have three hot Boston, Massachusetts dates tonight." They casually invited us to go to the club here, *The Canyon Roller* here at *The Diamond Club Casino*." Bethany put her towel on her chair.

 "Woo-wee, I definitely want to the wear my new dress and shoes." Megan took her reading glasses off and very cool-like put on her sunglasses and turned her focus on the three guys at the end of the pool. Studying them closely, she said.

"Sound like we already have dates for tonight!"

Chapter 4 – "Family Vacation Get-Away"

Jenny called Frank at the office. "Hey Frank, it's Jenny. "Real quick because I know you're a busy man. I just opened the mail and guess what? We just got 2 nights and 3 days at *The Diamond Casino* for 4th of July weekend in Las Vegas. I am so excited, I already booked us, but I can cancel if you say no." Jenny closed her eyes and held her breath and continued.

"They have three pools, a lazy river pool with donut tubes you can float around in and two other pools for swimming. They have $300 in food comps and $100 in playing comps. The kids Sofia and Laker will have a great time! What do you think?"

Frank sighed and thought for a minute. He needed a break from his fast-paced advertising job. He had two weeks' vacation left. It had been ages since they had taken a real vacation. It was summer time for the kids and would be a good time to get away from the hum-drum of every day in and out parallels of life. He paced back and forth in his office, contemplating.

"Okay, let's do it!"

Sofia and Laker, ears burning, came running into the kitchen all excited, jumping up and down.
"Mom? Mom? Are we really going to Las Vegas?"

"Shhh, shhh, okay honey. "Las Vegas here we come!" Jenny hung up the phone. "Yes! Yes! We are going to Vegas!" Sofia started screaming, running down the hallway yelling "Las Vegas here we come! I am going to pack!" Laker took off down the hall way yelling, "Me too!" Jenny looked on-line and found 4 airline tickets on United from North Carolina to Las Vegas.

Jenny sat down kind of relieved. She had already called *The Diamond Casino* and booked the three nights, Friday, Saturday and Sunday. July 3, 4, 5th. She thought that the kids would love the fireworks. Frank and her had been married 15 years and had been through some rough times. She knew every marriage went through its ups and downs. Trust was a big issue with hers' and Franks relationship.

After six years of marriage, Frank had had a brief affair with one of his associates at work. Jenny, of course, went through the denial and disbelief as most women do. They both ended up in therapy for a year. It had been a struggle for them. Jenny thought this would be a good break for both of them to get their marriage back on track.

Jenny, Frank, Sofia and Laker walked down the airline ramp and went to the baggage claim area. Laker was acting up, grabbing Sofa's cell phone. Sofia was pushing him aside. The kids had gotten their cell phones at Xmas. Jenny had reminded Frank that it was a necessary evil; the kids needed them for more or less safety reasons to call for back-up emergency reasons. The baggage claim area was packed. The flight was the usual get on plane, read, sleep, get off plane ride, go to baggage area and pick up baggage. Frank watched the luggage ramp go round and round, grabbing the suitcases as they swirled around. Jenny had told Sofia and Laker one piece of luggage each and one carry-on bag. Of course, they whined. But they knew when mom said "one she meant one."

They all headed towards the outside doors. The heat hit them all at once. "Ooh, it's going to be a hot one here!" Frank blurted out. Jenny took her shades out, put them on and smiled. "Yes, but it's going to be a good hot one". She saw a shuttle pulling up and pointed to it. "Come on", let's catch that shuttle over there to the casino." They all walked across the parking lot to the shuttle with their luggage.

Kinsey looked out the shuttle window and said "Welcome to Las Vegas!" Where are you folks headed? Frank said *"The Diamond Club Casino* on the strip". "Climb in, Kinsey said." "What brings you folks here? Kinsey asked. Frank climbed in the front, "Oh we are here just for a fun family get-away."

"Nice!" Kinsey said. *"The Diamond Club Casino* is a fun casino. You'll have a good time!" Kinsey looked in his rearview mirror at Laker and Sofia. "They even have three swimming pools you can choose from. Sofia put her ear phone plugs on and plugged them into her cell phone, playing her music. Sofia nudged Laker, rolled her eyes, then looked out the window. Kinsey smiled thinking of his kids when they were that age.   The typical brother, sister relationship.

Jenny handed the receptionist her driver's license and added Frank, Sofia and Laker to the room. The receptionist gave them each a key packet and they walked towards the elevator and pushed 12th floor button. Frank slid his card in the key holder and they all walked into the double room suite.

"Not bad," Frank said as he threw his bag on the bed. He opened his bag and grabbed his binoculars and looked down at the pool area. "Wow! They have three pools. There is one directly below us, a pool with yellow donuts riding around and two other ones." He wanted to check out the pools and the action. Jenny rolled her eyes thinking, "I brought the 16 year-old with the binoculars" and went in to the bathroom to change into her bathing suit. They had a suite with two rooms with two queen size beds in one room and one king-size bed with two bathrooms.

Jenny went to the bathroom. She looked around observing the two sinks, big shower and tub with jets in it. "This is great!" Laker and Sofia roamed around and found their room. "Hey mom, let's go eat" Laker said. "I am hungry". Jenny emerged from the bathroom.

"Okay, let's put our bathing suits on and go check out the food places and then go to the pool." Frank smiled and took out his swim trunks, head towards the bathroom, slapping Jenny on the behind as he passed her.

The food court was packed and noisy. Frank, Jenny, Laker and Sofia headed for the pizza. Frank ordered a large pepperoni pizza with 4 drinks. They found a table and sat watching the people interact. "Mom," Sofia said, I'm ready for the pool after we eat." "Okay," Jenny said. Laker took a big bite of pizza and looked at Sofia, "Me too! Jenny smiled and looked at Sofia and Laker and observed how they were growing so fast. Laker would be 11 and Sofia 9. They were good kids. Both of them were different in their own ways, somewhat competitive with each other. Laker a soccer player. Music seemed to be Sofia's love. The violin was her musical instrument of choice.

Jenny watched Laker and Sofia splashing in pool. There were three pools. She picked the pool with no music and less bodies splashing around and sat down. Ten minutes later, she glanced at Frank with his dark shades. She could hear his heavy breathing with small echoing snores. She loved him. She wanted her marriage to work. After his affair with an associate in his office named Charlene, she fell into a long depression. She didn't know what she wanted to do. She believed in "true love, trust and friendship, children, and long years of marriage. Pretty much she wanted the fabricated rose-colored fairytale life without the bullshit drama that goes with it. The kids were important. She wanted them to have their father.

She glanced across the pool. Lots of people here she thought. She saw a guy who caught her eye. He had his arms stretched out on the side corner of the pool in the shallow end near the stairs. He was smiling. His teeth were perfectly white. Dark shades, white/black skunk looking hair. Distinguished looking. His skin was a gleaming rose color. Jenny guessed at his nationality. He looked American Indian, but then again, he looked Hawaiian or maybe Spanish. Say 49ish. He wore bright florescent orange bathing trunks with black lightning bolts.

Jenny was in dreamland. "Handsome" she thought. The more she looked at him, the more she thought, somewhat of a look-a-like, "Ponch" on Chips, the Los Angeles Cop. That handsome Erik Estrada look. She wanted to stay in dreamland. Some older ladies started to swarm around him.

Handsome, she thought, and also charming. The ladies in the pool seemed to dance around him.

Jenny watched him, casually smiling at him. He seemed to smile back at her. In her mind, Jenny knew she was kind of flirting. She liked the eye contact. The stare he gave her behind his dark sunglasses. His beautiful white perfect teeth flashing against his rose -colored skin, smiling at her. It was the back-and-forth flirtation and teasing that was interesting. She liked playing with the rose colored, Golden fish. It gave her a sense of youth and beauty. Something she wanted to experience again and needed to gravitate to once again in her life.

From the corner of her eye, she saw a beautiful somewhat older girl walking towards the stairs. She had a gold one-piece bathing suit on. Her hair was long golden blond and her nails were French tipped, long. Jenny guessed she was 42ish, pretty. Her body fit, toned, but not perfect. She walked towards the stairs. She dipped her foot in the water and then she stepped down and casually tip-toed over to the rose colored, Golden fish. She made her way past the women still swarming around him. She snaked her way closer to his rose colored, Golden fish and wrapped her arms around his neck. Jenny watched in fascination. She took a long sip and her drink and thought "holy crap!" The golden blonde goddess put her lips on his. He kissed her back and smiled.

There seemed to be a whole lot of splashing of some sorts and all the women miraculously disappeared. Jenny laughed inside. Mr. Handsome splashed his hand in the water towards her and smiled. Jenny put one hand on the side of her sunglasses, tipped them forward so he could see her eyes and smiled back at him thinking, "One rose colored, Golden good-looking fish" already caught.

Jenny laid back in the lounge chair thinking. "I like that dream**." "What plays in Vegas, stays in Vegas!"** Frank woke up and rolled over on his lounge chair and looked at Jenny.   He sat up watching Sofia and Laker splashing in the pool, having a good time. He was happy they were all together. Jack yawned and stretched his arms in the air. Sweat was running down his back. In the back of his mind, he heard "shower" calling his name.

Frank jumped in the shower. He planned on taking Jenny to the Handel Steak House. It was going to be a date night out for just the two of them. The receptionist at the front desk had asked when they checked in at the front desk if he wanted to make a reservation at the Handle Steak House and he thought "why not?" They had $300 in food monies. Laker and Sofia were big enough to watch a movie in the room and snack on snacks.   He toweled off and yelled out to Jenny. "Hey Jenny, I made reservations for you and me at the Handel Steak House for tonight 7:00 p.m. Jenny who was glancing out the window watching the street strip people walking, turned from around from the window and smiled. "Sounds great!" she said. She turned to the closet and looked at her black silk short, backless dress and glanced down at the rhinestone black heels.

She pulled the curtains back farther and watched the people on the strip walking on one side and then the other. Laker and Sofia can stay in tonight and watch movies in the other room. They're big enough and they have their phones incase anything goes crazy. Laker and Sofia's ears perked up. They looked at each other, smiled and did the thumbs up. Jenny began giving them the "stay-in-the-room" lecture: absolutely no venturing out anywhere, only one soda each, watch two movies and we should be back by then. That will be about four hours. No making any loud noises, there are other people in the rooms next to us. Sofia and Laker looked at each other. Laker nudged Sofia and giggled. "Sure Mom." "We have everything under control."

Frank yelled from the bathroom, "Hey honey, let's go down a little early and check out the casino." Have a cocktail or two. Maybe try our luck and play some black jack?" Jenny grabbed her make-up bag, dress, and shoes and pranced pass Frank to the bathroom to take a shower, looked him in the eyes with a smile, and pinched his ass. Frank jumped, turned and slapped her butt. Frank threw his fake finger guns up in the air and grinned, "I've got eyes for you!" he said.

Jenny stepped into the shower and let the water flow all over her. She thought about the handsome rose colored, good looking, Golden fish. She put shampoo on her hair and laughed to herself. She finished showering and stepped out of the shower, grabbing a towel. She opened the shower door, letting the steam out of the shower, while wrapping herself with the one of the hanging white towels. She put a small white towel on her head and muffled her hair. It was long, black and wavy. In the back of her mind, she thought about cutting it at one time, but knew Frank liked long hair. Over time, it never changes, all men almost always like long hair. She looked at her face and ran her hand over her olive skin. The wrinkle lines had finally started catching up with her at the age of 39. Her mom of Italian descent always had nice beautiful olive skin, the Italian heritage. Sofia had gotten her grandma's skin also, olive in color. She opened her cosmetic bag and took out her face makeup and a brush.

She wanted to look good for Frank tonight. She took her time and painted her eyes with a light gold glitter and hot red lipstick with a touch of blush on her cheeks and a shimmering bronze. She took out her gold drop earrings Frank had given her for their 7th year anniversary. She smiled as she remembered him hiding them in his sock drawer, in a pair of his socks. She had been putting his clean socks away and felt a square box of some sorts. She opened the sock drawer and found a gold wrapped box. She quickly put it back, all the while her mind racing, thinking, she hoped it was for her and not someone else. Tears rolled down her face. She quickly wiped them away and pulled out her red lipstick. She closed the door, and looked at her black, short silk backless dress hanging on the door. She put her black bra on. She held up a black thong she had worn many moons ago and looked at it. It wasn't torn yet. She slipped it on. Black butt floss.

 "Okay I can do this." She turned around in the mirror and glanced at her butt with the black thong. Yep, I still got it!"

She slipped on her little black dress. The gold earrings looked stunning with the dress. She looked hard at herself in the mirror. Her makeup, she thought, was flawless. She

sat on the toilet and put on her black rhinestone medium
high heel sandals on with a black strap around her ankle.
It had been ages since she wore high heels. She got up,
balanced herself, and threw a kiss in the mirror and smiled.
"This was her night!" she thought. **"What plays in Vegas,
stays in Vegas!"**

Jenny turned and opened the bathroom door. Frank was
sitting on the bed bending over polishing his black dress
shoes. He looked up. "Wow! You look stunning!" Jenny
slowly spun around. All she could remember to say was
from the movie Pretty Woman. You like? Dear." Frank
got up and moved towards her.

"I like very much", he said. He took her hand and pulled
Jenny close to him and kissed her lightly on her lips, trying
to avoid the bright hot red lipstick.

Jenny looked up at Frank's eyes and smiled at him. She
knew she would have to look back at all the love they had.
Her parents had flown all the way from Italy and had spent
a lot of money on her and Frank's wedding. Not that the
money mattered. She had a catholic up-bringing and her
and their Italian wedding and vows were important to her.
She also knew she would have to forgive and forget if she
wanted their relationship to last. Frank looked deep into
her eyes and said, "I love you, Jenny." He pulled her close
and held her in his arms.

Jenny closed her eyes and the memories came flooding
back of earlier years. Memories of her and Frank walking
in the water on the ocean beach, holding hands and
laughing together. Memories of her seeing Laker and Sofia
for the first time when they each were first born. The joy

of being a mother and having a real family to take care of and love. She wanted to keep those good memories deep in her heart. She wanted to believe again it was all real. It was all still good. It was not just a dream and she was going to somehow get through the pain.

Sofia and Laker came running into the room. "Wow Mom, you look beautiful!" Laker said. Sofia grinned. "Mom you look young again!" Sofia laughed. "Okay Laker, Sofia, you guys know the rules. No going out of this room! We are having dinner and then going out. We will be back when you both are asleep. There are sodas, chips, left over pizza. Please behave." Frank grabbed his black jacket and Jenny grabbed her beaded black clutch purse and threw her cell phone in. "Love you guys! Jenny said." "See you later!" Laker flipped the TV channel. Sofia positioned herself on the bed with a piece of pizza. Watching the boob tube, they yelled back, "Love you, too, Mom and Dad! Have a good time!"

Laker switched the TV channel. "Cool! Captain Nerd. Ugh!" Sofia sighed. "Really?" Sofia sighed, "At least it's not a scary one." "I am not in the mood". It was getting dark and Laker went to close the curtains. As he was closing the curtains, he saw some lights in the air. "Cool", he said and he grabbed Dad's binoculars from the night table and looked at the lights twirling in the night.

"Sofia, Sofia, come look! Come look!" Laker handed her the binoculars. "What? What?" What do you see?" Sofia said. Laker pointed his finger. "Look up there! See the twirling lights over there above that casino?" "Wow, Sofia said. It looks like there are black birds flying with colored twinkling lights. That's awesome!" Sofia said. Laker grabbed the binoculars from her. Sofia watched Laker look through the binoculars and adjust them. "Let me see! Let me see!"

Laker noticed the birds flying around with red eyes and black/orange fur with white faces. The moon is huge. Look at all those casino lights and the billboards with all the singers and comedy stars in color on them. So cool!" Laker said. He could hear symphony music playing. "Sofia, they are playing symphony music somewhere." "I can hear it, the violins." Sofia perked up,

"Really? "Now, Laker! Give me the binoculars. I want to see, now!"

Laker handed her the binoculars. "Be careful. If Dad knows we were playing with his binoculars, he'll bury us!" Sofia took the binoculars and adjusted them to her eyes. "Whoa, did you see the light coming out of that casino on the far right, shining in the sky?" Laker grabbed the binoculars from her and looked out the window. Sofia got up and ran to the other bedroom and pulled her suitcase out from under the bed. She unlocked the locks on the suitcase and opened the lid. "Okay Laker, don't tell Mom and Dad, but I had to bring it."

Sofia pulled out a brown case and opened it. It was her violin. She looked at Laker. He turned around and said, "Nooo, you didn't!" She took out her violin out of the case along with the bow and started spinning around the room slowly playing her favorite song. A slow, sweet, tempo.

Laker's eyes smiled in amazement. He stood there staring
at his sister, her long blondish brown hair flowing around
her, in her pink butterfly pajamas, all the while thinking
how talented and, beautiful she was. A master of the violin
and the songs she created. She was always playing her
violin and winning so many awards at school. He knew
she loved playing her Violin every chance she could get.
He sat on the bed watching her twirling around the room
playing her magic Violin. He thought, **"What plays in
Vegas, stays in Vegas."**

"Bang!" "Bang!" "Bang!" Laker and Sofia both jumped.
"What the"? What was that?" Sofia stopped playing and
put the violin down beside her bed. They both went and
looked out the window. It had smudge marks all over it.
Laker quickly closed the curtains. The lights in the room
started flickering. The TV went to snow with a buzzing
sound. Laker and Sofia both jumped on the bed. Laker
grabbed his phone. "Call mom, Laker!" Sofia said.

Laker dialed his mom's cell phone as he put Dad's
binoculars on the end of the table. They fell off the end
table and landed slightly under the bed. "Dang it, Laker
said.

Laker reached down and picked up the binoculars. He felt
something metal when he picked the binoculars up. A
small object fell on the bed. He put the binoculars on the
table where his dad had left them. He picked up the small
object and looked at it. It was a penny. President Lincoln
was on the front of the penny. It was a silver looking
penny. "Hurry up Laker!" call Mom. He quickly put the

silver Lincoln penny in his pocket and called Mom's cell phone.

Chapter 5 – "The Whale" - Kinsey McDonald

Kinsey Jacobs looked at his watch. It was 10:00 a.m. He closed his eyes and rubbed his head. He was looking forward to the Poker Tournament at the Diamond Club on Friday, July 3rd in the Diamond Club Casino, Premier Conference Room. It was a big event. Every year the Diamond Club sponsored 200 players. Entry fee was $10,000.00 with a grand total win amount of $1 million dollars; 2nd place winner $750,000 and 3rd place winner $500,000. Kinsey had lived in Las Vegas for 24 years.

Kinsey had just turned 59. His wife, Doreen who also was 59, had divorced him 5 years earlier after the kids had grown and left the nest. It was when he decided he wanted to leave his career as a VP Industrial Engineer at a waste management company and play poker full time. He had taken out his pension retirement funds and 401K of $700,000.00 behind Doreen's back forging her signature.

He had won two small poker tournaments for $75,000 each. His three kids, Melody, 31, Kinsey Jr. 27, and Alice, 24, of course, were all grown and had moved on to different states. Melody and Kinsey Jr., married. He thought of them often but was pretty much estranged from them after his wife of 32 years Doreen had found out about what he had done with their nest egg.

Of course, the kids took Doreen's side. Why wouldn't they? Their Dad had ruined their mother's life, all their lives together; by taking the money and gambling it away.

 (Gambling, gambling, gambling, the addiction that left a hammering headache and a hole in my pocket every day.) To take his mind off his addiction, Kinsey had taken a part-time shuttle bus driver job from the Airport to the Strip. The hours were 9:00 a.m. to 3:00 p.m. each day. He didn't mind. It paid the cheap motel bill each month and a daily breakfast at a diner across the street from the motel.

Kinsey rubbed his head again. He got up, popped two aspirin, showered, dressed, tied his shoes and walked out of the tiny cheap motel room in old down town. He walked across to *The "Fun, Fun" Casino* and headed for the $3.99 breakfast at the Dude Café inside the casino. A place he ate breakfast a lot at.

"Good morning, Dorothy." Smacking her gum, Dorothy clicked her ballpoint pen and started writing on her pad. "Good morning, Kinsey. Will it be the same old breakfast daily special with black coffee? Kinsey smiled up at Dorothy.

"Now how did you know that?" Dorothy had been working at the café for 17 years. She was getting to be an old bird. Every day she looked the same white hair up in a tall bun with a striped pink and white dress uniform with white shoes. She looked like a Candy Striper. An old Candy Striper with worn white shoes and white hair in a bun hair-do.

Kinsey walked around *The Diamond Club Casino* for a while observing the casino crowd. Same old people he saw every day. He could spot the visitors and also the Las Vegas residents. He looked at his watch. It was 7:45 p.m. He walked towards the Premier Conference Room. He flashed the girl sitting there his badge and said, "Kinsey McDonald". She handed him his name tag. He pinned it on his shirt. It was noisy and crowded.

He looked around and walked towards his table. The 10 players were already next to their chairs. Kinsey introduced himself and shook each of their hands. There was six guys and one girl. Two of them he knew, Todd Bales and Leonard Galley. Both of the players were very good players. They had won thousands of dollars taking second, third in tournaments. Kinsey started to sweat. He was nervous. He knew he was in for a challenge. He took his place at the table. The dealer arrived and explained the game. Five-hand Texas Poker. The Standing Player at the end of the game with all the chips moves on to the next table. First place winner will win $1 Million, 2nd Place $750,000 and 3rd place winner $500,000.

Kinsey looked at his watch. He had already told his boss, Jake, from *Fly by Shuttle* he was taking off for a few days for the 3rd, 4th, 5th of July. Of course, his boss scoffed. But at the end of the day, Jake let him off for the holiday anyway. It was 3:10 p.m. Friday July 3rd. The poker game started at 8:00 p.m. This was the last of his monies for a buy in of $10,000. His last shot to make it big or go back to his lonely room broke, working as a shuttle bus driver the rest of his life. He walked back to the motel and took a shower. It was a hot one. Then he walked to *The Ritz*

Casino and played a few hands of poker and had a couple of drinks to get his nerves in check.

Chapter 6– Ed Johnson – General Manager, *The Diamond Club Casino*

Ed Johnson, General Manager of the Diamond Club Casino flipped opened his pocket watch his grandfather had given to him when he was 12 years old. It was 10:00 a.m. He had a flashback of when he first came to the Diamond Club Casino. He started out at 21 dealing the black jack tables. After three years, he was promoted to Pitt Boss of all the 15 black jack tables. After seven years he saw an opportunity to become General Manager. His boss, at the time, longtime friend, Donald Sullen helped him get the promotion. After given more years of hard work, he finally proved his smarts and skills and was promoted to General Manager of *The Diamond Club Casino*.

He walked back to his office, waving to Sally, his Administrative Assistant to come into his office as he passed her desk. The phone rang as Ed was sitting down. He picked up the phone. Sally came in and sat down across from Ed. Sally Evans and her husband Ramsey Evans had moved to Las Vegas 3 years ago with their 13 year old son, Jacob Evans. Ed thought the Evans family was nice. He had met them all at an Employee Picnic at Jefferson Park.

Sally's husband Ramsey was a truck **dri**ver for 13 years, but had finally gotten a job in Las Vegas as a taxi driver. It suited him after being on the road most of the time. Ed Johnson had interviewed 7 top candidates, and Sally appeared to have the professional skills and appearance Ed was looking for and she had an ability to speak in-front of an audience which he liked.

Ed's phone started ringing. He turned to the side of his chair and positioned the phone on his ear. "Yes, Dr. Cooper". "What can I do for you?" "Oh, I see. Yes, yes, please keep me informed. I definitely need to know the outcome of your patient.   "What is her name?" "I appreciate your call." "Please feel free to call me anytime. Thank you. Have a good day." Ed hung up the phone and gave Sally a serious look.   "It seems they have a patient at Anderson Memorial Hospital who has a rash. It started on her abdomen and now it has spread to her back. Her friend and she were here at *The Diamond Club Casino* before she got the rash. Her friend doesn't have it. But she does. I really don't know how it relates to our casino. People come and go all the time from casino to casino.

Sally sat there for a moment. Then she shrugged her shoulders. "Yes, there are thousands of people in and out of the casino. I guess we'll just have to wait and see the outcome."

"Moving on Sally," Ed said. "It looks like we are on the verge of another big even, 4th of July. "The Casino is almost Sold Out." "Anything, we need to discuss?"

Sally set back in her chair. She studied her checklist and looked up at Ed. "No, everything on the list is in check. "I think we are good to go! Sally continued. Everyone is here and all assignments for the 4th of July event are in progress. Sally mentioned, "Oh the only person that is not available is the Executive Chef, Von Dorf at the Handel Steak

House. It seems his brother is very ill and he needs to take some time off. Ralph Trop the 2nd Chef will be available to step in." Sally went down her list again and filled Ed in on all the details. "We also hired 2 new Valet Personnel under Dan Largo, the Valet Supervisor.

Ed listened carefully and said, "Great Sally." "I think we are on target!" He got up from his chair and pulled his pocket watch out. It was 11:30 a.m. "I'll see you later Sally". Sally followed Ed out the door and headed toward her desk in front. "Oh", Ed yelled back as he headed towards the Casino lobby, "Sally, please make sure the maintenance crew has all landscaping trimmed and garage parking areas cleaned."

"Sure thing, Sally yelled back." Ed marched through the casino black jack area. He saw Jack, a longtime college friend of his, shuffling the cards. Ed nodded and Jack smiled back. They were childhood friends. Both grew up in Michigan and attended Michigan State University together. They liked fishing. It was basically the lake boat scene before they eventually found their way to Las Vegas and started their careers there.

Ed passed the cashier cages and waved at Kim. She waved back and smiled. Kim was counting money and turned to Penny her friend and giggled. "That Mr. Johnson is so cute". Penny eyed her friend and casually replied "Yes, he's cute alright and also is a married man. "Mind your manners, Kim. There are plenty of other Las Vegas man machines out here for your taking." Penny laughed.

"Yes, all 40 million visitors a year, some of them are Las Vegas drinking, woman chasing, gambling fools." Penny laughed, rolled her eyes and turned towards the next customer in line. "May I help you sir."

Ed knew the casino by heart now. He knew most Supervisors by their first names. He knew the layout of the casino and where all casino machines were outlined and when they were going to be moved to in other spots in the casino. He walked across the receptionist area and walked behind the receptionist desk. "Good morning, Sir" he said to one of the guests checking in.

Ed turned to Linda one of the Check-in/Check Out receptionists. "Everything good Linda?" he asked.

"Everything is great Mr. Johnson." Ed walked past her and looked at the lobby floor of the receptionist area. The floor had black and white large marble squares. He noticed some white and brown streak marks on the black squares. He glanced at the customers in line looking at each of the rollers on their luggage. He could see dark brown and white smudge marks from the luggage roller wheels. He bent down and took his handkerchief out and wiped the floor. It needed to be cleaned. He radioed Sally.

"Can you please have the cleaning crew come to the lobby entrance with a mop and strong cleaning solution and clean the floor areas? Have them clean the front rotating door areas and front walk-in areas also. Also clean all of the casino entrances. Let them know there is some kind of white or dark brown streaks of something. Have them put some orange cones out signaling 'wet floors' be careful.

41

Also, let Maria Sanchez, Supervisor of Housecleaning tell all cleaning crews to vacuum the carpets in each floor hall area and all rooms when they start cleaning."

"Okay, Mr. Johnson, no worries. I'll take care of it, Sally said.

"Also, radio Dan, Supervisor of Maintenance and have him clean all the garage parking structure areas with a strong cleaning solution and sweep. "Also have his crew clean all elevators on each parking garage structure floor. All seven, parking garage structure floors.

"Yes, Mr. Johnson." "I'll get on it right now."

"Thank you, Sally."

Chapter 7– *The Diamond Club Casino* Maintenance Crew

It was July 1st and the casino was already filling up in the parking garages. Dan Largo loved his job as Maintenance Supervisor. He had been with *The Diamond Club Casino* for three years and it was his dream job. Dan took the elevator to the 6th floor garage structure, where the golf carts were stored. He radioed Jimmy. "Hey, good morning, Jimmy". Meet me on the 6th floor" at the elevator, I'll pick you up. I need your help making sure the parking garage structures are in good shape".

"Okay boss, I'll meet you on the 6th floor elevator area; over and out." Dan put the key in the golf cart and pulled

up to the elevator. The elevator door opened and Jimmy
jumped in the golf cart.

"Good morning, Jimmy." "Ready to start?"

Jimmy started laughing. "Yep, let's do it!"   They circled
the parking structure and headed toward the 6th floor garage
floor storage closet. It had double doors with a heavy lock.
Dan grabbed his keys and opened the storage building
closet. It was 6 feet high with a thick wire rope up high
with hanging brooms and mops on it and 20' feet long.

Jimmy switched on the light and walked around. It was
packed with janitorial supplies and maintenance tools. The
light flickered. He noticed moths flying around the light.
Heard a small scuffling somewhere in the storage unit. Dan
grabbed a mop and broom, not thinking much of it,
thinking rats were probably lurking around. He got back
into the golf cart, turned to Jimmy, "You ready for today?"
Jimmy smiled,

"Yes, I am ready for a big Monster hamburger and French
fries for lunch!"

Dan started laughing. "You're too much!"

Sally called Dan on his radio. "Hi Dan, its Sally, Kirk
Noble from Party Fireworks is here. Meet him in the front
of the casino by Valet now"

"Okay, Sally, I am on my way". Dan and Jimmy rode the
golf cart down around and around and down the parking

lot. The parking garage structures were packed. It was a
full house.

Kirk shook Dan's hand. "Hi I'm Kirk Noble." Kirk let Dan
know, "I need to pick up the fireworks around 2:00 p.m. on
Saturday July 4th so the team can start setting them up on
the 7th open air garage structure floor.

"Okay, no worries, Dan said. Dan took a card out of his
front blue uniform pocket and handed it to Kirk. "Call me
at this number when you get here." Kirk smiled, okay can
do!"

Dan called Sally. "Sally, just to let you know, the 7th floor
is actually taped off with yellow caution tape at all
entrances with a "Do Not Enter" sign and several orange
cones. Put "No parking" signs. Dan parked the golf cart
and walked over to the white "Party Fireworks" logo on the
van. We will take you up to the 6th floor in the parking
structure to the storage area." "We have three garage
storage units." One is on the 2nd parking garage structure.
One is on the 4th level and the largest one on the 6th level.
You can put the fireworks on the 6th floor garage storage
unit."

Dan yelled for Jimmy. "Hey, let's grab some of that green
cleaning solution, two large buckets, brooms and mops. I
saw some white bird crap around the edges of the parking
structures and there's dark brown pellets everywhere.
There are some foot prints where people had stepped in the
bird crap and roller marks where they rolled their luggage
bags to the elevator.

44

"Not good," Dan said. "The boss says we need to have all parking garage levels in tip top shape.

Jimmy made his way to the back of the storage unit. As he reached down to grab the handle of the cleaning solution, he saw little red eyes staring at him. Not one but about 10 pairs of red eyes staring at him. He grabbed the green cleaning solution and jumped back, quickly hustling out of the storage unit. He put the large green plastic jug of cleaning solution and jumped into the golf cart, shaking and breathing hard.

Dan laughed, "What's up? "You look like you saw a ghost in there?"

"Jimmy wiped his sweaty forehead." "Damn you! That lighting in that storage place is so low, you can't see anything! You know there are rats in that place." Dan spun the golf cart around, laughing all the way.

Dan walked to parking garage elevator and hit the 6th floor garage structure button. It was 79 degrees already at 8:00 a.m. 4th of July. "It's going to be a hot one!" He opened the storage room and heard some noise in the back. It sounded like birds chirping or singing. He radioed Jimmy.

"Hey Jimmy, remember that guy Kirk Noble from Party fireworks will be here around 2:00 p.m." Jimmy finished cleaning up the stinky bird shit and swept the small dark brown pellets (like dark brown grains of rice) that were all over the edges of the parking garage structure. Dam birds, shitting all over the place. He looked up and saw bird crap on the edges of the parking structures, in every corner of the structures.

Dan and Jimmy worked all day on the parking structure, cleaning all the bird crap and dark brown pellets everywhere. Every one of the parking garages had the same bird crap and small dark brown pellets near the open-air ledges. He stepped on his step stool and took the mop handle and lifted up towards the ledge of the parking garage structure. A bird flew out from under. He ducked and started flinging the mop around as if he was going to beat the bird to death. "What a shitty mess he thought!" Jimmy's thoughts raced to the storage room on the 6th garage structure floor. Visions of rats started appearing in his mind along with snakes sliding out of the firework containers. He felt the sweat on his forehead and hands. He had made sure to wear his tan heavy steel toe construction tie up boots today.

The Monster Burger restaurant was never looking so good when they arrived. "I am starving, Dan said." Jimmy sat down and said, "hey just wanted to let you know that Sally called and wants us to meet Party Fireworks, Jim Noble at 2:00 p.m. and take him to the 6th floor garage storage unit to store the fireworks until 4:00 p.m. On the 4th of July when him and his crew will pick them up and set them up before 9:00 p.m. 4th of July. The fireworks show begins then.   I told Sally there was plenty of room.

Jimmy took a big bite of his Monster burger, "Cool!"

Dan and Jimmy in the golf cart followed Kirk Noble and his crew of five from Party Fireworks in his white van circle around the parking garage to the 6th floor garage structure parking. Dan and Jimmy got out of the golf cart and walk towards the storage unit and ask if they needed help. Dan opened the storage unit, turned on the light and started walking toward the back of the garage storage unit. "Damn light!" He heard some rustling in the back area. Kirk Noble opened the back of his van and started carrying the containers. Dan and Jimmy helped him. There were 20 containers.

Jimmy noticed the light flickering again. "Dam light!" Jimmy turned to Kirk who was following him to the back of the storage unit.

 "Sorry, you would think we had extra light bulbs hanging around. These are special light bulbs. But we do have some on order." Kirk Noble followed Dan and then grabbed a container.

"Thanks! But I think we got this."

Dan handed Kirk the lock and key. "Here's the lock for key for the door. Just put it back on when you're done and give it to Valet before you leave." Dan drove Jimmy to an extra parked golf cart and told him to start cleaning on level two. Dan climbed back in his golf cart and headed for level 3 parking structure.

Dan looked at his watch. It was already 5:00 p.m. Dan radioed Jimmy. "Hey Jimmy let's go get a quick bite to eat. Ed Johnson wants us to work late and make sure the garage areas and elevators are cleaned before we leave.

"Okay, boss. I'm on level two. There are more white streaks on the second level floor." Meet you on level six parking garage near the storage area in 15 minutes." I need to get some more green cleaning solution.

Jimmy unlocked the storage unit. "Damn, Jimmy thought." "What is up with the lighting in the storage units?" He saw the green cleaning jug in the corner. As he grabbed it, something flew over his head. "What the hell?" Then several things started flying over his head and out the door. Crazy freaking birds he thought. He quickly got out of the storage place and loaded the green cleaning solution in the golf cart.

Dan came flying around the parking level, looked at Jimmy and yelled, "Hungry?"

"Starving, Jimmy said." "Let's go get a Foot-long chili dog and hot fries at "Speedy's Foot-long Hot Dogs." "Sounds good to me!" Jimmy said.

Kirk Noble's crew arrived at 4:30 on 4th of July and started grabbing the firework containers that were locked on the 6th floor garage storage unit and drove to the 7th garage open air structure. They started unloading the fireworks for set up. Kirk Noble looked up at the sky. He saw some gray clouds to the east. He smiled to himself, thinking not tonight "Rain Cloud."   His Native American Indian Heritage starting showing. This time, he didn't want to do the American Indian "rain dance tonight."

**Chapter 8 – Jack Levin –*The Diamond Club Casino*
Black Jack Dealer**

Jack Levin shuffled the deck of cards again and put them in
the machine to be shuffled. There were three people
already at his table. Minimum $25 bet. He had gotten up
at 6:00 a.m. and went to the fitness gym, *Work and Play
Fitness Center.* His car was on the brink of collapse. It
had been running ragged for the past three days. He had a
hard time getting it to start. Every day for the past three
days he had cursed it all the way to work, "Piece of shit
car". He had worked three years at *The Diamond Club
Casino.* Even though the money he made at the casino
began to look somewhat good, Jack knew he was getting
older and this was not exactly where he wanted to be in his
career with his college education. Nor did he know if he
wanted to stay in Las Vegas at all.

His college sweetheart, Sarah Kramer, had pretty much
dumped him when he decided to pursue his dreams in Las
Vegas with his friend Ed Johnson. He loved her, but he
also knew she was a Michigan girl and would always be a
Michigan girl. Since coming to Las Vegas he had only met
one other girl, Denise who was a waitress on the floor at
The Diamond Club Casino. She was nice, but not quite the
girl he wanted to marry. Jack dealt the deck and stood
back. He watched the players, hit, or stay and and/or paid
them out one-by-one or gathered their chips.

Jack folded his last deck of cards, clocked out and headed
for the parking structure. He got in the elevator and hit the
6th floor button. The elevator jumped and above he heard
some fluttering noise. Brushed it off and got in his car.

Turned the key and it wouldn't start. "Damn it!" He hit the steering wheel. "What the hell". He climbed out of his car and called Denise. "Hey, Denise, it's Jack." "My car won't start". I'm going to take a taxi home and I'll meet you at *The Canyon Roller Club* at 9:00 p.m. tonight okay.

"Wow that sucks, Jack!" "I'll see you there!"

Jack knew that Denise worked until 8:00 p.m. every night. He called AAA and had given them the details to pick up the car and take it to Henderson's Garage off the strip. He called Henderson's and talked with Mac, the owner. "It's a 2000 Chrysler Sebring convertible with 168,000 miles. Betsy starts when she wants to start. "Damn Bitch". "What?" Mac said. Jack put his hand to his throbbing head, "Oh nothing." Mac told Jack he would take care of it and call him when he knew what was going on. "Ok, thanks Mac."

Jack hailed a taxi and jumped in the back seat of the taxi. From the back seat, he eyed the taxi cab driver. "2123 Sole Avenue" he told the taxicab driver. Jack noticed his name badge hanging in the rearview mirror, "Ramsey". Jack rolled down the window. He took a sip of his energy drink, and started gagging. The energy drink sprayed all over the taxi cab drivers back seat. Jack's nostrils filled with a strong order that illuminated in the air. It smelled like "shit" mixed with something that was dead. He couldn't bear the shitty, gagging smell. He stuck his head out the window trying to suck in the air, holding his breath; seeing how long he could hold his breath and then trying to breathe fresh air again. All the time thinking, he hoped he made it home without throwing up. He opened the door, jumped out of the taxi before he saw his house and tossed the driver a $20 bill. Holding his breath, he tried not to puke. He threw his energy drink that now smelled like "shit and skunk into the trash before he climbed the stairs to his apartment. He opened the front door. Tokyo his grey stripped, green eyed cat came running, "meowing," rubbing his fury body between Jack's legs.

Jack picked Tokyo up and started petting him. "Hungry, Tokyo?" "Okay, buddy let's get you some chow." Jack immediately went to the bathroom and turned on the shower and gagged at the memory of the smell that still illuminated him. The shit he smelled in the taxi cab and something other really bad smelling that stayed in his mind and nose and mouth. He closed his eyes and let the cool water take over and clean his body as if he needed to be germ free of any speck of shit he felt stuck to his body. After 20 minutes, he reached for the water knob to turn it off and saw on his hand a red rash, the size of a quarter. His mind started racing. He thought of the gym where he worked out; the equipment he worked on. Then he thought of the deck of cards he shuffled and the red velvet table his hands touched every day.

He got out of the shower and took out some ointment from the medicine cabinet. Annoying, he thought. This crap better go away in a day or two. Dammit", I'm going to lose players and tips, he thought. His mind was racing. He went to the hallway closet and pulled out his black golf glove. He put it on. He smiled. "Perfect!"

Jack poured himself a Jack Daniels and coke. His cell phone rang. "Hey mom, how are you?"

"I am fine Jack, how are you?"

"Okay, I guess, Jack said.

"What do you mean you guess?" His mom asked.

"Well, my car died today and it was towed to Henderson Garage. I took a taxi from hell home today. "That's another god-awful story." "But other than that, I am going to grab something quick to eat and then I am going to meet Denise tonight at *The Canyon Roller club* at *The Diamond Club Casino* around 9:00ish. It had been a crazy week. It's the 3rd of July, Friday night and it's crazy. The casino is packed and they plan on having fireworks tomorrow night. They are launching them off the 7th garage parking floor. Never done that before, should be interesting. I talked with Ed. You know my friend from college, Ed Johnson. "The General Manager of *The Diamond Club Casino.*

"Yes, Jack of course I know Ed, his mom said. Jack continued talking. "He said it was going to be a big 4th of July night."

They start the fireworks at 9:00 p.m. Denise and I plan on seeing that. "That's great Jack." I am glad you are doing well. Do you think Ed will promote you to Pitt Boss soon? Yes, mom, Ed and I talked about that too. He said possibly in a couple months.

"Okay Son, you have a great time tonight with Denise." Be careful, love you."

Jack shifted the phone to his other hand, "How's Dad, Mom?" "He's sleeping on the couch now, but I am sure he would say "hello" if he were awake."

Jack laughed to himself.

His Mom whispered on the phone, "I'll call you again soon"

Jack picked up his watch from the night stand, "Okay mom, I love you." "Bye." He thought about his mom and dad. They both were retired. His dad retired from the phone company and his mom was a retired teacher. They were 67, now had worked hard for him to have the best and also to get him to college. Jack finished his drink and headed for the front door. Tokyo quickly ran after him, rubbing his fury body against Jack's legs, meowing all the way.

Jack looked at his watch as he walked to the front of the line of *The Canyon Roller Club*. It was 9:10 p.m. He smiled at JJ the bouncer, shook his hand and flashed his *Diamond Club Casino* Employee card. JJ lifted the rope and Jack walked past him. Jack looked at his watch and walked towards the bar. Denise picked up her *Sleazy Mary* drink and turned around on the bar stool.

Denise saw Jack coming towards her and waived. It was, of course, kind of loud. The music was the usual 24ish to 39ish dance scene sometimes rap music. Jack walked up and stood next to Denise. "How are you, beautiful?" he said. Denise kissed him on the check, "I'm doing great now that you are here, handsome!" Jack turned to the bar

tender and ordered two *"Rattle Snake Venom Shots"*. He
wanted to forget the day, but smiled at Denise and said,

"As you know my dear, life can be shitty." "My day was
the day from hell!" He told her about his car not starting
and the taxi cab stink ride from hell. She laughed and said,
"Welcome to Las Vegas, Sweetheart! Let's make your day
better. Let's party!" Jack handed Denise the *Rattlesnake
Venom* shot glass and they both clinked. "Cheers! "To a
better night!"

Jack ran his hand through his hair. He was sweating.
Denise and he had danced about three dances, all the while
ordering drinks in between each dance. Jack grabbed
Denise's hand, "Hey let's split this scene. It's getting
crowded and I am kind of worn out." Denise shook her
head.

"Let go!"

They headed for the outside double doors. The air felt
great! Jack took a deep breath. "Man, it was getting hot in
there!" Denise tossed her head back, her flaming red hair
blowing in the soft wind and lit a cigarette.

"Hey you want to come back to my place and have a night
cap?" she asked. Jack looked at her smoking her cigarette.

Jack shook his head. "Na, I don't think so tonight. I've got
to be to work at 10:00 a.m. tomorrow morning. It's 4th of
July and I'm working a late shift tomorrow until 9:00 p.m.
They got the fireworks going off on the 7th floor of the

casino at 9:00 p.m. But hey, let's meet at 9:30 p.m. and watch the fireworks.

"Okay, Denise said, "I forgot all about that. I've got to work starting at 10:00 a.m. also. Sure! Let's meet at the front of the casino where valet is at 9:30 p.m. tomorrow, July 4th. Denise headed for the parking structure. Let's go get my car," Denise said. "I'll drop you off at home."

Jack took his key out and unlocked the apartment door and headed to the bedroom. He climbed into bed and turned off the light.

The alarm went off. Jack thought it was a fire siren. His head was aching. Tokyo romped over Jack, purring. His claws were pulling the blanket up and down as he walked over Jack. He knew that was the "I need breakfast now" wake-up call. "Jack grabbed Tokyo and rolled over and looked at the alarm clock. It was 7:00 a.m. Ugh. He looked at his right hand. The rash had spread up to his wrist. He winced. "This does not look good, Tokyo", he thought. He rolled out of bed and went to the kitchen and grabbed a can of cat food out of the cupboard. Tokyo as usual was hungry.

"Meow. Meow." If only, cats could talk. They would say. "I'm hungry, Jack! Put the damn can of cat food in my dish and make it quick!" Jack started some coffee and headed for the shower. Today was going to be a big day, the 4th of July.

Jack wondered how his car was doing. He dressed, ate some cereal and picked up his phone and called Henderson

Garage. "Hey, Mac how are you doing?" Good morning
to you." "Yes, I was wondering if my Sebring is fixed."
"Oh." Hi Jack. "It looks like it needs a starter." "We'll
need to order it." It will be in a few days. "So, I would say
Tuesday morning the 7th, it should be ready."

Jack winced. "How much is the cost of all that, out the
door? "Estimate of $375.00, out-the door".   Jack sighed.
"Okay, go ahead. Order the part and get it fixed."

"Okay Jack, Mac said. "Sure thing." "Thanks Mac" Jack
said and hung up. He grabbed a can of cat food from the
cupboard. He noticed his right hand again. Ugh! He
remembered the black golf glove he had put on his bed
stand. He went and put it on.

Jack paid the taxi-cab driver and walked in the casino to his
black jack table. There were three players who walked up
to his table. Two young girls and an older guy. He shuffled
the cards and dealt the first hand. Ed Johnson walked by
and waved to Jack. He nodded. Ed immediately noticed
the black glove on Jack's right hand. Ed walked over to the
Pitt Boss Sam and told him to have Jack take the glove off.
People would think he was cheating. After the black jack
hand, Sam walked over to Jack and whispered in his ear.
Jack looked at Ed. Ed nodded.

"Give me 3 minutes, folks, "I'll be right back." Jack
walked over to Ed and told him about the rash on his hand.
Ed looked at Jack's hand then looked Jack in the eyes.

"Jack, I understand totally, but people are going to think
you are cheating and we can't have that in this casino.

Jack winced. "They are going to think I have leprosy. The rash on my hand is bad, Ed."

Ed looked Jack square in the eyes. "Hey, I'm your best friend, Jack. Take a few days off. Ed looked at Jack's hand again with the black glove on it. Jack, go see a doctor and see if you can get hid of this rash. I will make sure you get paid." Jack looked at the golf glove still on his hand. He knew he couldn't take it off in front of everyone.

"Looks like, I have no choice." Okay then, I'll call you in a few days." The Pitt Boss walked over to the Black Jack table. "Give us a few minutes ladies and gentlemen and we will have a new dealer." The two girls and the guy got up and walked away. Jack gathered his belongings and went home.

Jack went to the bathroom to assess his hand. He took off the glove and then took off his shirt. He winced. The rash had spread from his hand up to his wrist area. His cell phone rang. It was his mom. "Hi Mom, how are you doing?"

"Jack, I don't mean to scare you but your dad has had a massive stroke and is in Detroit Memorial Hospital." "I am here with him". Jack's heart and mind started racing. He started to get sick to his to his stomach.

"Is he alright Mom?" "What did the Doctor's say? Slow down Jack. He is in a coma and is in critical condition. But Doctor's aren't sure if he will recover or not.

"It is a matter of time," they said. She started crying. Jack held his tears back and said.

"Mom, please don't cry. I will be there soon. I am flying out tonight. Mom, I will call you when I get to the Hospital."

His Mom sniffled. She knew she needed his support. He was the only son. We are on the 14th floor, room 2006. "Love you, Jack."

"See you soon, Mom". Jack hung up the phone. He ran both of his hands through his hair and sat down. He put his hands over his face and started to weep. He knew he had to pull himself together.

He picked up his cell phone and called his work. Hey Sally is Ed in?"

"Hi Jack. No, he is out on the floor."

"Can you please tell him I have an emergency at home? He knew he could tell Sally. He wanted his best friend Ed to know. Jack tried not to crack as he said. Please tell Ed that my dad had a massive stroke and I have to fly home to Detroit, Michigan tonight and I don't know when I will be back. I'll keep you posted."

Sally gasped. "Oh, Jack, I am so sorry. Sure, I will let Ed know. Please give my regards to your family Jack. Have a safe trip home." Jack wiped his tears away from his face.

"Thank you, Sally. Jack dialed the airport and got a flight
to Michigan airport. He then called Denise and told her the
bad news and asked her if she would watch Tokyo. He
would put an extra key was under a plant by the front door.
She assured him no worries. She would take care of Tokyo
and watch over the apartment for him. Jack poured a
strong Jack Daniels and coke and got his suitcase out and
packed.

Jack took a shuttle to the airport. Kinsey, the shuttle bus
driver took Jack's luggage out of the back of the shuttle and
told Jack. "Have a nice trip!" Jack walked to the terminal
gate and gave his ticket to the boarding agent and walked
down the long plank to the airplane. He had gotten a 6:00
p.m. flight to Detroit, Michigan airport. He should be at
the hospital by no later than 10:00 p.m. He found his seat
12C next to the window and put his bag over the overhead
baggage department. The captain came on the air.

"Ladies and Gentlemen, we will be ready for takeoff in a
few minutes." "Please buckle your seat belts. Put all seat
backs up and relax!" I hope you have a wonderful flight.
Stewards and Stewardess please prepare for takeoff. Jack
buckled his seat belt, closed his eyes and leaned his head
against the window. He thought about his dad and Mom in
the hospital. He always wanted them to have money to
travel a little when they retired. It was what both of them
talked about all the time, even before they retired.

Before his parents both left for work, they would sit at their
tiny kitchen table having breakfast. Mom, holding a strong
cup of black in her hand with a gleam in her eye. She
would be talking to Dad about where she wanted to go first.
Greece? Italy? And then Spain. She would get Dad to

watch all the TV Travel shows so he could get a glimpse of where she wanted to go. Vividly now, he remembered when he was a little boy walking down to the mailbox in front of the house. Always, five days a week, waiting for the school bus to arrive, sometimes wearing rubber yellow rain boots with a yellow raincoat. Before getting on the bus, Jack would always turn and waive back good bye to his mom who was staring out the window while raindrops fell. He was seven years old then.

His Mom began her teaching career when he was 12 years old. Old enough for him to be at home alone with Snickers, his brown colored dachshund, who thought he was a big hunter when he went outside. Chasing rabbits and squirrels in the large wet-grass front yard. Mom would open the door when the bus came and Snickers would go running. Snickers became his bedside sleeping buddy. He would hold Snickers tight under the covers. Snickers always snuggled next to him, making him feel safe at night from the boogieman or when it was thundering too loud.

He thought about his dad. Slowly in his mind he started collecting the adventures they had together. Jack loved to go fishing with his dad at the Silver Lake Pond down the road. Every other Saturday morning, Dad would get up early 6:00 a.m. or so, start his coffee, pack two sandwiches and some sodas, Mom's homemade cookies and chips and come wake him up. They would both put on black rubber booths and walk to the shed and get our fishing poles and worms and walk down the dirt road to Silver Lake Pond about ¼ mile from the house and find a grassy area where we would sit down and throw our fishing lines in. There were many cool mornings. Usually, the grass was wet from the dew. Often times, Dad would ask me about school.

60

How I liked it, what I wanted to do when I got older. Jack remembered his dad fondly. He worked hard but was a quiet, simple man. After a few hours of fishing, his dad and he would head home. The house always smelled like cinnamon apple pie or something good to eat.

They would find Mom with a flowered printed cotton dress with her apron on bustling around the kitchen singing a little tune as she played Mrs. Susie home-maker. Jack knew her favorite place in the house. She would always yell out when she heard us come in the back door.

 "You boys take off those muddy boots!" Dad would look at me and wink.

"Yes!" "Yes dear! Then Dad would give Mom a kiss on her cheek and say, I'm going to go lie down in the Study awhile." I'd usually end up taking Snickers out to the front yard and throw a ball to him, while he tried to be the "big hunter," chasing everything he could see.

His mother was the typical house wife and mother. Always humming a tune or singing in the kitchen. She would have a special treat for him when he got off the bus. He would run down the path, opening the front door, running to the kitchen to see what she had made. Snickers by his side too, wanting some kind of treat. Being the only son, Jack knew he had it made. Most times, always the one, the only adoring Son. He thought it would be fun having another brother and sister. Then he thought again and easily dismissed it. Knowing in his mind, it was not going to happen. Jack knew, there was not going to be any "Leave it to Beaver" re-runs.

Jack opened his eyes and looked out the airplane window. The plane was coming to a stop. There was a light drizzle falling, which was normal. On average there are only 183 sunny days per year in Detroit Michigan. He never knew when the rain would come and go.

"Good evening, Folks. This is Captain Briggs. Welcome to Detroit Michigan. Light showers expected for the next two days. Have a wonderful evening!" Jack stood up, looked at his watch. It was 11:30 p.m. He waited for the people in front to move and got his bag from the overhead luggage compartment. He walked down the ramp and got his cell phone out. He called his mom. "Mom, I'm here."

"Jack, I am so glad you arrived and you are safe. "Joe, I mean your dad, is still not awake. We are hoping for the best. I'll see you soon." She hung up and drifted back to sleep in the hospital chair. Jack hailed a taxi. He thought of the last one he was riding in Las Vegas. He looked at the name tag hanging from the rearview mirror, "Simon." He opened the taxicab window and took a whiff of air. "Fresh." "Thank God!"

He walked into the hospital and went to the Admissions Desk. "My name is Jack Levin. My mother Trudy Levin is here with my father Joe Levin. My Dad Joe Levin suffered a massive heart attack. I am Jack Levin, their son. Can you please tell me what room they are in? The Admissions Clerk looked up at Jack's pain strained face, and then she looked down at her computer. Peering over her black reading eyeglasses, she whispered.

"Yes, Mr. Levin, they are on 14th Floor, Room 2006. The elevator is down the hall to your right."

"Thank you." Jack hurriedly walked to the elevator pushed the 14th floor button. He took a deep breath and composed himself. He didn't want his mom to see that he was grief stricken and tired.

He walked down the corridor and pushed the room door 2006 open softly. His Mom was resting in a chair next to his dad's bedside with her head back and her eyes closed with a blue hospital blanket over her. Jack stood for a moment and looked at her. He thought about all the traveling dreams she wanted to spend with his dad when they both retired. He flashed back to his mom changing TV channels on Dad to have him watch all the traveling shows with her. She would be sitting with her cup of tea next to Dad who was trying not to fall asleep in his big chair.

Jack wiped a tear from his eye. Somberly, he looked at his dad. He had tubes down his throat and IV in his arm. His breathing was raspy. He walked over to his bedside and picked up his hand. Tears started flowing. "Oh, Dad," he thought. His Mom sat up. Jack quickly wiped his tears. Jack walked over to his mom.

Jack took her hand while she stood up and they hugged. "Oh, Mom," he whispered.

His Mom wiped her tears away, "I am so glad you are here Jack."

A nurse came in the room. She started whispering. "Hi my name is Callie Jenkins." "The cafeteria downstairs is open 24 hours if you would like to go down and get a coffee or something to eat. It is on the first corner, down the hall on the left-hand side. Jack looked at his mom.

"Come-on Mom, I need a bite to eat. Let's go downstairs." Jack took his mom's hand.

In the cafeteria, Jack asked. "Do you want anything Mom?""

"Yes, I haven't eaten a lot lately. I'll take an orange juice, some scrambled eggs." Fumbling with her hands, she looked down at the table. Jack ordered and brought the tray to the table. He sat down and put the food in front of her.

"Here you go Mom." Jack took a drink of his coffee and forced the food down his throat. His Mom took a bite of her eggs and looked up at Jack. "I really don't know what to say." It happened so fast. He was going out to the garage to look for something, but ended up lying on the kitchen floor clutching his hand to his heart. I picked up the phone and called 911 right away. They came quickly and took him to the emergency room. While we were driving to the hospital, they had an oxygen mask on his nose. He was staring up at me, breathing hard. I took his hand and put it in mine. He looked up at me again, squeezed my hand and then slowly closed his eyes." Tears began to run down her face.

Jack reached over and took his mom's hand. The pain was evident on both their faces. "Mom, it's going to be okay. Whatever happens with Dad, please know that I am here." We will get through this together. Right now, we have to be strong and that means nourishment and trying to get some sleep. The nurse told me that Doctor Willow will be in today and is going to stop by Dad's room around 4:00 p.m. today. Hey, mom, let's go home and get some rest."

Looking at her son with sorrowful eyes, she wiped her eyes and patted Jack's hand. Now, she was feeling tired. "Okay, she said." She stared at Jack's hand. "What's the black golf glove on your hand all about?" Jack quickly re treated his hand and put it under the table. Not wanting her to worry about something else. He shrugged off her question, Oh, it's nothing Mom. Let's go home and rest."

He fell into bed as soon as he got his mom to bed and slept a hard six hours. When he woke up, he lay his bed thinking that he was lying in the bed he was grew up in. After he left home to go to college, his mom never changed the bedroom. Everything seemed little. There was a little twin bed. There was a little desk on one side of the wall, with a little lamp on it. Little shelves above the desk with little books. Little closet door where he had his clothes. Little clothes drawer. Little night stand with a lamp on it and a little window looking out to the front yard with little blue curtains. He picked up his watch on the bedside. It was 3:00 p.m. He got up, turned on the shower knob. He let the warm water flow over him. He looked at his hand in the shower. It still didn't look good.

Ed's phone call earlier to him was alarming to say the least, letting him know there was a rash that had possibly started and broke out at *The Diamond Club Casino.* Jack looked at his hand again. The rash had spread past his right hands' wrist. Ed had given him all the other signs to watch for. He knew he had to talk to Dr. Alexander Willow when he got to the hospital again. He did feel a little hot and at times a little faint and his chest hurt off and on. He wanted to brush it off as jet lag, but he knew better. He felt his head thinking "I can't get sick now. He banged his head lightly against the shower wall. "Not now God." "Please not now."

 He toweled, shaved, brushed his teeth, dressed, put his golf glove back on and went downstairs to the kitchen. His Mom was sitting at the kitchen table holding a cup of coffee. Jack kissed his mother lightly on the check and went and poured a cup of hot coffee. It was 3:30 p.m. Time didn't seem to matter. He sat down at the kitchen table across from his mom. Even though he hoped she had slept a few hours, she looked tired. "I'm going to start the ca,r Mom." With a blank stare on her face, she got up and said "I'll make some sandwiches for us." Okay, see you in the car Mom. Jack got in the car and started it.

They met Dr. Willow in Dad's Hospital Room. Extending his hand out, Dr. Alexander said, "Good afternoon, I'm Dr. Alexander Willow. You must be Jack?" Jack shook Dr. Willow's hand.

"How is he Dr. Willow?" Your Dad is actually awake. He woke up a few hours ago. He is just is taking a rest. Jack sighed with relief.

"Thank God!" His Mom rushed over to her husband's side. She squeezed his hand. His Dad opened his eyes and looked up staring at his mom. She started smiling, laughing and crying all at the same time. Dr. Willow stepped over to the bed.

"How are you doing Joe? "How are you feeling?" Joe finally spoke up.

"I am feeling good now." "Now that I know I can open my eyes and I'm alive." They all started chuckling.

 "Good, Dr. Willow said. You should be home in no time. No time at all. Joe smiled.

 "Thank you." He peered over at Jack. "Jack!" "Jack!" Holding back tears, Jack rushed over to his dad's side and took his other hand.

"I'm here Dad." "I'm right here."

Jack took Dr. Alexander Willow aside and walked out the door so his mom and Dad could not hear. "Do you have a moment?" He took off his golf glove and showed him his rash. "Dr. Alexander Willow looked at Jack's hand and said. "Come with me."

Jack popped his head back into the room. "Be back in a minute mom and dad."

He followed Dr. Alexander Willow down the hall to a vacant room. Dr. Willow closed the door. Jack explained what Ed Johnson, his friend had told him and what was going on in Las Vegas and how the garage parking structures were contaminated due to the bat droppings that had been there for a while and rain added to the moisture in the structures. He also explained what happened the night of July 4th with the brown bats flying around the huge full moon and all the details of the disease he had been told by Ed Johnson.

Dr. Alexander Willow sighed and put his hand on his hip and looked down at the floor and spoke.

"Yes, Jack, I am aware of the episode that happened in Las Vegas on July 4th and understand the details of this case. "There was a National Alert Bulletin put out late July 5th evening to all National hospitals with all the details and to watch for the symptoms. The rash, of course, was the first symptom." But there is much more to come if we don't get this virus with the new methods and applications ramified and disposed of before it explodes to other humans and populations.

Dr. Willow took Jack's hand. "Let me see your hand again." It appears it has spread to your wrist area." The good thing is it's not contagious as of now from what we know.

I am going to give you an antifungal prescription. It will be a strong antifungal prescription antidote. The prescription will be good for 90 days. You can get this prescription filled at the Pharmacy Department on the first floor. It is important you take this pill for 90 days. No exceptions. Are you experience any other symptoms you are

experiencing? Any fatigue? Flu-like symptoms? Any
Dizzy spells? Coughing? Any chest pains?"

Jack knew he was tired, very fatigued. He told Dr.
Alexander Willow. I've had a slight fever, fatigue and off
and on chest pains."

"Not good." Dr. Alexander Willow said. "If you continue
with these symptoms a week after you start taking the
prescription, I recommend you seek medical help
immediately.

Dr. Alexander Willow patted him on the back. Do you
understand? Most people that have a strong immune
system can beat this. Be sure to take one pill for 90-days.
There was a strong urgency in Dr. Alexander Willow's
voice. No exceptions, Jack!" Dr. Willow looked him
squarely in the eyes. "Do you understand Jack?" Jack saw
again the concern in Dr. Alexander Willow's eyes. Jack
knew it was critical to his health.

"I understand," he said." "Thank you."

Jack walked back into his dad's hospital room. Dr.
Alexander Willow stood in his white coat with his hand on
his dad's bed rail whispering to his mother and dad. Jack
walked over to the other side of the bed and took his dad's
hand. Dr. Willow said. "Jack, as I told your mom and dad,
your father is doing great! We are going to have your dad
stay a couple more days for observation and then I have
advised your mom to hire an in-house Nurse and a
Therapist to help your Dad for the next month. I will

evaluate the reports from the in-house Nurse and Therapist and let your parents know about the current situation is.

Jack looked at his mom and then at his Dad. They both nodded. Jack looked at his dad again. "How are you doing Dad?" His Dad looked up at him and smiled. "I'm starving!" They all started laughing.

Before turning to leave, Dr. Alexander Willow said. "I can see your dad is doing just fine." "I'll be in touch. Jack rang the nurse. A nurse came in and looked at Jack. Jack read her name tag. It said, Nurse Callie Jenkins.   She had coco skin that contrasted with her white uniform and white shoes. Jack knew she was from the south.

"Can we please have some real food, please? My Dad is starving! Dad spoke up again.

"Maybe, some meatloaf with mashed potatoes, some green beans and a big glass of milk." Nurse Callie Jenkins rolled her eyes. This was an everyday patient dialogue for her.

"Sure, of course, Mr. Levin! No problem! She waived her hand in the air and rolled her big brown eyes, coming right up!"

Jack watched his dad eating. He was starting to look good. He was happy he was awake. His Mom stood over him making sure he was doing fine. After Dad had eaten, he took his mom's hand and said, "I'm going to be just fine. No need to worry anymore. I'm going to rest a little and then he closed his eyes.

Jack went over to his mom and they walked outside his dad's room. His Mom took Jack's hands in hers.

"Listen Jack, the doctor said we are off to a good start. I am thankful your dad is alive and is in good spirits."

Jack knew his mom would not leave his Dad's bedside until he was escorted out of the hospital and reached home where she could watch over him. His Dad was in good spirits, sitting up, eating, drinking and seemed to have some glimmer in his eyes. Dr. Alexander Willow showed them the x-rays. Dr. Willow said it looked good. His heart showed slight scaring, but no real major damage.   He would just need to take medicine plus an aspirin the rest of his life and rest until his strength came back. "I still would suggest a Home Registered Nurse for about two or three weeks until he is on his feet." Dr. Willow reiterated.

Jack's Mom looked Jack straight in the eyes. "I am good Jack. I can take it from here. You go back to Las Vegas, to work. Jack smiled at his mom. He knew she was right. He needed to get back home and to work. He touched her cheek with his hand and looked her straight in the eyes and kissed her lightly on the cheek.

"Thank you, Mom." "I love you. I'll talk with you soon." His Mom watched him walk down the hallway and turned and walked back to his dad's hospital room.

Jack walked out the glass doors. He got his cell phone out and called a shuttle to pick him up and take him to the house. He told the shuttle driver to wait 5 minutes while he packed his bags. He looked around his little room one last time, picked up his bag, walked out, hid the key under the flower pot and climbed in the shuttle, "Detroit Michigan Airport, please."

Jack got off the plane. It was still hot in Las Vegas. He made a quick call to Henderson's Car Repair. He recognized Mac's voice.

"Hey, Mac is old Betsy fixed yet?"

"Yep, she's ready." "She had some kind of sticky white crap and some dark brown pellets floating melted into the engine. We cleaned her up and put a new starter in her. She's purring now. You can come pick up your car anytime.

"Thanks Mac", Jack said. "I'll be there soon."

Jack hailed a taxi. He saw the tag on the rearview mirror, "Ramsey." "Not this nasty-ass, stinking asshole, again!" Jack waited for the god-awful smell to fill his nostrils. It didn't. "At least he got hid of the God-awful stink out, he thought. In the back of his mind, still remembering it, he turned his head towards the window, opened it, took a long deep breath and gave "Ramsey" his home address.

Chapter 9 – Kinsey McDonald's NIXON Watch

Kinsey looked at his watch on his wrist. It was a steel NIXON watch. A, "New Year's Special Edition." The Dials were made on the left-hand side of NIXON not the right side. He had always thought that was interesting and the watch was a heavy steel watch. He always thought

NIXON watches were cool. They had that heavy-metal, tough-guy look. For about two years, every time he and Doreen had gone shopping he was always looking at the watches in each store for the same watch. Doreen caught him one time looking at the watches at Neiman Marcus and a finally asked him. "What are you looking at? Kinsey showed her the NIXON watch he had been spying on for about two years. Doreen bent down and looked at the watch and then at the price tag. "She turned to him and said "$450.00!" "In your dreams! Buddy!" She turned and walked away.

It was their 30th Anniversary and it was also around Xmas. They sat down on the couch next to the Xmas tree. The kids were of course grown and they were not coming over for Xmas. Doreen and Kinsey decided they would only buy a few small presents for each other. They had a small fake tree in the corner with lights and Doreen's favorite ornaments she had collected through the years. Kinsey had bought her a heart shaped necklace he had found at a pawn shop and a bottle of her favorite perfume she wore all the time.

Doreen handed him a present. It was socks. Something she always bought him every Xmas along with new under ware, knowing that most of his undergarments had holes in them. He finished opening all his presents and looked at Doreen with her cup of coffee. She looked happy.
"Doreen smiled and turned to Kinsey, "Well, I guess that's all that Santa brought us."

Doreen patted Kinsey's knee and got up. "Want another cup of coffee?" Kinsey laid down on the couch, ready to take his Xmas morning nap.

"No, I'm good, honey" he said. Doreen walked over to the tree and reached way behind the tree for a silver foil wrapped box with a silver ribbon tied around it. She walked over to Kinsey, "I think Santa left you one more present. Kinsey opened his eyes suspiciously, eyeing her up-to-no good mischief eyes. It looked like it just saw a silver foiled box with a silver ribbon. Doreen sat down beside him. Kinsey sat up and looked at Doreen all the while thinking "is it what I think it is? Doreen smiled.

"Open it!" "Open it!"

Kinsey tore the silver paper off and looked at the watch box. He opened it. And, there it was! The steel NIXON watch he had wanted for two years. He grabbed Doreen and put his arms around her. "It's perfect! "It's just perfect! I love you honey!" Doreen sat back and watched the little boy, she had not seen in a while, in her husband emerge.

"Merry Xmas, Happy 30th Anniversary, honey." She leaned over and kissed him lightly on the lips. I love you too. Enjoy!" Doreen got up to get another cup of coffee. As she walked to the kitchen, she turned and smiled at him, "Now I can call you my "Man of Steel."

Kinsey, still lying down in bed, looked at the "Man of Steel" watch staring back at him. It was the last thing he had in the world that reminded him of the love Doreen had for him and the love he lost. Sometimes he wanted to bury it somewhere so he could forget the shame he felt and the lost life he threw away. The life, he knew, he wanted back so desperately. He wanted Doreen back and the kids he missed so desperately. He had not seen Melody, Kinsey Jr. and Alice in almost five years. He knew he probably had grandkids by now. The good life he once had he wanted back with all his heart.

Kinsey looked around the casino. It was 6:30 p.m. He grabbed his poker chips and finished off his drink and put it down. "That's enough for me," he said. "You' all have a good evening," he said as he walked away. He walked towards the cashier's cage and cashed out $200 in chips. The sleazy motel night light turned on as he unlocked the motel door. Another crappy night.

Kinsey woke the next morning, took a shower, ate breakfast, stepped to the side of the curb and hailed a taxi. He climbed in the back seat. "Where you going?" the taxi cab driver asked. *"The Diamond Club Casino"*, Kinsey, said. A strong stench came over him. "Someone shit in here?" It smells bad! Like shit and a dead cat or something. Man, you need some air freshener!" Kinsey took out his handkerchief and held it to his nose trying not to gag, hoping he would make it through the strip lights before throwing up. He looked down at his new shoes. "Nope can't do that," he thought. His mind switched to the poker tournament. He had been playing poker for over 5 years now. The stench was too much for him. "Right here, buddy, he yelled! This is good!"

Kinsey opened the taxi cab back door and threw the cash in the front window to the taxi cab driver. As the taxi cab driver drove away, Kinsey yelled, "You need to get that stink out!" Kinsey threw his handkerchief in the trash near the entrance of the casino. He pushed *The Diamond Club Casino* double doors open and headed to the Premier Conference room to place his entry $10,000. He was down to his last $10,000. He watched the last of his monies being counted in front of him. "Ok, Mr. Kinsey, you are good to go. Good Luck!" He clipped his sign- in card to his waist and surveyed the room. There were seven tables with eight players each. He knew he would need to put his best poker face on. The odds would be heavy. He knew who some of the players were. And, they were good.

He had won $500 at the high roller poker machine, gathered his money and headed for the sports bar area. He watched the circle of TV screens with horse races. Tables and chairs with people sitting around staring at the TV screens. He wanted to sit and watch the people. He knew it was getting late and he had to get up early. While watching the TV screens, he turned towards the Sandwich shop. There were three guys standing around looking down the game aisle and talking. They all looked in their late 20s. He saw them all laughing together, obviously having a good time.

One of the guys almost stumbling into his friend, took out a cigarette from his shirt pocket and was having a hard time lighting it with his lighter. He definitely was very drunk. Kinsey laughed inside. Watch for it?" Watch for it?" He knew that, as soon as the drunk guy lit that cigarette, he knew the puke was a-coming next and everywhere. Sure enough, he lit the cigarette and there it came, the puke, all over the aisle carpet. His friends backed off. One of the guys grabbed him around his shoulders and they all stumbled down the aisle. Kinsey laughed inside. He had seen that picture scene over and over again, many times. Thank God, he thought, he wasn't a big drinker. "Yep, time to call it a night," he thought.

Before he left, Kinsey walked by the Poker Tournament Board and looked up at the names on it. Five Players were listed in yellow neon lights. He saw his name Kinsey McDonald at the top, listed as number one. He saw Todd Bales listed as number two. And then, Vu Tong, number three, Jake Walters, number four, and Michael Mendez number five. "Good," he thought. "Leonard Gallery didn't make the list." Funny how time slips away fast in Las Vegas, Kinsey thought. He got up and walked towards the casino entrance and hailed a taxi. He told the cabby, "Satellite Motel 5th Avenue and Florence." The motel neon was light barely shining.

Kinsey rolled over again and looked at the alarm clock. He had already told his boss at Las Vegas Shuttle he was taking his vacation days. It was finally the big tournament day, 4th of July. He had not slept well at all. He didn't want to take a sleeping pill for fear he would not wake-up on time. He looked at the clock again on the nightstand table. It was 7:00 a.m. Awe, he sighed, lying in bed a few more minutes reminiscing about last night.

He put his arm over his aching head and closed his eyes thinking. Should he make a deal with the devil or should he not; should he make promises he knew he probably couldn't keep? He had a list of them he thought about every day: totally not gambling was at the top of the list. Trying to be a good person, diligently making an attempt to call his ex-wife Doreen and be congenial; find his three kids and grandkids and at least talk with them once a week. His eyes began to water. So much time had passed, wasted time. Wasted life! On, what? On gambling what else? He knew that he knew better. Shame always seemed to creep into his very soul every time. He wiped his cheek, okay, enough of this self-defeating crap.

He rolled over and looked at the alarm clock again, turned on the TV to the News. *"In the past two weeks, two women have been found sexually assaulted, strangled and stabbed to death. Both victims were dumped in garbage bins in old town Las Vegas. Police have identified the two women as working prostitutes in the Las Vegas area. Although there is an investigation at this time, there are no suspects at this time."* Kinsey flipped the TV off. "Crime never changes in Las Vegas," Kinsey thought.

Kinsey got up showered and walked across the street to *"The Fun, Fun Casino*, the Dude Café for breakfast. He sat down at his favorite booth and stared out the window. Today is the big day. A waitress came over and asked what he wanted. Kinsey looked up at her.

"I haven't seen you before." Are you new?"

"Yes, my name is Virginia, "what can I get you?"

"I'll have the $4.99 daily special with black coffee." "Where is Dorothy?" Virginia clicked her black pen and looked at Kinsey.

"Oh, she got fired yesterday." He looked up at her shocked. "What? She's been here for 17 years." She smacked her gum.

"From what I hear she had her hands in the cookie jar." "She was embezzling money for 17 years and she finally got caught."

She looked at him still smacking her gum, "I'll have your order in a few minutes." Virginia tore the order receipt to give to the chef, turned and walked to the next customer. Kinsey sat there flabbergasted, shaking his head.

Chapter 10–Girls Night Out – Let's Party!

"Damn old bird finally flew the coop." **"What plays in Vegas, stays in Vegas."**

Stephanie climbed out of the shower, brushed her teeth, gargled with some mouth wash and called out "I am starving!" They have an Extreme Pizza Restaurant downstairs. "You guys want to go?" Megan and Bethany both yelled back,

"Yes!" Yes, let's go! "I am starving too," Bethany yelled back,

"I'll be ready in 15 minutes Stephanie said and then we can go try out luck."

Stephanie grabbed her wedge red shoes. She started to lace them up and noticed her right food had a rash on it. She thought that dang pool with all the pee and body germs. Fungus? Casually ignoring it, she put on her earring and grabbed her purse. Bethany and Megan met her at the door.

"Let's go eat and have some fun!"

The girls, Megan, Bethany and Stephanie stepped off the elevator and looked around. They went to the Extreme Pizza Restaurant and ordered a pepperoni pizza with lots of cheese. They had full view of the casino area. The round booths only went to their shoulders so they could see all the people coming and going around the casino area.   They ate, watched the people and talked girl chat. After they finished, they all got up.

Stephanie, Bethany and Megan walked around the corner to the Mystic Bar and sat down. A waitress came over.

"Hello, ladies!" Stephanie noticed her name tag, Denise. "We have a special shot *called "The Pink Slipper"* which is a double shot of rum for $4.00 if you ladies are interested?" Megan and Bethany both looked at Stephanie.

"Sure, that sounds good."

Bethany looked at her watch. It was 9:00 p.m. Megan asked, "Hey, are we going to *The Canyon Roller Club to* meet those guys? Hell yay!" Stephanie giggled.

Bethany chimed in, "sounds good to me!" "Hey girls, they have a shopping mall across the street from us called *The*

Clothes Forum. "I want to go over there tomorrow." "I'm in." "Shopping is always good," Bethany said.

Megan said, "me too". "I need a new purse.

"Hey, let's go find a roulette table, Stephanie said. The floor was buzzing. People were everywhere. Also, lots of noise everywhere on the casino floor coming from all the casino machines. There were people from all walks of life, walking by, talking, rolling their suitcases, dragging their kids. Ca ching, Ca ching, Ca ching. Stephanie headed toward a roulette table. Megan and Bethany followed.

There was a waitress there. Her name tag said "Denise." "Hi, my name is Denise. What can I get you, ladies, to drink?" Denise leaned forward and said we have a special drink tonight. "It's called "*Shut up and Smack me Good*" drink. All the girls started laughing. "It is a vodka double shot with orange liquor and lime juice mixed together and poured into a long shot glass. They turned and looked at each other and nodded. The girls still all laughing, Bethany put three fingers up in the air. "Yes, we will all have one of those!"

"The Roulette guy stood in his black vest, black pants, white long-sleeved shirt with a red bow. The Roulette guy took a hold of the spinning wheel. "All bets down." Megan and Bethany watched Stephanie throw a $20 bill down. The roulette guy gave her chips. She then placed all her chips on 27 and 21. They all watched the roulette wheel spin and the bouncing ball spin around and around. Red! Black! Red! Black! It slowly passed black, then Red

and landed. Bethany screamed. "Yes!" The black ball
stopped. It landed on number 27.

The Roulette guy smiled. "This must be your lucky night!"
He paid Stephanie $80 in chips.   He looked at each of the
girls. "You, girls, have a great evening!" Stephanie picked
up her chips and they all walked back to their table.
Stephanie turned and yelled back, "Thanks, we will!"
Denise came back around to their table and gave each of
the girls their drinks. "Have fun ladies!" Still holding their
drinks in their hands, they all lifted their shots and cheered.
Megan cheered!

"Cheers to Las Vegas!" Bethany cheered!

"To us" the three BFFs!" and Stephanie cheered.

"To the three Boston guys we are going to have fun
tonight!" Megan looked at Bethany and then both looked
at Stephanie and started busting out laughing out loud.
They all downed the shots. Megan taking two long sips
instead of one. "Bethany looked at Megan, only you Ms.
Megan!"

Once again, the machines were making their music sounds.
People were walking hurriedly everywhere. It was fun
watching them all roaming round. There were waitresses
walking around, getting drinks for everyone. Diamond
Club Casino employees were walking around in their black
suits, and the Pitt Bulls, observing players playing at the
tables. Stephanie, Bethany and Megan all sat, drinking
their drinks and watching the people. It was fun taking in
the whole Las Vegas scene. Stephanie got up.

"Hey, I need to run to the ladies room."

"Okay, let's all go. It's this way," Megan said. There was
a small line.

Stephanie glanced down at her right foot. She noticed the
rash had spread below her ankle. Staring at it, she winced.
Bethany looked down at Stephanie's foot also. "Oh my
God, Stephanie, are you alright? You have a huge rash on
your foot."

Stephanie winced again. "I know I saw it when I got out
of the shower. I am thinking it might be from the pool
water. You know people do sometimes pee in the water
and who knows what else."

"I think it might just be a pool fungus." The drinks were
starting to make her feel nothing. "I'll be okay. It doesn't
hurt that much." Stephanie looked down at her right foot
again. "It's just really ugly and annoying."

It was 9:30 p.m. Stephanie, Bethany, and Megan were
standing in line waiting to get into *The Canyon Roller
Club*. She looked around to see if she could see Johnny,
Brett and Darren. Bethany's phone started ringing.

"Hey, she said, we are here at *The Canyon Roller Club*."
"We are standing in line".

"Hi Bethany, it's me Brett. We're inside."

"We will see you when we get in. Okay, we'll be looking for you." Bethany hung up and jumped up and down. "They're here!" "They're inside the club already!" Stephanie and Megan started jumping up and down. "Yes!" Yes! Yes!"

Bethany looked up at the bouncer as they entered the club and smiled.

"Finally, I can't believe it's already 10:00 p.m. and we are finally in the club."

Bethany, Megan and Stephanie headed for the bar. Bethany spun her head and looked down the bar to the left. Ah, there they are. Brett leaned over, elbows on the bar, and did the tw- finger signal over his brow, as if to say, "we are down here girls, end of the bar". Bethany waived. "They are down at the end of the bar, Bethany said. The girls headed through the crowd to the end of the bar. It was starting to get crazy packed. "Hey, you finally made it" Brett said.

Johnny eyed Stephanie up and down and smiled. "Oh, I get to finally see you with clothes on and no sunglasses." Stephanie laughed, "And I get to see you with more than your swim trunks." The bar tender looked at them. What will you ladies and gents have?" "Darren looked Megan and then at the bartender.

"We will have the *Long Legged Sally,* " a shot of gin in the long-Island Tea."

Brett turned to Brittany and smiled. We will have one
"Pink Slipper Whiskey Shot" and one *"Lie Down Lucy"*
double tequila shot, each for $3.00 each.

"Wow! Stephanie said. Megan and Bethany and shrugged
their shoulders. As the hours lingered in the air and
between the loud music, Johnny leaned over to the bar
whispered, loudly.

"We'll take *six* *"Lie Down Lucys."* "Good enough!" the
bar tender yelled as he headed down the bar for the shots.

Each one took the double shots of the *"Lie Down Lucys"*
with the limes in the other hand. "Cheers", Johnny said.
They all clinked shot glasses and downed the hatch.
Megan started coughing. "Whew, I'm not use to this snake
oil." They all laughed. Johnny smiled at Stephanie and put
his shot glass down on the bar and grabbed Stephanie's
hand.

"Put your drink down, let's go dance!" She put her drink
down on the bar, rolled her eyes at Megan, while Johnny
weaved them through the crowd to the dance floor.

Megan turned to Darren at the bar.

"Hi, my name is Megan." I really didn't get a chance to
meet you guys at the pool, since I was guarding the harems
chairs and accessories, while they played in the pool."

Darren laughed.

"So, you were the chair chained harem? Megan smiled.

85

"Right?" That would be me.

Megan looked at him casually up and down. She liked his cool, casual protector demeanor, his Massachusetts and his brown eyes. She couldn't see any tattoos. Thank goodness she thought.

Darren grabbed Megan's hand and they both squeezed through the crowd to the dance floor. Darren swirled Megan around and pulled her close to him. Megan's head was spinning. She had drunk four shots and was feeling no pain. It was 2:00 a.m. and she waved to Stephanie and Bethany. Stephanie waved for her to come to the bar. Megan grabbed Darren's hand pulled him off the dance floor.

Stephanie took her last shot and moved closer to Johnny.

"Hey, I hate to be a party pooper here, but its 2:30 a.m." Johnny put his shot glass down on the bar and smiled at Stephanie. "Let's go get some breakfast." "They have a breakfast diner down the road. Stephanie looked at Bethany and Megan.

"Sure, I am starving, Bethany said." Megan shrugged her shoulders.

"Sure."

The guys waived three taxi cabs in the entrance area. Johnny and Stephanie got in the back seat of the first taxi cab. Darren and Megan got in the second taxi cap and

Bethany and Brett got in the third. *"The Breakfast Dinner* down the Las Vegas Strip, each told the cab drivers."

Megan put her hand to her stomach. Her stomach was churning. She put her hand to her mouth. Darren put his hand over her hand and turned to her with a concerned look.

"You, okay?

Megan started heaving. "I think I'm going to be sick." The taxicab driver adjusted his rearview mirror.

The taxicab driver's name tag swung back and forth on the rearview mirror, "Ramsey."

"There's a barf bag behind my seat in the pocket."

Darren grabbed the bag and gave it to Megan who was starting to heave again. Darren looked at the asshole taxicab driver in his rearview mirror.

"What the hell is that smell in here?" It smells like a dead smelly skunk!"

The taxicab driver looked at both of them through his rearview mirror. He didn't flinch. Nor did he say anything, while staring hard at each of them in the back seat.

Darren put his hand on Megan's back and patted it and whispered, "We'll be there in a minute sweetheart." Put

87

your head out the window and get some fresh air.   He looked at the taxicab driver again with a look.

"Just get us there and fast dick head!"

Darren tried to take in the fresh air as he held Megan's hand. They both got out and Darren threw a $10 through the taxicab driver's front window. The taxi cab idiot yelled back at Darren.

"Where's the tip asshole?" Darren turned and flipped him off!

"Shove it up your stinking ass!"

Chapter 11– Dinner for Two – The Handel Steak House

Frank and Jenny walked into *The Handel Steak House*. Frank greeted the hostess, reservations for Frank Zimmer.

"Sure, this way Mr. and Mrs. Zimmer. We have window seating for you so you can see the Las Vegas lights. Jenny smiled at the hostess.

 "Sounds great!" Frank pushed out Jenny's seat.

"Wow, it's so glamorous here with all the lights and movie and comedy stars, Jenny said as she sat down.

The waiter came over dressed in white and black. Towel on his arm, he handed Frank the Wine Menu.

"My name is Kevin and I will be your waiter for this evening." Jenny looked at his name tag on his vest with a black bow tie. "Here is the wine menu madam." The Sherri Blanc Red Wine here on the list is the favorite here at *The Handel Steak House*. Frank asked Jenny.

 "Does that sound good to you?"

"Sure." Frank smiled at her and turned to the waiter.

"Please bring a bottle of the Sherri Blanc Red. "Thank you."

Frank looked at Jenny who was playing with her white cloth napkin and admiring all the lights. He reached for her hand on the table. Jenny turned and looked at Frank.

"I just wanted to tell you how beautiful you look tonight, Jenny." Jenny looked Frank in the eyes and smiled.

"Thank you, Frank. It's been a while since I played dress up for you."

Frank looked Jenny in the eyes to see if there was any kind of sincerity. He searched for a glimmer of hope.   He said in his best sincere voice.

"I know we have had some hard times Jenny, but I promise you, from now on, it's going to me and you and Laker and Sofia." All the way!"

Jenny looked at him and then looked down at her napkin. Her heart wanted to believe Frank. She still had a deep wound. She often thought and once again played the same recording over and over in her head. "All girls dream of the fairy tale life". "That one dream, the most important dream, every girl wants in her life." But she also asked?" "How many girls really get that fairy tale dream? That, one-time and forever fairy tale dream in each of our lifetimes?" She moved her hand from Frank's hand, took the white napkin, wiped her mouth and put it back on her lap and picked up the Menu.

Frank frowned and picked up his menu. All the while, Jenny was aware of the hurt that still there. She still had that same old thought in her mind, "he's still an asshole for cheating on her."

All Frank knew is that he still loved Jenny and he was trying. He wanted to make it right with her again. The waiter came back, opened the wine bottle and poured Jenny and offered Frank a glass of the Sherri Blanc. Frank picked up his glass, smelled the wine and said "to you Jenny, my lovely wife."

Jenny picked up her glass and smiled, "cheers!" She took a sip of wine and stared out the window.

The waiter said, "Our special for tonight is the Handel Black Angus Rib Eye Steak or notably worldwide called the *Blonde Aquitaine*. It is prepared by our Executive Chef, tonight Ralph Trop. It is served with your choice of vegetables and potatoes, scalloped. Jenny looked at the waiter.

"That sounds good." "Yes, I will have that".

Frank handed the waiter his menu and said, "I'll have the same."

Jenny turned and looked out the window again at the Las Vegas lights. She put her hand to her chin and smiled. "The lights are really beautiful at night in Vegas." The waiter brought their entrees while they both enjoyed small conversation of home and the kids.

The waiter put the receipt in the black book on the table.

 "Is there anything else I can get you?

"No thank you, that was exquisite!" Frank said. Jenny finished her chocolate mousse desert and sat back looking at Frank. Frank finished the last of the Sherri Blanc Red Wine and put his glass down and looked at Jenny. "Where are we off to my dear?" Jenny's cell phone rang.

"Hi Laker, how are you and Sofia doing?

"Mom, we are doing great, but the lights went off for a few minutes and it kind of freaked me and Sofia out? Jenny sat back in her chair and looked at Frank.

"Okay your dad and I just finished dinner and we'll be right up."

Jenny saw the disappointment on Frank's face. She looked at him, say listen Frank, "if you want to just go and see Las Vegas night life and gamble a little, that's okay with me."

It's 11:00 p.m. now and I'm tired. Jenny looked at Frank for a sign.

Jenny yawned, "I'm a little tired. I think I'll go up to the room and see if the who got eaten by the boogieman."

Frank laughed, okay sure." Frank got up from his seat, threw his napkin on the table and paid the check.

"I think I'll take a stroll around." I'll be up later." Jenny stood up and gave Frank a quick kiss on the cheek. "See you later."

Frank walked out of the *Diamond Club Casino* and walked six blocks east and decided to go into *St Patrick's Casino*. It was not a big casino at all, but it sure was noisy for sure! But after viewing the casino, nothing he saw was that great or spectacular. There was an escalator straight ahead. He took it upstairs. He went to the bar to order a drink. The bar tender looked at him. "We have a special tonight. It's called, the *Grab Me Baby* which is a double shot of rum with a splash of coke for $3.00 Frank looked at the bartender. It sounded like a drink he needed.

"Sure, I'll take one of those.

He took his drink and looked around at all the machines and people playing. He wasn't much into gambling. He just liked watching the people. Outside, there was a small balcony with two iron chairs, an iron table with a white railing. Below him was a long strip area. He looked up and saw a huge curved hanging ceiling. It had a lighted show all the way down the strip. There was a night show going on with Elvis Presley's in parachutes coming down from the sky.

"How cool is this!" he thought.

Below there were lots of people walking around. "What a mix?" he thought. There were all kinds of dudes in Elvis costumes. Some of them wore costumes of white, some wore red, some wore blue and, of course, some wore black. Some were playing guitars, some without guitars. Some were with Marilyn Monroe look- a-likes on their arms wearing white crisscrossed strapped flowing dresses.

Frank took a sip of his drink, "Awesome costumes!" he thought. "Now this is entertaining." **"What plays in Vegas, stays in Vegas."** He observed the Elvis outfits again. There were all kinds of outfits. White, Red, blue in color with black wigs. Frank laughed. "What a riot!" he thought.

On the corner was a big, fat, beer bellied guy with a aqua blue woman's swimsuit with a with white plastic boots dancing and pretending to hold a microphone singing. Frank laughed. "That guy has to be on drugs."

Frank sat watching the fun and ordering more drinks. He looked at his watch. It was 1:30 a.m. It was getting late. Before he got up to leave, he heard some screaming down below. He leaned over the railing and heard a woman screaming "I knew I would find you there" The guy was walking drunk across the strip to her. She started screaming again. "I knew it, I knew it!" "I just knew you would be at some cheap strip club, whoring around again!"

She took her wedding ring off and threw it across the strip
in his direction. You could hear the bing!, bing!, bing!
When it hit the ground. She yelled out again, "It's over!"
You asshole!" She grabbed his ear, turned and stormed off
holding his ear.   Frank thought

"Wow!" "Now that's a sight to see." "A real wake-up call
for sure!"

 It was one of those moments that made him realize how
lucky he was to have his family, Jenny, Laker and Sofia.
And how crazy life is around you and how safe you feel
when you know you're going home to people who really
care about you. "Only in Vegas", he thought.
"What plays in Vegas, stays in Vegas!"

He sat thinking staring at the crowd and thinking how
stupid he had been having a one-time fling with Charlene,
one of the new associates who had just started with the
firm. They had lunch together. At first, he didn't think
anything of it, but then it began to get sticky. She was 27
and single; career-minded, pretty and adventurous. He
knew he had to keep his distance. He also knew that she
could be dangerous. Soon she started coming on to him.
He played around at first, just flirting. Then the flirting
became something more, a kiss here and there on his cheek.

His ego got the best of him. Pretty much, after that, his ego
took over him. They both ended up in a cheap motel
having cheap sex. It was nothing ever worth talking about.
It was only when Jenny noticed too many text messages
and too many after work phone calls that she got
suspicious. The lipstick on his white shirt was the kicker.

He had come home and she walked by with the shirt with a post-it on it*! "Crazy Asshole!" "What were you thinking?" "Pack your shit and get out!"* He knew she knew.

Frank didn't say a word to her. He knew better. He packed some clothes and spent two weeks in a cheap motel kicking himself in the ass every minute and eating sand every second. Jenny ignored his calls. He knew she was pissed. "

"Well, I guess any married woman would be. Marriage and vows are important and should be kept." Frank realized Jenny was his soul mate and the kids Laker and Sofia were his pride and joy.

When she finally did answer his call, he was so elated he didn't know what to say. She simply said, "I told the kids you had to go on a long trip for work." They don't know. They miss you. We need to go to therapy. If we both can't fix the work of destruction you have caused in our marriage, we can each say our goodbyes." Jenny gave it her best angry voice.

"Understood?" Frank held the cell phone and put his hand over his eyes, tears running down his face. Trying not to have his voice break, he whispered, "Understood!" Jenny shifted the cell phone to the other ear.

"Don't tell me you miss me and you love me! I don't want to hear your bullshit! You can come back tomorrow around 6:00 p.m. The kids will be anxious to see you." Jenny hung up.

Frank hung up the cell phone and wiped his tear-streaked face. He knew he would have been begging Jenny on the phone like a dog if she hadn't asked him back. His heart was hurting. He wanted to go home so bad. He knew he had screwed up. And he screwed up bad. He wanted a second chance to make it up to Jenny. But he also knew there would be hell to pay. Jenny would not let him off easy. In her own way, she would make him pay!

Frank got up from his seat on the balcony railed terrace. Those six blocks walking back to the hotel seemed like an eternity. All he could think of was Dorothy in the Wizard of Oz saying, *"There's no place like home!"* *"There's no place like home!"* And the witch dressed in black with a green face, (Jennys) with green hands, long nails, saying, *"I'll get you my pretty and your little dog (bitch at work) too!*

Jenny looked at the alarm clock. It was 9:30 a.m. She rolled over and looked at Frank fast asleep. Thank God, he was here with all arms, legs and hands intact. She didn't know what time he had come in. But she definitely had the worry mind tick-tock away she goes. Why wouldn't she? It was Las Vegas! All she knew was, **"What plays in Vegas, stays in Vegas!"**

She had come back to the room to hear Laker and Sofia's night episode. After calming them both down, they all climbed in the king size bed together and started to watch a cartoon movie. Jenny looked at Sofia and then at Laker. You'd think at age nine and 11, they would be big enough to handle anything now-a-days. She wrapped her arms

around Laker and Sofia and laughed inside. Guess it was
all the big sounds and glitter of Las Vegas that spooked
them. She rolled over in bed and tucked her pillow under
her head. Before her eyes slowly closed, she whispered.

"Hey, you guys head for bed now. It's 1:30 a.m. I am
tired. We have another day to play tomorrow." Forgetting
all about the evening charade, Laker asked."

"Can we go to the roller coaster ride at the *Arrow Landing
Casino* tomorrow? Jenny rolled over and turned off the
light. Sleepily she said, "We will ask Dad tomorrow." "He
should be coming in soon."

Jenny opened her eyes. She could hear the TV in the other
room.   She got up and sleepily walked to the kid's room.
Sofia was sitting up on her bed with her bathing suit on.
"Hey Mom, I want to go to the Lazy River pool." "The one
that has the yellow donuts you get into and ride around the
pool in.

Laker rolled over. "Shhhhhh, I need my sleep." Sofia
rolled her eyes.

"As usual", she thought."

Jenny put her finger over her mouth and said "Shhhhh".
She whispered, "Okay! Okay! Let's let the boys sleep in
and go downstairs, have some breakfast and go to the pool.
I'll leave your dad a note by the bed to call me when he and
Laker get up." Sofia jumped up off the bed.

"Okay Mom, cool! Hurry, Mom, go get your bathing suit on and let's go!"

Frank turned over and looked at the clock. It was 10:00 a.m. He saw the note Jenny left him saying they were down at the Lazy River Pool. As he turned on the TV, he rolled out of bed.   Laker called out from the other room. "Hey Dad you think we can go to the casino that has the crazy roller coaster ride today, *The Arrow Landing Casino*? Frank yelled back.

"We'll see. Your Mom and Sofia are by the Lazy River Pool. Take a shower!" Frank yelled.
"Then we'll eat and go get them."

Jenny watched Sofia playing with the other kids in the Lazy River. The yellow donut rings with kids and adults in them slowly floating under the cascades of waterfalls and a manmade cave with steamy fog coming down from the top of the cave. The Lazy River waves gently carrying everyone down its path. She smiled as she listened to the sounds of laughter coming from the lazy river and the sounds of people talking around the pool area.

Jenny put her striped blue and white hat on, along with her dark sunglasses. She waved at Sofia and sat back in the lounge chair. She closed her eyes, listening to the sounds of The Lazy River. This was the first time she felt relaxed in a long time. She smiled to herself feeling the warm sun on her body.

"May I sit here?" Jenny quickly opened her eyes and looked at the lady standing next to her pointing to the empty lounge chair. She was Jenny's age, 37ish. Jenny put her hand over her brow.

 "Sure, no one is sitting there."

"Thank you" the lady said and put her orange towel down and positioned her body on the chair and turned to Jenny. "Hi, my name is Peggy," she said. Jenny turned and looked at her. "Hi Peggy, my name is Jenny. Nice to meet you." Jenny looked at Sofia floating around with some other girl. She could see that they were playing hide and seek, all the while giggling, trying to get away from two boys about the same age. She took a deep breath and closed her eyes again. She lay there for 10 minutes, relaxing.

She heard a muffled sound from Peggy next to her. Jenny opened her eyes and sat up. She took her sunglasses off and looked at the Peggy. She saw tears running down her face. "Peggy looked down at her fumbling hands and then quickly removed her sunglasses and wiped away her tears.

"Excuse me, Peggy said. "I didn't mean to be rude."

Peggy gave Jenny a quick glance and then stared down at her lap, not wanting to pry into Peggy's moment of unexpected sorrow. Peggy sat in silence and looked across the pool into the distance.

 "I am sorry. I didn't mean to disturb you."

Jenny pulled a Kleenex from her purse and handed it to her.

Peggy blew her nose and turned to Jenny.

"Everyone now and then I get weepy." "As time goes on, the crying seems to get less and less." "My husband Jeff is upstairs in the room sleeping". "He has terminal cancer, she said and he is dying."

Jenny, horrified, sat up and leaned over and touched her hand. "I am so sorry." "She looked down at the tissue, tearing it apart. "It happened so fast." She looked up and stared in the distance. "Funny how you think you have your life planned out and you want to be married for 35 years or more, like your parents did and watch your children grow and have children of their own" she said.

Jenny sat dumbfounded. She didn't know what to say. And then the words came to her.

"Life can throw some shitty curve balls." Just when you think you got it good, out of the blue, you get shit on". Jenny looked at the pool again and softly said, "My husband, Frank threw me a shitty curve ball by cheating with one of his girly colleagues at work." Peggy very softly started laughing.

"Well, I thought my situation was a dead-end one. You have the rest of your life to live wondering if he's going to cheat on you again. Well at least, it's a girl and not a guy." Jenny looked at Peggy who started chuckling and then she started chuckling. "Sorry, Peggy said." "I just find some irony between your life and my life situation. Peggy leaned over to grab her water to take a drink. A ring fell off her finger on the cement.

"Oh here, let me get that for you Jenny said. Leaning over, Jenny picked up the ring and looked at it before handing it to Peggy. "It's an absolutely beautiful ring!" "Peggy took the ring from Jenny and sat there staring at the ring and twirling the ring on her finger.

Peggy remembered the first time her husband Jeff had given her the ring. It was their 1st wedding anniversary. Peggy held the ring in her fingers and swirled it around, remembering how proud he was giving her the ring and how lovingly she looked in his eyes. Knowing all along it took him a long time to save to buy the ring. Peggy took a few more minutes admiring the sparkling green emerald marquee with 10 karat gold. All of a sudden, she realized, the ring would always torment her when Jeff died. It would be a reminder of their love. It was something she wanted to keep inside her, but not live staring at her when he moved on out of this world. She turned to face Jenny and extended her ring out to Jenny.

"I want you to have this."

Jenny turned to look at her. "What?" Jenny looked at her in shock. Peggy looked at her and smiled. "I want you to have this ring for good luck."

"No, I can't take your ring, Jenny blurted out."

Peggy took off her sunglasses again and looked at Jenny with sincerity in her eyes.

"No, please, I truly want you to have this ring for good luck." I am hoping when you wear it, your marriage will last 35 more years". She smiled at Jenny, took Jenny's hand and placed the ring in it. She got up from her chair, grabbed her water and purse, put her sunglasses on, smiled at Jenny for the last time and walked away.

Jenny looked at the ring in her hand. It was beautiful. The green marquee emerald sparkled. She never had anyone give her such a gift. It was the most "enlightening" experience she had ever had with another person she never even knew. She put her hand over her brow to shade the sun again and softly yelled "thank you." Peggy never looked back. Jenny put the ring on her middle right-hand finger. It fit perfectly. She put her hand over her brow and looked up again. Peggy was gone.

Jenny watched Sofia and her new little girlfriend in the Lazy River pool. Two boys were behind them, diving under the water, in the chase chance to splash them and tease them. She smiled and looked around the pool. Maybe, just, maybe? She was hoping to see the "rose colored gold, good-looking Golden-Like fish" one more time. She laughed out-loud, as her dreamland wishing faded, when she caught a glimpse of Frank and Laker making their way towards her.

Jenny waived for Sofia to come out of the pool. Laker looked at his mom.

"Hey Mom, I was wondering if we could all go on the Rollercoaster called the "Caterpillar" at the *Arrow Landing Casino*?

Seeing Sofia floating in front of her, Jenny got up, waiving
to Sofia, she yelled, "Let's go!" She looked at Frank and
shrugged her shoulders. "I don't see why not." "How far
is the casino from here?"

"Oh, it's right down two doors from our casino", Laker
said. "I saw it from our hotel window." Jenny toweled
Sofia off. "Okay game plan is, let's go to the food court
and get something to eat first," Frank said.

The food court was amusing, Frank thought." It was fun
watching all the tourists bustling around from all walks of
life, Asian, Indian, European, old people, young people.

On the way to *The Arrow Landing Casino*, Frank noticed
several people with a tall drink. I think I'll try one of those
drinks. The really long looking bong drink with a huge
straw. He wanted to order one of those. He found a
waitress at *The Arrow Landing Casino* and ordered one.
Jenny looked at him crazy.

"Hey its Vegas, Frank said. All the while she was thinking
"You Go Boy!" Frank took a long swig from the straw.
"Whoa! This stuff is strong! It's a strawberry daiquiri with
vodka in it.

"Probably a bottle of Vodka," Jenny thought.

Laker and Sofia headed for the roller coaster ticket area.
Jenny and Frank followed right behind them. Four tickets
please, Laker said. "Oh no, no, not me", Jenny said. "I'm
crazy, but not that crazy!" "You guys go!" Frank handed
her his drink. "Okay baby cakes see you in few." Jenny

took Frank's drink letting him know, "I'll meet you guys at the end of the ride". She walked outside to the end of the ride area, sat on a bench and watched all the crazies on the ride." She thought, "four-minute ride tops."

She took a sip of Frank's drink. "Ick", she thought. All she could taste was vodka. She'd be drunk after a few sips, she thought. She saw Frank, Sofia and Laker get on the Roller coaster. It had three big loops; a back-me-up to the end and stop motion and that was it. They were all in the front seat row. "Laker is going to really like this ride," she thought. Front row seats. She watched as the ride took off. It started out slow and then it got faster on each loop. She glanced up and watched them. Laker and Sofia were laughing and screaming all at the same time.

She could see Frank's face. It looked white. His hands were gripping the bar tightly, his eyes closed and his whole face turning white in a frozen look. Thank God she had her dark sunglasses on. She tried not to smile. It was too much seeing Frank's face turn white as a ghost, frozen in time on the roller coaster. Holding Frank's drink, she took another sip and started laughing. She put her head down so they couldn't see her laughing. She couldn't stop laughing, all the while thinking "You Go Boy!" Everyone exited the ride. Laker and Sofia came running over.

"Can we do it again?" "Can we do it again, Mom?"

"Okay, okay, one more time and that is it! Jenny gave them a $20 bill. Frank looked at Jenny in terror. Jenny was laughing hard inside. Frank sat down on the bench holding his stomach with his head down trying not to gag. Jenny looked at Frank trying not to show her smirk on her face and asked.

"Want to go again, dear?"

 Frank still with his head hanging down whispered, "No, I'm good."

Laker and Sofia took off to get round two tickets. Frank reached for his shades in his pocket. They were gone.

"Whoops, lost my new Ray-bans, Frank said."

Jenny was still laughing hard inside.

"That's not all you're going to lose," she thought.

Frank bent over to the side of the bench and lost it in the grass next to the bench. Vomit all over. Jenny put her hand on his back, "you okay honey?" "Yep, give me a minute." Jenny handed Frank his drink and said, "Want your drink?"

Frank looked up at her crazily.

"You think?" he said. All the while Jenny was smiling and laughing hard on the inside. "Didn't think so, Jenny said." She couldn't hold it anymore. She started laughing.

"Mmm, that tall Yard drink is really good!"

Frank didn't say anything. He just sat, bent over on the bench, with his hands on his forehead. She thought a little humiliation was good for him.

Jenny looked at her watch. It was 4:00 p.m. Sofia and Laker came running over to the bench. Out of breath Laker shouted.

"That was so cool!"

"Mom, Sofia put her hand on her mom's knee, "I'm hungry. Can we go get a hamburger and French fries somewhere?"

Sofia then looked at her dad. He had his head hanging down with both hands on his head.

 "Dad, you okay?" Sofia asked. Frank slowly raised his head and got up. He ruffled Sofia's hair.

"I'm good sweetheart."

Jenny got up and said, "Okay hamburger and French fries it is!" Frank still looking green, rubbed his stomach.

Frank, Jenny, Laker and Sofia walked across the street from their hotel, The *Diamond Club Casino*. They ordered their food and sat outside at *the Sam's Hamburgers and Hotdogs* eating their hamburgers and French fries watching everyone. It was always noisy with lots of interesting people walking around. There were people walking fast everywhere that Laker and Sofia have never seen before.

Men looking like women dressed in short paisley skirts with long legs, high heels, black wigs and make-up carrying a purse. Laker would nudge Sofia and point his finger indiscreetly on the table towards the walking crowd. Sofia would look with wide eyes and then put her eyes down on the table so the quick walking passer-byers would not see her staring. Laker would end up eating and laughing all at the same time. People would leave their uneaten food on a trash can and two minutes later a homeless person would walk by and quickly pick it up.

Sofia thought that was a good thing. People in Las Vegas, on their last leg, needed to eat something, anything. Jenny turned to Frank and said, "I think this area would be a good place to stand and watch the fireworks. It faces *The Diamond Club Casino* hotel. The fireworks start at 9:00 p.m. tonight. Laker and Sofia looked at each other, smiled and both at the same time did a high-five. Yes!"

Chapter 12– Kinsey - 1St Round Poker Tournament – Who Will Win?

It was now down to three players at the table. Him, Todd Bales and Leonard Gallery. Kinsey eyed both of them, thinking if one of them had the 10 of Hearts he would be out. Or if one of them had 2 Aces he would be burned.

"This was it!" It was either, "go big or go home broke" he thought.

Kinsey had about $30,000 in chips. Kinsey quickly glanced at his watch. It was 10:00 p.m. Kinsey rubbed his forehead; he looked hard at his hand again. He had three good cards. It was a King of Hearts, A Queen of Hearts and a Ten of Hearts. He looked at the river cards in front of Paul, the dealer. The Ace and Jack of Hearts were on the flop. He just needed the 10 of Hearts for a Royal Flush and win would be his. Kinsey moved his chips to the middle of the poker table, "All in!" Kinsey said. There was a gasp from the crowd watching in the bleacher seating area. Kinsey eyed Todd. He had black shades on, so he couldn't see his eyes.

Kinsey looked at his two cards. He quickly glanced at his watch. One o'clock. He had been playing for three hours. Three players remained. Himself. Of course, Todd Bales across the table and Leonard Gallery another great poker player. Kinsey knew in the past few years, Leonard Gallery had won two major poker tournaments. He asked the waitress for water. The dealer announced they were going to break for 30 minutes after this hand. His adrenalin had worn off and he needed some energy, a bite to eat to relax his mind and stop the madness of his stomach telling him he needed to eat. "How can you think of food when you're in a battle for your livelihood? He shook his head. "Ridiculous" he thought.

Kinsey fumbled with his chips and then eyed Todd who then quickly, threw the rest of his chips on the table. "All in!" Todd declared. Leonard looked at Kinsey and then at Todd. His card hand was fair, but he knew if Kinsey had a full house he would be doomed. Bluff or fold? Leonard threw the cards on the table. "I fold." You could hear a pin drop. It seemed like minutes ticking by. The dealer

finally flipped the last river card on the table and said, 10 of
Hearts. Kinsey got up and threw his cards on the table, and
put both of his hands folded to the back of his head, while
shaking it. He couldn't believe it! Todd stood up and
flipped his cards over. One Ace and one King. The crowd
stood up and all clapped. Kinsey had won! Dealer
announced.

"Mr. Kinsey McDonald is the winner of the table."
"Congratulations to Mr. Kinsey McDonald!"

All players but Kinsey got up and left the table. The dealer
turned to Kinsey. "Congratulations again, you will attend
the final Poker Tournament table of 10 players tomorrow
July 4th. The winners will be announced at 12:00 p.m.
tonight on the Casino Poker Players Board at the High
Stakes Gambling Area. The Poker Tournament will begin
at 12:00 noon tomorrow, July 4th, here in the Premier
Conference Room. Please be here at 10:30 a.m. Your
current chips on the table will be accounted for. I see there
is a total of $100,000. They will be in safe keeping for you
until tomorrow.

Kinsey thanked the dealer and told him to take three $100
chips for his tip. The dealer gave him a pink slip for the
$300 tip and thanked him. Kinsey walked to the high roller
club and sat down at a poker machine at the bar and
ordered a drink, bourbon straight. He put a $100 bill in the
machine and played the max of $5.00 a hand, all the while
his hands were shaking. The bartender came over and
asked. "What can I get you sir to drink?"

Kinsey looked up at the bald bar tender. "I think I'll have a *"Ball-headed* Be*nny*." The bald bar tender shook his head and laughed. Bald head shining he turned around and walked down the bar saying, "All righty sir, still laughing, one *"Bald-headed Benny"* coming up." Kinsey put another $100 in the machine.

Chapter 13– *The Diamond Club Casino - Relax With Us Spa*

Megan opened one eye and then the other. She rolled over and looked at the alarm clock. "Ugh!" It was 4th of July, 9:45 a.m. They had all gotten back to the room around 4:30 a.m. She put her hand on her head and got up and headed to the bathroom. She couldn't remember how many *Lie Down Lucy shots* she had drunk.

Megan looked at her and pulled the covers over her head. Then she slowly got up and walked by Bethany like she was some zombie. "Good morning." She looked in the mirror. The mirror told the whole ugly story behind the bloodshot eyes and smeared mascara. She brushed her *"Lie Down Lucy"* stinking breath and teeth and opened the shower door, turned on the water. She took a wash cloth and soap and pretended she was going through a car wash with all the extras, including a superior wax. *"Lie Down Lucy"* began to run down the drain. She started to feel somewhat better. If she could just get her head to say *"Lie Down Lucy"* she'd be in good shape.

She barely ate any breakfast. She was trying to work her magic with Darren. Sitting close to him, feeling lightheaded, in the Diner, and smelling his cologne was a good ending to a great night. She put both of her hands on her head while sitting on the toilet. Thinking of Darren's cologne smell now made her gage. And thinking of all the *"Lie Down Lucy"* shots made her think she was Lucy and needed to lie down. Her heading was woozy. She stepped out the shower, towed off, dressed and opened the bathroom door to let the steam out.

Bethany heard the bathroom toilet flush. Megan walked out of the bathroom brushing her teeth. "Good morning, Sunshine!"

Bethany sat combing her hair. "Hey remember, its Spa Day today at 1:00 p.m." Megan came out of the bathroom. She sat on the bed a minute to make sure the *"Lie Down Lucy"* and her head wasn't going to *"Lie Down Lucy"* anymore. She watched Stephanie prancing around, opening the shades and then sitting at the desk and putting her make-up on.

Bethany raised her eyebrow as Megan stood by the bed.

"I saw you and Darren in the taxi this morning." Lips in a vise lock".   Megan laughed.

 "I think my lips where in the barf bag!" What about you and Brett humping and bumping on the dance floor? Or was that the "Back-it-up grind dance? Bethany starting laughing,

"I really think they are nice guys!" "Megan sat on the bed with Bethany smiling. "I do too!"

Megan, I'm starving! "Hey, listen, I'm going to grab us some coffee and breakfast sandwiches downstairs." She grabbed her purse, "I'll be back up in a few. Bethany yelled to her.

"Can you please bring me an orange juice and breakfast burrito? Megan yelled back,

"How about a "*Lie Down Lucy*" to go with your orange juice?" Bethany put her finger in her mouth as if to gag. Megan started laughing as she closed the door.

Stephanie heard the girls from the other room. She put her arms in the air and yawned. She lied in bed awhile longer and did a flashback of last night. "Oh, that Massachusetts boy, Johnny, she thought. "Wow, what a great kisser!" They had made their way to the bathroom of *The Canyon Roller Club* and he had grabbed her hand, spun her around and kissed her hard on the mouth. She looked in his dark brown eyes and smiled. Of course, the "*Lie Down Lucys*" were doing their magic, she thought.

Still lying down in bed and trying to keep her wits about her, trying not to let the "*Lie Down Lucys*" take control, she got up slowly. She put her hands to her throbbing head. She walked slowly to the bathroom and opened the shower door. Her feet were killing her from dancing all night. She looked down at her right foot. "Ugh!" she winced. The rash was still there. It was still red and now it had white bumps all over the red parts. It was ugly looking. She didn't want to think about it. She felt tired and hot. She could feel a slight pain in her chest that would come and go. She didn't want to think about it now. But, for sure she knew she was going to have it checked out when she got home.

Megan opened the hotel suite door and placed the tray of coffee, orange juices and bag of breakfast sandwiches and a burrito on the bed. Stephanie and Bethany were sitting there brushing their wet hair. "Thanks Megan. You're the best!" Megan put her hand in the air and high-fived Bethany. Bethany took a bite of her sandwich, "Well girls, it's our Spa Day, today!" Megan took a sip of her coffee and looked at Bethany.

"I am so ready!" Okay the game plan is this." Bethany looked at her watch. It's 11:00 a.m. Our appointment is at 1:00 p.m. at *Relax While You Can* Day Spa which is on the 3rd floor. "I guess we have just enough time to eat, put some makeup on and go."

Bethany's cell phone started ringing. She picked it up from the bed table and said "hello".

"Hey Bethany, its Brett. The guys and I were wondering if you girls would like to meet us at *The Aero Tower Casino*. They have an elevator that takes you up to the 102th top open-air floor. Say around 8:00 p.m. tonight. We thought it would be a good place to watch the fireworks."

"Mmmm that sounds great! Let me ask the girls."

Bethany put her hand over the cell phone. Stephanie and Megan were already nodding their heads, "Yes! Yes! Bethany laughed. "Yes, of course, sounds like fun!" We'll see you guys at 8:00 p.m. in the entrance area of *The Aero Tower Casino* tonight.

"Great!" Brett said, "Don't worry about getting there." All the taxicab drivers know where the famous *Aero Tower Casino* is. It's one of the tallest casinos in Las Vegas."

"Okay, see you guys there!" Stephanie said again. She hung up and they all looked at each other, entwined the girly pinky fingers together on the bed. "Yes! And it's our last day night in Vegas!" Megan said.

"On that note, Stephanie chimed in, check-out is a late one at 1:00 p.m. Sunday, tomorrow. I suggest we all pretty much pack-up before we go out tonight."

"Sounds good," Megan said. "I wanted to thank you, Bethany, for inviting me and Stephanie,"

Bouncing off the bed, Bethany smiled, turned and said, "Oh, my BFF Megan!" She gave her a big hug, "Megan, always being the best friend with perfect polite manners." Bethany got up off the bed and grabbed Megan's hands. Megan got up off the bed and grabbed Bethany's hands and they both spun around and around. Megan laughed.

 "What are best friends for?" I'm ready for the spa!" "Let's go!"

Bethany pushed the 3rd floor button that *read "Relax with Us Spa"*. Bethany handed the Spa receptionist her Driver's License. "A reservation for three under Professor Grant Bishop, my dad." The receptionist smiled.

"Yes, I see your reservation." Here are your locker keys.
The receptionist handed each one a locker key with a
number on it. The receptionist then pointed to Sandy.
Sandy will be your tour guide for the day. She will show
you around our *Relax with Us Spa.*

Standing beside them was a tall Swedish looking girl with
long braided blonde hair. "Hi, my name is Sandy. I'll be
your tour guide for today." "Right this way please."
Bethany, Megan and Stephanie looked at each other and
giggled. Megan said.

"Oh, the royal treatment. I am beginning to like this
already."

Sandy took the girls on a tour and showed them the Locker
Room, the Jacuzzi, the Sauna Room where the massage
rooms where also the shower room and the sitting room
with bold trimmed, white cushioned lounge chairs with
small round tables with ice containers with lots of lemons,
looking out on a small tropical flower garden. "Heaven
just arrived," Megan thought. Bethany smiled at Stephanie
and high-five her. Bethany looked around in awe and
exhaled a long sigh.

"Dad, you did it again!" she thought.

Bethany, Stephanie and Megan put their stuff in the Spa
locker. They had a small bag with makeup, a hair brush,
tooth paste, tooth brush and other necessities. Bethany and
Stephanie grabbed the white fluffy robes and put the white
slippers on.

Stephanie opened her robe to the girls, she said "Walla!" showing her bathing suit. Megan froze. She had forgotten to put her bathing suit on before she left the room. Turning bright red, she blurted out, "Holy crap! I forgot my bathing suit." Bethany and Stephanie looked at each other and starting laughing. Stephanie said, "Look, Megan, Las Vegas!" **"What plays in Vegas, stays in Vegas!"** No one is going to know you. With all the people that come here every day, to the Las Vegas playground, who are you going to bump in to?

Megan thought about it for a minute. "Stephanie you're right let's go get our massage."

"After our massages Bethany said, "how about we all meet at the Jacuzzi spa?" One hour later, Megan walked through the open-door spa area. She observed the area with its wooden lockers and a wet floor. The Jacuzzi was square, not very big, with about five stairs down. She casually peeked into the area. There were three ladies in the Jacuzzi. Two of the three ladies were wearing bathing suits. She wrapped her soft white robe tighter and tried to calm her nerves. "Okay, she thought." Good". One of them was not wearing a bathing suit." She closed her eyes and whispered, "I can do this." "I can do this." Remember what Stephanie said, **"What plays in Vegas, stays in Vegas!"**

Bethany and Stephanie cruised through the open door to the spa, smiling. They both dropped their white robes showing their bathing suits and climbed down the five stairs into one corner of the Jacuzzi. Looking up at Megan, Stephanie whispered.

"Come on Megan! It feels great! Nice and warm with lots of bubbles."

Megan closed her eyes for a moment, she pulled her robe tighter and then thinking all the while, **"What plays in Vegas, stays in Vegas!"** "Okay here goes!" She dropped her towel. She slowly walked down the five stairs into the Jacuzzi.   She wanted to act cool in front of her friends. She held her breath and pranced down the stairs like she was Cleopatra with a gold crown on her head.

All of a sudden, she heard some commotion behind her. Stephanie and Bethany tried to keep her eyes on Megan. As if to say, "Yes you can do this!" "Just a few more steps, Megan, just a few more steps and you are good." They both shifted their eyes and casually looked behind Megan to see what the heck was going on with all the commotion.

 As Megan reached the last step, Bethany and Stephanie both looked at each other. Bethany put her hand over her mouth; they both started laughing. Then Stephanie and Bethany turned to each other and put their hands over their mouths and started laughing. Laughing, more hysterically. Each second seemed like an eternity for Megan. And then the commotion behind her turned into sounds. Loud sounds behind her. It got louder and louder. Megan quickened her step and slid down into the bubbly water and turned to Stephanie and Bethany. Bethany turned and looked at Megan and said, *"I didn't know you brought your entourage with you!"*

Megan, with a horrified look on her face, looked at the Spa entrance. There was Sandy, the tour guide, smiling, waving, with a group of six women. "Oh my God," Megan blurted out! She slid down again under the water and held her breath as long as she could. The girls were still laughing uncontrollably when she emerged. Her long wet brown hair draped over her eyes. The other three women had already gotten out of the Jacuzzi quickly. The trail of six women standing at the Spa opening had disappeared.

Still laughing, Bethany put her arm around Megan. "Oh, Megan," she whispered. "You looked like Cleopatra, Egyptian Queen, with her high crown, making an entrance to her kingdom, walking down those stairs." Bethany tried to make Megan feel better. Remember what I told you Ms. Megan, **"What plays in Vegas, stays in Vegas!"** Megan still in somewhat of a comatose trance, closed her eyes and put her head under the water again. She wanted to quickly fade away, hide somewhere, and erase from her mind just what happened to her.

She came up for air. Bethany and Stephanie, trying not to laugh anymore, got out of the Jacuzzi and handed Megan her white robe. She took the robe and walked up the five stairs as gracefully as she could and wrapped the robe tightly around her. Bethany and Stephanie both looked at each other and started laughing again. The image of Queen Cleopatra seemed to play over and over in their minds. It was just too funny. Megan stood there with her arms wrapped around her robe holding it tight. Bethany looked into Megan's terrified eyes and patted her back. Still trying not to laugh. But knowing the eyes always tell everything she said, "Okay Ms. Cleopatra, it's time for the Sauna room."

"I am ready for the Sauna room!" Bethany said. The Sauna had two floor-length, side-by-side glass mirrors with handles on each side. Bethany opened them and they walked in. Bethany and Stephanie headed for the top seat. They both looked like white furry cats in their robes crouched in their corners. Megan took the seat in the front level facing the two glass doors. Her feet dangled against the tile seat.   There were two girls to the left of her and two to the right. It was a packed sauna room.

The glass doors slowly closed, the lights dimmed and steam started rising from the floor. It was so quiet that you could hear a pin drop. Steam started rising from the floor in front of Megan. It was getting hot. The steam kept rising. It was getting hotter. It was so dark and so steamy you couldn't see your hand in front of your face.

Megan closed her eyes and tried to relax. But nothing was relaxing to her. All she could think of was "Jack the Ripper" coming out of the fog from nowhere with his surgical knife ready. She tried to be cool and breathe slowly. But all she was feeling was panic. "Okay, be cool, be cool, she thought. Breathe slowly." She kept chanting to herself, "You are not going to be the first one to leave. You are NOT going to be the first one to leave. Everybody, for sure, would know you were the chicken. She felt her breathing becoming rapid and uneven. She thought she heard a "click" on the doors. "Jack the Ripper" had arrived. The girl next to her jumped slightly, got up hurriedly and said,

"Yep, I think I'm done!" Megan knew that was her exit.
She quickly jumped down from the tile seat and said "Me
too!"

Megan yelled back at the two white silent cats in the
corner, "Hey guys, I am going to the shower. I'll see you in
the locker room." No response from any of the girls.
"Okay, Megan thought. "They're taking a cat nap. Good
for them! I'm out of here!" She opened the doors and
breathed in the fresh air thinking, "Awe, fresh air, no "Jack
the Ripper."

The Spa locker room was getting full. Megan quickly
grabbed her clothes from the locker and started putting her
make-up on. Bethany and Stephanie came in, where Megan
was looking in the mirror. They both turned to each other
and started laughing. Megan holding her mascara brush
said, "Okay, okay guys, I am sure it was funny, but not that
funny."

 "Okay, Queen Cleopatra, Bethany said. And once again
she and Stephanie once again both started busting up
laughing again. Megan rolled her eyes and finished her
mascara. Bethany looked at Megan and gave her a hug.
Megan looked down and put on her frown face. Bethany
patted her knee and stopped laughing. "Okay, I say we all
go and have dinner at the Lobster House before we meet
the guys. I hear they have a two pound lobster."

"I'm in!" Bethany looked at Stephanie in the mirror and
put her hand over her mouth not to start laughing again. It
was just the funniest thing ever.

"Me too!"

Chapter 14– July 4th – Kinsey McDonald – "Win Big! or Go Home!"

Kinsey walked *toward The Diamond Club Casino*, Premier Conference Club. It was 10:00 a.m. He glanced across the casino floor and saw Todd sitting at the bar. Kinsey showed the front door girl his badge who checked her computer screen and handed him his name badge. Kinsey looked around the conference room. The final poker table was in the middle of the room. He walked over to the table and saw his name on the chair. Todd Bale's name was right across the table from him. Kinsey knew that Todd Bale was going to be his major challenge. All the other players were new to him. Todd walked in and nodded to Kinsey. He nodded back and they both took their seats. The other players arrived right behind Todd and they all took their seats and shook hands.

Todd put his dark sunglasses on. The dealer, Paul, began reciting the rules. "Once again, we will be playing, Texas Hold'em Poker. The dealer, Paul, placed chips in front of each player, declaring how much each player had. The First Place Winner will receive Title for one Year "The 4th of July Poker Tournament at the Diamond Club Casino and will receive one year's complimentary stay in the Poker Winner's Suite, along with $1,000,000.00. Second Place Winner will receive $750,000 and Third Place Winner will receive $500,000. The other two players left will receive a consolation prize of $20,000 each. "Okay, everyone on board?" the dealer, Paul asked. Each one of them nodded. "Okay, let the game begin! "Good luck to you all!" The dealer, Paul dealt the first hand and flipped 2 cards in front of each of the player. After everyone had played one hand, the dealer Paul flipped 4 cards on the river flop.

Kinsey looked at his two cards and quickly glanced at his watch again. Seven hours had slipped by intensely, but quickly. It was now 5:30 p.m. He had $100,000 in chips. Todd had about $100,000 in chips and Vu had about $100,000. Two cards, two Aces is all he needed. That would give him the highest hand for the win. This could be the hand he needed. The Dealer, Paul, made the flop. He turned over one King and one Queen, and an Ace. Kinsey didn't move. He didn't even blink. He sat there looking across the poker table at Todd and staring at the Ace of Clubs, Paul, the Dealer had dealt.

He wondered if Todd or Vu had the other Ace and they had three pairs. "Okay Gentlemen," Paul said. "Mr. Bales, please start the bidding." Todd looked hard at Kinsey. Kinsey looked hard at Todd. "All in" Todd moved his chips in the middle of the table. Vu looked at Todd and Kinsey. Vu looked at his cards again and announced his call, "All in!" Vu moved his $100,000 into the pile. Kinsey looked hard again at Todd. Then he looked hard again at Vu.

Kinsey then took his time and looked at his two cards again. This was it. He knew it! *It was Go Big or go home broke!* He moved his chips to the center of the poker table, "All in". You could hear the crowd in the background. The Dealer, Paul announced. "All players are all in." Then the Dealer, Paul, flipped two more cards: One Ace of Diamonds and one Queen of hearts. All players laid

their cards on the table. The Dealer, Paul announced aloud
on the microphone. "Winner of the Diamond Club Casino
4th of July Poker Tournament is Kinsey McDonald,
$1,000,000! The Second Place Winner is Todd Bales
$750,000 and Third Place Winner is Vu Tong $500,000.

Kinsey jumped up and placed both hands folded on the
back of his head staring down at his cards and the pile of
chips on the table. He had won! He had finally won!   He
spun around with his hands in the air. He took the Poker
Tournament Belt and held it high in the air and displayed it
to the crowd.   The crowd stood up, clapped and yelled,
"Kinsey! "Go Kinsey!" Kinsey shook Todd and Vu's
hands and nodded. Kinsey instructed Paul, the Dealer, and
the head of *The Diamond Club* Poker Tournament, John
Adams to deposit all the funds except $2,000 for his pocket
change into his bank account at Las Vegas Windfall Credit
Union and to give Paul, the Dealer $3,000.00 tip monies.

Kinsey had left his account open with $20.00 checking and
$5.00 in savings and vowed not to touch it, knowing that in
hard times he would not be able to get another account.
After all, he was entitled to some play monies and $2,000
was a good start. Especially, after living in a dumpy motel
room, living off of nickels and dimes.

Looking at his watch, 7:00 p.m., he also figured that if
anyone tried to steal his $2,000.00 he remembered Doreen
telling him. "You are the "Man of Steel!" One quick
whack with his lucky NIXON watch would bring anyone
down! Or, Kinsey thought. At least the looser would end
up with a bloody lip or broken nose, hopefully. After all
the monies and contracts were disclosed and signed, John

Adams handed him a (2) room keys to The Poker
Tournament Pent House Suite located on the 20th floor.
"These two slide keys are good for you and one other
person of whom you need to register for one year. Enjoy,
Mr. Kinsey."

Kinsey walked by the Poker Tournament neon light board.
It read "*Diamond Club Casino* Texas Hold'em Poker
Tournament; CONGRATULATIONS to "Kinsey
McDonald" 1st Place Winner; 2nd Place Todd Bales and 3rd
Place, Vu Tong. Kinsey walked into the high roller bar
area. It was a little crowed. It was, after all, 4th of July.
Kinsey took a seat at the bar in front of a poker video
game.

He took out a hundred and put it in. It was $5.00 each
hand. Wiping a glass, the bar tender walked over and
asked him "What would you like?" Kinsey looked at the
bar tender. "Same old "*Bald-headed Benny*" the bartender
asked?" Kinsey looked down at the poker machine, pushed
the bet button while chuckling and said "*Bald Headed
Benny*" it is. Then he looked up. The bartender came
close, bent closer, looked at Kinsey hard, picked up a dirty
napkin and walked away shaking his bald head. *"Bald-
headed Benny"* coming up! Kinsey ignored him and
pushed the poker video machine button. He glanced
around the bar area. As usual it was quiet, low music with
a few heavy players playing. He took a sip of his *"Bald-
headed Benny"* and looked across the bar area.

He noticed a lady sitting across the bar from him, pushing
the buttons on her video machine game fast. It was
obvious she did not play video games, and, if it was poker,

she didn't know what she was doing. The bartender walked over to her and put his hands on the bar. "What would you like to drink Miss?"

"I'll take what that gentleman ordered, a *Bald-headed Benny*." Kinsey stared at her long and hard. Her hair was brown cut below her ears with bangs. She was wearing a low-cut green dress and her fingernails were long and painted red. But he knew those eyes. She looked up and stared back. Kinsey sat back on the bar stool and looked again hard. He shut his eyes and then opened them. "I'll be dammed! Kinsey thought. He sat there. He couldn't move.

She got up from the other side of the bar, took her drink and grabbed her purse and walked over to him. Kinsey's eyes followed her every move. She sat down on the bar stool next to him. She flashed her green eyes while batting her black fake eyelashes at him. "Hello Stranger!" Remember me?" Kinsey sat there flabbergasted. He couldn't even breathe. Low and behold!

"Is that you Doreen?   Doreen looked at him with shifty eyes.

"You didn't recognize me after 32 plus years together? Thought you'd never see me again?"

Kinsey wanting to be a gentleman for once, knowing it had been a hell of a long time, got up and put his arms around her, kissed her on the cheek and sat back down. "Hello Doreen. Yes, it has been a long time." Doreen shifted on the bar stool.

"I think it's been at least five years, Mr. Kinsey McDonald."

She took a sip of her drink. Kinsey looked directly into her eyes. "And what brings you here to Las Vegas, Doreen?" She eyed him closely, thinking he probably thinks I'm here for his win monies.

"You remember my good friend Grace, whom we knew here when we were still together, called me and said that *The Diamond Club Casino* was having a big Poker Tournament. I had an inkling you might be in the tournament since *The Diamond Club Casino* is your favorite casino. So, she invited me out here for a few days for the 4th of July and she gave me a ticket to watch the tournament."

Kinsey took a sip of his drink and looked at her. "You were here all the time?"

"Yep, you got it! I was up in the crowd watching you." She took another sip of her drink. "So how does it feel to be Mr. Poker Tournament Winner?" Kinsey knew by her saying that, and by him answering her question, he was taking her stab. He looked down at his drink, took another sip, put his drink down on the bar and looked straight into her green eyes. "Damn he thought, I still love her!" His heart welled up.

"To be honest Doreen, winning was not as much fun as I thought it was going to be after losing you."

Doreen looked into his eyes. She wanted to see the man
who she married a long time ago. She wanted to see if he
had any ounce of sincerity. Kinsey waited for the second
stab. He knew he had to take everything Doreen was there
to say. Before she could answer, he took her hand and said.

"Say, listen, I know this is not what you probably want to
hear, but since you are here now, let's go to dinner
somewhere and talk?"

She looked again at Kinsey in the eyes and then looked at
his hand on hers. Even after all those years together, she
still felt herself flush. Her green eyes flashing all the while
saying, no, her beating heart was saying yes." She got off
the bar stool, "Okay, Kinsey, why not? It's just dinner."

Kinsey smiled, "where would you like to eat?" "Pick any
place you like. Las Vegas is on me tonight!" Doreen
looked up at Kinsey.

"As long as there no gambling involved, "I'm good!"
Kinsey smiled. In the back of his mind, Kinsey wanted
Doreen back. He had always loved her. He missed her and
the kids.

Lying in the broken-down cheap motel, he had thought
about Doreen and the kids every night.   He knew that if he
ever had the chance to get Doreen and the kids back, he
could never gamble again. He looked at his NIXON watch.
It was 7:30 p.m. "Dam, I'm the luckiest man tonight!"
Doreen turned and looked at Kinsey. "Let's go to the Blue
Moon Chinese Restaurant here at *The Diamond Club
Casino.*" It has a window table where we can look outside

and see all the lights on the Las Vegas Strip." Kinsey looked at Doreen and smiled. "That sounds good to me!"

Kinsey and Doreen walked into the Blue Moon Chinese Restaurant. Kinsey looked at the hostess. Table for two, please. The waitress smiled at them. Kinsey turned to her again. A booth next to the window if you have one, please." The hostess smiled, looked at both Kinsey and Doreen and grabbed two menus.

"Right this way." The booth was light pink. Kinsey immediately thought of a pink flamingo.

They sat facing each other. Doreen stared out the window at all the lights. She opened her menu and looked at Kinsey. "Boy, it's been a long time since I've seen these lights." Kinsey took his reading glasses out, put them on, opened his menu, scanned it, and then looked up at her.

"Yes, I believe it's been five years, six hours and 30 minutes since we last seen each other."

The waitress came by. "Do you want anything to drink?

"I'll just have water with a lemon Doreen said. "Me too" Kinsey said.

"And what would you both like to order?" Kinsey looked at Doreen. Doreen looked up at the waitress.

"Yes, I think I will have the Duck ala carte with fried rice. She handed the menu back to the waitress. Kinsey looked at the menu again.

"I'll have the Lobster chow mien and an order of green hot tea please for both of us.

Kinsey handed the menu back to the waitress, took off his reading glasses and smiled at Doreen. Doreen placed her napkin in her lap. Kinsey was anxious to know everything that Doreen had been doing. Where did she live? What had she been doing with her life? How the kids were? What was going on in their lives? How many grandkids did he have? He looked at her again. She was still beautiful he thought.   Kinsey asked. "So where are you living now?" Doreen fumbled with her napkin under the table.

"When we divorced, I moved to Cripple Creek Colorado. The population there is about 1,172. I found a nice three - bedroom log cabin 5 miles away from downtown."

Doreen continued. "I eventually got my Real Estate License and started all over again. The children moved on their separate ways, but decided to come visit Colorado to visit one summer and loved Colorado. Kinsey, Jr. and his wife, Sherri, found a home close to Cripple Creek have one daughter, Julia. Kinsey, Jr. got a good job as a Postal Carrier.   Julia is three now. Sherri is a stay-at-home wife." The waitress brought their waters and then their food. "I visit them often. Julia is a doll. Melody moved to Florida. She's 30 years old now. She became a Swimming Coach for the YMCA and loves her job. She's is dating a guy named Bruce. "I met him last summer when they came to visit. He seems good for her. Alice is 28." She's has gone through some hard times. She actually lives with me now."

129

Doreen started playing with her food. She was the one that took our divorce hard. She left Las Vegas when we divorced and moved to the big city, New York with a girlfriend of hers. She stayed there for two years." Doreen looked up at Kinsey. "Mostly, she was living on the streets in New York, I never knew about. She called and asked me for money to come home last summer. Of course, I wired her the money! I was in shock when I picked her up from the Airport. She looked awful! Underweight, hair stringy, wild looking eyes. She looked strung out." Kinsey's eyes filled with tears. He, of course, had no idea.

Kinsey put his fork down and reached over and touched Doreen's hand. "I am so sorry Doreen. I had no idea. I am so very sorry. I have missed you so much and I have missed the children too. Every night I would lie in bed beating myself up over all the mistakes I had made." Doreen took her napkin and wiped her tears away. She knew Kinsey still loved her and she also knew she still loved him. It was those married 32 years she had spent with him and the three beautiful children they had.

The waitress came and put the check down on the table. "Anything else I can get you?" Kinsey looked at Doreen.

"No thank you." We're good." Kinsey wanted to hear more. But not now. All he wanted was them to be together tonight. He looked at her and said, "I know this is crazy, but I would like to go back to the motel, get my belongings and go to *The Diamond Club Casino* Poker Tournament Penthouse." Doreen looked at him like he was crazy.

"What? She asked. "You're being crazy again!"

Kinsey looked at her and laughed. "No, for real Doreen! When I won the Poker Tournament at *The Diamond Club Casino* they gave me *The Diamond Club* Poker Tournament Penthouse Suite for one year on the 20th floor." She looked at him crazy-eyed again. He got up and reached for her hand. Doreen took his hand and stood up next to him.

"Okay, I don't see why not. It's not like I'm going home with a stranger in Las Vegas." He laughed.

Kinsey looked at her again. This time more seriously. "First, I need to go back to the motel and pack my stuff." Kinsey opened the door to the cheap motel. Doreen walked in and looked around. She was horrified at what she saw. It was dingy and dirty looking. Old cigarette holes in the carpet with an old smelly blanket on the bed. Mold growing on the bottom of the edges of the walls. The curtains had moth holes all over them. The furniture was old, worn and dirty.

Kinsey went to the closet, got his green duffle bag out and started shoving his dirty clothes in it. Kinsey grabbed two shirts off the hangers from the closet. He opened the cheap motel drawers and started shoving his socks and under ware into the bag. He went to the bathroom. "I'll be just a minute, Doreen." Doreen sat on the bed and put her purse down beside her. She looked around again. She suddenly felt sad and her eyes welled up with tears. She had no idea her ex-husband had been living for five years in Las Vegas in a broken-down cheap motel room!

Doreen sat on the cheap, smelly motel bed, deeply saddened. Kinsey emerged from the bathroom holding a worn-out black shaving case in his hand. He looked at Doreen sitting on the end of the bed. He dropped the shaving case and stared at her. Doreen started crying. She had taken off her brown wig and was sitting there fumbling the wig in her hands, helpless.

Kinsey looked in horror at her sitting there with her fumbling hands twirling the brown wig. She had no hair. She was bald. Doreen wiped away her tears. Looking up at him she said. "I have cancer." "I have stage4 breast cancer." The doctors told me I have six months to live or less."

Kinsey's face went white. "Oh my God, Doreen!" he said." Kinsey went over and sat down next to Doreen and put his arms around her. His heart broke. He couldn't take it anymore. "It's okay. It's okay my love. I'll take care of you." Don't worry, sweetheart. Shhh. Please don't worry." I will take care of you." He sat rocking her back and forth and the tears began to fall. "Oh my God, poor Doreen, he thought. In that horrible moment, holding Doreen, in her sorrow and grief he knew his gambling days were over. He was going to take care of Doreen, no matter how long she had.

Kinsey looked into Doreen's eyes. He got up from the bed and grabbed his green beat up dirty duffle bag, started shoving the rest of his dirty clothes into it. "Let's get out of here, honey!" Doreen wiped her tears, picked up her wig

and went to the bathroom and put it back on. She came out
and grabbed her purse and put some red lipstick on.

Kinsey stopped by the Motel reception area and told Hank.
"Here's your money for the last month. I'm out of here
tonight! And you can bet your last cheap-ass dollar, I am
never coming back here again! Hank shifted his cigarette
in his lips, counted the money and looked up at Kinsey.

"Okay Mr. McDonald, if you say so." Hank stared at
Kinsey and Doreen. As he put the money in the cashier's
box, he looked at Doreen. "You have a fine young lady
standing beside you that I hope will keep you happy the
rest of your life." Hank winked at Doreen as her face
flushed red. Kinsey turned and kissed Doreen on the cheek
and looked at Hank.

"You got that right! Kinsey hailed a taxi and said "*The
Diamond Club Casino*!" Doreen sat in the back seat with
Kinsey and looked out the window. Kinsey put his arm
around Doreen in the taxi. He knew she was suffering. He
also knew he had to be strong for her.

Doreen looked at Kinsey and softly asked. "Can we stop
by Grace's so I can get my suitcase? I have all my clothes
and medicine in my suitcase at her house." Kinsey looked
at Doreen,

"Sure-thing honey, no problem, whatever your heart
desires." The taxicab driver looked at Kinsey and Doreen
in the backseat. Doreen looked at his name tag hanging
from the rearview mirror, "Ramsey." She looked at his

133

brown eyes in the rearview mirror and leaned toward him.
Can you please go to 3232 Santa Maria Street.

The taxicab driver nodded, "Yep."

It was late in the evening, 11:30 p.m. Grace had given
Doreen an extra key to her house. Kinsey told her he'd
wait in the taxi. Doreen opened the door. It was dark
inside except for a hall light. She didn't see anyone. She
thought Grace was sleeping. She crept down the hallway to
the spare bedroom and put her stuff in her bag and crept
back down the hallway. She got a pen from her purse, a
receipt of some sorts. At least it was a piece of paper. She
went to the kitchen and flipped on the light and started
writing fast. *"Grace, I hooked back up with Kinsey tonight.
I will be with him. I promise to call you soon! Thank you
for everything! "You're the best friend ever! Love you,"
Doreen.* She left the note on the kitchen island, turned off
the light, picked up her shoulder bag and rolled her suitcase
out to the taxicab. Kinsey was waiting outside the taxicab
by the trunk.

The taxicab driver, Ramsey, opened the trunk as soon as he
saw Doreen coming with her luggage. Kinsey was
standing there also and stepped back, "Whew!" The aroma
he had smelled before in the taxi-cab came rolling back out
of the trunk. He had no choice; he threw Doreen's luggage
into the trunk and shut the taxicab trunk quickly. He
opened the taxicab door for Doreen and got in. Kinsey
looked the taxicab driver in the rearview mirror, *"The
Diamond Club Casino!"* He eyed the taxicab driver
closely in the rearview mirror again. "And make it quick!"
Kinsey and Doreen got out of the taxicab. Kinsey handed

the taxicab driver a $100 bill. "Keep the change!" All the
while thinking, "You're nothing but a dam stinky asshole!"
The taxicab driver looked at Kinsey and nodded.

Kinsey and Doreen got in the elevator and he pushed button
for the 20th floor The Pent House Poker Tournament Suite.
Doreen was quiet. She didn't have any expectations. She
just wanted to be with Kinsey. He took his slide card out
and opened the suite door. It was white double doors with
gold painted inside frame moldings. Doreen walked in
while Kinsey dropped her bags in the doorway and reached
for the lights. He turned the dimmer on the shades on the
far wall, opening the shades.

Doreen walked in and looked around. She walked into the
living room and looked out the-wall to-wall window at the
lights.   The curtains were drawn wide. She stood staring at
the full yellow moon. Kinsey walked over, stood behind
her and put both his hands on Doreen's shoulders. "It's all
ours Doreen. All ours to enjoy for one year anytime we
want to." Doreen put her hand on his hand.

 "I almost forgot what Las Vegas looked like at night."
"It's still as beautiful as I remember it." Kinsey went over
to the bar. "Do you want a drink?" Doreen turned and
walked over to the round circle couch and sat down.

"Sure. "I'll take a gin and tonic if you have it." Kinsey
went to the kitchen and looked through the refrigerator. It
was stocked with everything. He knew Doreen couldn't
drink a lot with her medicine. Kinsey poured her and him a
small drink. He sat down next to her on the couch looking
out the window at all the lights. On the table in front of

135

him was an envelope with his name on it, Mr. Kinsey along with five boxes, each gift wrapped in silver foil paper with big silver ribbons tied around all of them and a large silver bow on top. He got up and moved all the boxes and the card to the suites entrance table.

Kinsey looked at his NIXON watch. It was 12:30 a.m. He sat down and put his arm around Doreen who was sipping her drink looking out the window at all the lights. Kinsey suddenly felt tired. He took a sip of his drink and reflected on the day for a brief moment. Everything about it was good. For once, in his life, he felt relieved. After five years of a crappy life, living in a cheap run-down motel. He finally felt happy. The puzzle had finally come together.

Doreen turned and looked into his eyes." "I love you Kinsey. I never stopped loving you. Thirty-two years is a long time to be with someone and then totally stop loving them. That's unless they want to kill you". Kinsey started laughing.

"I don't think so!" Kinsey pulled her close to him. He looked into her eyes. "I never stopped thinking about you and the kids, Doreen. I loved you then and I still love you now." He leaned forward and gave her a long kiss on the lips. His heart began beating fast. Kinsey could see that Doreen was tired.   "I think it's time to call it a night." Doreen smiled "I'm tired."

Kinsey showed her all three bedrooms. Doreen put her luggage in the first bedroom, got her medicine and a nightgown, and went into the bathroom. She pulled her

wig off and looked at herself in the mirror. She took out
her bright pink headband and put it on her bald head. She
ran warm water and took a wash cloth and wiped her
makeup off. It all felt seemingly familiar. It was like old
times when Kinsey and she were living together. When he
wasn't out night after night gambling, playing poker and
coming home broke.   She stood there thinking.

"I hope he never goes back to gambling."

It was the only thing that destroyed their marriage. She
knew his gambling ruined and took everything they had
worked together for. She looked again in the mirror. She
was 59. Kinsey was 59. In all reality she didn't have much
time to think about anything.   All she knew now is that she
wanted to try to stay healthy and spend her last 6 months
with Kinsey and, the kids, and grand kids.

She took off her dress and shoes and looked at the pink
stretch soft band the doctor had given her to put around her
chest after she had her double mastectomy   When the
doctor had sat her down in his office and announced to her
that she had cancer and that it had started spreading to other
parts of her body, she knew she would not be needing fake
boobs. She put her silk green short nightgown on and
walked to the bedroom and climbed in bed. Kinsey came
in and sat down next to her and took her hand.

Doreen looked into his eyes. She knew he was tired. They
were getting older. Why wouldn't they be worn out and
tired? She patted his hand. "Come. Climb in bed with
me." Kinsey got up took off his clothes, climbed in bed
and pulled the covers over them both. Doreen turned and
put her hand on his chest and her head on his right

shoulder. "I've missed you Kinsey." Kinsey kissed her forehead. A tear fell down his cheek.

"I've missed you too sweetheart."

Kinsey woke up at 8:00 a.m. He turned his head and looked at Doreen peacefully asleep. He got up quietly and walked to the closet. There were his and her white robes and slippers. He wrapped the robe around him and closed the closet quietly. He turned and looked to see if Doreen was still sleeping. He wanted her to sleep as long as she could. He went and walked around the suite. It was huge. Three bedrooms, two bathrooms, a kitchen with a stainless-steel refrigerator, an electric stove, toaster, 10 cup coffee maker and lots of cabinets. The refrigerator was stocked with all kinds of different soft drinks, two dozen eggs, bacon, orange juice, plastic fruit container, bread, a fruit cake, ground coffee, coffee creamer, sugar, butter, peanut butter, jelly, oranges, two large salads and salad dressings, lemons, limes.

He got the coffee grounds out of the refrigerator, found the coffee filters and started the coffee maker. He looked in all the cabinets and drawers. There were dishes, silverware pots, pans, drink glasses and all the basic utensils to cook with. "Nice, he thought". He got a coffee cup from the cupboard and poured himself a nice strong cup of coffee. He walked over to the entry desk and picked up the silver envelope with his name on it. He walked over to the couch, put his coffee down and opened the envelope. Forgetting his glasses on the night stand, he tipped toed back into the bedroom and grabbed his eye glasses. He

tiptoed out and sat back down on the couch. He pulled out
a one-page letter and started reading it.

*"Greetings, Mr. Kinsey. Welcome to the "Poker
Tournament Winner's Suite.   You are now a part of our
Elite Registration for one year. For one year you will be
entitled to all the benefits of the Diamond Club Casinos
Elite Players Programs which include two FREE dinner
reservations per week to any of our three restaurants, the
China Moon Restaurant, the Handel Steak House
Restaurant and the Diamond Club "All you can Eat"
Buffet. Also feel free to visit our Elite Club which is located
on the first floor next to the High Limits gambling area any
time at 4:00 p.m. and relax with FREE hors d'oeuvres and
drinks on us.*

*Also, you will receive a 20% discount when you visit our
gift shops and you will also receive a monthly any Spa
Massage Package for two at our "Relax with Us." The
"Relax with Us" Spa located on the 3rd floor. Just call 211
from your hotel phone to make a reservation from 9:00
a.m. to 9:00 p.m. any day of the week. Last but not least,
we have a Casino Financial Accountant here for your
convenience. Winning! And Winning Big! It can sometimes
pose a monetary challenge. So, we invite you to call Ed
Johnson, our General Manager here if you are interested at
Ext. 201. You are most welcome to call Ed Johnson at any
time with any questions you may have. Also, we welcome
you to charge any charges you desire to your Room, also
any outside charges that Vendors include in their services.
We hope you enjoy your one-year stay with us in our
beautiful Poker Tournament Winner's Suite at the
"Diamond Club Casino! Cordially, Mr. Richard Jenkins
CEO.*

Kinsey folded the one-page letter and put it back in the envelope. He took a sip of his coffee and put it down on the coffee table. He got up and walked over to the gifts on the entrance table and carried them to the coffee table. He smiled to himself. "It's Christmas in July! He took the bottom box and opened it. There was a pair of dark blue trousers. He pulled them out and looked at the size. Yep, 38-inch waist. He whistled. "Boy those are sharp!" He opened the next box. There was a off white golf shirt with blue trim around the sleeves with a small green alligator on the front.   He read the label, IZOD Lacoste Crocodile.

He opened the next box and there was a pair of black, shiny shoes, size 11, with black socks. He slipped them on. Perfect! He opened the next box. In it was a bottle of men's cologne. He looked at the bottle; 'Cartier Les Heures for Men.' He whistled again, and held the bottle high in his hand." "Now that's a $380 bottle of cologne. He had seen it in the gift shop in some high-end casinos. As most men aren't. Kinsey was included in this one. "Most men aren't" category, Kinsey was not a shopper.

Kinsey heard the bathroom toilet flush. Doreen walked out of the bathroom and sat down next to Kinsey on the couch. Kinsey put the cologne bottle down and turned to Doreen. "Good morning sleepy head." Kinsey noticed her pink headband on her head. "You look good in pink." She looked up at him with sleepy eyes as she sat down beside him on the couch.

Kinsey smiled and patted Doreen's knee. He then got up and headed towards the kitchen. "Do you still like your coffee with cream, no sugar?" Doreen pulled the white robe she found in the closet tighter around her waist.

"Yes, thank you!" She looked at all the opened gifts on the table and yelled back at Kinsey in the kitchen. "I see the *Diamond Club Casino* likes you a lot! She gave him one of those lifted eye-brow looks. Must be all that money you won!" Kinsey handed Doreen the cup of coffee and sat down next to her.

"Say listen, I was thinking we could go shopping today." "I have money now." Kinsey took a sip of his coffee, all the while staring at her, "And don't think I'm trying to buy you, because after 32 years of marriage, you and I both know better!"

Doreen took a sip of her coffee, got up and looked out the large full-length window. It was sunny and she felt good this morning. Her nausea would come and go, but she was good so far. She was not going to think too much about anything. She didn't want to. She was back with Kinsey now and that's all that mattered. She wanted him back in her life and the kid's lives. She turned around to Kinsey, shrugged her shoulders and said, "Sure why not? "Sounds like fun! I don't have to be anywhere."

Kinsey got up and walked over to her and put his arm around her and said, "Now that's my girl!" Kinsey gave her a light kiss on the lips and turned and headed towards the kitchen. "They have stocked the refrigerator with lots of good things to eat. I'm going to make us breakfast!" Doreen walked to the kitchen and leaned against the island in the kitchen.

"Good, I'm starving!" Doreen went around to the kitchen and poured herself another cup of coffee. She looked in the refrigerator for the coffee creamer. "Wow, you weren't kidding when you said they stocked the refrigerator!" She poured creamer in her coffee cup and looked at Kinsey. He was busy trying to locate a cooking pan.

"I am going to go take a quick shower while you cook." Without looking up and still trying to locate a cooking pan, Kinsey said.

"Okay, hon."

Doreen took a shower and dressed in a light blue silk blouse and a short jean skirt and then put on her sandals. She still had her legs to show off. She took her medicine bag out and walked to the bathroom and turned on the water. She opened all her pill bottles and started popping each one, splashing water in her mouth after each one. She washed her face and then went and sat on the bed to put her make-up on. Not too much. She took a blonde wig out of her suitcase and put it on and walked down the hall to the kitchen. Kinsey was setting the kitchen table.

"Okay, I think we are ready to eat." Kinsey pulled her chair out and Doreen sat down. Kinsey took a bite of his omelet. "Are we ready to do a little shopping today?" Doreen took a bite of her omelet;

"Sounds good to me!"

Maybe, she thought, a massage at the *Relax While You Can* Spa would be great. Doreen looked at Kinsey, all along debating if she should say something to him about "it may be uncomfortable for her with no boobs and scars. But she thought again and let it go. He was being charming and she wanted to enjoy every moment she had doing whatever she wanted. Tossing her head back and forth, she said "Maybe?" Kinsey finished his breakfast.

"I am going to take a quick shower, my dear."

He gave her a quick kiss on the check and walked down the hall singing carrying his gift boxes with him. All Doreen could think of the movie star Roger Dangerfield whistling his way down the hall to the shower. She laughed to herself.

Doreen held her coffee in her hand and looked out the window again at the Vegas Strip. She felt safe with Kinsey. When she was with him, it was like, "old times." Aside from his gambling, which went on for years, they had some pretty good times together with the kids. He was a good father. He took Kinsey, Jr., fishing and they all went to the park for picnics when he wasn't working late. He attended their school functions. Kinsey, Jr. liked baseball and watched all the sports channels with his Dad. Melody liked reading and writing poems. She was the ever-so romantic one. She also liked baking cookies and having sleepovers in the back yard with a tent and flashlights with her girlfriends. Alice, on the other hand, the younger daughter, liked playing her music, all different rock artists on her CD player in her room and with her ear plugs. They all had different things they liked in their growing up years.

In the five years Kinsey was away, she had struggled.
Divorcing and moving away with three kids was hard. The
kids had eventually left the nest. Alice, her youngest
daughter, of course, returning home from New York, strung
out, with major drug problems. And then, of course.
Knowing her fatal illness would rear its ugly head. It had
taken a toll on her. But as it was and as it is now she had
tracked Kinsey down and she knew she wanted him back.
Time was her enemy now.

Again, in her mind she thought. Thirty-two years, she still
loved him. Even though for four years her anger vented
out and she was madder than a scorned demon woman.
Her illness gave her a reason to forgive. She knew it was
all about "forgiveness" in the end. She chuckled to herself
and asked. "Why does it always take something drastic for
some people to wake-up,
"Hello?"

Kinsey walked out to the front room and put his arms and
hands out in front of him and did a little tap spin. "Ta-da!"
"New threads my dear. Compliments of "*The Diamond
Club Casino*." Doreen turned and looked at Kinsey and
said,

"You clean up good."

He had his polo shirt on with his new pants, socks and
shoes with his Nixon Watch. Doreen could smell the
cologne. She walked up to him and whispered. "You
smell nice too." He grabbed her hand.

"Come-on. Grab your purse! Let's go shopping!"

Chapter 15– Los Angeles Girls – Massachusetts Boys 4th of July

Megan sat on the bed, put her thick black glasses on and got her sketch pad and black chalk pencil out. She knew she needed to get up and get dressed and freshen her make-up. It's was 5:00 p.m. Bethany had made a reservation at *The Lobster House* for 6:30 p.m. and then they were going to head over to the *Rocket Aero Tower Casino* to meet the guys in the lobby area. She was anxious to see the guys again and to see the fireworks on the 98th top floor. S

Stephanie stepped out the shower. It was steamy in the bathroom. She wrapped a towel around her hair and muffled her hair, drying it with another one. She opened the bathroom door and shouted to Megan. "Hey Megan what are you wearing tonight?" Megan, still sketching on her sketch pad, yelled back.

"I brought a white satin short dress with a silver rhinestone neckline with black rhinestone strapped high heels and long silver dangly earrings. "Wow that sounds HOT!" "How about you, Stephanie?" What are you wearing?"

"Well, Stephanie took a long sigh." "I think I am going to wear a sleeveless, high collar, short red dress with red wedge shoes and long silver earrings. The steam had evaporated out the bathroom. Stephanie looked down at her foot. Uhgg. The red rash had spread from her foot up, past her ankle. All of sudden she felt sick. The rash was not going away. It was getting worse. She sat down on the stool in the bathroom. She felt faint. She felt her head. It felt hot, feverish.

She yelled back to Megan. "I think I am going to wear the long, off the shoulder stretch red dress with red velvet closed shoes with the gold earrings."   There was no way Stephanie was going to give up her last night with her friends and the guys because of a rash.

Stephanie spun around in her red long stretch dress and red velvet shoes. "You look fabulous my dear!" Bethany said. Megan stepped out of the bathroom and did a twirl also. "Wow Megan!" "No one would ever know that you're a bookworm!" "You look sensational!" Megan took a bow.

"Thank you!" Batting her eyes and fanning herself with a pretend fan, Megan blurted out, "Queen Cleopatra has arrived. This time with clothes on!"   Stephanie and Bethany looked at each other and started laughing so hard, tears were running down their faces. Grabbing their purses, they headed for the door. Bethany, closed the door, bowing "Au revior!"

The Lobster House Restaurant was beautiful. It was filled with white linen tables and white folded napkins. The waiters wore white shirts with black bow ties and black pants and black shoes. "I have a reservation for a table for three, please. The name is under Bethany Bishop." The host looked down the reservation list and smiled. "Yes, please come this way." Bethany whispered to the host. "Is there any way we can sit by the large window over there so we can see the Las Vegas strip lights.

"Sure, come this way please."

Megan and Stephanie walked graciously as if they were princesses, giggling, all the way to the table.   The waiter, Kevin, walked over and handed each of them the wine menu. Bethany asked.
"What is the favorite wine choice here for the Lobster?" Kevin turned to her and said, "well, I suggest a good Chardonnay, a Sauvignon Blanc or simply good Champagne. They all looked at each, smiling while chiming in together.

"Champagne!" "Very good!" "We have a splendid house Dom Perignon 2009" the waiter said. Bethany looked at the waiter and said, as long as it's not more than $150 a bottle, that's fine"

The waiter bowed. Yes madam, it is within that price range. I will leave you each with a menu and bring you our best house Dom Perignon Champagne." They all knew what they wanted. The tw- pound stuffed Lobster. Megan leaned over her tall menu.

 "Is he gay?" "Stephanie and Bethany starting laughing.

"Gay as Queen Cleopatra in drag". The waiter brought a bucket with the Champagne on ice. He poured each of them a glass of Dom Perignon.   They all raised their glasses and cheered! "Cheers, to Las Vegas!" **What plays in Vegas, stays in Vegas!"**

Bethany turned and looked out the window. "Wow, look at the lighted billboards and hotel lights on the Las Vegas strip." "Amazing!" Stephanie started talking about the boys and the fireworks. "So what do you gals think of Johnny?" Megan then stepped in.

"So, my question is, "What do you guys think of Darren?" And then Bethany stepped in smiling a big smile, "So what do you two think of Brett? "The Massachusetts Boys?"

"Cute!" Cute! Cute!" They all started laughing.

Kevin brought the main course and placed the huge plate in front of each of the girls. "Lobster a la carte (2 pounds)." Megan's eyes got big! "I've never seen a Lobster this big." "Yummy!" Kevin threw his hand in the air. Enjoy!" "Bon Appetite!"

Chapter 16 – Doctor's Prognosis

Emily and Sylvia stepped into Dr. Cooper's office. "Hi, Dr Cooper." Dr. Cooper looked up at Emily and Sylvia and motioned them to take a seat. Hoping they both had something good to report. Dr. Cooper asked "What do you have?"

Emily looked down at her chart. "We ran 16 biopsies from urine to blood tests and the last biopsy came up with some sort or rodent droppings or feces called histoplasmosis which is rare but can be fatal. If the fungal spores are airborne inhaled, an individual the person will get a fungus or rash with high fever, flu-like symptoms, chest pains, severe lung problems with dry cough, tuberculosis which can worsen over the months leading to death. The incubation period is typically 3-17 days for acute disease.

148

Ninety percent of infections are asymptomatic or result in a mild influenza-like illness. Some infections may cause acute pulmonary histoplasmosis, manifested by high fever, headache, nonproductive cough, chills, weakness, pleuritic chest pain and fatigue.

"What is the treatment?" Dr. Cooper asked.

"Itraconazole is one type of antifungal medication that is commonly used to treat histoplasmosis. Depending on the severity of the infection and a person's immune status, the course of the treatment can range from 3 months to 1 year." Dr. Cooper sighed.

"Good work Emily and Sylvia." I will inform Dr. Emily Madera of the prognosis and to have her start treatment on our patient Rose Davis. I will also advise Admissions to put out a Disease Alert Notice for all other individuals coming into the hospital with these symptoms. Thank you." Emily got up, smiled and handed Dr. Cooper the chart with all the notes.

 "I am glad we were able to help Rose." She and Sylvia walked out, turned the corner, smiled at each other and high-fived. "Another team star for the two team stars," Emily said.

Dr. Cooper picked up the phone and called Dr. Emily Madera to tell her of Rose's diagnosis. The doctor's Admin picked up the phone. "I'm sorry Dr. Cooper, Emily Madera had a family emergency and we don't know when she will be returning." "Dr. Madera put out an email last night with your name on it as the contact physician for all patients.

"Thank you, I will take a look at that." He sat in his chair thinking of what and where the bat (guano) feces were coming from? He remembered Rose saying she and her friend were last at *The Diamond Club Casino*.

He picked up the phone and dialed *The Diamond Club Casino* and asked for the General Manager. The main receptionist transferred the call to Sally. She picked up the line. "Hi my name is Dr. David Cooper. I'm the Director of the Preliminary Disease Immunities Department at the Anderson Memorial Hospital here in Las Vegas. "Is Mr. Johnson in?"

"Yes, one moment." Sally transferred the phone to Ed. "Dr. David Cooper from the Anderson Memorial Hospital in Las Vegas is on the line."

"Okay, Sally. "Thank you." Ed picked up the phone and pushed the blinking line. "Ed Johnson"
"How may I help you Dr. Cooper?"

Dr. Cooper asked Ed if he was aware of any dark brown rodent droppings in The *Diamond Club Casino* floors areas or garage structures. "Funny that you mention that, Ed Johnson told him. "I have noticed dark brown chalk streaks in the receptionist area and have requested the cleaning team take care of all entrance areas and carpets in hallways and the rooms be shampooed. The maintenance crew has been cleaning up dark brown pellets on parking garage floors 2nd, 4th and 6th and bird droppings around the edges of the 2nd, 4th and 6th parking garage areas also."

Dr. Cooper continued. "It seems we have a patient here that has a rash on her abdomen and her back. We have concluded it was caused by some kind of rodent. We are not sure what type. It is not contagious from person to person, but it is transferred to humans by airborne spores." Ed took a deep breath and froze on the phone. He flashed back to Jack's hand and Jack telling him he had a rash. Dr. Cooper waited on the phone. "Mr. Johnson." "Mr. Johnson, are you still there?"

"Yes, Dr. Cooper I am still here." Ed took another deep breath. "Is there any way I can meet you tomorrow at the hospital?"

"Yes, yes, sure". How does 9:30 a.m. sound? Ed looked at his calendar.

"That works within my schedule."

"I'll see you then." Ed hung up and sat back in his chair. His mind was racing. All he could think of was an epidemic. Ed buzzed Sally. "Sally, can you please come to my office. Yes, Mr. Johnson, I will be right there.

Ed took a seat behind his desk and began. "I just received a call from Dr. David Cooper who is the Director of Preliminary Disease Immunities at Anderson Memorial Hospital here in Las Vegas. Apparently, one of his patients has a rash. And that patient was last here at *The Diamond Club Casino* with her friend. He has assured me that it is

151

not person-to-person contagious. But, with that being said, I am still concerned because it is an airborne infection.

Dr. Cooper continued, "Here is what I want you to do."

"Please contact HR and have them contact all head of departments via email to let them know we are looking for a list of any employees that may have a red rash anywhere on their bodies.   House Keeping, Valet, Maintenance, Receptionist, Cashiers, Bell Boys, the Restaurants German, Chinese, Buffet, Food Court, Waitresses, Pitt Bulls, Hand Payouts, Rewards, Bar tenders and all Table Employees. I am going to call HR and advise them of this dilemma and have HR put a memo out to all *The Diamond Club Casino.* We do not want to cause any panic anywhere."

Sally sat there looking at Mr. Johnson in shock. She couldn't find her voice for a moment and then she asked. "Is this rash contagious or deadly and do they have a cure for this rash?" Sally could see the worry in Ed's eyes.

"I am sorry Sally. I wish I had more to tell you. But for right now, I don't know yet. "I am to meet with Dr. Cooper tomorrow morning at 9:30 a.m. I will know more after our meeting." Sally's head was spinning. Sally got up to leave. "Please close the door on your way out, Sally and oh, please let me see the list when you are finished. Oh, Sally, there is one more thing. Please call Grant Benedict, The Diamond Club Casino's Financial Advisor and schedule a meeting with him for 5:00 p.m. July 5th.

"No worries Mr. Johnson." "I'll have the list done by 3:00 p.m. today."

"Thank you, Sally. That will be all. Please close the door on your way out."

Chapter 17 - Rose Still in Hospital - July 4th Fireworks

It was 7:00 p.m. the fireworks would be starting soon. Rose asked the nurse to lower the lights and open the curtains so she could look out the window. "Sure honey, she said." How are you doing?" she asked. "You need anything?" Rose lowered her eyes. Yes. A new life she thought.

"No thank you, I'm good for now." She closed her eyes. Her mind started racing again. It's funny how when you're stuck, time stops but your mind doesn't. It wants to remind you of all the things you should have done instead of all the good things that could be. She lay there resting. Again, her mind went back in time. A few months ago, she remembered getting up from the bar and putting Grant Benedict's card in her purse.

A week later she once again sat at the coffee shop and ordered water. She sat there thinking. Still no work. She took the card out of her purse and started flipping it between her fingers. Should I call? Should I not. Should I call? Should I not. She knew things were not improving. Rebecca had called an old friend and they were kind enough to give her $1,000 to bail us out of our crises until we both found some kind of work. She thought, "What the heck?" She dialed Grant Benedict's number.

153

He answered. "Hi this is Rose. The girl you met at the bar a week ago." Of course, Grant remembered. She was the one with the long red wavy hair and green eyes.

"Oh, Hi Rose, how is it going with you and Rebecca?' "Well, I would like to say it's going fabulously, but it's not." Grant's thought "as usual most the time". Rose took a long breath and put her pride aside as asked, "Hey I was wondering if you might know of someone who is hiring?"

Without thinking and not knowing what else to say, Grant blurted out. "Well, why don't you and I meet for drinks and dinner and we can talk, okay?" "Are you free tonight?" Rose thought. Am I free tonight? I'm free every night.

"Sure."

"Okay then, Rose, let's meet at *The Diamond Club Casino* at 7:00 p.m. "Do you like seafood?" "I love seafood." Rose fumbled with her hair.

"I'll see you at 7:00 p.m. Oh Rose, by the way, bring your friend with you. What's her name?"

"Rebecca, Rose said. Sure, okay, I'm sure she would love to come too."

"Okay Rose, see you and your friend at 7:00 p.m. at *The Diamond Club Casino* at the Lobster House Restaurant.

"See you there." Rose hung up. She was so excited. She knew Rebecca would be too. All she could think about was

what she had to wear. She wanted to look nice. She got up
from the Coffee Shop and headed towards the motel. She
opened the motel door. Rebecca was lying on the bed
watching TV. Rose told her the whole story. Rebecca's
eyes lit up. Rebecca took a deep breath. Finally! Rebecca
thought, "Some light at the end of the tunnel Rose."

Rebecca looked at Rose in the eyes. All of a sudden
Rebecca started crying uncontrollably. Rose put her arms
around Rebecca. "Shhhh, shhhh. "It's going to be alright."
"It's going to be alright my friend." While holding her
Rebecca, tears began to roll down Rose's cheeks. All she
could think of was the months of struggling to survive and
the same pain Rebecca was feeling.

"Hey, hey, hey." Let's get out our best dresses and shoes
and let's play make-up. "I'll put your make-up on and you
put my make-up on. Rose sat back on the bed and took
Rebecca's hands.
"Deal?" Rebecca looked up at Rose, wiped her eyes and
smiled.

"Deal!" Rose, my little Rose. You are such a little girl at
times. I think that's why I love you as my best friend."

Grant and his friend Ben walked in *The Lobster House
Restaurant*. They immediately saw Rose and Rebecca
sitting by the front desk. Grant recognized Rose right
away. He walked straight to Rose.

"Hi Rose." Grant leaned forward and gave her a light kiss
on her check while taking her hands in his." He turned to

Rebecca and said, Grant then reached for Rebecca's hand while looking her in the eyes. "You must be Rebecca?"

"Yes, nice to meet you, Grant." Grant turned to Ben and said, "This is Ben, my good friend." Ben shook Rose's and Rebecca's hands. Rebecca liked what she saw. He was Italian looking, dark black hair, nice olive skin with greenish blue eyes and a nice smile.

Grant told the receptionist his name and party of four. She ushered them to a table by the window of the Las Vegas strip. Grant pulled out Rose's chair to seat. Ben did the same for Rebecca. "Lovely restaurant" Rose said. The waiter came over to the table.

"Wine ladies?" Rose looked at Rebecca.

"Ye,s that sounds great!" Grant looked at the wine list and ordered a nice bottle of wine. The waiter handed them the Dinner Menu and told them the specials of the evening.

Grant looked at Rose and Rebecca. "Order anything you want." Dinner is on me and Ben. Rose looked at Rebecca and turned and looked deep into Grant's eyes. She smiled.

"Thank you." "I think I will have the two-pound lobster."

"Me too!" Rebecca chimed in. Grant turned to Ben.

"You good?" "Yes, I'm good with that"

Grant handed the waiter his Menu first and then they all handed him the menus. Grant looked up at Kevin. "That will be four two-pound lobsters. Kevin asked what they wanted for sides. Taking the orders, Kevin told them he would bring them some bread, butter and waters and put the food order in.

 Grant looked at Rose. "You look lovely, Rose". She had decided to wear her only blue chiffon dress that wasn't too out of date and not too old looking.

"Thank you."

Ben looked at Rebecca and said basically the same. "Rebecca thought he was charming, smiled and said, "thank you". They all made small conversation until the food came. As the meal and small talk continued, Rose began to feel her old self coming back.

At this moment in time and for some crazy unknown reason, Rose actually felt happy. She felt like a real person again. She looked at Grant sitting across from her talking about his clients in Vegas the last 3 years and Ben who was a General Manager at a Mercedes car dealership in Las Vegas. He had worked there for four years and he liked it. Rose was thinking he was about 32. Grant explained how he met Ben three years ago when Grant went to buy a Mercedes. As Rebecca took a mouthful of Lobster she asked. "Okay so gentlemen, without being too forward, are you both single? Married? Divorced?" Rose could feel herself flushing while holding her breath, not only for Rebecca's forwardness but for the answer she was hoping for.

Grant turned to Ben and they both chuckled and looked at
Rebecca and then they both looked at
Rose. They both turned and looked at each other again and
raised their wine glasses. Rose and Rebecca raised their
wine glasses. "Dun Dun Da Da"--- They all clinked
glasses together at the same time.

Both Grant and Ben looked at each other at the same time
again and blurted out. "We are both single!" While they all
took a sip of wine, Rose almost choked, while covering her
mouth and laughing at the same time. "What a relief,"
Rose thought. Kevin then came over and asked how
everything was. Grant looked at everyone, "Any dessert
for you girls?" Rose didn't want to over indulge. "She
smiled at Grant and said, "No thank you." Rebecca did the
same.

Kevin handed Grant the bill. Rose gasped. She noticed a
large red rash on Kevin's, right hand. Before anyone could
see the slight terror in her eyes, she lifted her napkin up to
wipe her mouth and looked out the window, admiring the
lights. She watched the beautiful night lights. The bill
boards flashed with their colored signs and casino hotels all
glittering with their night lights. Rose was wondering
when Grant was going to let her know he might have a job
for her. She and Rebecca were having such a grand time;
she didn't want to push it. She wanted to enjoy the
evening. She definitely would wait for Grant to bring the
subject up.

Grant paid the bill and looked at his watch. "Say listen Ben
and I were wondering if you two would like to go dancing
at *The Canyon Roller Club* tonight?" Rebecca turned to
Rose with a huge smile on her face. Rose knew that look.

"Yes, of course we would!" Before they all got up from the table, Rose said, excuse me "I am going to the Ladies room". Rebecca following Rose, chimed in.

"Sure, sounds great!"

Rose and Rebecca make their way to the Ladies room. They both used the bathroom quickly. Looking in the mirror they both put their lipstick on. Rebecca put her lipstick back in her purse and turned to Rose and asked. "When are they going to talk about a job for us?" Rose put her lipstick in her purse, turned to Rebecca and said,

"Don't worry! I think Grant is a good person. If he doesn't bring it up, I will ask him by the end of the night." Rose grabbed Rebecca's hand. "In the meantime, let's go dance have fun with the guys!"

Rebecca wiped her lipstick, chuckling out of the Ladies room, "By the way, I think Ben is super cute!"

Rose and Rebecca met Grant and Ben by the restaurant entrance. *The Canyon Roller Club* had a line a mile long. Grant grabbed Rose's hand and Ben grabbed Rebecca's hand. Grant walked to the beginning of the line and flashed JJ the Bouncer his Employee ID Card. Ed Johnson had given him when he first signed the contract for the Financial Advisory position. The bouncer opened the rope and let them in. Grant headed for the bar. The bar tender came over. Grant asked. "What do you ladies want to drink?

"Uh, I think I will have a *Rattlesnake Venom Shot* with a lime, Rebecca said.

"I'll have the same," Rose said.

Grant looked at Ben and smiled. I like these '*Ladies of the Night*' drinking style." Grant said "I'll take the same and Ben chimed in. "I'll have the same also." They all cheered! The music was loud and it was crowded. Grant grabbed Rose's hand and pulled her on the dance floor. It was a fast song and Grant was twirling her around like a spinning top. She looked over at Rebecca and Ben. They seemed to be having a good time getting to know each other. The lights dimmed and a slow song started playing.

Grant looked into Rose's eyes and pulled her close to him. She could smell a weak scent of shaving cologne on his neck. He held one hand in hers upright and his left hand on her back. His body felt strong, warm and exciting. She closed her eyes. She wanted this moment to last forever. She felt a slight nudge. It was Rebecca and Ben dancing next to her and Grant. She smiled at Rebecca and winked. Rebecca smiled and winked back. The song came to an end and Grant took her hand and spun her around again pulled her close to him and kissed her lightly on the lips. At 2:30 p.m. the disc jockey called out. "Last drink call and last song of the night". Ben and Rebecca came back to the bar.

Grant casually looked at Ben. "Hey, is anyone up for coming back to my place for a late-night cap? Rebecca looked at Rose with desperate eyes. Her feet were killing her and she was tired. Rose looked at Rebecca as to say "don't leave me!" Ben looked at Grant. The alcohol was talking.

"Sure, I'm game." Grant looked at Rebecca.

"How about you, Rebecca, are you in?" Tipsy, Rebecca looked at Rose again.

"Sure, why not?" "I'm in," Rose said putting her thumb up in the air. Well then, the good news is we don't have to drive anywhere.

"I happen to know the General Manager here at *The Diamond Club Casino* and I work for this hotel. I have a three-bedroom suite here at *The Diamond Club Casino*." Rebecca took off her shoes.

"I hope you don't mind, but my feet are killing me."

Ben started laughing. "You are not the first girl Rebecca to take off your shoes off in Las Vegas. And, I know, you won't be the last girl to do such again!"

Grant grabbed Rose's hand and told Ben. "We are going to take a tour of the casino. We'll be up in a few. Rose was impressed that Grant knew all the areas of the casino.

Grant pushed the 19th floor elevator button. He walked to the end of the 19th floor. There were two white double doors with gold trim. He took out his hotel card and slid it over the magnetic key slot. Both doors opened. "Voila!" He said with his hands opened wide. "Welcome to my hotel home". They both heard some giggling and stopped

and looked at each other. Grant knew it was Ben. He had
given Ben a key to his suite a few months ago when they
had become good friends after buying a Mercedes and
having a few drinks with him. He trusted Ben. He had to
trust someone in Las Vegas.

Rose walked in and took her shoes off. Grant pushed a
button and the lights dimmed inside and the curtain shades
opened to an expansive floor length window. Rose walked
towards the window. "Wow! Look at all the lights of
Vegas!" Rose said, spinning around in her bare feet. She
looked at Grant and smiled, "it's beautiful!"

Rose asked Grant where the bathroom was. She made her
exit. She stood and looked at herself in the mirror for a
minute. She looked a little drunk, but not too bad. She sat
on the toilet, took a pee and flushed the toilet. The
bathroom had two sinks and a fabulous large bathtub for
two easily with jets, plus a huge shower. Maybe four
people could fit in that shower she thought. She felt like
she was in the movie "Pretty Woman."

She walked down to the hall to the living area. She heard
giggling coming from one of the bedrooms. She knew it
was Rebecca and Ben. She thought, Rebecca's a big girl.
She can do what she wants.

 Grant was on the phone with room service. "I

"I am ordering some food for us." Grant looked at Rose.
"What would you like Rose?" Rose sat down on the couch
next to Grant. She shrugged her shoulders.

"Oh, I guess some peel and eat shrimp and maybe some jalapeño poppers."

Grant picked up the phone again and placed the order.

"Yes, that will be it." "How long will that take? Okay, 30 minutes sounds great. "Thank you." Grant hung up the phone and walked to the bar. "What can I get you to drink Rose?" Rose was not in the mood to drink anymore. She knew she had had enough to drink and it was early morning.

"I'll take a Seven Up." Grant looked into Rose's eyes while giving Rose her drink. He sat down, reached over to the end table that had a radio and turned on some nice soft jazz music.

A knock came to the door. Grant got up to answer the door. A man with a butler looking suit wheeled in a large silver tray with lots of domes of food. Opening each one, he told Grant and Rose what each kind of food was in them. Rose looked at Grant with eyebrows raised. "Impressive she said." "Now I really feel like I'm in the movie, Pretty Woman.

Grant finished his drink and looked at Rose. "You look tired." Grant got up and took Rose's hand. Pulling her along down the short hallway, he said. "There are three rooms here, Rose." He opened the door and pulled her into one of the empty rooms. She turned and looked at him and then looked down and then looked up at him and whispered.

"Thank you, Grant, I had a great time." Grant touched her cheek with his thumb. He brushed her hair with his hand, looked her in the eyes and gently kissed her on the lips. It was a sweet kiss. Roses head started spinning. Grant looked into Rose's eyes and brushed her hair away from her face with one hand and said, "I really like you Rose."

Grant gently closed the door and whispered, "Sleep well Rose."

Rose opened her eyes. Awe, it's Sunday. Sundays were always good. She yawned and stretched her arms out. She rolled over and looked at the clock on the bedside table. It was 1:00 p.m. She sat up. She had forgotten where she was for a moment and then she remembered and smiled. There was an envelope on the bedside table with her name on it. "Rose". She picked up the envelope and looked in it. There was a note with 20 one-hundred-dollar bills in the envelop.

Rose took the note out and started reading it. *"Good morning 'Lady of the Night.' "Rose, I want to let you know I had the most wonderful time with you last night. You are a beautiful woman I would like to get to know you better. Please don't think the money is for anything else not proper. The money is for you 'My Lady of the Night.' For my special Rose. It's for you taking the time to share yourself with me for one night with your kindness, your beauty and your wonderful spirit. Please feel free to stay as long as you like in the suite. I will be gone for two days on business. Also feel free to call room service and order anything you and Rebecca would like. Have a wonderful day, Rose. I will call you soon. Always, Grant."*

Rose lay back down on the bed holding the envelope and note to her chest. She didn't know what to make of it. She didn't do anything sexually with Grant. So, the money was not for sex. Her mind kept racing. "What did he want? What did he really want from her?" He was so sweet in the note. She read the note again.

She pushed the bad thoughts out of her mind. "Maybe he really did like her. She pinched herself just to make sure everything was real. Then she got up, put the envelope in her purse and went to the bathroom. She saw the fabulous tub with the jets with bomb salt balls and bubble bath too. She threw in the bomb salt balls and put some bubble bath in the water also. She slid into the tub and pressed the button for the jets.

Rose was actually beginning to like Grant's place. It was nice and she felt safe. Anything was better than the run-down cheap motel she and Rebecca had been staying in the past year or so.

"Awwwww…" the warm water and soothing jets flowing felt good. She leaned her head back and closed her eyes. A warm feeling of happiness came over her. She was finally happy. He thought about Grant and what a really good guy. He had totally surprised her. I guess she thought spending time with him was her job now. If that is what he wanted, then that is what she was going to give him. She heard tapping on the bathroom door and then it opened. She sat up and opened her eyes. "Oh, you scared me." It was Rebecca.

"Hey girly girl, how are you?" Rebecca whispered while giggling all at the same time. She threw off a blue man's shirt and got in at the other end of the tub. She leaned back her head and closed her eyes. Awe, this feels so good. Her eyes still closed she said.

"Good morning, Rose. And how was your night?" She was being the sneaky, quirky Rebecca, Rose always knew. Up to no good at times when you should not have been up to no-good.

Rose splashed some soapy water in Rebecca's face. Rebecca sat up quickly and spit out the soap and splashed back at her. They both started splashing each other and laughing. They both leaned back and closed their eyes enjoying the jets and warm bath water. "Oh, just to let you know, Ben is going to be busy at the Mercedes dealership". But he left me an envelope with a note on the bedside table. "And?" Rose asked.

"And? And, what?" Rebecca said.

Rebecca closed her eyes and then opened one eye and looked at Rose. They both knew what each other was thinking and started laughing again.

"And? "And?" Rose asked again. Rebecca crinkled her nose and put on a smirk on her face with a Alice in Wonderland, chemise cat smile.

"Ben left me 20, one-hundred-dollar bills, Rebecca said. And what about you? Being a little secretive, are you

Rose?" Rose closed her eyes and leaned back and put her soapy leg up in the air and said "Nothing."

Rebecca looked at Rose to see if she could see what Rose's eyes were saying. Rose opened one eye again to see if Rebecca was staring at her. She started laughing out loud!

"Gotcha! "The same!" Rebecca splashed Rose again in the face with soapy water. Rose spit it out and put her soapy leg up in the air. Rebecca screamed.

"I knew it! "I knew you were fibbing Rose!" Rebecca lay back and put her leg up in the air and they both touched their feet together, to *'The Ladies of the Night,'* Rose said.

To *'The Ladies of the Night'* Rebecca said. Both sinking their heads under the soapy water together.

Rose opened her eyes and looked out the hospital window. She wanted to keep that special memory forever. It was four days now that she had been lying in a hospital bed with a smelly hospital gown. She was beginning to smell like the hospital. And she didn't like it. Who would? Nurses came in every hour and poked her with needles. They finally put some kind of IV in her vein in the arm and told her it was an antifungal antidote. She knew she had to get rid of the rash. She looked at the clock on the side of the hospital bed. It was 8:30 p.m.

She carefully rolled over and pushed the Nurse button on the side of her bed. The Nurse came in and she asked. "Can I see the fireworks at *The Diamond Club Casino* from my bed here? Nurse Betty went to the curtains and pulled them back.

"Yes, you sure can. "Let me pull these curtains back a little more." The nurse walked over to Rose's bed. "Anything else I can get you honey?"

"Yes, can you please bring me some bottled water and a Sprite."

"Sure thing hon. I'll be right back. Oh, by the way Rose, Dr. David Cooper will be in to see you tomorrow sometime. Rose turned off her bedside hospital desk light. She wanted it dark so she could really see the fireworks. She lay there and stared out the window, looking at the full yellow moon.

Chapter 18– "Let's Dance!"

Rebecca woke up and looked around the dumpy cheap motel. It was 7:00 a.m. and she had to get ready for her dancing interview. She was excited and nervous all at the same time. She and Rose had kept their $2000 in a safe place and were spending it very wisely. She was grateful for the money. Rose was too. She called the hospital and asked for Rose Davis. Rose answered. "Good morning, Sunshine! How are we doing this morning?"
"Good morning my friend!" Rose sat up. Happy to hear Rebecca voices, "I am going home in a couple of days."
The rash is going away?

"Oh I am so happy for you Rose!" "I have missed you!"

Rose stared out the window, "I missed you too!"

"Say listen, Rose, I have an interview today." Rose sat up in the hospital bed. "What?" "Yes, I have an interview for a dancing job working evenings. I have to be there by 7:00 pm. tonight. I wanted to tell you, real quick before I left."

"Oh Rebecca, I am so happy for you!" "Good luck!" "My cell phone has not been in service since I have been here." "I need to pay my cell phone bill today sometime when I get out of here." So, I will call you later. "Go! Get them!" "I'll be back at the motel later Rose." "I'll call you later when then." "Good luck Rebecca!" Rose hung up the phone and tears began to fall. She started crying uncontrollably.

All Rose could think of was how her and Rebecca came to Las Vegas and wanted to make it big and how they ended up in a cheap motel almost begging every day for some kind of mercy. No jobs insight. Every day, thinking about, always needing money to survive. She remembered Grant and Ben and the money. It was a Life-saver. Rebecca and her needed that money so desperately. She wiped her tears away, closed her eyes, bowed her head and silently prayed. She prayed that things would get better. She prayed her rash would never return.

She prayed Rebecca would get the dancing job. Somehow! Some way! She prayed and prayed. She prayed for good things to come. She prayed for life to get better for both her and Rebecca. She had seen it all in the last two years. When she and Rebecca first came to Las Vegas she would grab Rebecca's arm and would point to girls on the Las

Vegas Strip sitting on the cement with their hands out, young, 15ish with ragged clothing, dirty waiting, looking with anguished eyes for someone to give them food or money. You could tell by looking at them they had been living in Vegas for months, scarcely with no food or money. They were a sign of the desperate, not being able to make it in Las Vegas, living on the streets with no one to help them.

It was heartbreaking and disturbing, all at the same time. She looked at Rebecca with serious eyes. "I don't want to ever end up like that. Promise me, Rebecca, we won't ever end up on the streets like that!" Rebecca looked deeply into Rose's eyes and both pinky-fingered.

"I promise you Rose, we won't ever end up on the streets like that." Rebecca put her arms around Rose and hugged her tight while looking down at the two homeless girls who were dirty, hungry, probably stung out on drugs with their hands out to anyone who would give them money. She closed her eyes and said a silent prayer. *"God, I know you are with us and I know you will help me and Rose."* *"Amen."*

Rose sat up in the hospital bed. She heard *Boom! Boom! Boom!* She opened her eyes and looked out her hospital window. The fireworks had begun. She saw a huge full moon in the sky. A big, bright, yellow moon looming in the dark sky. It was beautiful. She watched each explosion of color out her window in the black sky. So many colors appeared in the night, red, blue, green, yellow. So much splendor. She wondered where Grant was and if

he could see the fireworks. She wished she was with him
this night watching them together.

Boom! Boom! Boom! Boom! Boom! Boom! Colors were
exploding in all directions in the night sky. She knew it
was the Grand Finale. It started to sprinkle. She could see
raindrops on the hospital window. Then the rain was really
starting to come down. She looked at the moon. It had
turned black for a few seconds.

She looked at the moon again. There were black birds with
red eyes flying all over the moon.
The moon turned black again for a few seconds and then
yellow streaks began to shine through. Rose watched in
amazement. Big black birds were flying everywhere; all
over the raining black sky. She pushed the Nurse button
three times. She wanted someone else to see.

Rose watched in wonderment. All the beautiful colors in
the sky exploding everywhere! *Boom! Boom! Boom!
Boom! Boom! Boom! A*nd big black birds flying
everywhere around the huge full yellow moon. It was
amazing!

A Nurse came running in. Rose pointed to the window.
The Nurse stood there with her hand to her chest watching
out the window. "What the…?" She ran out and then ran
back in with six more hospital personnel who all stood
gazing out the window. The rain was still falling. Each
pointed out the window. "Look at that?" Black birds, with
red eyes flashing, flying around the moon and over the
black sky. Sandra was the first nurse on staff that night.
She looked at her watch. It was 10:45 p.m. She

immediately ran out of the room and went to the front desk. "Call Dr. David Cooper, she yelled, "Call Dr. David Cooper! Do it now! Tell him to turn on the 11:00 p.m. *Tonight's News.*"

Chapter 19– July 4th – Jenny, Frank, Sofia, Laker

Frank and Jenny, Laker and Sofia finished their hamburgers and walked across the street to The Diamond Club Casino Hotel. Jenny could tell Laker and Sofia were tired. She looked at Frank. He looked tired also. "Okay game plan is to watch TV and rest, take a nap if you want in your room," Jenny said. By the time she and Frank hit the room and flopped on the bed, she was exhausted. Frank turned on the TV. Jenny got under the covers and closed her eyes. She didn't know how long she slept. She awoke with hands all over her, mainly massaging her breast. Familiar hands, she had somehow felt before. She rolled over and looked at Frank. Wide-eyed, looking into her eyes, frisky as ever. Frank smiled, pulling her close to him. "Play time" he said as he kissed her hard on the mouth.

It had been some time before Jenny was even thinking about play time in bed with Frank. She put her arms around Frank and looked at the green marquise ring on her middle right hand finger. She thought about what Peggy had said, *"I want you to have this ring for good luck. I am hoping when you wear it and your marriage will last 35 years."* She closed her eyes and gave Frank a long, hard, sweet kiss. Frank looked into Jenny's eyes and whispered, "I love you, Jenny. I will always love you. Forever!" Jenny smiled. She knew it was time to start healing and trying to forgive him. Frank waited for a sign from Jenny.

She put her hand on his ass and pinched it and kissed him
hard on the lips.

Jenny could hear Frank in the bathroom shaving. She lay
there in bed a few minutes. She put her hand over her
forehead, thinking about their time in Vegas. She could
hear the TV in the other room. Sofia and Laker were
probably lying in their beds watching TV. "It's been great,
she thought!" She took her hand and put it in front of her.
She looked at the green emerald cut ring on her right
middle finger. It was her good luck charm. It was her
good luck ring. To give her strength. She needed strength
to believe. To save her. She needed strength to save
Frank. She needed strength to save their marriage.

She heard some music coming from somewhere. She got
up and went to the other room. Sofia had her violin out and
she was dancing around in her pink butterfly pajamas. She
was spinning around slowly while she played beautiful
music. Laker pulled the blankets up with both hands over
his head. He closed his eyes. All he could think about was
Mom is going to raise a holy cow argument for her
bringing her violin. He waited for his mother's mouth to
start firing fireworks out at Sofia. Jenny eyes flashed red
for a second and she began to say something. Then she
stopped herself and leaned against the doorway watching
Sofia dancing and playing her beloved violin. She smiled
at Sofia. Sofia smiled back as she danced around playing a
lullaby on her violin.

But in those moments, watching Sofia, all Jenny thought
about was she wanted her daughter, Sofia, to remain
captured in that timeframe. Laker peeped his head out
from under the covers and looked at his mom smiling.

"Ok, we are good?" Laker thought. "We are all good." He watched his sister Sofia smiling, dancing on her tip toes in her pink tinker bell pajamas playing her violin with her long hair swirling around. Laker peeped his eyes out from under the blanket again. He saw his dad standing in the doorway behind his Mom. He put the covers down and smiled. He never wanted this moment with of all them together to go away. He closed his eyes thinking again for a brief moment, **"What plays in Vegas, stays in Vegas!"**

Jenny, Frank, Sofia and Laker hurriedly crossed the crowded street to Sam's Hamburgers and Hotdogs where they had decided to watch the fireworks from. The police had already barricaded the Street Strip area with yellow tape. The Strip was car silent. No cars. There were huge crowds all lined up down each side of the Strip. Huddling together, they all looked up in the sky.

Laker nudged Sofia and pointed to the huge moon. "Cool! Look at that big moon Sofia. Now that's a sight to see!" Sofia looked in amazement. Sofia pointed to the moon.

"That's the biggest yellow moon I've ever seen".

Laker wished he had his dad's binoculars. He grabbed his cell phone out of his jean pocket and started taking pictures. Sofia pointed to the black night sky, "Mom, Dad, look at that huge yellow moon! It's gigantic!" Jenny put her arms around Sofia's shoulders.

"Yes, yes, we see it, honey." *Boom! Boom! Boom*! The fireworks had begun.

"Wow! Sofia pointed again to the black sky, Look at that!"
Colors exploded everywhere. They were beautiful.
 Sofia tugged on her mom's arm. "Mom, I feel rain
sprinkles on my arms". Jenny felt some raindrops fall on
her face.

"It's okay Sofia, the fireworks will be over in a few
minutes and we can go.*"* *Boom! Boom! Boom!* Sofia
watched in wonderment. There were magnificent, rainbow
colors exploding all over in the black sky.

They stood in the crowd watching the fireworks. Jenny
looked at Frank. Everyone was watching the Grand Finale
with rain coming down. For a split second, the huge
yellow moon turned totally black. When the Grand Finale
began, the rain started to fall harder. Laker pointed to the
moon. "Look mom! Look dad! Look at the moon!" It
was covered with black birds with red eyes. They were
flying everywhere in the night. Sofia grabbed her mom's
hand and held it tight.

There was a loud noise from the crowds on the streets and
then a gasp with everyone pointing towards the moon.
"Look! Look! Look at that!" There were black birds flying
everywhere, covering the moon at times and then splinters
of yellow appearing again. Frank took Jenny's hand.
Jenny grabbed Sofia's hand and told Sofia to grab her
brother's hand. They all started running, pushing their way
against the crowd to across the street to *The Diamond Club
Casino*.

Laker ran into his mom's and dad's room and grabbed his
Dad's binoculars on the side of the table, ran to the window

and looked out. He looked at the still bright yellow moon.
The rain had stopped. The birds were all gone. "Okay,
enough," Laker, Frank said taking the binoculars from him.
"I think we have had enough excitement for one night.
You and Sofia go dry off and get in bed. We check out
tomorrow at 1:00 p.m. and have to be to the airport by
3:00."

"Awe, I don't want to go home" Sofia said. Lakers chimed
in, me neither. Jenny looked at Frank.

"Okay kiddos, time to go to bed."

Frank woke up the next morning. He rolled over and
looked at Jenny who was peacefully sleeping. It was 7:00
a.m. Sunday, July 5th. He knew everyone would be up
early to finish packing. Check out was at 1:00 p.m. The
flight was at 4:00 p.m. Vacation was almost over. He
didn't know if he was ready to go home or if he wanted to
stay and have more time to hang with Jenny and the kids.

 Well, that was an easy answer, he thought. "Stay!"

**Chapter 20–Los Angeles Girls with Massachusetts Boys
- July 4th**

Bethany, Stephanie and Megan stepped through the double
glass doors at *The Rocket Aero Tower Casino*. They
looked across the lobby and saw Johnny, Brett, and Darren
standing there with their hands in their pockets. Johnny
saw them and waved them to come over. "Hi, how are our
beautiful girls doing tonight?" Stephanie smiled.

"We are doing just fine. And how are you boys doing tonight?" Johnny rolled his eyes, "Boys?" Johnny said and started laughing. Johnny smiled grabbed Stephanie's hand "this way my dear." Darren and Brett followed suit with Megan and Bethany.

They all headed to the elevators. The elevator had clear glass on all sides except the door entrance. Johnny hit the 98th floor button. The elevator took off slowly. Wow! Megan's stomach turned a summersault. The lobster that was already cooked and eaten by her was rotating in her stomach. She put her hand to her mouth trying not to gag. "I've never seen nor been in a glass elevator before." Everyone looked out the glass elevator while going up and up. It was fun and exciting all at the same time. Johnny pointed out various electronic bill boards and hotels to Stephanie. Darren squeezed Megan's hand. "You, okay?" Megan smiled.

"Yes, I'll be fine. Thank you for asking." He smiled at her and squeezed her hand again.

Megan looked down at the elevator floor trying to maintain her composure.   The elevator doors opened and they all stepped off the elevator onto the 98th floor. There was a large crowd already hanging around. There was three white, small, Xmas lighted strings around the bar areas and two bar tenders for each bar. The moon was a huge full moon. All Megan saw was a bright yellow moon and a black, clouded sky canvas. All of a sudden Megan wished she had her sketch book in her hand with her black charcoal.

177

She closed her eyes for a minute to capture the beautiful night and hold the imagine in her mind. They all went to the bar. The bar tender asked. "What will it be?" Johnny looked at Stephanie. Then he looked at the bar tender again.

"We'll take four *"Lie Down Lucys."* They all started laughing. Johnny put his shot up in the air and said, "Cheers! Cheers to a beautiful 4th of July night with three lovely ladies, with three gents from Massachusetts." They all clinked their glasses, drank their *"Lie Down Lucy"* shots and then made their way to the high railing. The fireworks had begun. *Boom! Boom! Boom!* Colors exploded in the night sky. They exploded everywhere, red, green, purple, yellow. Beautiful!

Bethany turned to Stephanie and Megan and the guys. "Did you feel that?"

"Feel what?" Darren asked.

"It's sprinkling." Johnny put his hand up in the air.

"Yep, it sure is!" The fireworks will be over in a few minutes. We should be good for a few minutes."

Boom! Boom! Boom! Boom! Boom! Boom! There was an explosion of colored fireworks shooting up in the sky all at once with magnificent colors; red, blue, orange, yellow, green, purple. It was the Grand Finale. The rain began to come down, first slowly and then it came down harder.

Boom! Boom! Boom! Boom! Boom! Boom! Bret turned to Bethany and pointed to the sky.   Rain began to fall. Bethany, Megan, Stephanie, Darren, Johnny and Bret all stood in the rain looking at the sky with all the colors and then they noticed the moon. It had turned black for a few seconds and then there were black birds flying everywhere. The moon was again covered black with yellow streaks coming through it. Everyone was pointing towards the moon.

"Look!" Look!" Look! They all watched in amazement. Cell phones were flashing pictures in the night everywhere. The rain began to come down harder. Darren heard slight fluttering noises. Darren grabbed Megan's hand and they all ran towards the elevators. There were only three elevators.

One of the elevators opened. Darren pulled Megan in and turned to the crowd to see if Johnny, Stephanie and Bethany and Brett were in. Someone was holding the elevator door open. It was Johnny. He looked at Darren in the back of the elevator. He put two fingers up high in the air. "We're all in!" Darren put two fingers up in the air back to Johnny to say, "We are all in." It was packed like sardines. Everyone was murmuring. "Did you see the huge yellow moon?

Yes! Yes! Yes! Lots of people saying "Yes! Yes! Yes!

"Did you see those black birds?" "Yes. Yes. Yes." "Now that was a sight to see!" someone said. Another guy in the back of the elevator chimed in, **"What plays in Vegas, stays in Vegas!"**

They all stepped out of the elevator.   It was 12:00 a.m.
Stephanie didn't feel well. She started coughing. "You
okay," Brett asked? Stephanie put on a brave face. "Yes, I
just look like a wet puppy now." They were all wet from
the rain. Darren was looking at his phone, "Did you see all
those black birds around the moon?" "That was
awesome!" "Crazy! if you ask me," Brett said. They all
started laughing.

Johnny turned to Stephanie, "Where would you gals like to
go for your last night?" Johnny asked?

"Let's go play black jack!"

"Sounds good to me!"

"Me too! Megan said. Stephanie held back, shrugging her
shoulders.   She was not feeling well. She touched her
forehead with the back of her hand. It felt hot. She knew
she was getting a fever and she had the chills. Stephanie
spoke up, "Let's go back to *The Diamond Club Casino* to
play!"

The Diamond Club Casino was rolling? They all sat down
at a $5 Black Jack table. Johnny ordered the usual *"Lie
Down Lucys"* with limes for everyone. Stephanie looked at
the *"Lie Down Lucy"* and put her hand over her mouth,
coughed and slide *"The Lie Down Lucy"* shot over to
Bethany. Bethany looked at her. "Stephanie, are you
alright?" You don't look so good?"

"No, actually, I feel like I am getting the chills and I am
hot, like I am getting a fever."

180

Megan turned to Bethany. "Hey Bethany, I'm going to take Stephanie up to the room. She is not feeling well." Megan got up and took Stephanie's arm. Stephanie leaning on Megan turned to the guys, "Hey sorry guys, "I hate to be the last night in Las Vegas party pooper. I'm just not feeling well. Please excuse me." Everyone looked at her. She looked pale, faint, sweat on her brow. Her words were coming out of her mouth soft, barely auditable. Johnny got up immediately. Megan could see a look of disappointment on his face.

"Hey, Megan do you need some help?"

With helpless eyes, Stephanie looked at Johnny. Holding on to Megan's arm, she said, "I am sorry Johnny. I want you and everyone here to know I had a great time. It was a pleasure meeting you all. Maybe we will meet again in Las Vegas someday." With that Megan and Stephanie both walked to the elevators. Stephanie turned back slightly and yelled. "Don't drink too many of those *"Lie Down Lucys,"* or you will be lying down with Lucy!" They all looked at Stephanie and laughed. Johnny looked down at his cards. He didn't want the guys to know how disappointed he was. His hand showed an Ace and King. He turned the cards over and yelled, Black Jack!

Megan turned the bedside lamp on and helped Stephanie to bed. Stephanie lied down and passed out. Megan removed Stephanie's long red dress and started taking her red shoes off. She could see a red rash that covered her right foot. It had started up her right foot and had reached up toward her ankle. She put her hand over her mouth and gasped. "Oh my God!" she thought. She looked at the bedside clock. It was 2:00 a.m. Megan bent down and touched Stephanie's forehead. It was hot. She ran to the bathroom and got a cold washcloth and put it on Stephanie's head. She got two aspirin out of her bag and a glass of water. Here sweetie, sit up. Take these two aspirin." Stephanie sat up groggily and took the aspirin and water. She flopped back down on the bed, closed her eyes again and slept.

Megan looked at her friend. She sat there wondering what was the best thing to do. She was really concerned. She took off the wash cloth and felt Stephanie's head again. She leaned forward and put her hear to Stephanie's mouth. Her breathing was okay.   Selfishly thinking, it was there last night in Las Vegas. She knew Stephanie would sleep until morning. She got up and went back downstairs. Everyone was yelling at the Black Jack table. "Yes!" "Black Jack!" "Johnny was shouting, "Another round of *Lie Down Lucys*," please!"

Chapter 21– Anderson Memorial Hospital – Code Green

Dr. Cooper's cell phone rang. He had retired early to bed after a long shift. His wife, Miriam rolled over. "Aren't you going to answer your cell phone? It's been ringing for about five minutes now."

He picked up his cell phone and read his texts. Code Green. Code Green. Please turn on TV to the 11:00 p.m. tonight's, channel 8, KLVG News.

"What the?" Dr. Cooper sat up in bed and grabbed the TV channel and turned on the 11:00 p.m.

"This is Tom Solis with KLVG Las Vegas News on the Las Vegas Strip here. *It appears this evening when the Grand Finale fireworks went off, there were hundreds of huge black birds flying around the large yellow moon and then the rain began to fall. We don't know exactly what the birds are nor do we know, as of this moment, where they came from. We will give a more inclusive update as we follow the story. And now here is Rachael Summers with the seven-day weather report."*

Dr. Cooper watched the TV in amazement as the News continued. *"The Diamond Club Casino had their 4th of July yearly firework event tonight. It started at 9:00 p.m. and the streets were lined in hundreds and spectators. The fireworks were splendid. There were huge crowds lined up on the Strip' streets but it seems everyone has taken shelter inside due to a rain shower that come through when the Grand Finale was displayed in the air. The News room has received several calls in from spectators that there were black birds that covered the huge full yellow moon and they were flying everywhere. Spectators sent images from their cell phones to our website for view. We are not quite sure what the birds are or where they came from. We will definitely keep you updated on this news broadcast and soon as more details come in. This is Tom Solis KVLS Las Vegas New."*

Dr. Cooper picked up his phone and texted Emily, Sylvia with a Code Green. Code Green was an Alert Text term used to say "meet at hospital at your usual station."

Miriam rolled over and looked at her husband. "Are you off to the hospital tonight?" He rolled over and kissed her.

"Yes, my dear. Go back to sleep." Miriam looked into his deep brown eyes and brushed his silver haired wings behind his ears. She was use to the Doctor's wife life after nineteen years of marriage. "Love you."

Dr. Cooper rushed down the hallway to his office. The hospital was in somewhat of a panic mode. He knew something was happening. Emily and Sylvia were outside his office waiting. "Come in." "Come in." "Please sit down." He looked at them both. "You both already heard the black flying around the moon?" They stared at Dr. Cooper a moment.

"Yes!" "Yes!"

The hospital has had all kinds of variations of talk content of what went on. But they have all pretty much said it started to rain when the Grand Finale was exploding in the air and then there were black birds flying over the moon. Dr. Cooper looked concerned. "Okay here's where we are at. I want you both to go back to the 16 biopsies, including Rose Davis's and see if we can identify any "bat feces" in any of the biopsies." Emily and Sylvia looked straight at Dr. Cooper and his concerned face. He looked like a statue in deep thought.

Emily could feel her face draining from red to white. She knew that whatever was going on now, could be serious. She also knew that bat's feces (guano) if inhaled airborne by an individual could be deadly if not treated properly and that bats carried rabies.

Dr. Cooper stood up and started talking fast. He looked at his watch. It was 11:30 a.m. "I'll be around the hospital. Please have the floor receptionist page me on the intercom when you are done. Thank you,Sylvia and Emily for getting here to the hospital so quickly. "I think it's going to be a long night and morning. He swiftly walked away down the long corridor. He got in the elevator and pushed 8th Floor and then he stopped by the Admissions desk. Rose Davis's chart please."

"Yes, Dr. Cooper, here it is." He took the folder, flipped it open reading the notes as he approached room 810. He gently pushed the door open. Rose was still awake looking out the window. She turned her head towards Dr. Cooper.

Nurses were coming out of rooms and walking hurriedly down the corridor trying to catch up to him. "Did you hear about the black birds Dr. Cooper? Dr. Cooper turned around and put his hands up.

"Yes, yes ladies. Thank you all for your concern. But as of now I can say everything is fine. I will keep everyone at the hospital informed as soon as I know more. Just be calm and let me know if any patients start arriving tonight or tomorrow with a fever and a rash."

The intercom rung out. "Dr. David Cooper! Dr. David Cooper!"

"Excuse me ladies." He walked towards a phone on the wall and pushed 2 and then 0. "Yes, this is Dr. Cooper."

It's Emily. "We have concluded the biopsy results."

"I'll be there in a few minutes." Dr. Cooper hung up and rushed to the Lavatory. Emily was reviewing the specimen again. Dr. Cooper rushed into the Laboratory. Emily stepped back. Dr. Cooper covered his mouth and nose with a blue surgical cloth. He looked into the Microscope and carefully took his time to look at the evolving cells and tissues. He looked up at Emily and then looked at Sylvia.

"Good work Emily and Sylvia. It is confirmed. It is bat droppings known as "bat guano". "Histoplasmosis is the disease you can get from bat droppings. Bat droppings have a very distinct order. If not treated, patients will have acute respiratory disease, ill feelings, rash, fever, chest pains and a dry cough. It can lead to death if not treated properly. Itraconazole is one of the type of antifungal medications used to treat histoplasmosis.

He looked up at Emily and Sylvia. "Good thing it's not contagious." Emily and Sylvia looked at each other. They knew in the back of their minds it could be contagious. And it could spread like wild fire around the world if the pills they were prescribing didn't work in 90 days. And they both knew an epidemic could arise around the world and the totality of lives would be severe.

Dr. Cooper looked once at Emily and once at Sylvia. He studied both of their composures. He recognized their body languages. He knew then, there was a second of terror in both their eyes. He quickly shook the notion so they could not see in his eyes, his own fear and turned and said,

"Let's go to my office to discuss this further." Dr. Cooper closed the door. He sat down and looked at Emily and Sylvia. What I am going to tell you is Confidential. The patient, Rose Davis, on the Isolated 8th Floor had all the symptoms of this disease. "She had a red rash on her abdomen and her back and a high fever when she came in. "We have been treating her with an antibacterial IV for the past two days. I just checked on her and her rash on her back is gone and the rash on her abdomen is disappearing. I am going to give her a 90 day prescription of antibacterial Itraconazole. The rash should be gone by then. Viewing the worst scenario of this disease and depending on the severity of the infection and the person's immune status; the course of treatment can range from three months to one year. I am putting the hospital staff on a Code Yellow Alert. Meaning I am asking all hospital personnel to inform me if they have any incoming patients coming into the hospital with a rash and high fever or bite marks from any kind of animals.

"Rose was last at *The Diamond Club Casino Hotel.* She has informed us, her friend and her spend a lot of time there. I am going to contact the National Animal Health System, who also manages emergency animal disease control. I will keep you both informed."

Sylvia spoke up. "Dr. Cooper, I did my thesis on bats when I was in college. I would like to share this information with you plus more up-to-date information. May I?" Dr. Cooper nodded. "Sure, Sylvia, anything you have, please share with us.

"During the day bats sleep in trees, rock, crevices, caves and buildings and usually sleep during the day, roughly 19 hours. Bats are nocturnal (active **at** night) leaving daytime roosts at dusk. Upon leaving their roost, bats fly to a stream, pond or lake where they dip their lower jaw into the water while still in flight and take a drink. Bats are not flying mice; they are not even remotely related to the rodents. There are 1100 different species of bats. They are such unique animals that scientists have placed them in a group all their own, called "Chiroptera," which means hand-wing. Chiroptera is the name of the order of the only mammal capable of true flight, the bat. The name is influenced by the hand-like wings of the bats, which are formed from four elongated "fingers" covering by a cutaneous membrane. Generally, bats are **not aggressive by nature** and unless you are threatening them, they won't act aggressively toward you. **Most bats are quite timid and prefer to avoid people.** Bats are definitely not blind, but have accurate vision. They also avoid natural and artificial lights. Being nocturnal animals, they are adapted to extreme low light conditions. When bats are in flight during the night, they are conscious of artificial lights and avoid them as much as they can."

Sylvia took a deep breath and continued. "Most bats are predators of night flying insects, like mosquitoes. At night, their ears are more important than their eyes. They use **special sonar systems called "echolocation**, meaning they find things using echoes. "Unlike birds, bats cannot launch their bodies into the air from the ground, because their wings don't produce enough lift to take off like a helicopter. If sleeping bats need to escape quickly, hanging upside-down means they are already in the perfect position

188

to spread their wings and fly. Hawks and owls regularly
kill and eat bats. Snakes and predatory mammals such as
weasels and raccoons climb into the bat roosts during the
day and attack bats when they are sleeping."

"In a six-year time frame nearly 5 million bats died of
white rose syndrome, a fungal disease introduced from
Europe or Asia that's common in the Northeast and is
spreading south and west. Several hundred thousand bats
die annually after flying into wind turbines. The risk to
humans might increase over the next couple of decades as
climate changes bring species like the so called, Vampire
Bat of Mexico and Central America into the southern states
of which feeds on cattle, dogs and people. They account
for 90 percent of human rabies. But to date there have only
been 26 human deaths due to rabies and only half in the last
decade were from bats.

But with that being said, bats are good for the ecosystem
because they produce guano, the gold standard of animal
fertilizer and the majority of the North American species
eat bugs. Sylvia paused. Dr. Cooper said.

"Very good, Sylvia, thank you for sharing that piece of
information." "I will also do some more research, myself."
Anything further you find, please email me a report.

 Emily turned to Sylvia. "May I? The biopsy shows that
this bat is part of the big brown bat colony. That may be
more or less of a good thing. We do not want the Vampire
bat."

"Yes, thank you Emily for that information, Sylvia said and continued. In one year, 100-Vampire bats known as the Desmodus rotundas, colony can drink the blood of 25 cows. They are nocturnal and utilize pointed fangs to feed on blood. They are a main vector for the human vampirism virus. During the darkest part of the night, common vampire bats emerge to hunt. Sleeping cattle and horses are their usual victims, but they have been known to feed on people as well."

Dr. Cooper looked at his watch. It was now 3:00 a.m. He looked at both Emily and Sylvia. "I must say, well done! I don't get impressed very often by individuals, but I am impressed with you both! I want you to know that I hired you as my Preventive Disease Biologists because you both are very intelligent and helped me immensely on several cases. And I am grateful to both of you." Emily and Sylvia smiled.

"Thank you, Dr. Cooper."

With that being said, "It has been a very hectic evening and morning. Both of you please go home and rest. I have some rounds and meetings this morning." I will text Code Green if I need you."

Standing up Emily turned to Sylvia. "I am looking forward to that nice comfortable bed." Sylvia smiled. "Me too! Dr. Cooper got up from his chair and walked them both out of his office.

"Enjoy your comfortable beds this early morning."

Dr. Cooper smiled at both of them. "Thank you again ladies. I'm looking forward to a nice hot cup of hospital coffee!" Sylvia and Emily laughed. They knew the coffee was not the Starbuck coffee.   Dr. Cooper immediately picked up the phone and dialed The Diamond Club Casino and asked for the Ed Johnson, General Manager.

Ed Johnson walked out of his office and waived to Sally. "I'll be at Anderson Memorial Hospital. I have an appointment with Dr. David Cooper. I'll be back later."

Dr. Cooper sat down in his chair with his black coffee. He picked up the phone and called the Admissions Clerk, Renee. "This is Dr. Cooper. Can you please get me the phone number for the *Federal Animal Preventive Disease Control Administration.*

"Yes, Dr. Cooper, right away. "Oh Dr. Cooper, a gentleman by the name of Ed Johnson from *The Diamond Club Casino* is here to see you."

"Okay, please let him know "I'll be right there. Thank you."   As Dr. Cooper approached Ed Johnson, he extended his right hand and shook Ed's hand.

"Welcome to Anderson Memorial Hospital. This way please, Mr. Johnson, to my office. Please have a seat Mr. Johnson. As I told you on the phone, I am Dr. David Cooper and I am the Director of Preventive Immune Disease Department here at Anderson Memorial Hospital. I will get right to the point Mr. Johnson. I don't want you to take what I am saying as accusations."

"Because of our recent research and with sound evidence we can confirm that your casino, *The Diamond Club Casino* may be infected with brown bats and brown bat fungus. I have called the Federal *Animal Preventive Disease Control* and they are going to send a task team of five to your casino, *The Diamond Club Casino* to perform a three-day Animal Control Preventive investigation. They will be arriving today at July 6th Tuesday at 4:00. I have advised them to meet with you today before they start their research at The Diamond Club Casino. They will be performing various research tasks and also will advise you on what cleaning measures need to be taken for your casino, especially focusing on all garage parking structures, storage units and elevators on each floor."

Ed looked at Dr. Cooper. He thought back to all the streaks he had seen on the floors. Dr. Cooper continued. "We have a patient here in the hospital. I cannot tell you, her name. It is because of a patient confidential. But she was at your hotel and came in with a high fever, slight cough and a red rash on her abdomen and back. We ran several tests and biopsies and finally concluded that she got the rash from bat guano, feces. It can be airborne. She somehow breathed it. It is not contagious. We do have the antifungal IV antidote and the prescription pills to cure this disease; but only if the patient comes into a nearby hospital and it is caught in time. Dr. Cooper folded his hands together and looked Ed Johnson sitting quietly in his chair. Still staring at Ed Johnson, he sat back in his chair and took a long sigh. "And, only if the patient has a good immune system."

Ed looked down at the floor and inhaled slowly and then exhaled. He looked back up at Dr. Cooper with concerned eyes. He rubbed his forehead with his fingers. "Whew, this is a lot to take in. I want you to know I saw white and dark brown streaks in the receptionist area where visitors pull their luggage bags in. I told the cleaning and maintenance crew to take a janitorial green solution and clean all floors, entrances included and also the carpet in the hotel room hallways and the garage parking structures, elevators included. Well, I guess there is no choice in this matter." "I would appreciate it if you would please keep me informed of any other out breaks.

Dr. Cooper unfolded his hands and asked. "Did you see the black birds last night flying around the huge yellow moon when the fireworks were going being displayed?"

"Yes, I did. I looked out the window to view the fireworks and noticed birds flying around the moon. I did not stay long to watch since I was being called by one of my Pitt Bosses on the floor. But I did see them."

Dr. Cooper leaned forward in his chair. "Let me fill you in on what I heard from the News broadcast and what we know for actual facts. It started to drizzle and then it started to rain before the fireworks Grand Finale. There were black birds that took flight when the fireworks Grand Finale began. *Bats have supersonic ears.* I am thinking that th,e *Boom!, Boom!, Boom!, Boom!, Boom!, Boom!* noise sounds made them take flight. People everywhere took pictures from their phones of them shadowing the moon. There was a huge yellow full moon. I believe they took flight from your parking garage structures. They were hiding out there. Maybe in the storage areas and also on the garage floors. They hung from the side beams around your garage parking structures unnoticed by all your visitors. Their droppings, guano feces, were dropped on your garage floors. While feces were exposed on the garage floors, visitors rolled their luggage bags into your casino. This is why you see the white and brown streaks on your casino floors." Ed knew Dr. Cooper was right. Dr. Cooper continued.

"What we need to do is let the *Animal Preventive Disease Control* task team do their job and advise us on what we need to do next. I will also be getting their report. I have contacted the News Channel and I will be giving a five-minute Local News Press Conference at 2:00 p.m. today so everyone in Las Vegas is aware of this situation. The staff here at Anderson Memorial Hospital has been informed. We will most likely receive thousands of calls."

Dr. Cooper looked at his watch. "I am sorry, Mr. Johnson, I have a patient I need to go see now. I want you to know that we are prepared. I am sorry I have to be the bad bearer of bad news. But at this very moment, I am just happy we can help our patients here and hopefully you can take care of the Casino and your guests. Do you have any questions? Ed looked at Dr. Cooper. Ed shook his head.
"Not at this moment."

Dr. Cooper stood up. "Please call me if you have any further questions or concerns." Ed got up and shook Dr. Cooper's hand.

"Thank you for your time." Ed got in his car. He put his hands on the steering wheel and bowed his head. He knew he had to keep things under control so no one panicked at

the casino. He quickly sat up. He thought of his friend
Jack.   Sally said Jack had to leave to go home for a few
days because his dad had a major stroke and was in
intensive care in the hospital. He thought of his rash. He
immediately dialed Jack's cell phone.   He heard his voice.

"Jack, Jack!" Oh my God! Jack, listen to me very
carefully. First of all, I am sorry to hear about your Dad."

"What is it Jack asked? What's the urgency?

Ed continued. "The rash you have. How bad is it now?
Jack pulled the golf glove off his right hand. It had spread
up to the middle of his arm.

"It's getting worse."

"Listen to me Jack. We have had an emergency here in Las
Vegas. Please turn on the TV and look at the news. There
seems to be a bat problem. And, as far as we all know, it
originated from *The Diamond Club Casino* in the garage
parking areas and then it contaminated the casino floors by
guests wheeling in their luggage."

"There is an Animal Preventive Disease Control task team
that will be exploring the situation in more depth. In the
meantime, please go to the physician at the Detroit
Memorial Hospital and ask them for the brown bat
antidote. They will probably give a strong antidote pill.
Please take them according to the doctor there. Jack could
feel his body go slightly faint. Ed continued,

"Jack, this is serious. You cannot take this lightly. It can be deadly. Do you understand?"

"Yes, yes, Jack said. I understand. Jack wanted to ask more questions, but he was too fatigued and needed to sleep more. Thank you, Ed. I will be in touch."

Dr. Cooper called his wife Miriam, "Hello, my love. It's going to be a long day. I'll call you later before I come home." Miriam took a bite of her sandwich.

"Is it the bird thing from last night I've been seeing it all over every News channel on the TV? He knew he needed to say something.

"Yes. Watch for the TV/Radio Media News Press Conference today at 2:00 p.m. I will be explaining everything. I'll tell you more about it later. Miriam took another bite of her sandwich, hung up the home phone and looked out the kitchen window.

Dr. Cooper met the TV/Radio News journalist/broadcasters outside the Anderson Memorial Hospital. In a brief seven-minute statement, Dr. Cooper began informing the public about the circumstances of the night of July 4th, the fireworks, the brown bats, their origin, the airborne bat feces matter and the rash. He did not release the name of the casino. Reporters were thrusting their microphones at him everywhere with questions. His final answer was: "We are currently doing an investigation which will take at least three days. There will be another TV/Radio News Press Conference once we have concluded the investigation and all reports are finalized. Thank you and have a good day."

Dr. Cooper called Miriam. He was exhausted. "I'll be home for dinner. See you around 7:00 p.m. Miriam could hear his tiredness in his voice. She softly whispered.

"Okay. See you then."

Chapter 22 – Roses are Red and Violets are Blue

Dr. Cooper approached Rose's bedside and touched her on the shoulder. "Sorry to bother you at this early morning time, Rose." Rose rolled over.

"No problem, Dr. Cooper. It's not always very comfortable sleeping in a hospital bed." Dr. Cooper smiled.

"It appears you have been on a fungal antibacterial IV for the past day and half." "May I?" Dr. Cooper pulled Roses' hospital gown over and studied her rash on her abdomen. It looked as if it was slowly disappearing. Can you roll over Rose, so I can see your back? Rose rolled over. The rash on her back was gone.

Dr. Cooper smiled. "Good news Rose. Your rash is slowing going away. I am going to release you tomorrow at 12:00 p.m. Please stop by the Admissions Desk out front. They will have a prescription for you. Please take one pill in the morning for 90 days. If the rash does not go away completely in 90 days or you experience other symptoms, like the fever you had when you came in, please call here at the hospital and I will get in touch with you." Rose smiled. She was tired.

"Thank you, Doctor Cooper." Dr. Cooper turned and walked toward the door. "Oh, Dr. Cooper, by the way did you see the moon and those black birds? It was amazing!" Dr. Cooper turned and looked at Rose.

"Yes, I heard, Rose. Rest well, Rose."

 Dr. Cooper walked past the Administrator's desk. Wanda stood up from her desk, "Did you hear? "Did you hear Dr. Cooper about the big black birds around the huge yellow full moon last night?"

Rose rolled over in bed. It was 10:00 a.m. July 6th Monday. A nurse came in carrying a big vase of 24 red roses with a card. She placed the roses on the bedside table and smiled. She looked at Rose and said, Umm, someone special?" Rose sat up and took the card out of the roses. She opened it. It read. *"My Dear Rose... As corny as it sounds, I am going to say it anyway. Roses are Red and Violets are Blue, you are my Rose, my Rose come True? Get Better! I miss you! Love Grant."*

She heard a male voice talking behind the nurse. She strained her neck looking around the Nurse for the owner of the voice. It was Grant. He smiled at her while taking off his sunglasses. He walked over and took her hand. "Hello Rose." He bent down and gave her a light kiss on her lips and looked into her tearful eyes. "I hear you've been very sick." Rose wiped away her tears and reached for Grant. He put his arms around her and whispered in her ear, "My little Rose, my beautiful, little Rose."

Rolling her eyes, the nursed blurted out before she left the room, "I heard you are going home today Rose." Dr. Cooper will be here in a few minutes and then you can start dressing to go home." Rose smiled at her.

"Thank you."

While holding Rose's hand, Grant turned and yelled out to the Nurse, "Don't worry, I will take good care of her". The nurse stuck her head around the corner of the door. "Rolling her eyes once again, "I'm sure you will!"

Dr. Cooper knocked lightly on the hospital door and walked in. He noticed a man standing next to Rose's bedside. He walked over to him and said, Hello my name is Dr. David Cooper. Grant shook his hand.

"I'm Grant Benedict. I am here to pick up Rose and take my *"Lady of the Night"* out to dinner tonight.

Dr. Cooper looked suspiciously up and down at Grant. He remembered Rose telling him the first day that she came in she worked for *"Ladies of the Night"*. Rose looked at Dr. Cooper's face and gasped.

"Dr. Cooper, I am sorry, I wasn't totally truthful the first night I came into the hospital. I told you I worked for *"Ladies of the Night."* Truthfully, I didn't know what to tell you. Rose looked down at her fumbling hands.

"At that moment in time, I don't have a full-time job and it was the only thing I could tell you. With sincerity, Rose looked into Dr. Cooper's eyes. "I am sorry."

Dr. Cooper's face relaxed. He felt relieved to know that Rose was not some young girl known on the streets of Las Vegas working as a hooker or a prostitute.   Of which Dr. Cooper had seen many.

"May I?" Grant moved away from the Rose's bed. Dr. Cooper pulled Rose's hospital gown up to look at her abdomen. It was clear. The rash was almost gone. "Please roll over Rose. Rose rolled over. The rash on her back was gone. He looked at her anxious green eyes.

"Very good Rose. It looks like the rash is gone." Dr. Cooper smiled. "You're free to go home now, Rose." Please remember to stop by the Admissions desk when you check out and pick up the 90-day prescription of the fungus antibiotic. Please take one pill a day for 90 days. If you notice anything else strange going on, please call." Dr. Cooper headed for the door and turned and looked at Rose and said, "I wish I could tell you to come back and visit. But, I know, as a doctor, and from experience, most people who come to the hospital don't want to come back for a visit or even for that matter anything else."

Rose looked at Grant, and for the first time in days, finally laughed. "I'll be back in a few minutes. Rose got up, grabbed her purse and clothes and went to the bathroom. She looked in the mirror. She looked dreadful. No makeup and smelling like an old hospital bed. She quickly got in the shower and let the hot water and soap take over. She

200

toweled off. Grant yelled. "Need any help in there?" Rose
rolled her eyes.

 "No, I'm good. I'll be out in a minute." She quickly put
her clothes on, brushed her teeth with the hospital tooth
brush and toothpaste. Looking in the mirror she winced.
No make-up. "Yuck!" She grabbed her purse and walked
out the bathroom, picked up her beautiful vase with the
roses. Elated she was getting out of the hospital, she
looked at Grant in the hospital chair and said "Come on!
Let's get out of here!"

Rose walked towards the Admissions Desk and gave the
Admissions Clerk her name. "I'm Rose Davis and I'm
checking out." She looked up at Grant and smiled. The
Out Patient Admissions
Clerk looked at Rose and smiled. "Okay Ms. Rose Davis
here is your prescription for 90 days.
Please take one in the morning for the complete 90 days.
Rose smiled back at the Out Patient Admissions Clerk,
"Thank you."

Rose reached behind her and put the rose vase secure on
the back car floor behind her. Grant got in the other side of
the car and started the engine and then casually sat staring
at Rose. Rose turned and looked at him.

"What are you staring at?"

"You!" "I think you're beautiful!" Rose could feel her
face turn bright red. She smiled and casually punched his
shoulder.

"Come On!" You've seen me looking better than this."

Rose was starting to feel herself come alive. She felt free.
Free from days of hell in the hospital. There was no one
here to really talk to for days.

"Where too? Grant asked. Rose blurted out.

"I'm starving!" "I need some real food!' Grant started
laughing. Rose started laughing too.

Rose blurted out again, "Let's go get a big fat juicy burger
at Sam's Hamburger and Hot Dogs and a very large order
of fries with a large chocolate shake!" Grant put his right
hand out in a high-five! Rose put her hand out in a high-
five and they both said together.

 "Game On!" "Let's go Eat!"

Grant looked at Rose devouring her hamburger and fries.
He didn't know what it was about her, but he liked her
flashing green eyes and her long red hair. She had a sweet,
naïve side to her and he really liked that about her.

"Hey Rose what do you say we go shopping? Rose looked
into Grant's eyes.

"You're serious?" Grant smiled at her.

"Yes, Rose, I am serious." I know that I am a guy. But I
am human and I do go shopping every once in a while.
Nodding his head to the left and then to the right, Grant

took a bite of his hamburger. While talking with his mouth full he said, okay, only every once in a while.

Smiling at Grant, Rose cocked her head to the right picked up a French fry, popped it in her mouth and said, "I only have $100 with me." He reached for Roses hand.

"No worries my dear." Remember, you have a financial accountant wizard beside you. Rose started laughing.

"Oh, okay, I forgot about that one!" She took another French fry and popped it into her mouth and high-fived him. She bounced her head to the left and then to the right and flashed her green eyes at him.

"Okay, I'm in!"

Grant opened his hotel suite door. Rose ran in and went to the bedroom and threw all her shopping bags on the bed and squealed. Grant came in and dropped the rest of the bags. Rose ran over and threw her arms around his neck. "Thank you!" "Thank you!" "Thank you!" Grant put his arms around her waist and pulled her close to him and pressed his lips against hers. He liked seeing her happy. It made him happy.

He kissed her long and hard. Rose began to melt in his arms. Grant moved toward the bed and brushed off all the bags in sight and laid Rose down on the bed. Rose took her arms and swished the remaining bags off the bed. Grant looked at Rose's eyes. He got up pulled her down at the end of the bed and unzipped her jeans. While standing in front of her at the end of the bed, he unzipped his jeans and

pulled them down. Rose put her hands over her brow and
looked at him. He climbed on her, pulled her shirt over her
head and unsnapped her bra.

Rose put her hands around his neck and pulled him close to
her. She could feel his breath before he kissed her wet lips
again. She could feel his hands touching her breasts. She
could feel his hardness against her soft, young,
womanhood, her legs wet and then closer to her woman
cave.

She felt his throbbing manhood enter her woman cave. She
closed her eyes and moaned. "Awe." "Yes. Yes. Yes, she
whispered. Grinding, grinding. Up and down and all
around. Grant moaned. Her heart was racing. Her
breathing got faster and faster. Faster and faster their
bodies were moving in motion together. Every sensation
was wild, hot, wet and throbbing. Rose's mind was racing.
"Manhood come, manhood come! "Womanhood come!"
"Womanhood come! All she could think of was the 4th of
July Grand Finale and Fireworks everywhere! Uh. Uh.
Uh. "Awe, Awe, Awe." "Yes! Yes!   She moaned.

With sweat dripping from Grant's brow, he took a deep
breath, looked down at Rose, kissed her and collapse on
bed. He could hear Rose breathing hard too. Grant took
her hand and kissed the back of it. Then he rolled over and
looked at Rose. On one elbow, he said. "You're amazing!

Rose looked at Grant and got up on her elbow and ran her
finger down his nose, "You're amazing too!"

Grant leaned over and kissed her softly glaring into her eye passionate eyes.

"Let's do this again later."

Rose started laughing. She got up slowly off the bed. Standing naked she said, "I'm going to take a nice, long hot bath in your beautiful bath tub with the jets on and lots of bubbles. And then I'm going to look like a *real Rose* instead of an ugly, dirty hospital gown in a hospital room."

Still standing naked in front of him, she twirled around, put her hands on the up in the air, then on the sides of the doorway and said, "Then I'm going to put on something special you bought me. Something you haven't seen yet." And, maybe, just, maybe? Someone special will take me out on the town tonight?"

She blew him a kiss and then turned and headed towards the bathroom, closed the door, started running water, tossed a bath bomb in the tub along with lots of bath bubbles.

Rose turned on the jets, slid into the tub and leaned her head back against the tub. She closed her eyes. She felt happy. She still had some money in her pocket. She also knew she needed to find a job. She thought about Rebecca and her dance interview at 7:00 tonight. She said a silent prayer for her friend. She took a deep breath and played with the bubbles. She let the jets sooth her. She relaxed again. She finally felt really safe and at home.

In the back of her mind, she also knew that Grant liked, maybe liked her a lot. She could tell he really liked her by

the way he looked at her at times. As if he was fascinated
with what he saw. As if he were studying a new specimen.
He had been there when she really needed someone. He
was the only someone, the one that really took an interest
in her. In only a short time, she had seen his kindness and
his generosity. She was hoping in the long run he was "the
real deal."

Grant heard Rose singing in the bathroom. He smiled. He
liked her being there with him.   Grant got up from the bed
and looked at his cell phone. It was 5:00 p.m. He noticed a
call from Ed Johnson from *The Diamond Club Casino*. He
dialed Ed's cell phone number.

"Hello Ed, its Grant. "What can I do for you?"

"Hi Grant. I was wondering if we could meet Thursday
this week at 10:00 a.m."

"Sure thing, Grant said." Anything in particular you want
to talk about?

"Yes, I would like you to do a Quarterly Financial
Statement Audit for me *on The Diamond Club Casino*."
Grant held the phone closer. "Okay, sure thing. I'll be
there on Thursday at 10:00 a.m." He put his cell phone
down on the bedside and went to the other bathroom down
the hall and hopped in the shower and turned the water to
warm. He knew Rose would be awhile. He closed his eyes
and put his head in the warm water and put soap in his hair.
He put his hands against the shower wall. He thought of
Rose. Rose, Rose, Rose.

His heart beat faster. He wiped the shampoo out of his hair and opened his eyes and wiped his face with his hands. He took the soap and wiped under his arms. He looked up at the ceiling of the shower.   His mind started racing. He couldn't fight the feeling anymore. He knew. He knew his heart was talking to him and his soapy head was listening. He knew he loved her. He took his fist and hit the shower wall knowing in his mind, he had never felt such a feeling before. But he also knew it was a good feeling. He chuckled to himself. Turned off the shower, opened the door and grabbed a towel. He wiped himself off and put the towel around his waist.

He walked out of the steamy bathroom and walked to the shades in the living room. The window overlooked the Las Vegas Strip. He opened the curtains and let the light in. "Awe. It's gorgeous! Sunny. He went over to the bar, poured a drink and went to the bedroom and looked in his closet. He pulled out of the closet, a light purple shirt and dark blue slacks, dark blue jacket, black socks, a black belt and black shoes which he polished quickly. He felt good. He felt happy. Everything seemed to finally be going better for him. He went out to the living room and sat down on the couch. He turned the TV, drank his drink and started watching TV. Since nothing really was interesting on TV, he lowered the volume.

Grant's mind drifted back to six years ago before he came to Las Vegas. He was 26 years old living in Tennessee. He had one sister Patsy who was two years younger than he. His Dad Grant, Sr. was a true Tennessee Criminal Attorney. He had always wanted Grant to follow in his footsteps and become a Tennessee Lawyer. His Mom was the typical house wife. She had a part-time job at the

library. She loved books. But pretty much was a blue
belly Tennessee trophy wife.

More or less, Grant saw her as a typical Mom and house
wife who loved to cook, bake and look nice for his dad
when he came home while taking care of Grant, Jr. and his
little sister Patsy. His Mom was the ever-so-loving Mom,
always there for his dad. Mom always, handing his dad his
favorite drink. Usually, a couple shots of Bourbon in a
cold glass. Dad going to his study with his cocktail,
smoking a cigar before Mom came in to let him know
dinner was ready. The typical, "Leave it to Beaver" home.

His parents had been married 37 years. It was New Year's
Eve Day. His sister called him. She had chosen to go to
the University of Tennessee.   It was his 4th year in college.
His major was Law, but his minor was accounting.   He
was going to graduate that year.

His sister Patsy was right behind him with two more years
to graduate. She was studying to be a Nurse. He knew she
was going to be a nurse the moment she found her first
prize and brought into the house to show his mom. She
was 6 years old. Mom would get up every morning and
would have Pasty sit down on the floor in front of her. It
was always Patsy's mouth running like syrup pouring on a
pancake, carrying on about this and that, yapping like a
run-away cat. Mom would take Patsy's short very thin
platinum hair and bundle it up with a rubber band on top of
her head, making it into a tiny sprout. It was cute. She had
a perfect round onion head. I use to call her *"onion head"*
all the time. That was my favorite name for her. She was
adorable. She would always be my cute *"onion head."*

She was playing in the front yard and found a squawking
baby Red Robin under our large oak tree. She carried the
red robin into the house in both of her small hands.
Looking up at Mom, all the while pulling on Mom's apron,
with her big blue almost violet eyes with very thick long
eyelashes she said. "Mom! "Mom! See it has a broken
wing." Mom, please? We need to take care of him until he
can fly again."   All Mom had to do was look into those big
blue violet eyes with eyelashes flapping like the bird's
wings. Her heart gave in. She patted Pasty's onion head,
and then looked at me.

"Maybe Grant will build you a little bird house honey until
the bird gets well." Grant stood there staring at his mom in
disbelief. It took him years for his mom to finally say yes
to his Australian Shepherd "Aussie".   Best dog ever.

Grant ended up finding two cereal boxes and taping them
together to make a small cardboard house together. The
top roof of the house coming off so Patsy could inspect her
new prize. He cut the box so it had a small hole in the front
like a real birdhouse so Patsy's Red Robin could breathe.
She ended up calling him "Little Red Birdy". Not an
original name but one that fit the bird.

Patsy would jump off the bus, run down the path to the
house, drop her books, run upstairs to her bedroom and
open the top of the cereal cardboard bird box to see how
"Little Red Birdy" was doing. Then she would play with
him, inspect his wing, feed him, and put him back in the
cereal cardboard box. She did this routine every day. Until
the fifth day. She came home, ran up the stairs and opened
the box and guess what? "Little Red Birdy" took off in
flight and quickly few out her bedroom window. She

209

started screaming, running to the window. I had run to her room, thinking someone was torturing her.

She leaned out the window screaming, "Little Red Birdy! Little Red Birdy! "Where are you Little Red Birdy?" Mom came flying upstairs, out of breath, running over to the window. Holding her hand to her heart and breathing hard she asked.

"What?" What is it, Patsy?" Patsy looked up to at her with those big violet blue eyes and long eyelashes filled with tears.

"He's gone," she said. Mommy he's gone. Little Red Birdy is gone." She wrapped her arms around my mom's yellow, tiny blue cotton flowered dress and sobbed uncontrollably. Mom put her hand to her mouth while the other hand rubbed Patsy's back, feeling all her child's sorrow. She took a long deep sigh. Relieved there was nothing wrong with Patsy. Mom looked down at Patsy's teary violet blue eyes. She patted her on the head.

"It's okay Patsy." With a smile and a sincere gentle voice she said, "Honey, you took really good care of Little Red Birdy. I am sure you made little Red Birdy really happy. It was time for him to fly home."

Patsy looked out the window again and wiped her tears on Mom's apron. She looked up at Mom.

 "Okay Mom. Can I have some cookies now?"

Mom stood there staring out the window and then looked down at Pasty's tear-stained face.

Still looking into Patsy's violet blue eyes, she smiled and took Patsy's hand. She turned and saw me leaning against the doorway with my arms crossed observing.

For one moment, my mom's eyes met mine. She winked at me. In that one moment, I loved my mom more than anyone or anything in the world (including my true friend, my dog, Aussie).

Walking past me, she ruffled my hair with her hand and put her arm around my shoulder. "Come on, Grant, let's go eat some of Mom's homemade chocolate cookies." We all walked down stairs and sat at the small kitchen table eating chocolate cookies and drinking cold milk. It was a memory he wanted to keep forever. Then the phone call came. It was a phone call you never want to hear in your lifetime.

Grant sat remembering. He took a sip of his drink, then he heard the hall bathroom door open. He got up and got another drink and yelled down hallway.

"Rose I'm in the front room when you are ready."

Rose slowly walked down the hallway, her blue clutch satin purse in her right hand. She looked at Grant and spun around in the living room.

"You like?" she asked.

211

Grant turned away from making his drink and stared at her. She looked stunning! She had her flaming red hair up with large pearl bobby pins, dangling white pearl earrings with a double pearl bracelet and deep neck line pearl drop necklace. Her royal blue shoes even had a double pearl strap with rhinestones. Her deep royal blue dress was a wrap dress with a belt sash in front, ¾ sleeves and when she walked, it opened in the front to show one of her sexy legs. Her makeup was flawless. She had a small diamond glued to the side of her brow.

She looked like an Egyptian Blue Goddess.   Grant walked over and took her right and hand and spun her around. "Wow!" Smiling and looking at her up and down. "You look absolutely beautiful, Rose! "Rose looked at Grant.

"You don't look too bad yourself, handsome! Guess what?"

"What?" Grant asked.

"I'm hungry again!" She pulled him close to her and whispered. "I think it was that workout we had together that made me hungry!" He laughed and grabbed his jacket from the couch and said,

"I made reservations for us at *The Rocket Aero Tower Casino*. They have a beautiful French restaurant on the 98th floor that rotates around so you can view all of Las Vegas out all of its rotating windows while you eat." Grant opened the front suite door. Rose smiled.

"I already like!"

**Chapter 23– *The Diamond Club Casino* – Animal
Preventive Disease Control**

Ed called Sally into his office and explained the meeting to
her. "Well did you get the list of employees who may have
the rash?"

"Yes, I have it here. There is only one person on the list
that came back with a sign of a rash and that was Kevin
Grits, a waiter at the Handel Steak House. But the head
chief called me back and said he talked with Kevin the
waiter and observed the mark on his hand. It was just a
burn mark, not a rash.

Ed sighed in relief. "Well, it's looking good so far."

Ed rubbed his forehead. "Sally, I want you to know that it
might be a little crazy for the next few days. What you and
I need to do is not panic and stay calm. I have contacted
HR and informed them of our situation. They are on-board
and have contacted the hire-ups. So, we may be getting
several calls, one of them maybe from the CEO of the
Casino, Grave Jenkins. I just want you to be prepared."

Ed looked seriously at Sally again. "Are we good?" Sally
shifted in her chair.

"Yes Mr. Johnson. We are good."

Ed continued, "The *Animal Preventive Disease Control*
task team will be here at 4:00 p.m. I believe there will be a
team of five. They will most likely be taping off all seven

213

parking garage structures, elevators and storage units on the 2nd, 4th and 6th floors. Please radio me and let me know when they arrive."

Ed looked at Sally. "Do you have any questions?' She looked at him.

"I just wanted you to know that my family and I did watch the fireworks last night. And we did see black birds flying around the yellow moon when *The Grand Finale* began and it started raining. Everyone was pointing and taking pictures from their cell phones."

Ed swiveled in his chair.

"Well, I am sure the TV/Radio Media News will be broadcasting it for several days and *The Diamond Club Casino* will be the target of the news. I would like to keep it as low key as possible. But as you and I know both know, once the media Radio/News gets a hold of something, they don't let it go until it is exhausted.

Sally looked up from her tablet, looking Mr. Johnson in the eyes.

"So true."

The last two days the phone was ringing off the hook. It was Monday, July 6th 10:00 a.m. and Sally, Dan Largo the Supervisor of Maintenance had already met with the Director, Josh Kimble of the *Animal Control Preventive Disease*. The game plan for the next three days was to barricade one parking garage floor at a time and then have

214

the entire maintenance crew along with *the Animal Control Preventive Disease* task team on board directing and helping clean each garage parking floor, along with elevators and all garage structure hanging areas. Josh Kimble, from the crew, let Ed know he had the cleaning fluids that would totally disinfect every area, including casino floors, carpets, including linens and all furniture.

Josh Kimble had let Ed Johnson also know that it was illegal to kill/eliminate all and any kind of bats. They had to be physically removed. He also let him know that brown bats moved quickly. They did not stay in one spot very long. They moved to new areas where there were plenty of insects. Ed took Josh and his team to the parking garages. The task team wore green maintenance clothing. Ed, of course, told Josh he wanted his team to be as inconspicuous as possible. He didn't want to cause "panic" with the casino guests. Josh Kimble understood and assured Ed his people were experienced professionals and they were aware of this type of circumstance. Hearing that bit of information, Ed felt somewhat reassured.

At the end of the day, Sally went to Mr. Johnson's office and took a seat. Ed looked up from his paperwork and looked at Sally. "Mr. Johnson, I know this is bad timing, but I wanted to let you know that my husband, Ramsey, has found a job in California and we both talked about it and we have decided to leave Las Vegas to go to California. He has a college friend there and wants Ramsey to go to San Diego and start a Taxi Cab business in with him. Ed sat there speechless and looked at her for a moment. She was right. Ed did not want to hear this news now. He was happy for her, but at the same time he needed her now.

Sally continued talking. With that being said, "I am giving you my two-week resignation now." Sally handed Ed her two-week notice/letter. Ed sat back in his chair, looked at the two-week notice letter she had written and then looked up at Sally's tearful eyes. What could he say? He would miss her. She was a good worker. He pressed his fingers to his lips and said,

"I understand Sally. I wish you and your family the best. I will advise HR of your notice. I will be sorry to see you go, Sally." Sally got up from her chair. It was such a relief to get it out. The anticipation of having to tell her boss she was leaving him and *The Diamond Club Casino* was like weight on her shoulders. Ed got up walked past Sally who was standing there. Sally gave a sigh of relief and followed Ed out the door.

"Have a good day, Sally. Radio me if you need me for anything."

Chapter 24– Rebecca – Time To Dance

Rebecca stood in front of the building. There it was! Twent- six Twenty two Santa Moon Street. It was 4:30 p.m. and she had her dancing shoes on. She went up to the 3rd floor and went to the receptionist. "Yes, I am Rebecca O'Connors for the dance interview." The receptionist looked down at her computer.

"Yes, Ms. O'Connors here you are. Just take a seat and someone will come out the door over there". She pointed to the right door. "They will call your name when they are ready for you."

Rebecca looked around the receptionist area. There were
five other girls and four guys. She sat down, picked up a
magazine, and tried not to look at her competition in the
room. All the same height and same weight size. They
were all toned with little makeup. She had practiced a
seven-minute routine in her room. It was more of a ballet,
jazz movement. She had thrown all her clothes on the bed
and decided none of them were good enough.

She went to her hiding place in the cheap motel room and
took a hundred-dollar bill out. She put it up in the air and
kissed Benjamin Franklin's face on the $100 bill. "I love
you, Benjamin!" She said out loud. "Of all the monies I
have, you are my favorite."

She put Mr. Benjamin in her purse and headed out the
door to the mall. She had found a light pink leotard suit
with pink leggings and pink leg calf warmers. She got her
worn ballet shoes out. She slipped each one on and tied
the laces. "Good, she thought, they still fit." They hurt
like hell, but still fit. She had thought of a dance she
learned in high school to the music and she knew the one
song from the Titanic she would have the pianist play
while she danced. She turned her cell phone and turned
the song on from the Titanic. She played it over and over
again while practicing her seven-minute dance. She
wanted to show the director she could move fluently and
gracefully. The right door opened and a girl standing there
called "Rebecca O' Connors." Rebecca put the magazine
down and walked through the door. They both went down
a long aisle. There were rows of red felt chairs, in a large
movie theater auditorium with a large stage.

She heard a voice from one of the rows. "You can walk up the stairs to the stage." Rebecca walked up onto the stage and stood in the middle. It was bright. The seats below were dark with people in them. "State your name please."

"Rebecca O'Connors." She put her arm over her brow to see where the voice was coming from.

"Speak up, please." Rebecca belted out her name, "Rebecca O'Conners!"

"You understand, Ms. O'Connors, this is a seven- minute dance, right? "

Rebecca put her hand down and stood with her hands entwined in front of her. "Yes sir." "Yes, sir I do."

"What is the song you want the pianist to play Ms. O'Connors?" Rebecca looked at the pianist.
Rebecca walked over the pianist and bent down and whispered in her ear, "Can you please play the theme song from the movie the Titanic?" The pianist nodded. Rebecca walked back to the center of the stage and put her arms over her head and tilted her head. She wore a thick-stretch pink ban around her forehead. Her legs long-looking while standing on her tip toes in her pink ballet shoes. She bent her head down and lifted her arms in the air and began. She glided across the stage. She did several pivots and twirls. Dressed in pink, Rebecca danced. She danced, twirled and danced some more. She pivoted, bowed and curtsied across the stage with magnificent precision. All the moves she did on the stage in high school came back and now it was her stage again. The piano played and

played and then gradually ended. She stood on the stage, bowed and then looked up. It was quiet for a moment which seemed like several moments.

She heard a voice from the audience. "Thank you Ms. O'Connors. We will contact you within the next day if we are interested. Please make sure the receptionist has a good phone number to reach you at." Rebecca hurried off the stage. She grabbed her bag, took off her tutu and ballet shoes and put some flip flops on and walked hurriedly out the door. She knew this is how all performances went. You never knew if you got the part immediately. She sat down on the street curb and bowed her head. She thought. "I did my best. That is all I can do." She crossed her fingers and then uncrossed them. It was getting late. She thought of Rose. She wondered if Rose was back at the motel yet. She missed her. She got the keys out for the car and drove back to their cheap motel room.

Chapter 25 - BFFs - Leaving Las Vegas

Stephanie rolled over and looked at the clock. It was 8:00 a.m. She touched her head. There was a wash cloth on it. She laid in bed thinking, "what happened last night?" She heard the shower running. Bethany came out with a towel around her muffled hair and sat next to Stephanie. She felt Stephanie's head.

"You were a sick little girl last night? How are you feeling this morning?"

"I'm feeling better. Where is Megan?" Bethany looked at her pathetic-looking friend.

"She went down to get us some breakfast before we start our five- six-hour road trip back home." Let me get you two aspirin. You still feel a little warm."

Bethany got up from the bed and grabbed some aspirin, some water and handed it to Stephanie. "I think you should lie down in the back seat of the car. We can put the luggage in the trunk, while I drive. Then when we get home, you are going to the doctors. And I mean, immediately when you get home!" Stephanie sat up in bed.

"Okay, I know you are right."

Stephanie pulled back the blankets and looked down at her right foot. Bethany put her hand to her mouth and gasped. Stephanie examined her rash.

"I've had this rash ever since I've been in Las Vegas. I don't know where it came from? It's doesn't hurt. I actually thought it was something from the pool area and thought it would go away. But it hasn't gone away and it has gotten worse.

"Lordy- Lord." Bethany said. She looked at Stephanie's red rash on her right foot and going up to her ankle.

"Yes you are going straight to the hospital when we get home, girly, girl. I haven't answered my phone for fear it would be my Dad and I would have to tell him this ugly story. I didn't want to ruin our trip to Las Vegas."

Stephanie pulled the covers back over her foot and legs. Bethany stood up, grabbed her clothes and started dressing and packing all at the same time.

"I packed your suitcase as much as I could early this morning when Megan and I got in."

Stephanie looked at Megan and started laughing. "

You, my friend, look a little white faced. How many *"Lie Down Lucys"* did you drink last night?"

Megan rolled her eyes and got up.

"Too many, way too many!" I'm going to go get us something to eat. I'll be back soon. Oh, and we need to check out by 1:00 p.m. today. Stephanie changed the subject.

"How was last night?"

She heard a knocked on the hotel door. Bethany walked to the door and opened it. She looked surprise. It was Johnny holding a single red rose. Megan blurted out to the other room where Stephanie was.

It's Johnny!" Stephanie immediately slid the covers over her head.

"Come in!" "Come in!"

Bethany walked Johnny to Stephanie's room.

"Hey Stephanie Johnny is here."

Stephanie peeped her head out of covers. Johnny walked over and sat down next to Stephanie.
She put the covers down and sat up. "I look horrible."
Johnny smiled. "You look beautiful." He smiled and handed her a yellow rose. "This is for you."

"Stephanie took the yellow rose, looked at Johnny and smelled it and said, "Thank you, Johnny. That was sweet."
Johnny touched her hand.

"How are you feeling?"

Stephanie looked into his concerned eyes, "I am feeling better just looking like Godzilla now."

Johnny smiled. "As corny as it sounds from a New Jersey boy, I wanted to tell you how much fun it was being with you in Las Vegas. I had a great time. All the guys did too.

"Where are the guys?" Stephanie asked.

"They're downstairs sitting in the bar area."

Bethany sat on the other bed. She wasn't going anywhere. She wanted to hear. She wanted to hear everything. Nosey Rosie she was going to be. She smiled to herself.

"We know you girls are leaving today, so we figured we all would come over and say good-bye. We don't leave to go back to New Jersey until Tuesday evening.

Stephanie smelled the yellow rose again. "That's so sweet."

There was another knock on the door. Bethany opened the door and this time it was Megan with both arms full of drinks and bags of food. Johnny got up and put his hands in his pocket and looked at Stephanie.

"The boys and I are going to get some breakfast."
Stephanie laughed, "The boys? Hey, I was wondering if you wouldn't mind calling me, Stephanie and letting me know when you girls are all packed and ready to go."

Once again he smiled while standing to leave.

 "The boys and I will help you girl's luggage to the parking garage."

Stephanie looked at Megan and Bethany who were putting the bags of food and drinks on the desk area. They both turned around.

"Sure."

Stephanie smiled up at him and pulled the covers up.

"We'll be leaving around 1:00 p.m."

Johnny walked towards the door, turned and winked at Stephanie.

"See you then. We'll be here at 12:45 p.m."

Johnny looked at Stephanie, did a salute sign, smiled and said.

"No more *"Lie Down Lucy's"* for you little Lucy."

 The girls looked at each other and they all started laughing. Stephanie smelled the rose again thinking, "My Las Vegas, New
Manhattan Boy." **What plays in Vegas, stays in Vegas!"**

Johnny knocked on the hotel room at 12:45 p.m. Megan opened the door. "Come on in! Come on in!" Johnny, Bret and Darren stepped into the room. The girls had all eaten breakfast. Stephanie had taken a shower and was feeling much better. All the suitcases were packed and ready to go. Stephanie picked up the rose on the bedside and smelled it. Johnny smiled at her.

"You look much better. Which bags are yours?" She pointed and he picked up her bags. Darren and Bret picked up their luggage and they closed the hotel door and walked to the parking garage and pushed the 6th button floor. The *Animal Preventive Disease Control* task team was beginning to start their work on all garage structure floors. Starting tomorrow all guests were given a notice under their hotel room doors to move their vehicles to the 7th floor parking garage.

The girls and guys made small talk along the way to the parking garage. All making sure they all had each other's cell phone numbers. All jokingly saying and laughing at the same time walking to the parking garage elevator, "You better stay in touch with me! "You better stay in touch with me!" When they got to the elevator, there was a long silence between them all. They all knew the good time they had was coming to an end. Megan's eyes focused on the floor of the elevator. Her heart beating so loud she thought Darren could hear it. She really liked Darren. But she also knew long distant relationships were hard and most normally didn't work out.

Bethany clicked her keys to open the doors and pop the trunk. The boys lifted the suitcases and each one put them in one by one. Bethany closed the trunk. She looked at Brett. Megan looked at Darren and Stephanie looked at Johnny. Stephanie leaned over and kissed him on the cheek. "Thank you for a great time!"

Johnny grabbed Stephanie and pulled her close and looked into her eyes. "Now what kind of good-bye kiss is that?" He kissed her hard and long on her lips.

Darren pulled Megan close and gave her a hard long kiss also. Of course, Brett followed suit. After a minute or two, they let go of their embraces and hands. The girls got in the car and closed their doors. The boys stood watching and waving.

Bethany backed-up and circled the parking lot. The girls waved out the window yelling. **"What plays in Vegas, stays in Vegas!"** The boys put their thumbs up and turned and walked back to the elevators high-fiving each other. "Yes!" Johnny smiled,

"Now those California girls were really something!"
Darren chimed in.

"Yeah, they were really something special!"
Stephanie laid down in the back seat with her pillow and
blanket and put the damp cold wash cloth on her forehead.
She was tired. Bethany had her dark shades on listening to
the radio low. Megan took her thick black reading glasses
out of her purse, got her sketch pad out with black chalk
and started sketching.

Bethany got on the freeway.

"Okay, girls, you can definitely turn your cell phones on
now. "

Megan got her cell phone out. They had only used their
cell phones to sneak and take pictures. Megan had 10 calls.
Stephanie rolled over and got her cell phone out of her
purse and turned it on. She had 12 calls. One of them was
her mom. She dialed her mom's cell phone number.

"Hey Mom. I told you before we left that we were not
going to have our cell phones on. Only in case of an
emergency." Well, that was the deal me Bethany and
Megan made before we left to Las Vegas because we
wanted our time to be "our time. Okay, Mom, "I get it.
We will be home in about 5 or 6 hours. I'll see you then."

Stephanie put her cell phone back in her purse, leaving it
on. Megan turned around. "Stephanie, when you get home,
you really need to go see a doctor about your rash on your

foot." "You need to tell your parents you had a fever and you have a mild cough." Stephanie looked at Megan.

"Yeah, I know you're right. The rash is not getting any better and I am feeling really tired and I know I still have a slight fever.

"Promise me Stephanie, you will go." Bethany chimed in. "Stephanie, I know you don't like doctors, but it's important." "Promise me and Megan you will go as soon as you get home." Stephanie closed her eyes.

"Okay, I promise I will go." Megan turned to Stephanie again.

"As soon as you get home, right?" Stephanie put her hand on the cold rag on her forehead.

"Yes, yes, I promise."

It was a long drive home. Megan got her sketch pad out and colored charcoal pencils and started sketching. Stephanie laid in the back seat sleeping. Bethany finally rolled up in the garage-way to Stephanie's parent's house. Her Mom came running out. Bethany got out of the car and Stephanie sat up with her pillow and blanket. She was still tired and she felt hot. Megan got out and stood by the front passenger door.

"Hello Ms. Gables." "How are you?"

"Oh, just fine Megan. Thank you for asking."

"Megan, I hear you girls had a good time in Las Vegas."
Megan put her hand over her brow to block the sun."

"Yes, we sure did Ms. Gables."

Bethany opened the trunk and took Stephanie's suitcase
and bag out. She looked at Ms. Gables.

"It seems like Stephanie may have gotten a fungus on her
foot at the pool. She has a rash and it doesn't want to go
away and she's had a fever and flu light symptoms."

Stephanie looked at Bethany with eyes like "I'm going to
murder you". She put her finger to her mouth with a silent
shhhhh. Ms. Gables picked up Stephanie's suitcase and put
her arm around her and started walking to the front door.
Stephanie looked back at the girls.

"We will definitely see a doctor tomorrow." "Thank you,
Bethany and Megan!"

Bethany got back into the car. Megan shut her door. All
she could think about was it was good to be back at the
apartment. They both went to their bedrooms, wheeling
their suitcases behind them.   Bethany yelled as she shut
her bedroom door.

"I'm going to take a nap!" "See you later!" Megan yelled
back.

"I am right there with you girlfriend on that one!" She
closed her bedroom door.

228

**Chapter 26- *The Rocket Aero Casino* Restaurant–
Dinner for Two**

Grant and Rose stepped off the 98th floor elevator at *The
Rocket Aero Tower Restaurant*. The restaurant had a low
light setting with round half-moon booths that circled all
the windows. As you were seated in the booth, the floor
rotated the booths around and you were able to see all the
lights all around Las Vegas.

The waiter guided Grant and Rose to their booth. As Rose
sat down and placed her white napkin in her lap, she looked
out the window. "This is magical!" "Grant looked at Rose.
He once again was studying her. She was not only
beautiful. She was charming.

"You like?"

Rose looked at Grant.

"Like?"

She looked at Grant's amusing eyes staring back at her.
Grant turned and looked out the window and then looked
back at her.

"You like?" "You like this restaurant and the view?"

She smiled. "It's absolutely beautiful!" Her eyes watered
with tears as she smiled at him. In her mind. She was
grateful to be here with him.

The waiter came over to the table and Grant ordered a bottle of French wine from the Wine menu. The waiter came, poured some in Grant's wine glass to smell and sip. Grant sniffed it, sipped it and nodded to the waiter who poured each of them a half glass. Grant lifted his wine glass. "Let's toast." Rose lifted her wine glass. "A toast to a beautiful *"Lady of the Night,"* my beautiful Rose.

Rose picked up her wine glass and chimed in. "A toast to a handsome gentleman on a beautiful night!" They each smiled, clinked their wine glasses, and took a sip of their wine. Grant knew Rose probably did not know a lot about French food. He had been at this restaurant with clients and knew the menu.

He asked Rose if she liked duck. She told him she had eaten wild rabbit before but had never had duck. Grant told her it was somewhat like rabbit, a little gamey but richer in taste.

Rose closed her menu, "Okay, she smiled, let's go with that." While the booth rotated, they both looked out the window staring in the night at all the lights of the city. Grant pointed out the window at three hotels that he was working at.

He worked as a Financial Advisor for three hotels in Las Vegas. He had a contract for one year with each of them. He had just signed another contract with each one. So, starting in July, he had 12 months left with each hotel. The waiter brought their entre' of duck. It looked fabulous! While eating, Grant asked.

"So Rose, can I ask you about you? I don't know much
about you. I want you to know I am not trying to be a busy
body. I just would like to hear more about you. What
brought you and Rebecca to Las Vegas?"

 Rose looked down at her food and started poking her duck
with her fork. It was a subject Rose would like to avoid at
this magical moment, but she knew Grant was entitled to
know something about her. After all they had slept
together. Not only that but she knew in her heart she was
in love with him and he would find out sooner or later.

She just didn't want Grant to think little of her or to judge
her harshly. She would have to tell him that she and
Rebecca had taken up a little gamble coming to Las Vegas,
thinking they could win big and live easy.

She would have to tell him that Rebecca and she had both
decided to leave their small town in the cornfields of Iowa
and make a fresh start. Rose began her life in New Albin,
Iowa as a young girl. She was raised by her grandma, her
Nana Meme. Her mother's mom.

Her dad had left when she was young and her mom had
eventually left also. All she had there was her Grandma
Nana Meme and her best friend Rebecca.

She put her fork down and took another long sip of wine.
She looked at Grant and then looked down at her plate.
She started softly telling him her story. She was young
when her mom let her also. Her mom was a diner waitress
at Lou's Diner. Her mom had always hated the small town
with its small-town talk and small town ways. For a while,

she and her mom, Kathryn, lived with her grandma. It was
a small white wood painted house in New Albin, Iowa
which was located at the farthest northeast corner of Iowa
you could go.

Then one day when Rose came home from school, her
mom wasn't there. She would lie in bed hoping she would
hear the front or back door open and her mom would
appear. Even a creak would have made her happy knowing
she just might come back. But through the years, she never
heard it creak nor every open.

New Albin, Iowa, was the home to the late "Shooky" Fink,
the baseball wizard who spent a lifetime coaching baseball
to men and boys, included Babe Ruth. Grant looked at
Rose. He took a sip of his wine and said, "Interesting." He
knew it took a lot for her to tell him her sad life story. He
reached for her hand. "It's okay Rose. I do not judge
others."

Rose continued, "Rebecca and I knew each other since we
were six. We became best of friends. She didn't have a
lunch box or even for that matter, she didn't even have a
lunch most days."

She lived next door to me, we would always run to the bus
together and manage to get a seat to share together. I would
open my lunch bag and give her half my sandwich. "She
would always take it smiling. We would both sit together
quietly on the bus looking out the window at the rain fall
until we got to school. We would play after school at each
other's houses."

She was also from a broken home and her mom worked as a waitress at a small-town diner, called *The Sleepy Diner*. She would mostly spend the night with me.

"I had a small room upstairs in the attic at Grandma Nana Memes. There was a queen size bed up that had very old rusty springs on it and an old big patched quilt Grandma Nana Meme had made many moons ago. It was musty and cold up there.

There was a big sky window above my queen-size rickety bed. As little girls, Rebecca and I would huddle together in the big queen-size bed and look at the stars, point at each one and then look at the Milky-Way.

We would lie there for hours and start naming each star, like Princess Star-bright, Prince Galaxy and then we would end up giggling. Rose looked at Grant again to see if he saw any humor in her story. He didn't blink, he just sat there sipping his wine listening to her story."

"As we grew up together, many more years flew by. We spent a lot of time up in that cold attic. Rose took a bite of food, put her fork down and started laughing. Oh and the biggest memory of that attic was the rats. Grandma, Nana Meme had hidden a lot of rat sling traps all over the attic."

"I remember one night when Rebecca thought she felt a rat run across the bed. She sat up in the bed and screamed."

"What was that?" She started nudging me to wake up, Rose, Rose did you feel something on the bed? Rose, Rose, please wake up!"

Rebecca punched Rose's arm. "Rose, Rose, wake up!" I sat up. "

What is it? What is it, Rebecca?"

"Did you feel that?" Rebecca laid down, grabbed the covers and put them over her head.

"Rose, please get under the covers with me. I'm scared. I laid down and pulled the covers over both of us."

She whispered. "Really, Rebecca the sun is starting to come up?" Rose looked up at Grant again. Then picked up her fork and twisted it. "I had lied. I knew the whole truth of the matter.   I had known all along Grandma Nana Meme's rat traps would only catch some rats in the attic, but not all the rats. I said to her.

"Really Rebecca? I am your best friend. You should know me better than anyone else! I have slept in this room ever since I was a little girl and I never felt anything run across this bed."

"I held my breath hoping Rebecca would take the bait. But Rebecca kept on persisting. Whispering under the covers Rebecca asked again.

"Tell me, you felt something run across the bed Rose? Tell me? I pulled the covers down over both of us. Stammering again in a soft tone I said.

"Now really Rebecca? Don't be silly! It's almost morning, let's go back to sleep!" Rebecca took a deep cold breath of air. She didn't know if Rose was telling the truth or lying.

"Okay, but I am warning you, Rose. If I feel one more thing run across this rusty squeaky bed, I am so fast out of here!"

Grant started laughing. He started laughing so hard, he was rolling over in his seat. He could not stop laughing. Rose started laughing with him.

"Rose that is the funniest story I ever heard! Oh, Rose, you are too much! Grant took his wine glass and held it up to toast Rose. Rose smiled and raised her wine glass.

"Cheers to the rats in the attic!" Grant said.

"Cheers to the rats in the attic!" Rose said and they both sipped wine, looked at each other and started laughing again.

Grant put his wine glass down and looked at Rose and smiled. The hospital hoopla crazy nightmare had taken a lot out of her. Rose put her wine glass down.

"If you don't mind Grant, I would just like to relax."

Grant looked at her a moment.

"Okay, then I guess it's my place, relaxing on the couch with a nice night cap, cognac."

Rose raised her eyebrow, cocked her head to one side, smiled.

"So I take it we haven't called it a night yet? Grant smiled.

"I guess not."

Grant opened his hotel suite door and put his finger up to his mouth, "Shhhhh." Rose's eyes widened and she smiled. Not knowing Ben very well, she was hoping Ben was with Rebecca and not some fling he picked up somewhere.

Grant tip-toed down the hallway and knocked on Ben's door? The giggling stopped. Ben opened the door a crack. Grant looked at Ben whispering, "Tell me you have Rebecca in that room?" The door opened wider. Rebecca stood there behind Ben wearing something black and flimsy. She put her finger up to her mouth, smiled and said, "Shhhhh." Ben smiled at Grant. Grant smiled back. "See you in the morning, pal." He breathed a sigh of relief. He used the restroom and tip-toed back down the hallway to the living room.

Rose was lying on the couch. Her eyes were closed and she was sound asleep. He put his hands in his pockets and stood over her, looking down at her sleeping soundly. She looked like a tiny painted China doll. Grant smiled down at her, "My Rose. My beautiful *Lady of the Night,* " Rose. He got a blanket from the hall closet and put it over her, turned off the lights, and walked down the hallway to his room.

Chapter 27 - A Penny for your Thoughts

Frank walked over to a shuttle in the front of *The Diamond Club Casino*. The shuttle driver was out in front of the shuttle.

"Where to?" "Las Vegas Airport, please."

Simon smiled and helped Frank put all the luggage in the back of the shuttle. They all got in. Laker, Sofia and Jenny sat in the back seat. Jenny turned to Laker and Sofia.

"No cell phones until we get home."

Frank sat in the front seat. Simon fixed his rearview mirror.

"Did you all have a good time this 4th of July?" Frank turned and said, "Yes, we had a great time!" He turned and winked at Jenny.

"Did you happen to see those black birds flying abound the huge full yellow moon when the Grand Finale fireworks started *above The Diamond Club Casino*? Laker piped in.

"That was the coolest!" Simon looked at Laker in his rearview mirror.

"I watched the News Press Conference they had on TV. They said it was brown bats. Laker blurted out.

 "What?" Did you hear, Sofia? Brown Bats!" Real, live big brown bats!

Frank turned around and looked at Jenny, lifted his eye brows and widened his eyes. She stared at him. She shifted in her seat.

"Wow!" Now that's something! Can you even think of it, brown bats flying around in Las Vegas! Now, who would ever think of that?"

Laker put on his seatbelt and sat back in the airplane seat. He put his ear phones on and then reached in his pocket. He felt something metal. He took out the round metal object. He sat next to the airplane window, holding the silver penny in his fingers, staring at the silver metal object. It was the penny he found in the room next to the bed table. It was a Lincoln 1948 steel penny. Frank buckled his seatbelt and turned to Laker.

"What's that?" Laker shifted in his seat, staring at the penny.

"It's a penny I found by the bed table in the hotel room." Frank asked.

"Can I see it?"

Laker handed the penny to his dad. Frank studied it. He looked at it closely looking at the front and then the back of the penny. Handing it back to Laker he said.

"Hold on tight to it. It may be worth some money. It looks like one of the first steel pennies they made in that timeframe." Laker stared at the penny again.

"Really Dad?" Frank didn't want to get Laker's hopes up too high.

"Maybe? Just hang on to it. Put it in a safe place when we get home."

Jenny looked at Frank and Laker. She didn't know what they were talking about. She just wanted to get home. Laker put his hand to his mom's ear.

"Mom I just wanted to let you know, I was the one who flickered the lights in the hotel room. I wanted you and Dad to come back to the hotel and be with me and Sofia." Jenny looked at Laker square in his eyes. Laker closed his eyes and cringed up his nose and mouth waiting for the somewhat not nice words his mom was going to tell him. Jenny took Laker's hand and squeezed it.

He opened his eyes and saw his mom smiling at him with tears in her eyes. She opened her mouth and without saying any words, she mouthed.

"Thank you." Jenny looked across the aisle. Sofia was across the aisle sitting next to a little girl her age. Jenny though.

"Perfect! She put her head back on the headrest, took a deep breath and closed her eyes. "Good! Three hours away and we'll be home."

Chapter 28 - The Mermaid Swims to Las Vegas

Jack opened the door to his apartment. Tokyo came running meowing and rubbing his furry body along his legs. He dropped his bag and went to the kitchen and poured himself a strong Jack Daniels and coke. He thumbed through his mail on the table and saw a note from Denise.

He picked it up and read it while gulping his drink. *Jack: I got your voice mail. "Sorry I haven't called you back" I've been super busy with work!" I fed Tokyo and gave him water every day. He's fine, only lonely for his master. There was no one at home to pet him and keep him company.* Jack heard the front door open. Startled, he walked towards the front door.

A woman stood in the doorway holding the front door handle. The other hand held a bag full of groceries. He looked at her. "Sarah? Is that you?" She started to speak.

"Denise was here feeding Tokyo when I knocked on your door, yesterday. I told her who I was and she ended up giving me the key and said you were going to be home tonight."

"I just missed you at the Detroit Michigan hospital." I heard about your dad's stroke and I wanted to come by the hospital and see you. They told me I just missed you. You had left for the airport. So, I grabbed the next plane out here to Las Vegas. I thought you would be here before me. I was going to surprise you."

Jack took the grocery bag from Sarah and put his drink and
the grocery bag on the counter. He put his arms around
Sarah.

"Oh, my God! It's really you Sarah? After, all these
years, you are here in Las Vegas?" Sarah looked up into
his eyes.

"Yes, I guess it's been a few." Jack started talking fast.

"Have a seat."

Jack pointed to a chair in the kitchen. Sarah walked over to
the kitchen chair and sat down. She put her purse down
and looked at Jack again. He had changed. He looked
older. His black hair had silver side wings. Jack refreshed
his drink.

"Want a drink?

"Sure, whatever you're drinking is fine with me."

Jack held up the Jack Daniels bottle.

"Is Jack and coke good with you?

"Sure, sounds good."

Jack handed Sarah the Jack and Coke. Sarah took the glass
and said, "I put my luggage bag in your room. I hope you
don't mind?" Jack handed her the drink.
"No, that's fine." He leaned against the kitchen sink
standing there with his Jack and Coke staring at her while

she sat staring back at him. He didn't think he'd ever see her again. Being, she the Michigan girl she was.

Sarah took a sip of her drink. "So, I am really sorry to hear about your Dad, Jack." Jack took another gulp of his drink. "Thank you, Sarah for your concern. He came out of his coma and his heart chart showed scared but good. He'll be going home tomorrow. Mom says she has it under control. But we shall see." Silence fell between them for a few minutes. Jack spoke up.

"How long do you plan on staying?

"Well, I haven't decided yet. "My teaching job ended. I haven't really set up anything for the summer." Sarah looked down at the kitchen floor. "I was thinking about spending my summer visiting Las Vegas and spending some time with you."

She looked up to see what kind of reaction she would get. Jack looked at her. He was stuck in thought.

"Well then, if my roommate, Tokyo, says he wants a guest to stay the summer, then you can stay." Sarah sat there with a puzzled look on her face. Tokyo all ears, hearing his name, came running in the kitchen, rubbing his furry body against Jack's legs. Sarah looked at Tokyo. She started laughing.

"I take it, this is Tokyo?"

Jack smiled and looked down at Tokyo and rubbed his furry body. "Yep, this is Tokyo." He turned and opened the kitchen cabinet and got a can of cat food out, opened it with the can opener and poured it into Tokyo's dish and filled his water dish. Sarah watched Tokyo eating and then looked back up at Jack.

Jack looked at Sarah. She saw a flash of bewilderment in Jack's eyes. He looked down at Tokyo and then back up at her.

 "I think by the end of the summer, you and Tokyo will be best of friends!"

Jack took her glass and refilled it. Jack still had the golf glove on his right hand. His fingers touched hers. He felt that old flame come back. The spark, he felt when he and Sarah were together in college. She was his first love. He poured himself another drink.

"Let's go sit on the couch in the living room. It's more comfortable."

Sarah looked at his right hand and the glove but, at the moment, she shrugged it off. After all, she knew it was his dealing hand.

Another couple of drinks and the "old times" came flowing back between them. The college exams, the teachers, the frat parties, do you remember so and so, do you remember, do you remember when we did this? Reminiscing all the "old times." It was 7:00 p.m. when they had run out of things to say. Jack began to feel him old self with Sarah. More relaxed. Still sitting on the couch, Jack put his arm around Sarah.

"Are you hungry?" Sarah had enough to drink. Sarah smiled.

"Yes, I am hungry." Jack put his glass down on the coffee table.

"Are you up to going out, eating and seeing some of Las Vegas?

Sarah was feeling happy inside. The drinks also told her she was feeling "happy inside".

"Sure, why not! The night is still young!" Jack stood up from the couch.

"Okay then, I'll tell you what? Do you want to take a quick shower and then I'll jump in after you? Sarah stood up beside him.

 "Definitely she said." She put her hands up like a scary witch. The TV show, Fantasy Island came to her mind. "Z Plane! Z Plane! Cooties on Z Plane." Jack stood there laughing at her. Once again, Jack was seeing the quirky girl he fell in love with in college.

Jack looked at his hand in the shower. He was thrilled Sarah had showed up on his door step. He was looking forward to spending the summer with her. He had taken the prescription that Dr. Alexander Willow had given him for two days now. The rash was still there, but fading. He thought, "Good!" He told himself, he was going to call Ed and let him know about his dad's recovery and also take a

244

couple days off to give his hand some time to get rid of the rash in its entirety before he went back to Black Jack Dealing with the customers. Tomorrow, he needed to call Mac at Henderson's Garage and let him know that he would be by tomorrow to pick up the car.

Sarah wondered around the apartment looking at all the books while Tokyo sat in a chair watching her roam. She looked at the photos hanging on the wall and in the bookshelf. She picked one up from the bookshelf. It was one with Jack and her in college when they first met. It was her first year of college.

She remembered she was at a Frat Halloween Party with her friend Linda. Everyone was dressed up. The house was a two story, 1940's green framed house with a balcony on the 2nd level. Lots of college kids of course.

She was dressed up as a Mermaid. She had made her costume. It had light green mesh on the top half, with long silk green sleeves. From the waist down it had a deep aqua blue/green sparkling body cut below the knees to allow her legs and feet to walk and the back had a mermaid tail. She wore green stockings with green sparkling flat shoes.

Her make-up was green glitter with ruby red lipstick and long fake eyelashes. She had long red wavy strawberry blonde hair with a silver diamond crown on top and a hand-held mask with long green nails.

Jack wore a pirate costume. A big black hat with a red feather, billowing red and white puff shirt with a black vest, black pants, black belt with a large gold buckle and tie up black boots. He had a sword on his side and wore long gold medallions around his neck with a big black mustache with a gold earring in his ear and black brows and some black under his eyes making him look rough. He had even painted his fingernails black.

They had made eye contact when she and Linda were standing in the kitchen getting a drink. There was a large back yard. There were small white twinkling lights around the fence and a small wood platform that had a karaoke microphone and all kinds of music. It wasn't until later in the evening when everyone had a more than few drinks that the karaoke music started to get going.

Sarah and Linda had made their rounds trying to meet as many people as they could. They were new to the college and wanted to make some friends. She heard someone singing a song by Tom Jones. She walked to the back yard and stood by a oak tree. It was the pirate with the microphone singing *"She's a Lady"* by Tom Jones. He saw her by the oak tree and stared at her while he sang the song, bellowing out. *"While she's all you'd ever want. She's the kind I'd like to flaunt and take to dinner. She always knows her place. She's got style! She's got grace! She's a winner! She's a lady! Wowowa Wowowa, wha, She's a lady. Talking about that little lady." And that lady is mine.*

He pointed at her and smiled still singing the song. Sarah took a sip of her drink and smiled. He was somewhat cute she thought. But, didn't know what he really looked like outside of the costume. Amused, she took another sip of her drink.

A few weeks later she was in a class, large auditorium. The teacher would turn to the chalk board and she would see a small piece of paper in her lap. She could feel something wiz by her head. It was a post it note with a message. She picked it up and looked behind her. She didn't know who was throwing the post it notes. She inconspicuously opened the post it note carefully.

In small letters she read. *"My Fair Mermaid, the Pirate (Tom Jones) requests a dinner date?" Remember I have my sword if you say no. (And also, I don't think Tom Jones could take no for an answer).* She smiled, laughing all the while inside and thinking, *"Tom Jones? Yaw right? In your dreams buddy!"*

She turned around again and looked in the back rows. Two fingers with a salute sign went up in the air over his brow with a smile and a slightly bent head. The Professor said a out loud.

"Jack Levin you have a question?"

Everyone turned to look at Jack. Jack shifted his eyes to the Professor.

"No sir." "I'm good!" The Professor turned back to the board. Jack winked at Sarah. Sarah got up, took her backpack with her books and slung it on her shoulder and walked out of the classroom.

She heard a voice behind her. "So? Is it a date?" Sarah turned and looked at Jack. He put his hands in his pocket and smiled a big smile. Sarah turned and said,

"I don't even know you!" and she marched off. Jack kept
step with her.

"Well, this is your chance to get to know me, right?"

Sarah kept moving quickly across campus to her next class.
Sarah stopped and confronted the pirate again, eyeing him
more closely this time. "I guess you're going to hold me
hostage with your trusty sword on the plank until I say
yes?" She picked up her step and then stopped in front of
him abruptly and looked him square in the eyes. Jack
nearly bumping into her stopped in front of her. Jack
bowed down low before her.

"I am a noble pirate with only good intensions and good
deeds in-store for you my lady of the sea." Sarah started
laughing, remembering her Mermaid Costume.

In the back of her mind, she thought why not? "Okay, your
lady of the sea will be sitting on her sea rock at 7:00 p.m.
Friday in "The House of Mermaids" (Wick's Dorm House
Lobby). She raised her brow up at him. Jack smiled.

"My ship will await you at 7:00 p.m. Friday night my *"lady
of the sea."* He bowed down again and jumped in the air
kicking his heels with a gesture of his hands. Of course,
Jack arrived on time. He knew he couldn't be late for *his*
"lady of the sea." They ended up going to the *Pizza
House*, eating and talking. That was the night Sarah knew
her pirate would be a good "mate."

Jack walked out to the front room putting his cufflinks in his white long-sleeved shirt. He noticed Sarah had changed into a white linen dress hand embroidered flowers on it and that she had cut her hair so that it had long layers around her face with a twinge of bangs. Jack noticed her hair was very shiny. She wore a pink lipstick, brown eye shadow and her eyelashes were black and long with just a pinch of cheek powder.

Sarah stood up with her white embroidery flowered clutch in her hand. Her shoes were also white cloth wedges with embroidery flowers on them. She looked "well put together" and nice. Jack stared at her. She was the same girl he left in Detroit Michigan, only better. He grabbed her hand. Tokyo meowed and rubbed his fur body against Jack's legs. Jack bent down and petted him. "Okay buddy. You have enough food and water for the night. Guard the house!" Sarah laughed. Jack and Sarah walked down the block and hailed a taxi."

Chapter 29– Rebecca's Dance Rehearsal

Rose opened her eyes and stretched her arms up in the air. She sat up and looked around. She realized she was still dressed in her shoes and jewelry. She looked at her watch. It was 8:00 a.m. Grant walked in the front-room buttoning a white shirt. He had taken a shower and his hair was wet. "Hey, sleepy head," he said. Rose took the blanket off her and sat up and yawned.
"What time did I fall asleep?" Grant tucked his shirt in his pants and said.

"As soon as you sat down on the couch last night." Her hair was ruffled and make-up half on, half off. Rose yawned and stretched her arms up in the air,

"Dang, now that's not how you're suppose to end a nice evening." She felt gross. She needed coffee and a shower.

Grant sat down next to her on the couch. "I have an accounting project appointment I need to keep this morning at 10:00 a.m. with Ed Johnson my friend here at *The Diamond Club Casino*." Grant leaned over and kissed her lightly on the lips. Grant smiled. "Okay, sleepy head, there is coffee in the kitchen for her princess highness." There is also some bagels and orange juice in the kitchen. The toaster is in the cub board next to the refrigerator." Grant stood up and smiled down at her. "You know where the tub is." "I'll be back by 1:00ish. "I'll see you then?"

Grant grabbed his suit jacket. Rose got up and stretched her arms out in the air and walked behind Grant to the front door. Rose put her hands on the door knob, smiled, ever so slightly tilted her head to the right leaning her head on the door, "See you later, alligator." Grant touched her cheek and said

"See you later, alligator." Rose closed the door and went to the kitchen and poured herself a cup of coffee. She walked down the hallway. A door opened. It was Rebecca.

"Hey Rose. Good morning."

With coffee in one hand, Rose gave Rebecca a hug and whispered, "good morning". "I haven't seen you in ages."

250

Rose pointed to the door, "Is Ben in there?" "Rebecca softly closed the door.

"No, he had to go to the work at the Car lot." "He's working today. Rose held her coffee in her hand. She took a sip, "Hey, I'm going to take a bubble bath. "Come join me. Let's gossip." Rose brushed her teeth. One thing she had gotten on the shopping trip with Grant was a tooth brush and tooth paste. She threw a honeysuckle salt bomb in the tub and added some bubbles. She put her coffee cup on the side of the tub, turned on the jets. She undressed and slid into the warm tub.

Rebecca came waltzing in wearing a white, long means dress shirt. She put her cup of coffee on the opposite side of the tub, took off the shirt and slid into the tub at the other end. She stared at Rose a minute. "You look better now than I've ever seen you Rose." Rose put her hand in the water and brought up some bubbles and blew them in Rebecca's face. Rebecca giggled.

"Rebecca, I'm finally happy. "And, you, my friend? How are Ben and you getting along?"

Rebecca sipped her coffee slowly. Rose could tell she was deep in thought. Then she slowly looked up at Rose with glossy eyes. Rose's heart hurt. She knew Rebecca was thinking of all the rough times they she had somehow blanked out long ago. All she knew is she wanted Rebecca to finally have something good in her life. She wanted her to be happy.

Rebecca splash her saying, "I think he's great!" And then she sat up quickly and said.

 "Oh, the most important thing now for me is I auditioned for the dance part. It's a professional evening dance performance that plays at *The Gala Casino*."

Rebecca looked at Rose. "I did my ballet routine. Her eyes were gleaming. Remember, Rose, the one I used to do in high school?"

Rose sat up, looked at Rebeca and grabbed both her hands. They entwined their fingers together. With excitement in her eyes, Rose looked at Rebecca seriously and started talking fast. "And? And? Did you get the part? Did they tell you right away? What did they say?

Rebecca unlaced her fingers from Roses, sat back in the tub, lazily looking at Rose. Rose knew that sassy look also. Rebecca splashed her again.

They said. She hesitated looking at Rose's wide eyes, smiling. "They would call me today, hopefully and let me know if I got the job." Rose sat back in the tub.

"Well then." Rose started laughing. "I guess we will both be staring at your cell phone all day long today? Right?" Rebecca shifted her eyes to the sink area where her black cell phone was lying on the sink. Rose followed her eyes to the sink area and saw Rebecca's phone lying there staring at both of them. "I guess so!"

Just then Rebecca's cell phone started ringing and vibrating all at the same time! Rebecca looked at Rose wide eyed and jumped out of the tub, all the bubbles following her while grabbing a towel. Putting the towel around her with one hand and grabbing the phone with the other, Rebecca's towel dropped to the floor. Standing there in front of the mirror, butt ass naked with bubbles running down her legs, Rebecca gasped, "hello? Hello?" She bent over to pick up the towel, still wet bubbles running down her ass and legs and wrapped it around her with one hand. She turned to Rose. "Yes! "Yes! I can be there tomorrow to register for the training class. Three o'clock? Sure! Sure! I will be there!"

Rebecca hung up her cell phone and started jumping up and down. "I got it Rose! I got the job! I start tomorrow rehearsal at 3:00 p.m. with Registration and Rehearsal. I will be working with the folly dancers in the Celebration Performance at *The Gala Casino*. Rebecca started jumping up and down again. "I am so excited!"

Rebecca's towel dropped to the floor again. Rose's eyes widened and she started laughing at Rebecca standing there naked with her boobs bouncing up and down. "Oh brother".

Rose slowly slipped down in the soapy water. Her head went under the water into the bubbles. Rebecca grabbed her towel again. "Rose?" Rose?" she yelled. Rose sat up with bubbles all over her wet head, running down her face. She put her hands to her face and wiped away the bubbles. "Yes?" "Yes? Let's go have some fun today while the boys are working. Let's go celebrate, my new job! Let's go eat somewhere and maybe do a little shopping."

Rose got out of the tub and grabbed a towel. She lifted her eyebrow to Rebecca. "Okay one question before we go to lunch today. How much of the $2,000 do you have left?" Rebecca got her coffee cup off the tub and took a sip.

"Oh Rose, I have about $1500 left."   Rose looked at Rebecca.

"You know and I know we have to stretch that money as long as we can, right? Rebecca kept on chanting, "I know. I know, Rose." We need to put gas in the car, pay our cell phone bills, and the motel monthly bill of $600 this month. Okay, let's go have a little fun!"

Rebecca glanced at Rose's stomach. There was a rash but it was fading. "What did the doctor say about the rash?" Rose tucked the towel around her tighter and looked in the mirror. She took a wash cloth and started washing her face with soap. Dr. Cooper said. "I need to take an antidote fungal prescription for 90 days. One a day and it should disappear completely." Rose looked at Rebecca in the mirror. Rebecca began washing her face also. Rebecca gave her a look like, "okay be sure to take that medicine and said, "I don't want to see that rash ever again." Rose looked down at the fading rash.

"Okay, Okay I get it girlfriend! Me neither."

Rebecca bellowed out. "Hey Rose let's dress up and go have a nice lunch." "Does Italian sound good to you? Rose looked up from the sink bowl. "Sure, sounds great!" Let's do it!" Rebecca turned and walked to her room. She had packed a small bag when Ben picked her up. She had been honest with Ben from the get go. She had told him that she and Rose were staying in a rundown cheap motel in Las Vegas and that it was the only place they could afford until she found some work. Rose went to the bedroom.

Of course, the bed was messy. Typical bachelor she thought and then she thought. "He probably has maid service." She walked over to the curtains and opened them. It was nice and sunny. She walked over to the dresser drawer and pulled a pair of white underwear out and a white bra she had bought when her and Grant had gone shopping.

Rose walked to the closet and pulled out a white silk skirt. It had little blue and green roses on it. She then pulled out a white peasant blouse with big wide ¾ sleeves and grabbed her burlap wedge tie-up shoes. Put green dangling earrings on and her watch. She liked the fact that her clothes were here in Grant's closets and drawers. Grant, obviously, didn't care about her clothes being here. She didn't want to feel guilty about it. She shrugged her shoulders and dressed. She was definitely not going to put too much thought into it.

Rebecca came out of Ben's bedroom. She had on a short jean skirt with a pink top tucked in with pink earrings and a pink headband with pink slip-on shoes.   She spun around in front of Rose, "Walla?" You like?" "Rose looked up.

"Yes, I like, Ms. Pretty in Pink!"

Sally escorted Grant into Ed Johnson's office. "Mr. Benedict is here". Ed got up and shook Grant's hand. "Let's go into the conference room. I think we will be more comfortable there." Ed looked at Sally as he passed her desk. "Sally brings me the 2nd quarter financial earning statements."

"Okay, Mr. Johnson."

Ed and Grant took a seat in the small conference Room next to Ed's office. Sally came in and put a heap of papers on the conference room table.

"Okay Grant, this is where we are at. I need you Grant to go through these 2nd quarter financial earning statements and give me a projection or insight on where we need to proceed before the 3rd quarter. You can take these with you and you can either work here in this conference room or you can take them with you and work on them. I need this report from you in three weeks. "Does that work for you?" Grant briefly looked at the documents.

"Sure, no worries." If I have any questions, I'll be sure to call you. I don't see a problem getting these back to you in that time frame."

Ed stood up, gave Grant a business card and shook Grant's hand again. "Okay, let's say first week of August?" Grant picked up the paperwork and put it in his leather satchel.

"Okay, sounds like a plan." They both stopped at Sally's desk on the way out.

"And this is Sally my superb Administrative Assistant. Please call her if you have any questions." Ed waved as he walked out to the casino floor. Sally handed Grant her business card.

"Oh Mr. Grant I just wanted to let you know, I gave my two- week notice. So, by the end of next week, they will have a new girl working here."

Grant took Sally's card and thought about Rose. He looked at Sally and said, "Sally not to sound like I'm taking your job right now, but I do have a girl in mind. Sally folded her hands and looked up at Grant.

"What is her name?"

"Her name is Rose Davis. Grant fibbed because he really didn't know. All he knew is Rose needed a job. "She has done Administrative work before and I am sure she would be good here." Sally picked up her pen.

"Do you have her cell phone number?" Grant gave her Rose's cell phone number. "Mr. Johnson is in definite need of an Administrative Assistant right away. I'll let Mr. Johnson know and maybe we will call her for an interview in the next day or so." Grant smiled a huge smile. Great, Sally, I appreciate it". He asked her, "You have my phone number, right? Sally looked down at the cell phone number and looked up at Grant again.

"Yes Mr. Benedict, I have your number."

Chapter 30 - Rose and Rebecca – Girls Lunch Out! - Bon Appetite

Rose and Rebecca drove down the Las Vegas Strip to the cell phone store where they both paid their cell phone bills for the month. Then they drove to Gino's Italian Restaurant. The restaurant was on the second floor facing the strip. It had seating outside on a small terrace facing the strip with glass windows surrounding the terrace. The tables had white linen tables with white napkins. A bit formal but the girls thought it was grand. They both wanted to feel special; after all it was a celebration for Rebecca and her new job. The waiter seated them both outside. They put their napkins in their laps. The waiter came over to their table and handed them a menu.
"What would you ladies like to drink?" Rebecca looked at Rose.

"I think I'll take an ice tea with a lemon." Rose looked up at the waiter.

"I'll have the same, thank you." She looked at the menu. "I think I will have the Chicken Alfredo and a house salad."

Rebecca looked at her menu. "Mm, I think I will have the Veal with Lasagna with a house salad."

"Very good the waiter said, taking their menus."

Rebecca looked at Rose. "I am so happy Rose for both of us. I finally got a job!" Rose smiled.

"I am so happy for you too Rebecca." Rebecca looked at Rose.

"They said the pay is $200 per night for six nights, so that is $1200 a week."

Rose looked at Rebecca, smiling. "I'm going to be looking hard for a job too. You know I was thinking that if I find a job soon, maybe in a month, we could find a small apartment together." Rebecca looked at Rose.

"You know Rose it's been a long time coming. We had such high hopes when we came to Las Vegas and it just got worse for us. "Thank God for Ben and Grant and the money they gave us." Rose looked down at the table. "I know Rebecca it wasn't at all what I expected. I am very grateful for Grant and Ben too. They were really our saviors in disguise. I don't want to think about the hospital medical bills that will be pouring in."

Rose took a sip of her tea and looked Rebecca square in the eyes. "How much do you really like Ben?" "Rebecca looked at Rose. She knew what she was getting at. Rebecca leaned over and looked her square in the eyes.

"Rose, I really do like him a lot. It's just a matter of if he really likes me. When we are out together, he gets a lot of cell phone calls. Who they are from, I don't know. I don't ask. And I don't want to know."

The waiter came by and placed their plates in front of them with their salads. "Bon Appetite!" he said and walked away. Rebecca looked at her plate.

"Okay, let's just enjoy today and our good fortune." Rose
started eating. "I want to go shopping today." We can pay
the motel rent and then walk around the shopping mall
downtown. And not spend too much money!"

Rebecca looked at her plate. "This food is amazing!
Sounds like a plan, girlfriend!" The waiter came back and
put one vodka glass in front of Rebecca and one vodka
glass in front of Rose. They looked up at the waiter.
Rebecca pointed at the drink in front of her and looked up
at the waiter. "We didn't order these!" The waiter said.
"These are called *"Smooch on the Lips"* vodka drinks. The
waiter pointed to two guys to the right of them sitting on
the terrace, both of them also with the same vodka glasses.
Both of them smiling put their two fingers to their brows
and saluted Rose and Rebecca. The guys took off their
sunglasses and winked at them.

Rose and Rebecca looked at each other and shrugged.
Rose looked up at the waiter. "Please thank the two
gentlemen for us." Rose and Rebecca took their *"Smooch
on the Lips"* glasses and raised them to the two guys. The
two guys lifted their vodka glasses and everyone took a sip.

After a few minutes, the two guys got up and walked
toward Rose and Rebecca. One of them spoke up. "We
thought you two beautiful would like a *"Smooch on the
Lips"* drink.

"What?" Rebecca blurted out. The other one spoke up.
He had a French accent also. "The drink is called "Smooch
on the Lips. It is made with a twist of lime and lemon to

make it very tart. Like a Vodka Lemmon Drop." Rose took another sip and puckered her lips.

"Oh I see. Thank you both."

 "Do you mind if we join you for a moment?" Rose almost choked on her bite of food.

"Well, we are actually getting ready to leave and go shopping." He took a card out of his pocket and gave it to Rose. "My name is Jean-Paul." "Here is my card. I live here in Las Vegas. I own a jewelry shop at *The Gala Casino*, first floor called "Jean-Paul's Finest Jewelry."

He took Rose's hand and gave it a light kiss and his hazel eyes met her green eyes. She blushed. Then she sat frozen in time for a moment. She was at a loss for words. She quickly pulled her hand back. The other guy put his hand out to Rebecca, bent down and kissed her hand, "My name is Pierre".

Rose looked down at her napkin on her lap and then looked up. "My name is Rose." She looked at Rebecca who was staring. "And this is my best friend, Rebecca." He smiled at each of them.

"Well, it is a pleasure to meet you two beautiful ladies. Have a great time shopping! Please come by and visit me at my jewelry shop. He smiled, "I'd love to see you again." They both put their sunglasses on and walked away and waved back. Rose looked at Rebecca who was following their every move, their every step all the way out the restaurant as far as she could see. Rose snapped her fingers

in front of Rebecca's eyes. "Snap out of it girlfriend!
"Don't get any ideas!"

Rebecca came to. She looked at Rose with one of her
eyebrows up in the air. "You're the one who has his
business card, not me!" She started laughing. Rose got up
from the table and put the card in her purse. As if she was
just dismissing the whole charade that came upon them in a
moment's flash. "Really? Rebecca. Remember, you've got
Ben and I've got Grant."

Rebecca picked up her "*Smooch on the Lips*" drink,
finished it off and put it on the table. "That *"Smooch on
the Lips"* drink was a close one! And then came the kiss
on the hands. Whew!" Rose laughed all the way out the
restaurant.

"Come on crazy!" Let's go shopping!"

Grant dropped his brief case on the kitchen table and pulled
out his laptop and *The Diamond Club Casino* Financial
Earning Statements. He took his tie off and poured himself
a Gin and Tonic. He got his phone out and texted Rose.
"Can you do dinner tonight?" Rose texted him back.
Rebecca and I are shopping at the mall now, but yaw
dinner sounds great." "What time? 7:00 p.m.?" Rose
texted him back. "I'll be there!"

Grant took a drink and sat down at the kitchen table. He
thought about Rose. He actually missed her. He put his
drink down and started thumbing through the stack of
papers.

The shopping mall was busy. Rebecca and Rose tried on clothes, perfume and shoes. They both bought a cute tie around the neck 60's looking silk jumpsuit with a pair of wedge shoes to match Rose's green paisley prints and Rebecca's purple paisley prints.   Rebecca's cell phone rang. "Hey, Ben." "How are you? "Okay, sure. I'd love to go to happy hour with you. "I'll meet you at the Gable's bar at *"The Diamond Club Casino.* First floor? Right? Okay, I'll be there at 6:00 p.m. "By the way, I've got some great news to tell you! "See you!" Rebecca hung up. Rebecca turned to Rose. She squealed. "It's date night tonight! "Let's go pay the motel rent and get ready!" Rose walked to the car, got in and she started it.

"Okay, Rose said. "The game plan for tonight is that you take the car tonight to meet Ben and I'll take a cab to Grant's hotel suite."

Rose got dressed and then looked around the cheap motel room. She kept thinking, "Things will get better!" She grabbed her purse and looked at Rebecca. "I will most likely be at Grant's place tonight. And, I am sure if you and Ben have too many *"Smooch on the Lips,* you will be back at Ben's place or Grant's place, whichever."

Rose started to reach for the door to leave but quickly turned around. "Hey listen, before I leave. She went over and sat next to Rebecca who was putting her high heels on. Rebecca looked over at Rose's serious face.

Rose looked Rebecca in the eyes. "Not to alarm you, but I got a glance of the news on TV this morning and it was saying there is a serial killer on the loose killing prostitutes.

So, please Rebecca, please make sure you watch yourself, okay?" Rebecca looked at Rose's eyes and saw the terror. Rebecca grabbed Rose's hand and said, "Don't worry, girlfriend, I've got eight eyes, all rotating around my head at all times!" Rose started laughing as she got up. She looked back at Rebecca again, "Okay, you know we've got each other's backs? Right? She blew Rebecca a kiss. "Have fun, girlfriend!" Rebecca looked down at her watch and called Ben to tell him she was running a little late.

Rose got in the back seat of the taxicab and said "*The Diamond Club Casino*" please. She looked at the driver's name on the rearview mirror, "Ramsey". She opened the back window a little. It smelled like some kind of flower freshener with a smell of old shoes. She couldn't figure it out. She took a small roll-on perfume bottle out of her purse and started rolling the perfume on her neck and arms.

She looked at the taxicab driver in the rearview mirror. He was staring at her with dark black eyes. She was getting the creeps. Then she started to panic. He had pulled off the strip and was going down a secluded alley area. She turned around to look out the back window. And then she turned around and leaned forward said aloud frantically.

"Where are you going?" She reached for the door and as he slowed down, pulled it open and jumped out. He quickly stopped the taxicab.

"Miss, Miss?" The road is blocked off. I have to take you on another route." Rose, not for a second, believed a word he said. She waved him on and walked three blocks back down the alley to the Las Vegas strip and hailed another taxi. She gagged at the thought of the smell in his cab, "Dam dickhead!

Rose knocked on Grant's suite. Grant opened the door.

"Hi stranger," he said and pulled her in and gave her a long kiss. He smelled of some kind of cologne. Rose kissed him back. She liked the smell. "You look smashing my dear!" Rose, pressed on the bottom of her skirt and smiled. Her hands were shaking. She had a flash back of the Taxi Driver and quickly composed herself and gave Grant a big smile. "And you smell great!"

Grant smiled. "It's Men's Versace cologne?"

She walked over to the kitchen table and looked at the paper trail and computer on it and then turned to Grant.

"What's all this?

Grant walked over to the table, "Oh, I'm working on a special project for *The Diamond Club Casino* for Ed, my friend. Remember he's the General Manager there?" Rose glanced up at Grant. Oh. "Yes, yes.

Grant finished his drink and looked over the table. "I'm working on a financial statement earnings audit. It's going to take a few weeks or so. Want a drink?" Rose ran her fingers along the kitchen table.

"No, I think I'll wait. "Where are we going? I am starving!" Grant looked out the window.

"We'll it's a hot evening tonight. They have a nice seafood restaurant at *The Gala Casino* called *Bubba's Lobster Hut*."

Rose walked to the door. Grant held the door open for her, "After you, my dear!" "By the way I like your jump suit. It reminds me of the 60s'. You know the Beatles era. Believe it or not, my mom wore the Culottes which was the short version of what you're wearing before our time. She showed me pictures."

Grant and Rose walked into *The Gala Casino*. Rose noticed several shops. She passed a jewelry shop and looked at the name "Juan-Paul's Fine Jewelry". She saw someone wave at her. Grant noticed also but kept on walking. "You know that person in the jewelry shop?" Rose lied.

"No. Don't know who that is." Grant put his hands in his pocket and kept walking and said, "Weird."

The restaurant's atmosphere was a large straw hut with wooden tables. It looked like you were on an Island in Hawaii with a tall tropical fruit drink. They sat around a wooden table outside with a large straw umbrella above them. It was a couch with Hawaiian painted flowers. The sun was fading a little so it wasn't so hot. The waiter came over and they both ordered a drink and Lobster.

Grant looked into Rose's eyes. "So how was your day?" Rose smiled placed her cocktail napkin in her lap and looked at Grant. "It was good. Rebecca and I finally spent some quality time together. Oh, and she got a job as a

Dancer as a matter of fact at this casino." Grant took his sunglasses off.

"I am so happy for her!" Rose took her sunglasses off.

"She starts rehearsal tomorrow at 1:00 p.m. and the money is good." Grant took a sip of his drink and looked at her.

"How good?" Rose took her napkin and folded it in her lap.

"She mentioned she is going to make about $200 per night five maybe six nights a week or about $1200 per week. That means we can start looking for an apartment. Probably start looking next week."

Grant smiled at her. "I am happy for you and Rebecca!" Grant took her hand. "That's really great Rose. Oh, and I forgot to tell you. Sally Evans may be calling you for an interview. She is the Administrative Assistant for my college friend, Ed Johnson the General Manager of *The Diamond Club Casino*. She is giving her two-week notice. Rose's eyes widened.

"Really? That is awesome! I gave her your cell phone number and she has my cell phone number also." Grant handed her a drink. Rose took the drink and gave it a sip.

"Perfect!" With desperate but excited looking eyes Rose blurted out. "That would be so good if I got that job Grant". You know as well as I do, I really need a job!"

Grant looked at Rose with her flashing green eyes that were
filled with excitement at the prospect of a real job and
started laughing. "Don't worry Ms. Rose. I really hope you
get the job too! "I'll put in a good word for you. I will let
Sally know you did Admin work before." Rose froze.

"Well, I am good on the iphone and I have done computer
work and know some programs."

 "Sally will probably train you for a week and half maybe
before she leaves. She has to hire someone really soon, so
I am hoping she calls you by tomorrow."

The waiter brought their plates of Lobster. Rose looked at
her Lobster on the plate. "This looks great!" She looked
back up at Grant who had already started devouring his
lobster. Obviously, he was hungry. She smiled.

 "Thank you, Grant. "I really do appreciate all your help!"

Grant put his lobster down and glanced at Rose. "Hey after
dinner, let's go sit in the High Roller's bar at *The Diamond
Club Casino* and have a drink and relax. I've got this audit
project for *The Diamond Club Casino* I need to start
tomorrow morning. Rose took a bite of lobster. She
looked up at Grant. "Yeah. Sure. Let's do it!"

"I just want you to know Rose that I will be working from
home and going to and from *The Diamond Club Casino*, so
I am going to be pretty busy for the next three week or so.

Meaning I am not going to have much time in the coming
weeks." She looked at him with serious eyes. What could

268

she say? He wanted her to understand that he would not have much time for them being together this upcoming week. She looked up at him.

"Okay, I understand."

Grant looked at the disappointment in her eyes. "It's business, Rose."

Rose took a bite of lobster and put her fork down and took a sip of her drink. Rose took her napkin and wiped her mouth.

"I understand. I get it Grant. I'm a big girl. It is what it is." But in her heart, she was hoping he wasn't saying this just to dump her. Letting her down slowly. In the back of her mind, she knew she had to be strong. Strong for him. And also, strong for herself.

Grant looked at her again. He knew she got it; but he also knew she didn't like it. They finished their lobster in silence and headed for the High Roller's bar at *The Diamond Club Casino*. Grant knew Rose wasn't being herself. She was normally bubbly and now she was not so bubbly. But now she was sulking. They found a booth area in the High Rollers bar area. Grant put his arm around Rose. The waitress came over and told them the drink specials. The *"Play it Again Sam"* for $3.00 each. The waitress smiled.

"It's a tall double shot of rum and coke." Rose looked at the waitress.

"I'll have one of those." Grant chimed in. "Me too."

He knew he liked Rose a lot and he wanted her to know he liked her a lot. She was basically the only girl that he was seeing. He really didn't have a lot of time for anyone else. He took her hand and looked into her eyes. He wanted to break the ice that seemed to have come over her.

"Rose, I just want you to know that I really like you. I more than like you." She looked at him.

"What do you mean you more than like me?"

Rose was smart. Grant just got himself into a pickle and in her mind Rose was amused at what he would say.

Grant looked down at their hands entwined together and then looked back up at Rose. "Rose you know what I'm saying." She smiled at him with amusement in her eyes.

"Really? Tell me." She saw him squirm a little. She also knew when men were to tell their true feelings. It wasn't an easy thing to do for some.

He took his hand and scratched the back of his head and looked out across the bar and then back at her. "Okay, you win. I think I'm falling. And falling hard.

Rose looked straight into his eyes. She wanted to witness the seriousness of what he was about to say. She wanted to see if he was "real."

I know we haven't known each other for very long, but I feel we know each other pretty well. "We are two of the same, in mind and in souls. At least that is what I see between us."

Rose took a sip of her drink. Now she really wanted to play him hard. "Falling hard where?" Grant cocked his head to the side and looked at her. Now he knew she was playing with him. He took her hand.

"Okay, I am being serious now. I want to ask you Rose. Have you ever been in love before?"

The waitress came by and put two more *"Play It Again Sam"* drinks in front of them. Rose picked up her drink and looked up at the waitress. "Thank you."

Grant nodded and paid the waitress.

Rose looked down at her in her hand. She twirled the straw and then she took a moment and reflected back in time, then she looked back into Grant's eyes and slowly began to speak.

"I was in love one time. It was a long time ago. I was 17. It was my senior year in high school. Rebecca and I would sit in my room in the attic and talk about the boys at school. There was one boy I liked. He was on the baseball team. He was the pitcher of the team. Where we lived in the small town of New Albin, Iowa, there was baseball scouts that came out to see the good players were for possible college scholarships."

"Remember I told you New Albin, IA is the farthest northeast town in Iowa. It's located on the Mississippi River and Minnesota border. It was named after an11 year old boy who on July 4, 1872 was celebrating the holiday by jumping over a large bonfire on the street. His name was Albin Rhomburg. His pockets were filled with gunpowder. He accidently stumbled and fell into the burning flames. The town tried frantically to save him, but his burns were too critical and he died the next day."

Grant took a sip of his drink and looked at her in horror. "That's horrible!"

Rose took a sip of her drink.

"It was horrible, but it was also true.

Anyway, Rebecca and I would go to the baseball games sucking on purple "Winner" suckers." Then, during the winters, as you know, it snows in New Albin, Iowa. As crazy as it seems, Rebecca and I would go to a big hill behind the school called Killer Hill. After school, we would take our cookie sheets and slide down Killer Hill together.

It was a fun pastime we did together for laughs! We had been doing it since we were eight years old. There were lots of other kids that were there also. We would all take turns riding our cookie sheets down Killer hill. Then one day, Rebecca and I got our cookie sheets and started sliding down the hill together and there were two boys that came up behind us on their cookie sheets and toppled us off our cookie sheets."

One of them was Ryan Colby who played pitcher on the New Albin's High School team. The other boy was Josh Baker who also played third base on the New Albin's High School baseball team of whom I found out later had eyes for Rebecca. Anyway I was mad when he pulled me off my cookie sheet.   I got up and threw a snowball in his face." He just stood there and laughed at me." Grant put his head back and started laughing.

"Really, now? Who does that?" Rose looked at Grant's amused smile. She took another sip of her drink.

 "I remember me and Rebecca going home and running up to my attic room going sitting on the bed saying, "what the crap?" What was that all about? At school the next morning Rebecca and I would pass Ryan and Josh in the hall way to class. They would throw paper notes at us. Of which Rebecca and I were stupid enough to pick up and read. They would write, "Let's do it again at Killer Hill!" Rebecca and I would look at the notes, then each other, and start laughing. The typical, usual, 17 year-old girl thing.

And, of course, they both would meet us at Killer Hill after school, and do it all over again. It was annoying at first but then it got to be fun. Rebecca would wait for them to go down first." "Then we would both topple them off the cookie sheets and start throwing snowballs in their faces."

Rose looked at Grant. She could tell he was still amused. She took another sip of her drink explaining, "Two can play the game! Ryan had a locker three down from mine and I would see him coming.

He would get his books out, close his locker and look at me. Then he would walk by, get real close and smile at me as he was walking by. Grant took a drink of his drink. He could feel some real old competition going on in his mind. He couldn't resist asking, "Was he cute?"

Rose sipped her drink and looked at Grant thinking that that was a weird question. "Yes he was cute. For some reason I started noticing that all the girls wanted to date him. I guess you can say he was popular.

It was March around Prom time. I opened my locker and Ryan came by and threw a note in my locker. I picked it up and read it. It said, will you go to Prom with me? I looked at him passing me in the hallway." "He turned and looked back. "I nodded my head, "yes". He smiled at me and put his hands in the air. "Yes!" Rebecca had gotten the same note from Josh, Ryan's best friend and buddy.

"That day, we both ran up to my room in the attic. We both sat on the bed giggling. Can you believe it? We both grabbed hands and entwined our fingers together in the air. Can you believe it, the most popular guys in the school? We are going to the Prom with them! We high-fived each other, "YES!" I remember Rebecca suddenly got a frown on her face. "What are we going to wear?"

I looked at her sad face and took both of her hands in mine and said. Don't worry, Rebecca, we will find something. Let's go ask Grandma Nana Meme if she has anything. We both ran down stairs to Grandma.   She was sitting in her big old flower chair reading a book with her legs on her

274

ottoman by the fireplace. Rose sat on the ottoman and looked at her Grandma. "Grandma, we were wondering if you had anything for me and Rebecca to wear for a Prom?"

Grandma Nana Meme took her eye glasses off and looked a little puzzled. "Well? she said. I believe up in your room in the attic is a chest in the closet. Let's go look and see if we can find something. Oh, Grandma that would be so great! We all got up from the fireplace and marched upstairs to the attic. Rebecca and I pulled the cedar chest out the closed and opened it.

There were all kinds of clothes, diaries, pictures and different kinds of jewelry, brooches, necklaces, earrings and bracelets. Grandma knelt down and started taking out the clothes. Let's see what do we have here? We both took the clothes from her and put each dress or gown on the bed. Rebecca picked one up and held it to her. Oh Rose, look at this one! It was a long, fully laced red-maroon gown with a silk red lining underneath with red lace sleeves. Rose looked up. Beautiful!

The waitress came by. Grant raised two fingers up. She smiled and returned with two more *"Play It Again Sams."* Grant turned back to Rose and said "Please continue." Rose took the last sip of her drink.

"Anyway, Grandma pulled out almost the same dress but it had blue lace from the top down to the floor with a blue silk lining. I held the dress up for Rebecca to look at. "Oh look Rose, it's like this red one but in blue. They both happened to fit perfectly. Grandma pulled out a red rhinestone necklace and also a blue rhinestone necklace and two bracelets that matched. Grandma said that she and her sister wore the dresses when they attended a fancy wedding. That's where she met my grandpa. They called my grandpa, Pauley because he owned *Pauley's Grocery Store* in the small-town square.   So, Rebecca and I had our Prom dresses and fake jewels. We were so happy! I had told Ryan and Josh to be at my house Prom night at 7:25 p.m. sharp."

"Prom Night started at 7:45 p.m. and the school was about three miles away.   Remember, we are a small town. So, there was really no place elegant to host a Prom.   It was on a Saturday night, March 29th to be exact. Rebecca and I had spent all day getting ready. The next morning, we both took showers and put pink curlers in our hair. Grandma had hand washed the dresses and ironed them lightly. "She even gave me $10 to buy shoes.

Rebecca and I had found some in a hand-me-down town store in the square. Nothing, fancy. We didn't have money to buy fancy shoes. So, we did the best we could. Rose looked at Grant to see if he was appalled at the thought of her buying something at a hand-me-down store. He didn't blink. She thought. "Good!" Because, she'd probably would have punched him in the eye and walked out. She was intolerant of people who thought they were too good to buy in a hand-me-down store.

"Ryan and Josh arrived on time. Ryan drove a dark green SS7 with a black stripe down the middle and Josh drove a late model Firebird.   Grandma got her old camera out and took pictures. Rebecca and I didn't have cell phones then.

We couldn't afford them. Ryan and Josh both looked
handsome.

 They had brought arm corsages. Rebecca and I had made
our hair-dos up high in ribbons with Grandma Nana
Meme's pearl bobby pins everywhere" We wanted to look
the same. We both put on white satin gloves up to our
elbows. We wanted to look somewhat different from the
other girls. We put each other's make-up on. She looked at
Grant again. He still seemed amused listening.

Rose looked at the waitress and held her two fingers up.
She was getting a little tipsy, but not tipsy enough to tell
Grant the rest of the story.

Grant started laughing. "Now you're getting to the good
part and you don't want to tell me."

Rose started laughing. "Okay, okay. The Prom ended at
12:00 p.m. I kissed Rebecca on the check and told her to
have a good time and to be safe. Then Ryan drove us to the
town baseball park and we talked. All the restaurants, of
course, were closed. He had brought a bottle of wine he
took from his parent's drink stash and two cups." Rose
could feel her face turn red. She took the drink napkin off
the table and started twisting it. "Then, of course, he kissed
me."

Grant put his arm around Rose and started laughing. "How
many times did he kiss you?" He wanted to tease her;
make her fidget. Rose looked up at Grant.

"Now you're teasing me!" Grant paid the waitress and
turned to her said.

"Yep, I sure am. And, I'm loving every minute of it!"
Rose pushed his shoulder with her hand.

"Now, you're being mean!" Grant took a sip of his drink
and put the drink down.

"It's just getting good now!" "Come on!" Tell me the rest,
Ms. Rose! Spill it! You know." Grant looked at her.

"And?" "And?

Rose took a sip of her drink. "And what?"

"Well, I know you guys danced all night and he kissed you.
Right? Well? Rose looked at Grant's teasing eyes.

"Well, what? She was playing with him and she liked it.
Grant squeezed her shoulder.

"Well, did you guys do the wild thing?"

 Rose took another sip of her drink. She started giggling
and talking real fast. "So, we drove back to Grandma's
house and we snuck upstairs to my room in the attic and we
did it!"

Rose put her hands over her face but looked at him with
one eye. Grant was laughing hard! He couldn't stop
laughing. Holding his sides with his hands he burst out
loud, "You are too much, Ms. Rose!"

"Well, there's more to it. But the final chapter to my story is for another time. She folded her arms across her chest. That was all she was going to tell. So, I guess you can say Ryan was my first love. And I guess you could say, I was in love. So, the answer to your question is "yes," I have been in love."

The waitress came by again. Grant looked up at her and shook his head "No!" He looked at Rose. "Ready to go?" Rose stood up.

"Yes, I'm ready." Grant took her hand.

"Steady there girly girl." Rose giggled.

"It's the shoes." Grant looked at her and laughed. "I bet!"

Grant opened his hotel suite door slowly holding Roses' hand behind him. They both took off their shoes and started tip toeing down the hallway. Grant pulled Rose behind him and turned and put his finger to his mouth. "Shhhh." Grant pulled Rose into his room and closed the door. He turned on the bathroom light adjacent to the bedroom and closed the door slightly so there was some light to see. Rose threw her shoes and purse on the side of the bed. Grant grabbed Rose from behind, turned her around and gave her a long slow kiss on the lips.

Grant started taking her clothes off. Piece-by-piece, he slowly undressed her. One-by-one he stripped all her clothes off. Rose laid down on the bed and put her arms

over her head watching him. Grant undress slowly in front
of her.

Watching her eyes, as he unbuttoned his shirt sleeves and
unzipped his pants, pulled them down and stepped out of
them. He looked at her lying there like a porcelain China
doll. He slowly bent over moving up her body from her
feet kissing her legs and then looking at her. Rose
squirmed. He moved his lips and tongue over her cave. He
reached her mouth, lying on top of her, he gave her a long,
wet kiss.

Rose could feel the passion oozing from every part of her
body. Her heart was beating faster and her breathing
became erratic and louder. She could feel his hardness
against her. She could feel his hands roaming her breasts
as he kissed her. She came up for air, took his hands in
hers and rolled him over and slid her body on top of him
and looked him in the eyes and ran her hand through his
hair and kissed him hard.

She was wet, very wet. She sat on top of him with her
hands entwined in his hands that were over his head. She
teased him by rubbing her breasts on his hairy chest. She
positioned herself on him. His man-hood found her
womanhood cave and it was on! Rose was riding the ride
of her life! And Grant was giving it to her! And for sure
loving every minute of it!

Rose opened her eyes. She looked over to the other side of
the bed. Grant was not there. She remembered he told her
that he was going to be busy for a while with *The Diamond
Club Casino* Audit project. He probably was up having

coffee and working in the kitchen. She lied there, naked, feeling happy.

She wondered if she really wanted to tell Grant. Tell him, that not only at 17 years old, Ryan was her first love, but that they did do the wild thing up in the attic. But also the reality of that so called first love good time had gotten her pregnant.

A tear rolled down her cheek. And that same year, a NCSA New York Baseball Scout had been watching Ryan play for two years as the pitcher and had signed him for one of the baseball colleges, Clarkson University in New York.

And that when she had told Ryan she was pregnant, he dumped her. He didn't want to have anything to do with her.

She remembered going home from school early. Rebecca came over and found her upstairs in the attic sitting on her rickety old bed springs crying silently so her grandma would not hear her.

Rebecca had sat down next to her on the bed. When Rose looked up with her face red and swollen from crying, she blurted out. "I'm pregnant and Ryan doesn't want to have anything to do with me." He got a baseball college scholarship at Clarkson University in New York." Rebecca reached over and put her arms around Rose. She could feel the hurt in Rose's heart. And her heart broke.

Rebecca was devastated at the fact that Ryan would dump Rose. She really thought Ryan was "into" Rose.   She got up and got Rose a Kleenex, handed it to her and thought, "Typical high school jerk! What a dick!"

Rose remembered Rebecca taking both her hands in hers and softly saying, "Whatever you decide to do Rose, I'll be right here for you." Rose looked up at Rebecca in the eyes, blew her nose and put her arms around her. "Thank you, Rebecca. I really need you now."

With tears running down her face, Rebecca patted Rose on the back, "I know. I know you do Rose." Rose sat back. She looked at Rebecca with concerned eyes. "Promise me something, Rebecca. Promise me you won't tell a soul." Rose's eyes flashed with fear. Rebecca looked at her and a tear fell down her cheek. "I promise you Rose." I'm your BFF forever. I promise you, Rose."

Rebecca was by her side every minute of every day. She would meet Rose every day at the bus stop, riding together to school, making sure she ate right. Even going to the bathroom with her when she had morning sickness and guarding the door to the bathroom not to let anyone hear Rose throwing up. Rose would become silent at times. Rebecca felt her sadness. They both would walk down the hall to their classes with their backpacks, never looking at Ryan and Josh passing by. They never went back to "Killer hill" again.

A month later, Rose was at home getting ready for school when she had tremendous pain in her stomach. She went into the bathroom. She was in so much pain that she fell to her knees. There was blood running down her legs. The long nightgown she wore was wet and bloody. She sat on the toilet for about 30 minutes holding her stomach. Then she took off her night gown and washed it in cold water in the tub. She got a Kotex pad out. She sat there on the toilet for another 20 minutes more, holding her head in her hands feeling flushed and feverish with tears rolling down her face. She knew that she had lost the baby.

Chapter 31 -Dr. Cooper - Report Relief vs. Bad Blood

Dr. Cooper got his cup of coffee and walked down the long corridor to his office. He put on his coat and sat down. He turned on his computer and looked at the daily reports. He read the report from Ed Johnson, General Manager, *The Diamond Club Casino:* - Subject: *The Animal Preventive Disease Control Final Report.* It read. *We have completed our investigation. Our Team secured all seven garage parking structures individually, and cleaned all garage structure floor areas with a hig- power anti-fungus bacteria cleaning solution. We also cleaned all storage units and walls. We cleaned all elevators on each floor. We also met with all Housekeeping and Maintenance and Valet, Restaurant, Bartenders, Cashiers, Dealers, Pay Out, all inside facility Personnel and they were advised of the specifics on cleaning all areas in the Casino. The Conclusion? We did not find any bats of any source, brown bats included. They have left the casino.*

We ran detective scans of all areas and found that the there is no airborne BATeria in areas of The Diamond Club Casino. It is contamination FREE. If there are any other concerns, please contact us immediately. Respectfully, Simon Jenkins, Animal Preventive Disease Control Task Team Coordinator. 330-xxx-xxx.

Dr. Cooper leaned back in his chair and sighed with relief. "Thank God!" He then went to the In-patient Admissions Register for the last three days. He scrolled the list to see if any of the patients that were admitted had the rash or bites of any kind. He saw one patient who was admitted, a Mr. Ramsey Evans. He had been admitted two days ago and was on the Isolated Patient Floor. Dr. Cooper looked at his watch, 9:00 a.m.

He got up, grabbed his coffee and head down the long corridor, got in the elevator and pushed 8th for the Isolated Patient Floor. He stopped by the front desk. Wanda the receptionist said "Good morning, Dr. Cooper."

Dr. Cooper smiled at Wanda and said, "Good morning, Wanda. Do you have Mr. Ramsey Evan's chart?" Wanda flipped through the stack of charts on her desk and handed it to Dr. Cooper.

"Yes, here it is." He stood there and flipped through the chart looking at all the notes. The attending doctor listed on the front of the chart was Dr. Emily Martina, a well-known Disease Physician from Chicago Presbyterian Hospital. He asked Wanda if Dr. Martina was in. Wanda shook her head. "No, she actually took a leave of absence. There was some kind of illness in her family. We don't know when she will be back." Dr. Cooper tucked the chart under his arm.

"Thank you for that bit of information.

 He walked down the hallway to room 802. He lightly knocked on the door and walked in. Ramsey Evan's had

284

the TV on low. Dr. Cooper walked over to him and put his
hand out. "Good morning, Mr. Evans." My name is Dr.
David Cooper. I am the Director of Preliminary Disease
Immunities Department here at Anderson Memorial
Hospital." "How are you feeling today, Mr. Evans?"

Ramsey looked at Dr. Cooper, studying him closely. "I am
not feeling very well. I am really tired and weak and my
chest is hurting me." Dr. Cooper looked at him. He could
tell Ramsey had a fever.

"Mr. Ramsey, I'm going to ask you a few questions. We
want to help you get better so you can get out of here."

Dr. Cooper, look through the chart again, took out his pen
from his pocket and clicked it open. "Okay Mr. Evans." "I
have reviewed your chart here. It says, you have a high
fever and you have a rash and you have a cough. Dr.
Cooper looked up from the chart at Ramsey. "Am I
correct?" Ramsey turned off the TV.

"Yes, that is correct."

"Okay, may I see where you have the rash?" Ramsey
opened the front of his blue hospital gown. A red large
rash area appeared between his thighs and his groin area
and penis and up towards his abdomen area. The entire
area was covered with the red rash. Dr. Cooper took a step
back. "Turn to the side, please." Dr. Cooper moved the
hospital gown to look at his back. Dr. Cooper noticed a
rash on Ramsey's buttocks area also.

285

Dr. Cooper tightened his lips. "How long have you had this rash?" Ramsey covered himself with his hospital gown.

"For about two weeks now. I'm a taxi-cab driver and I couldn't really afford to be off work. "I have a wife and son I have to support.

"How long have you lived in Las Vegas and how long have you been a taxi-cab driver?" Ramsey looked down at his nervous fumbling hands.

"I've lived here for about five years and have worked as a taxicab driver for almost five years."

Dr. Cooper started writing on the chart. "I am going to ask you some personal questions." "It is for medical record reasons only and is classified as "confidential information. I want you to answer them as honestly as possible. "Have you had any extra-marital affairs in the last five years while you have lived here?"

Dr. Cooper studied Ramsey's face to see if he was going to be truthful or not. "Ramsey shifted his eyes away from Dr. Cooper looking out the window and sighed. "Yes, Dr. Cooper, I have had extra-marital affairs in the past five years." Dr. Cooper studied him again.

"Okay, how many?" Ramsey looked at Dr. Cooper. "About 15, maybe 20." Dr. Cooper's pen was writing again.

"And in those five years and 20 individuals did you ever get any kind of venereal diseases?"

"No, I was careful to wear protection measures at all times."

Dr. Cooper studied Ramsey's face and asked.

 "Were any of these extra-marital affairs with call girls or prostitutes?"

Ramsey looked down and pulled his hospital gown tighter around him and pulled up the covers to his chest area. He looked up at Dr. Cooper. "Yes."

"Have you noticed a yellowish discharge from your penis and is it itching and burning?" Again, Ramsey looked down.

"Yes, to all three."

"When was the last time you had sexual relations with your wife?"

Ramsey looked out the hospital window. "Not for about one year now. We are both kind of estranged from each other. "Our son is the one that is important to us." Dr. Cooper patted the bedside side bar, okay Mr. Evans, I am going to have the nurse take some blood tests today and then run some more tests.

"How bad is your cough?" Ramsey shifted in the bed.

"It comes and goes".

I am going to have a technician run a MRI on your lungs to
see if they are clear. We need to keep your fever down also.
I am recommending you to stay here at Anderson Memorial
Hospital for another three to five days."

Dr. Cooper looked him square in the eyes. "I know your
job is important Mr. Evans, but it is also critical to your
health and your Families welfare that you stay here and we
find a cure for your condition. Do you understand? Please
make arrangements with your Taxi Cab Supervisor and let
him know your circumstances. And let your wife know
also. Ramsey looked him square in the eyes. "I told my
wife that my brother Gabriel was in the hospital in Atlanta
Georgia and I needed to go visit him for a few days. I
didn't want her to be alarmed."

Dr. Cooper studied Ramsey. "I think it is time you come
clean and tell her the truth." "You are in no condition now
to be hiding these circumstances.

Mr. Evans, I am letting you know now that you have a
serious condition and it borders on deadly. It is not a good
time for child's play. "I am suggesting only, as your
Physician and Doctor, you put your affairs in order with
everyone you know." "Ramsey's worried face said it all."
"Yes, I know Dr. Cooper." "I understand Dr. Cooper."

Dr. Cooper walked toward the door and turned. Okay then,
I will see you again tomorrow morning around the same
time. Let the nurses know if you need anything." Ramsey

looked at Dr. Cooper standing in the doorway. Ramsey closed his eyes.

Dr. Cooper stopped by Wanda's desk and handed her the file. "Please make sure the hospital staff follows my directions today for Mr. Evans. I need the blood results on my desk today. Also, schedule an MRI for Mr. Evans today and email me the medical report when it is completed." Wanda wrote all the notes down. Wanda looked up at Dr. Cooper and smiled.

"Okay Dr. Cooper, I got it." Dr. Cooper smiled.

"Thank you, Wanda." Dr. Cooper walked down to the elevator and turned.

 "Have a great day!" Wanda waived.

"You, too, Dr. Cooper!"

Chapter 32– Time to "Shop Till You Drop!"

Kinsey held Doreen's hand as they stepped on the escalator to the second level leading to the outside shopping mall stores. "You let me know what store you want to go in and if it's a women's store, I'll just sit outside here in the sunshine on a bench and wait for you." Doreen felt like a kid in a candy store. In the past five years it had been hard for her with the kids. The Real Estate market was a bust at times and she really struggled. She saw Nordstrom's and pointed.

"Let's go to Nordstrom's.

"Okay, let's go!" Doreen casually moseyed around the
shoe department while Kinsey parked himself on a sofa
seat in the store and took off his sunglasses.   He looked at
Doreen. He wanted her to have anything her heart desired.
He looked down at the floor, trying not to think about her
six months being her last days.   Doreen looked at Kinsey
sitting down. Kinsey smiled at her,
"I'll be right here."

Doreen came back with three pairs of shoes she liked. The
salesman came over and asked. "What size would you
like?" She looked up at the shoe sales rep with his suit on
and name tag of Tim Simpleton. She sat down next to
Kinsey, "Size 8, please." She looked at Kinsey. "It's been
a long time since I've been shopping." Kinsey patted her
on the knee. "Well today it's your special day." "Buy
anything you want." "It's our treat together." Doreen
smiled and leaned over and gave a kiss on Kinsey's cheek.
He smiled. She tried on each shoe and pranced around in
front of Kinsey and looked in the shoe mirror. She ended
up getting all three. Kinsey told the clerk they were doing
more shopping and he'd be back to pick up the packages
after they finished their shopping.

Next was the perfume and make up area. Doreen tried on a
few and ended up buying one Versace perfume, Yellow
Diamonds and one Este Lauder perfume, a soft tropical
one. Kinsey paid the clerk and then they went upstairs to
the women's clothing. Doreen tried on some sun glasses.
She picked on out with small daisies on top and put them

on for Kinsey. Kinsey did a thumbs up! "Look's good honey!"

She found some nice short skirts and a white peasant blouse and a few silk short dresses, a sun dress, two bathing suits, 3 pairs of shorts, 3 pairs of cotton Capri pants. Kinsey took a seat next to the fitting room again. He was enjoying watching Doreen shop. She was like a kid in a candy store. She came out each time and twirled in front of Kinsey with her new digs. He would, of course, nod and say, "That's looks great, honey!" It was the typical man thing to say.

Doreen put the clothes she wanted next to Kinsey and said I'll be back in a minute. Kinsey sat there and watched her trot off to some other clothing area. She came back and rushed into the fitting room telling him. "I'll be out in a minute!" Kinsey didn't know what she had in her arms and he really didn't care. This was her day. She came out and said, "Okay, I think I am done shopping." Kinsey looked up at her. "What?" "I thought we were just getting started?" "Well, I want all of these."

Doreen started laughing aloud. "I meant I was done shopping here at Nordstrom's." Kinsey got up laughing. "Oh, now I see." It had been so long since they had joked with each other. He was taking all of Doreen in at once and loving every minute of it. Kinsey paid the clerk and they took the hanging clothes and bags down to the shoe area and asked the clerk to hold them. He asked them if they had anyone that could deliver the shoes and bags to The Diamond Club Casino, the Poker Tournament Winner Suite on Floor 10. The clerk behind the shoe desk called the manager.

The manager came over Valarie and said there is a delivery service called "Begi's Delivery Service" that will come here and pick up bought merchandise from our store and deliver it anywhere in Las Vegas. Valarie handed Kinsey their card. "Here is their card." "Where are you at here in Las Vegas Mr. Kinsey?"

Kinsey took the card and put it in his back pocket. "We are at *The Diamond Club Casino*, The Poker Tournament Pent House Suite on the 20th Floor. Have the Delivery Service take these to our room, please. Kinsey pulled out Ed Johnson's card he had given him and put his name on the card and handed it to her.

He had gotten several business cards from Ed and had five with him in his back pocket. The phone number is 330-xxx-xxx for the General Manager, Ed Johnson at *The Diamond Club Casino* if you have any questions. Valarie handed him her card and then a receipt with delivery charges of $125.00. That will be One hundred ten for the service and $15 dollars for Nordstrom's service. Kinsey handed her his ATM Debit card. She ran it and handed it back to Kinsey. Kinsey held his breath. It went through. Kinsey put his ATM card away and sighed a sigh of relief and signed the receipt. Kinsey thanked Valarie and took Doreen's hand. Doreen put her sunglasses on and they walked out down the outside shopping mall. They both stopped and got an organic smoothie juice drink.

Doreen saw a purse shop, Coach and she pointed to the store. Kinsey took a seat on the bench. "I'll be right here when you're ready to check out." Doreen walked around the store. She picked up a small shoulder length light blush

pink Australian alligator purse with a matching small
wallet.

She then walked around and found a little bit bigger,
tomato colored cross shoulder purse with a matching
wallet. She thought Alice would like that one. Then she
walked around and found two more a medium turquoise
blue colored with matching wallet one and a striped blue
and white canvas looking beach bag to put her swimwear in
for the pool. She put the bags on the counter and said "I'll
be back in a minute."

Doreen waived to Kinsey. He came in and went to the
sales desk cashier counter. She picked up each bag and
wallet for Kinsey to see and let Kinsey see and showed him
the one for Alice along with a wallet to match. Kinsey
smiled. "They look nice honey!" He handed the clerk his
ATM card and signed the receipt asking her if they used the
Begi's Delivery Service?" "Yes, we sure do! The
manager gave him a Card with the business name "Coach",
Sandra Levy, Manager. Kinsey pulled another card out
with The Diamond Clubs Casino, Ed Johnson, General
Manager.

"It will be $110.00 delivery and $10 service Charge."
Kinsey looked at her.

"That seems to be the going rate for delivery around here
for the mall area?" "Yes, it is." He gave her all the
delivery information and she gave him a receipt.

Doreen smiled and gave Kinsey another kiss on the cheek.
"I'm having so much fun!" He looked at her and laughed.

"I'd have fun too, if someone was treating me like a precious jewel!" She took her hand and slightly slapped his shoulder. "Now don't get crazy on me!" "You told me, "It was my day!" "You told me it was my princess day!"

She laughed and took her hand they walked down around the mall. There were three stores next to each other. Doreen pointed to all three, MAC Cosmetics, Body and Bath, and Victoria Secrets. Kinsey sat down and pointed to his bench. "I will be right here dear sitting on this bench when you are ready."

Kinsey watched the crowds walk by and when Doreen waived her hand to him, he met her in each store. After paying for the merchandise and delivery, Doreen looked at Kinsey. "Whew, I didn't know how hard shopping could be." "I think I'm done shopping for the day!" I was hoping to find a toy store here so I could buy some toys for the grandkids. Kinsey took her hand and kissed the back of it. He smiled at her, "don't worry we have lots of shopping days ahead of us." "Can we go back to *The Diamond Club Casino* and go to the buffet?" "Anything you want my love! Kinsey bowed before her. "I am only here as your servant." Doreen put her head back and laughed. Her wig fell backwards and she put her hand on her head to make sure it was still on. Kinsey looked on in shock. Doreen started laughing. "Kinsey, Kinsey, my long-lost soul.

Kinsey could see Doreen was getting tuckered out. He turned to Doreen. "Okay, my love, one more trip to the Phone Store over here to get us new cell phones and with the same number and we are done." Doreen looked at Kinsey, "Okay good move!"

They walked back down the escalator and Kinsey hailed a taxi. They got in the back seat and the driver turned as asked. "Where to?" "Good! Kinsey thought, not the stink bomb Ramsey taxicab driver and the stink bomb cab." "*The Diamond Club Casino*, please." "He took Doreen's hand and looked at her with worried eyes.

"You okay honey?" She looked up into his eyes.

"I'm just a little tired." Kinsey looked at his NIXON Watch. It was 1:30 p.m. Kinsey squeezed her hand, "okay, let's go to back to *The Diamond Club Casino* to the buffet for lunch and then go up to the penthouse and rest a bit." Then we can decide what we want to do later."

"Sound good?"   She looked at him with tired eyes and squeezed his hand and smiled.

Kinsey hit the 20th floor Pent House button in the elevator. Doreen holding her hanging purse in front of her with both hands turned to him. "Thank you for the shopping trip and the nice buffet lunch." "It was wonderful!" Kinsey leaned over and gave her a quick kiss on the lips. "You are most welcome my dear!"

Kinsey opened the door with his slide card. All the gifts they had bought for the day where in front room lined up next to the wall to wall next to the opened curtained window. Doreen walked over to the couch and took her shoes off. Kinsey walked over and poured himself a cognac and turned around to Doreen.

"You want a drink hon?" Doreen looked at Kinsey.

"N,o I'm a little tired." I think I'm going to go lie down for a while.

"Okay love." "I'll be sitting on the sofa watching some TV."

Doreen got up and walked down the hallway to the bedroom. Kinsey took a sip of his drink and walked to the couch, sat down and turned on the TV. He turned on the News. *"There have been more updates on the killings that seem to be happening around Las Vegas. Two more girls were reported found in two different dumpsters. They were sexually assaulted and their necks were slashed with an army knife called an Engraved Stainless-Steel Knife. They both were identified as a 25 yea- old, and a 27 year-old, Caucasian. They both worked as call girls in the Las Vegas area. No names have been released yet.*

Kinsey flipped the TV channel. "Same old shit in Las Vegas." "Nothing ever changes!" Star Trek was on with Captain Kirk. He sat back and relaxed. "Now that's what I'm talking about!" He was happy Doreen got to spend some time shopping. The feeling of "real happiness" came over him. He was elated. He wanted to keep this feeling forever. He finished his drink and flipped off the TV.

He got up and took a note pad and wrote Doreen a note and put it on the kitchen counter top standing against a tall glass so Doreen could see it. "I am going to go out for a while." "No worries, I am going to be a good boy!" "There are snacks and drinks in the kitchen." "I'll be back later." "Love you, Kinsey".

Chapter 33 - Take Me to the Beach

Jack and Sarah got in the backseat of the Taxi. Jack looked
at the driver's name in the rearview mirror, "Pills-berry".
Jack glanced at the taxicab driver, who was adjusting her
rearview mirror and staring back at him. She had long
black hair with a black taxicab cap on. He had never seen a
woman taxicab driver. The taxicab driver turned around
and looked at Jack in the back. "Where to?"

Jack looked at the taxicab driver again, this time in shock.
The black stubbles on the chin were a dead give-away. She
was a He. *The Rocket Aero Tower*, please. He looked at
Sarah. She was looking out the window. It was 7:00 p.m.
and the sun was beginning to fade on the horizon. Jack
took Sarah's hand. Sarah turned and looked at him.

 "It's really kind of exciting being in Vegas." I didn't
know there were so many casino hotels and billboards with
different entertainers. "So many people from so many
countries walking the Las Vegas strip. This is definitely a
new adventure for me." Jack smiled at her.

"Yes this is definitely a very interesting and sometimes
strange place." Jack got out of the taxi and looked at the
taxicab driver as he handed him a $20. He had painted
black fingernails, manly hands and again he could see the
stubble on his face. It was as if he had not shaven in a
couple of days with a long black wig with bangs. He
looked down and saw he wore a mini shirt and his legs
were badly shaven with red high heels. "Strange she/he
was for sure."

Jack grabbed Sarah's hand and they headed through *The Rocket Aero Tower* and stepped into the elevator and pushed 98th Floor. The sun was gone and the sky was getting darker. Jack looked out the elevator glass window.

He could see gray rain clouds to the east. It very rarely rained in July in Vegas, but the weather could be as crazy as Las Vegas, doing what it wanted to do when it wanted too. The elevator went up slowly. Sarah looked at all the lights becoming visible in the as the sky darkened. The hostess escorted Jack and Sarah to a booth. The whole dining room was rotating around slowly, so you could see all of Las Vegas as you ate. Sarah was impressed.

She took a seat in the booth across from Jack. She smiled. "This is lovely Jack." Jack wanted it to be special for Sarah. He never stopped loving her. He just knew Detroit, Michigan was not the place he wanted to be. He made a choice three years ago when Sarah had gotten the teaching job there. He had met Ed Johnson CEO of *The Diamond Club Casino* now in college. They were both studying Business and both ended up with Business Management Degrees. And they both became good friends.

The waiter came by and handed Jack the Wine Menu. Jack asked Sarah if she would like some wine. The waiter turned to Jack.

 "Oh, and we do have two drink specials tonight." One is called *"The Snidely Whiplash"* which is a double shot of Canadian Mountain Whiskey with a splash of Canadian Mountain Dew. And then we'll have the *"Dudley Do-*

298

Right that is basically a double shot of Wild Cherry Rum of which you can drink straight or pour into a glass of *"Nell Fenwick"* which is a tall glass of coke with ice."

Sarah started laughing. "Now that's a new one!" Jack looked at Sarah and shrugged his shoulders.

"You're call?" Sarah looked at the waitress, Ann and said, "I think I will try the *"Dudley Do-Right"* with the glass of *"Nell Fenwick"* and hope *"Nell Fenwick's"* Dad does not show up and put *"Dudley Do-Right"* on the train tracks. Jack laughed and looked up at Ann the waitress.

"I'll have the same, please." She handed them the dinner menus and left to get the drinks.

Jacked looked over his menu and glanced at Sarah. "They have wonderful Veal, Steak and also Seafood here. Sarah scanned the menu.

"It all looks so yummy!" Sarah took her time looking at the menu. "The steak and lobster sounds wonderful with a house salad and baked potatoes." Jack took his time looking at the menu also.

"I think I will have the Veal with the Brussels sprouts and mashed potatoes." The waitress Ann came dropped off their drinks. Jack and Sarah poured the Canadian Mountain Whiskey into their cokes and stirred. Jack raised his glass to Sarah.

"To our summer together**!**" **"What plays in Vegas, stays in Vegas!"** Sarah raised her glass!

"Cheers!" "I like that!" **"What plays in Vegas, stays in Vegas!"**

Jack ordered two more, *"Dudley Do-Rights"* with the *"Nell Fenwicks."* He sat back and stared at Sarah. She was so refreshing. It had been a long three years for Jack dealing at *The Diamond Club Casino*. Denise was more or less a pass-time kind of girl. She was girl to spend time with when he was bored and lonely. He knew she was not the "real thing", the marrying type for him. His first love, Sarah, had always tugged at his heart. She was always in the back of his mind. He reached for Sarah's hand and looked steadily into her eyes.

"I am so glad you are here Sarah." Sarah smiled.

"I am too Jack." "I am too!" The waitress came with their food. "Sarah looked down at her plate, smiled and picked up her fork. "This looks wonderful!"

"Will that be all, the waitress asked? Jack looked up at her, "I don't see *"Snidely Whiplash*! I think we are good!" The waitress laughed and walked away.

Jack and Sarah finished their meal. Jack ordered a cognac for the both of them and they sat together looking out the window while the floor rotated around the Las Vegas skies. Jack told Sarah he had to call his Boss, Ed tomorrow and let him know he would be back to work in a couple of days and he needed to pick up his car from Mac at Henderson's Garage. Sarah smiled, "good that will give me and Tokyo time to get to know each other better." Sarah put her hand

over her mouth while yawning. Jack looked at her.
"Tired?" Sarah took a drink of her cognac.

"Yes, it's been a long day." Jack finished his cognac, stood up and put his napkin on the table, paid the bill and reached out his hand to take hers.

"Let's go home."

Jack opened the front door and as usual Tokyo came running meowing. Jack pointed to the bedroom. "The bedroom is all yours. I'll sleep here on the couch. It's comfortable." Jack bent down and petted Tokyo, right Tokyo?" Sarah yawned again. She walked up to Jack and gave him a quick kiss on the lips.

"Thank you for a lovely evening." She looked into his eyes, turned and gave a little waive. "See you tomorrow morning." Jack knew she was exhausted. It had been a long day for both of them.

Jack grabbed an extra pillow and blanket out of the hall closet. "Come on Tokyo, it's just you and me buddy." He turned off the lights and lied down on the couch. Tokyo followed, pawing his blanket, purring as he roamed over Jack. Jack closed his eyes and thought about Sarah and his first close encounters with her. Her college dorm was close to his.

He had a roommate Ed Johnson and of course she had a roommate also, Lisa Greenslave. On their fourth encounter together, he asked Sarah if she would like to go to Belle Isle's "Hipster Beach" for a weekend get-away. She said "yes!" He booked a hotel room on Saturday June 10th with a late checkout time for Sunday June 11th at the Detroit Club Hotel which was located downtown Detroit 2.9 miles to Belle Isle.

It was established in 1882 and is one of the nation's oldest private clubs in the nation. It had spa tubs, a 24- hour fitness center and dining. Many travelers there said the hotel rooms did not seem like a hotel room but rather an old historical charming mansion. His car back then was a dark midnight blue 1974 Pontiac Firebird with a large colored Firebird Eagle painted on the front hood.

Of course, Jack thought he was "hot" when he drove his car around the campus. Girls walking around the campus going to their next class would stop and whistle at him. Of course, he loved it! What guy wouldn't? He picked Sarah up in front of her Dorm. She a large shoulder bag and a medium roll luggage bag and her backpack. Jack got out and threw the shoulder bag in the back seat and the medium roll luggage bad in the trunk. She was grinning ear to ear. Opening the passenger door and climbing in she said, "It's been forever since I've been to the beach! "I am so excited!" It was a beautiful, sunny day.

Jack drove slowly down the district main street and then around "Hipster Beach." Sarah rolled her window down and stared at the beach and the people. Sarah put her head out the window and yelled "Whoo-hoo!" Jack valet parked the car and gave the valet guy a $5.00 tip.

A Bellman came with a large luggage rolling cart with gold round thick canopy bars and red fuzzy carpet where you put your luggage on. It looked like it came from the

"Titanic" ship. He was dressed in a brown/gold jacket, trousers, trimmed with black strips, black shiny shoes and a round hat on his head with white gloves.

 Jack and Sarah walked in and went to the reservation desk. "Jack Turner room for two, two queen size beds deluxe room with kitchen and patio and balcony." "Yes, Mr. Turner. Driver's license please."

Jack gave her his Driver's license. Jack looked at her name tag. "Two keys please, Ms. Clemons." She gave Jack two slide keys in two separate packets.

"Room709." The reservationist pointed to the right, elevators are to the right, 7th floor, Room 9."

Jack followed her hand pointing to the elevators. "Thank you." The Bell Boy followed with the luggage. Jack pushed the elevator button and looked at Sarah. She had her backpack and Jack had a carry brown duffle bag with him. It looked stuffed. Sarah looked at his duffle bag and asked him if he stuffed his whole closet in it? Jack laughed. "No but I thought about stuffing Tokyo in it." Sarah started laughing. "I am sure he would have enjoyed that one!"

The room was large with a kitchen, coffee maker, small electric stove and refrigerator. Two queen size beds and a bathroom that had a jet spa in it for two. The patio had French doors that went out to a small balcony in the heart of the Detroit district shop area with a small round glass table and two chairs.

The bell boy put the bags near the door and Jack gave him a $10 bill and thanked him.   Jack through his blue duffle bag on the queen size be and pulled out a bottle of Jack Daniels and a liter of Coke. "It's time for Jack's "*Dudley-Do Rights*" mixed with "*Nell Fenwicks*."

Sarah grabbed her bags and started unpacking them and putting her clothes in the drawers and closet. Sarah grabbed another bag and started taking out her shampoo, conditioner, tooth brush and tooth paste, shaver, baby oil, bubble soap, and make-up bag and put them in the bathroom. Jack handed her a large glass of Jack and Coke. "Cheers!" She smiled.

"Cheers!" They took their drinks to the patio and sat down. Aaaah, this is nice! "Refreshing".

Jack went back in and got some crackers, cheese and pepperoni out and put it on a plate from the kitchen. He placed the plate on the patio table in front of Sarah. "She took a long sip of her drink. Boy you don't go anywhere without the necessities. Drinks first, food second." He took a long sip of his drink, looking at her, he laughed.

"I saw you carry all your necessities to the bathroom." Sarah laughed.

"Oh now I get it! An eye-for-an-eye. A tooth-for-a-tooth!" Jack laughed.

Jack got up and made a couple of more drinks and they reminisced about their college days and their families. Let's go eat out somewhere and then go walk the beach.

"You game?" Sarah took a bite of cracker, cheese and pepperoni. Yep, I would like to take a bubble bath first. "Do you mind?" Jack stared out over the buildings and then looked at Sarah.

"Nope not at all, be my guest!" Sarah grabbed some clothes from the drawer and a summer dress she brought with some sparkly gold slip on strap around the ankle sandals with a small heel.

Jack sat, looking out, relaxing and drinking his drink and snaking on the crackers. He heard the tub water running and the jets being turned on. He wondered if he could make an appearance and join Sarah in the tub without her freaking out. Why not? He had three drinks and was feeling pretty good. He started reasoning with himself. After all, they were two adults. He'd probably never get the chance again. "Just do it!" He got up and knocked silently on the bathroom door and stuck his head around the doorway.

Sarah who was lying back in the tub with baby oil and bubbles everywhere "froze." She sat up quickly. "Yes?"

"Can I come in?" Sarah thought for a moment. The drinks were starting to do their own talking for her. What the hell?

"Come in." Jack opened the door softly and whispered.

"Can I come in?" Sarah slid back in the tub to cover her boobs with the bubbles. She looked at Jack with suspicious eyes. He walked in and stood against the bathroom sink area and looked at her in the tub with the jets running.

Jack pondered a moment staring at her and her boobs, of course, with the bubbles.

"I was just wondering if I could join you? I like bubbles and jets." Sarah started laughing.

"I bet you do!" You are too much!" He was daring her and she knew it. She looked up at him with a grin.

 "Only if you get me another drink and you stay on the far side of the tub." Jack took off running, "I'll be back in a second." Sarah started laughing and yelled.

 "And be sure to make that drink a double!" Sarah had her eyes closed when he brought the drink back. Of course, he brought him one also. He put her drink on the side of the tub.

 "Okay your drink madam is on the side of the tub next to you."

Sarah still having her eyes closed, "Get in the tub Jack and hurry!" Jack put his drink on the side of the tub and hurriedly took off his clothes and got in the other side the jetted tub opposite from Sarah. Jack sat back in the tub, not trying to touch Sarah in anyway. "Ah, now isn't this nice?" Sarah opened her eyes and looked at Jack sitting back with a huge white smile like the purple striped Cheshire cat in Alice in Wonderland.

Looking, at Jack closely, while putting one eyebrow up in the air, she took a long sip of her drink. "So, was this your way of hijacking me and holding me captive in a jet tub at Hipster Beach? Jack knew he had to be careful on this one. It was her way of daring him. He looked at her with suspicious eyes. "Are you daring me Ms. Sarah Kramer?" She lifted her foot out of the water put her soapy foot on his chest. Jack looked at her foot. He smiled. "Can I do the same?"

Sarah moved her foot back into the water and laughed. "Not!" She took another sip of her drink. "This was fun, but the bubbles are disappearing." "I think I am going to get out now." "Close your eyes!" Jack looked at her and splashed some bubbles toward her with his hand.

"Okay." "Okay." "I'm closing my eyes!" "Okay, I'm not going to be watching you with my four eyes, the ones behind my head included."

Sarah quickly got out and grabbed a towel and wrapped it around her. She turned to Jack, "you stay there in the tub for 20 minutes until I get dressed in the other room. Jack still had his eyes closed. Sarah grabbed her clothes and ran to the other room. Jack emptied the lukewarm water, refilled it with hot water and put back his head relaxing.

Jack opened his eyes and turned off the bathtub jets and got up out of the tub and grabbed a towel and wrapped it around his waist. He looked in the tub. The bubbles were gone. He figured, yup, 20 minutes is up!

He opened the door and walked out and looked at Sarah
sitting on the bed with a blue silk dress on with gold
sparkling sandals and gold long earrings with her hair
curled and her make-up on. Jack turned to get dressed.
His towel fell. It fell fast and it fell all the way down to the
ground. Sarah stood up and looked at him standing there
naked in front of her with his hands up in the air and his
eyes and mouth wide-open.

Sarah put both her hands over her mouth and starting
laughing. She put her head back and starting laughing
harder. Jack's face turned beet red. He just stood there not
knowing if he wanted to pick up the towel or what. "Game
on!" he yelled and started chasing her around the hotel
room.   She was still laughing hysterically when he caught
her from behind and turned her around and threw her on the
bed. He fell on top of her. Still laughing, Sarah looked at
him with eyes of sparkling amusement. She put her arms
around his neck and pushed his hair back on his forehead.
Jack knew he was caught. He looked into her laughing
eyes and kissed her long and slow. In the back of his
mind, he knew that she had won. He also knew their
dinner date would be later. Much, later. Much, much later.

**Chapter 34– Anderson Memorial Hospital – "Death's
Door Knocks"**

Dr. Cooper called Emily and Sylvia into his office. "Good
morning." Emily and Sylvia each held a cup of coffee in
their hands and looked at Dr. Cooper. "Good morning."
So, team, we have another patient who admitted himself a
day or so ago. His name is Ramsey Evans. And he has the

same rash as our other patient had, Rose Davis. But his rash is more severe.

First of all, it is located between both sides of his legs and his groin area and penis and it also appears on his lower abdomen and buttocks area. Listening carefully, both Emily and Sylvia took a gulp of their coffee at the same time.

Dr. Cooper continued, "I have ordered blood tests. The nurse will be calling soon with the blood tests. So, I guess our first task for today is to evaluate the blood tests.

With that being said, please read his medical chart in its entirety before you start the tests. "I just want to give you both a head's up." "No pun intended here." Emily and Sylvia gave a little chuckle. I want to advise you to know that Mr. Ramsey Evans is a taxi-cab driver for Las Vegas. "He is married and has one son." "He told me this morning that he has had extra-marital affairs."

"We are not talking just one or two." "He mentioned 15 to 20." "Dr. Cooper looked at both Emily and Sylvia straight on with serious-looking eyes, they were call girls or prostitutes." So, let's run tests for the air-borne bat infection, along with all venereal diseases and HIV.

Dr. Cooper tapped his pen on his desk, "Okay that will be all." "Do you have any questions?" Emily and Sylvia both looked at each other. Emily spoke up, "No, I'm good!" Sylvia chimed in. "No, I'm good too!" "Okay then, please let me know the blood test results, as soon as you have them." "Thank you."

Emily and Sylvia got up and walked back into the Lavatory. Dr. Cooper picked up the phone and called Ed Johnston at *The Diamond Club Casino* to make sure he had gotten the Animal Disease Preventive Control's final report and to let him know that they had one more patient that was admitted to the hospital with the same rash.

Dr. Cooper knew that it was patient doctor confidentiality and he could not release his name.

Emily paged Dr. Cooper. Dr. Cooper picked up the hospital hallway phone and waived to another doctor down the hallway, "I'll be right there!" "We have the testing done and the final results." Dr. Cooper walked into his office. Emily and Sylvia were there. Sylvia handed Dr. Cooper the Blood Test Analysis Report.

Sylvia softly said, "It clearly shows that our new patient Ramsey Evans has the airborne bat infection which was caused by a brown bat poop. They drop dark brown feces, pellets, (guano poop). The tests also show that Mr. Ramsey has Gonorrhea. And has had the venereal disease, Gonorrhea, for some time now. Sylvia looked down at her hands. "And finally, the report also shows that Ramsey Evans is HIV/AIDS positive."

Dr. Cooper put the report on his desk, sat back in his seat and sighed. "Apparently Mr. Ramsey Evans was not completely honest with me." He indicated to me he had worn protection in his extra-marital affairs.

Emily shifted in her chair and folded her arms, "obviously not, according to the test results." "I will start an IV on Mr.

Ramsey for the bat infection and also giving him a single, oral doses of Cefixime 400 mg plus a single dose of azithromycin 1.g for the Gonorrhea. Of course, advising him to avoid all sexual contact while being treated for at least 10 days." And also advising him, because of his HIV positive status to avoid all sexual relations.

Of course, as you both know and I know, to date, there is no cure for the HIV/AIDs virus. All we can do is suggest a strict adherence to anti-retroviral therapy (ART) to slow the disease's progress. Dr. Cooper looked at Sylvia and Emily. "Very well, is there anything else?" Sylvia looked at Emily and they both shrugged. Emily and Sylvia both stood up, "No, I think we are good." Dr. Cooper got up and they all walked out to the lavatory. Dr. Cooper started walking down the corridor. "I'll keep you both updated." "The updated report for Ramsey Evans will be on the computer for both of you to read."

Dr. Cooper headed towards the elevator, 8th Floor, Ramsey Evan's room to advise him of the results. He stopped by the clerk's desk and picked up his file before he gently knocked on Ramsey's door. He saw his wife sitting in a chair next to him talking softly. Sally stood up from her chair. Dr. Cooper walked towards her and put out his hand. "Hello, I'm Dr. David Cooper, Director of Preventive Disease Immunities Department. "You must be Ramsey's wife?" Sally put her hand out and shook Dr. Cooper's hand. "Hi, I'm Sally, Ramsey's wife.

Dr. Cooper put his head down, debating on telling Ramsey by himself the tragic news or telling them both. He looked at both of them. "He looked at Ramsey, unfortunately, Mr.

Evans, I do not have good news for you. "Would you like your wife here, when I tell you what the medical outcome is?" Sally took Ramsey's hand, put it in hers and looked into his worried eyes." Ramsey squeezed Sally's hand. His face went red and he closed his eyes and the tears fell. He shook his head yes.

Dr. Cooper proceeded. "Very well." "We have run the blood tests and the Analysis Report shows that you have an airborne bat infection caused from airborne bat feces. There was a Media News Conference on this outbreak a few days ago and they have been airing it daily. "Have you been following the News Mr. Ramsey?" Ramsey shook his head yes. "Yes, I have seen the latest Radio/News broadcasts that said they were brown bats that were flying around the moon on July
4th."

Okay, well if you parked in any of *The Diamond Club Casino* garage structures and got out of your car and or taxi-cab or you were taking luggage into a casino where the bats droppings may have been, you were susceptible to the airborne infection. So, with that being said we are going to start you on a bat antidote IV.

Dr. Cooper walked to the end of the hospital bed and looked at Sally first and then Ramsey. "You also have Gonorrhea." Sally quickly pulled her hand from Ramsey's hand and held it to her chest and gasped.

 Dr. Cooper looked at her. Then looked back at the chart and continued. We have two strong oral medications that you will be taking today to get rid of that infection." You are not to have any sexual contact with anyone for at least 10 days.

Dr. Cooper stood at the end of the bed and looked directly into Mr. Ramsey's eyes. "That is not all Mr. Ramsey. He looked at Sally first and then at Ramsey seriously, holding his eye contact with him. "The final medical blood test analysis report shows, you are HIV/AIDs positive". "And as you and I both know there is no known cure for the HIV/AIDs virus to date. "We can start you on a strict adherence antiretroviral therapy (ART) to slow down the disease's progress, but that is all we can do.

Sally put her hand to her mouth and gasped again. She looked at Ramsey in both eyes and then looked at Dr. Cooper. It was too much for her. She picked up her purse and rushed out of the room. Ramsey and Dr. Cooper watched Sally run out of the hospital room. With tears still falling from Ramsey's eyes, he looked at Dr. Cooper and whispered, "I have heard enough." Ramsey closed his eyes and rolled over, not wanting to hear anything more.

Holding the medical chart with Ramsey's fatal fate, Dr. Cooper put his head down and walked out of the hospital room.

Chapter 35 -Colorado *"There's No Place Like Home"*

Doreen got up and put a white hotel robe on, walked in the bathroom, looked in the mirror. She brushed her teeth and picked up the short bob medium ash blonde wig she had bought at the mall. She put it on her bald head and walked out to the living room. She didn't see Kinsey. She went to the kitchen and looked at the note on the counter. Picked it up and read it. Ugh, she thought. "I hope that man would stay out of trouble!" He said on the note he was going to be a good boy. Kinsey had promised her he was going to stay out of trouble.

But in the back of her mind, she wondered. She opened the refrigerator and got a fruit bowl out with a ginger ale. She sat on the couch and turned on the TV. The News came on with a Las Vegas News Conference Press. *We are definitely closer to finding the killer who has been sexually assaulting prostitutes, cutting their throats and dumping them in dumpsters around Las Vegas.*

Doreen thought. "I don't want to hear this crap! She took a bite of fruit and flipped the channel. "Yes, Wheel of Fortune" She took a sip of ginger ale. "Now that's what I'm talking about!" She heard the door open and she looked towards the door. She yelled out, "Hey you?" Kinsey came in the door, dancing a gig. "You look happy!" "Where have you been?" Kinsey spun around and pulled some keys out of his pocket and put them in Doreen's lap. "Here you go dear." "It's our new car!" Doreen almost choked on her fruit. "What?" "You did what?" "Look at the keys, Babe!" "It's our new car!" She looked down and picked up the keys. There was a Cadillac emblem and a Cadillac key. "Those are your keys!"

Kinsey pulled out another set of keys from his pocket and dangled them in front of her. "And these are yours." He pulled a folded brochure from his back pocket. "Here is the brochure." "I wanted to show you which one I bought for us." Kinsey opened the brochure and pointed. "It is a pearl white Cadillac SRX Luxury Midsize SUV with tan/beige leather seats that warm up and also seats up to five people. "It's top of the line, of course. It has been ranked #7 Luxury Midsize SUV by the U.S. News and World Report."

 Doreen took the brochure and looked at it. "Wow!" "This is really nice." She reached over, hugged him and gave him a big kiss.

"I love it!" "Good for you Kinsey!" Kinsey looked into her eyes.

"No" Good for us sweetie! He pulled her close and kissed her. Doreen was going to have to keep adjusting her mind set. "Okay, he's being really good."

Doreen knew within the six-month time period the doctor had given her to survive the shitty cancer she was diagnosed with she knew she would not be able to drive.

She also knew as long as she was alive now, breathing, walking and eating as much as she could, she was going to do whatever her heart desired.

Kinsey got up and poured a drink and turned to Doreen on the couch. "Hey Love's do you want a drink? She shook her head no and looked down. "I was thinking we could go for an "early bird special" tonight. Kinsey picked up his drink and looked at her. His eyes widened and his ears perked up. He knew Doreen too well after 32 years. He also knew what her "early bird special" was. He went over to Doreen and put his hand out and she got up and followed him to the bedroom.

Doreen woke up the next morning. She felt refreshed.
Kinsey had been so sweet. Never making her feel
uncomfortable while they made love. It had been a long
time for both of them. She felt like a school girl. And he
acted like a school boy the first time with a girl. She turned
and looked at Kinsey sleeping next to her. She knew she
still loved him. She knew she wanted the second chance
with him and the kids and grandkids.

She lied there thinking of when she stormed out leaving
him in the dust. After 32 years when she found out he had
taken their pension and 401 monies, $750,000 worth and
spent nearly all of it on gambling. Doreen was the very
least infuriated. She had stomped around the kitchen
staring at him while he was looking down at his folded
fumbling hands at the kitchen table.

She screamed at him, "This is it! Kinsey! "Do you hear me
loud and clear! I am done with you and your damn
gambling!"

She had left him in the kitchen watching his false tears fall
down his cheeks. She didn't care anymore. She had had
enough. She took whatever she could get out their bank
account together and packed as much as she could in a
small U-haul and drove her and the kids to Crippled Creek
Colorado, crying all the way.

She rolled over and watched Kinsey sleeping next to her.
She remembered sitting on his bed in the run-down motel
with cheap, dirty carpet, cheap dirty curtains and a old
musty bedspread with water barely running in the bath

316

room. A tear ran down her cheek. She had never known
how desperate Kinsey had become and how fast his life had
deteriorated from the time she had left him.

Another tear ran down her cheek. She thought about her
vows she had made to him 37 years ago. *For Richer or
for Poorer, In Sickness and in Health, Until Death Do
"Us" Part."* She knew she only had six months left at the
most. She wanted to make it right with Kinsey.

She believed he wanted to make it right for her and the kids
too. They were, after up their years, 59 years old. They
weren't 25 anymore. They had shared a life time together
with three great kids.

Kinsey opened his eyes, yawned and looked at Doreen.
"Hello, my love." He put his hand to her face and stroked
her cheek. She looked at him in the eyes, contemplating
what she wanted to say. "Kinsey, I was thinking." "I was
thinking, we could drive back to Colorado together." He
looked at her and wiped away the tears on her cheek and
whispered, "I think that sounds like a great game plan,
baby cakes." "I've already called my boss at the Shuttle
and told him, "I quit!" Doreen held his hand on her face
and looked into his eyes. "I love you Kinsey." "I never
stopped loving you."

Kinsey pulled her close to him and held her for a moment
in silence. He wanted to reassure her he was not going
back to gambling.

"I never stopped loving you either Doreen." "You always
were and always will be in my heart."   I made a promise to

317

me and to you Doreen, the moment I saw you in the bar. I am not going back to gambling. I want to spend the rest of our time together with our kids and grandkids." He squeezed her lightly and kissed her on her forehead.

Doreen kissed him on his tear-stained cheek. She finally felt safe.

Kinsey looked at Doreen. She had her eyes close. She was sleeping again. He gently rolled over and sat up on the bed. He picked up his NIXON watch on the bed stand and looked at it.

 It was 9:00 a.m. He got out of bed and grabbed the white hotel robe and slippers and walked down to the kitchen and started the coffee and looked in the refrigerator. They packed the refrigerator   eggs, bacon, orange juice fruit and bread by the toaster. Perfect! He'd whip them up a quick breakfast when Doreen got up.

He got a cup down and poured himself some coffee and went to the living room and flipped on the TV channel to News. He sat there sipping his coffee and watching. *"They have finally identified DNA that has matched the killer that was sexually assaulting prostitutes, slashing their necks with a Army Engraving Knife and dumping their bodies in dumpsters around Las Vegas." He was identified as a taxi-cab driver who worked in Las Vegas for 5 years, was married with a son. "His name was Ramsey Evans." Police identified it was Ramsey Evan's DNA that was received from a blood test that was done at the Anderson Memorial Hospital. An Army engraved knife he carried in his taxi-cab which had his initials was found with blood DNA on it from all four victims. That is all for now."* He flipped the channel thinking, "Dam bastard, hope he gets what he deserves!"

Doreen moseyed down the hall and poured a cup of coffee. She walked over and sat next to Kinsey on the couch. The "Wheel of Fortune." "I like Wheel of Fortune."

There was a knock at the door. Kinsey got up and opened the door. "Come this way please." There was a Bell Boy pushing a large gold handled cart with red velvet bottom wearing white gloves. Doreen turned and saw lots of luggage bags on the cart. "Right here please." The Bell Boy started taking the new luggage bags off the cart.

Doreen got up and walked over to Kinsey. "What's going on? Kinsey took a sip of his coffee. Well, my dear, I bought us Louis Vuitton luggage the other day when I was shopping for SUVs, so we could pack our things and head on home to Cripple Creek Colorado. We have one large bag, one travel hanging bag and a large duffle bag and a smaller Alize Poche bag for your make up and one for my tooth paste, razor, shampoo, personal items.

Kinsey knew she could put her medicine in it if she wanted. "Wow!" Kinsey took a purse off the hanging rack and handed it to her. And this, my dear is for you. She took the purse and held it twirling it around and looking at it. "Oh, my, goodness, blazing Hot Dogs!" She put it on her arm kissed him on the lips. She knew Kinsey had spent a pretty penny for this luggage. She also knew that the real Louis Vuitton was very expensive. The Louis Vuitton Monogram purse alone was $1285.00.

The Bell Boy turned. "Will that be all, sir?" "Just a moment, please." Kinsey quickly went to the bedroom and pulled a $100 out of his pocket. He came down the hall and handed to the Bell Boy. "Thank you." "That will be all." The Bell boy looked at the bill and stuffed it in his pocket. "Thank you, Sir." "Have a wonderful day!" The Bell boy tipped his hat to Doreen who was now walking around the luggage surveying it.

Doreen eyes lit up. She looked at Kinsey. "I want to go home!" "I want to go home today!" "And, I want to go home "Now!" "I called Alice at home and then I called Melody and Kinsey, Jr. They all want us, you and me, to come home.

 Kinsey looked at Doreen's folding entwined fingers together saying "please," and her begging eyes. He couldn't and he wouldn't say "no." He chuckled and threw up his hand in the air and looked down at the floor and then back up at her. "Yes!" "Yes!" Let's go home!

Doreen ran over and hugged him, gave him a smacker kiss on the lips, then hurried down the hallway. Kinsey grabbed the suitcases and started lining them up one by one in the bedroom for her to pack. Doreen came flying out of the bathroom with an armful full, her medicine bag, toothpaste, toothbrush, cosmetics, shampoo, conditioner, throwing them on the bed ready for packing.

Kinsey stood there watching her grab everything as fast and she could and fling it in the bags. He could tell she was in a hurry to get home. He pulled a large suite case out and opened it. "Oh, by the way I did a little shopping myself."

After buying the Cadillac, I went back to the mall to and
bought some more clothes. He grabbed some out the
luggage bag and headed towards the bathroom.   Doreen
looked quickly, but was too absorbed in getting all her new
stuff in from her bags in the new suitcases. She wanted to
go home.

Kinsey went to the kitchen and loaded some snacks, water
and some soda in his new duffle bag. He called the Bell
boy downstairs to come pick up their luggage. He walked
down the hallway and walked into the bedroom. Tip toed
into the bathroom to see if there was anything they forgot.
Doreen had everything already packed. She had crawled in
bed to take a nap. She seemed to get tired more often and
she needed rest.

Kinsey walked to her bedside and took the blanket and put
it over her. He quietly got his clothes out of his suitcase
and dressed, putting on a new pair of jeans, a polo shirt, a
new pair of socks and his new Bahamas tennis shoes.
There was something about his new clothes that made him
feel like he was somebody. Not that the clothes made him
who he was, but they just added a sense of fresh, well-
being after feeling like a bum, wearing the same old clothes
for so long. He picked up each piece of luggage and took it
to the front. He put his hands in his pocketed jeans, opened
the curtains and looked out the window viewing Las Vegas
for the last time. In the back of his mind, he knew he still
had the itch to stick a bill in a machine and play.

But then he would think of Doreen and her circumstances
and say "no". He knew now that he found her, he wanted

to keep her. He also knew she didn't have much time and he also knew he needed to kick his addiction.

 There was a light knock at the door and he let the Bell boy and told him that Valet had the keys under his name and to take all the luggage bags to the Bell Desk downstairs to store. The Bell boy gave him a yellow receipt and said very well. Kinsey gave me a $20. Then he said, wait give me the $20 back and he took out a $100 Benjamin Franklin and gave it to him. The Bell boy put the $100 in his pocket and thanked him while loading the luggage on the cart.

Thirty minutes later, Doreen came into the front room wearing a blond short bob wig, wearing jeans, tennis shoes and a Tommy Hilfiger white light cotton T-shirt. Kinsey looked up at her, flipping the TV off, "Ready to go home now?" "Yep, "I am ready!" Kinsey called the Bell boy downstairs and told him to have valet bring the Cadillac up and load the car with the luggage.

Kinsey took Doreen's hand and went to the door of the suite. He looked around the suite one more time. Doreen climbed in and the first thing she smelled was "new car". Beige leather seats with lots of room in the back.

The Valet boy opened Doreen's door on the passenger side and let her in and closed it. He then opened the driver's door and Kinsey got in. Kinsey turned the navigation on, GPS and said "Crippled Creek, CO". The navigation female voice came on "Las Vegas to Cripple Creek, CO, 776.7 miles, 11 hours, 51 minutes. Kinsey had already gotten a map and had highlighted the routes.

Kinsey knew they would be stopping whenever Doreen need to rest so it was going to be a long, but fun ride. He looked over at Doreen who was putting one of her purses down by her feet on the floor and adjusting her seatbelt. "Kinsey turned and patted her knee, you ready to go home honey?" Doreen put her hand on his. "Yes, I'm ready!" Kinsey put the Caddy in gear and drove down the strip one last time. He looked at all the billboards and hotels.

After several miles Kinsey read the road sign **"Leaving Las Vegas"**. He adjusted his rearview mirror and looked back one more time in the rearview mirror. The city behind him was slowly inching it's self away from him. Slowly, becoming farther, and farther away.

All his tormented, lonely days and nights of wasting his life of staying in a cheap dumpy motel, driving a Las Vegas Shuttle and gambling in Las Vegas of five years were fading. He knew that this was his second chance. He knew he still loved Doreen and the kids and that's all that mattered. He turned and looked at Doreen. She had her seat back with her eyes closed, resting. He smiled and thought, "I won my prize!" "I won my real prize!" "I'm going home!" **"What plays in Vegas, stays in Vegas!"**

Chapter 36- Resignation Time

Ed Johnson made his routine casino rounds. He walked back into his office and saw Sally sitting in his office sitting in one of the chairs crying hysterically. "Ed's face became concerned. He put his hands on her shoulders." He knelt down beside her and took her hands from her red swollen face. "What is it Sally? "What is it Sally? She

323

looked up at him and blurted out. "It's Ramsey." He's in the hospital and the Doctor told me he has a bat disease and gonorrhea.

Ed took the chair next to her and put his arms around her shoulders to comfort her. "Oh my God, Sally, I am so sorry." She looked at him again and burst into tears. "Not only that, the Doctor said he is HIV/AID positive." Ed shifted backwards in his chair in shock. He didn't know what to say.

 "I am so sorry Sally. Ed handed her some Kleenex. She took it, wiped her tears and looked up at him again.

"Mr. Johnson, I need my job back. "Would you consider giving it back to me please?"

Ed looked at her, knowing she would need her job to support her and her son and there was no future in California. Ed shuffled some papers on his desk. "Of course, Sally. Of, course. You know you have always been a good employee." The phone rang. Ed picked it up. Sally sat in the chair, listening to Ed on the phone. "Yes. Yes. I see. Thank you for your call." He hung up and got up and walked over to Sally.

Holding her Kleenex and purse Sally got up from her chair. Ed put his hand on her shoulder. "I want you to go home and rest. Take a few days off to evaluate your situation get your affairs in order. I will see Monday morning. Sally wiped her tears again. Sally composed herself, "I'm sorry Ed, I didn't have anyone to go to." Ed looked at her as she walked towards to glass doors to the casino. "No worries,

Sally, I'm here for you. If you need anything, please call me."

Sally wiped her nose. "Okay, okay thank you Mr. Johnson. I appreciate your help."

Dr. Cooper sat in his office going over the medical records on his desk for the day. The phone rang. He picked it up. "Yes." "Yes." "I'll be right there." He ran out of his office. Emily and Sylvia were standing at a station working on some lab testing when they both looked up at him. They could see that there was something wrong by the look on his face. As he was running out of the lavatory he yelled. "Emily, Sylvia we have a Code Blue, come with me!"

Emily and Sylvia looked at each other and took their blue hospital plastic gloves and eye goggles off and started running with Dr. Cooper down the hall. They all got to the elevator and he pushed the Elevator to the 8th Floor for Isolated Patients. Somewhat out of breath, he told Emily and Sylvia quickly while in the elevator. "They can't find Ramsey Evans anywhere!" Apparently, Mr. Ramsey threw his hospital gown on the floor and dressed and his bed was in disarray everywhere. Hospital Security has been notified to do a search of the entire hospital.

Dr. Cooper, Emily and Sylvia went over to the clerk's desk. "Wanda stood up." Dr. Cooper looked down the hallway to his Mr. Ramsey's room. There was chaos and talking commotion everywhere. Doctors and nurses walking quickly down the halls in all directions. Hospital Security, with their blue shirts and dark pants and hats were roaming the halls, looking in rooms, trying not to put the patients in a panic mode. Wanda looked at Dr. Cooper with worried eyes.

Nurse Shoemaker who was on the early shift went in to check on Mr. Ramsey early this morning around 6:30 a.m. and found Mr. Ramsey gone from the room with the hospital bed disheveled and his hospital gown on the floor and his walk-in clothes gone. Dr. Cooper turned to Sylvia and Emily and told them. Let's start with the EXIT Staircases. Sylvia, you take this Floor, 8, EXIT Staircase. I'll take EXIT Staircase 7 and Emily you take EXIT Staircase 6. T

There are four hallways with four EXIT Staircases on each Floor. If you find anything, pick up one of the hospital phones and say S8 for Sylvia North, East, South or West or E6 for Emily, North, East, West and I will do the same with DC7- "Code Blue", "Code Blue" North, East, West, south two times on the hospital phone. Dr. Cooper talking quickly, he turned to Wanda who was standing and listening to every word. "Wanda did you hear this?

Wanda stood with wide-eyes listening carefully. "Yes, Dr. Cooper." "I heard every word." If anyone of us calls on the hospital phone and says any of these words, you are to call Hospital Security immediately and have them meet us on the EXIT Staircase that would be a "Code Blue Alert." "I'll meet you back here in 30 minutes. "Got it?" Emily both stared at him. "Yes, Got it!" They all took off running down the hallways and EXIT Staircases.

Twenty minutes later, Dr. Cooper picked up the phone and said DC7 – "Code Blue". Hospital Security came to EXIT Staircase 7. Dr. Cooper looked over the railing. Ramsey was hanging from his hospital bed sheet. He had taken his belt and wrapped it tight around the sheet on the railing and then tied it around his neck and flung himself over the railing.

Dr. Cooper stayed and waited for the Las Vegas Police and Homicide to arrive. The Hospital Building Security secured all EXITs in the Hospital. Twenty minutes later the Las Vegas Police arrived with the Investigation and Homicide Department. Dr. Cooper looked down at Ramsey Evans hanging. He thought of Sally, Ramsey's wife and his son. He put his hands in his side pockets and shook his head, "such a deadly waste." "Dr. Cooper gave the Police, Homicide and Investigation all the information they needed and slowly walked back to his office.

Chapter 37– "Get Better Girlfriend!"

Megan and Bethany stood at the end of Stephanie's hospital bed at Los Angeles Memorial Hospital. Stephanie's Mom had called and said they had admitted Stephanie through the ER when she got home and she had an infection. Of course, as soon as Stephanie told Dr. John Wiley she was in Vegas. He knew he would have to do a biopsy and blood tests for the bat virus. Sure enough! That was what it was. She was to be in isolation for five days on a drip IV Fungus antidote and then take the antidote pills for 90 days. She was lucky. She is young and had a good immune system to fight the systems that can occur, including fever, chest pain, chills cough, fever, and joint. The more serious side is she could have lung disease and pneumonia and ultimately death would prevail. But once again, she is young and has a good health chart.

Megan touched her foot and said "Hey?" Stephanie opened her eyes. She looked at Megan and Bethany and smiled. "Hey, how is my Las Vegas BFFs?" Bethany had a vase of flowers. She put them next to Stephanie.

"I brought these for you sunshine!" Megan walked over to Stephanie and handed her an 8 x 10 picture framed. I thought you would like this. Stephanie took the picture and looked at it and started laughing. It was a picture of her and Bethany in the pool with Johnny and Bret. It was sketched in colored pencils.

Bethany was wearing a two-piece white bathing suit with big red polka dots all over it with a red polka dot headband. Stephanie had a hot pink two-piece bathing suit with hot pink ties on her hips with a gold belly button ring and hot pink round wood earrings and big round hot and a hot pink wooden balled bracelet

She was relaxing with her back against the side of the pool holding a 1 1/2 ft. hot pink flamingo souvenir Yard drink. Johnny was wearing blue long bathing trunks with yellow polka dots holding a 1 1/2 ft. football Yard drink. And Bret was wearing orange bathing trunks with green grasshoppers all over it. It had on the top of the sketch. **What plays in Vegas, stays in Vegas!*** *"To Stephanie, my BFF Forever!"*

Megan looked at her and said, "I thought this could be my next upcoming fashion line." They all started busting up! Stephanie wiped a tear away from the loud laugher. "It would be from Queen Cleopatra!" She reached over and took Megan's hand that was resting on her bed railing. "You're the best Megan!" "This is great! "I love it!" And they all started laughing again.

They all chatted about how she was doing and then they reminisced about their trip to Las Vegas, *The Diamond Club Casino* and how great it was with the three "New Jersey boys." They all said they got a call from them and they talked about each conversation they had. It definitely was a girl's day at the Los Angeles Memorial Hospital.

Chapter 38– *The Diamond Club Casino* - "Time to Move On!"

After Sally had left, Ed picked up the phone and called HR, Roberta Wallace and talked to her about the situation and got the legal advice he needed. He asked Roberta to bring in a Temp Administrative Assistant for two weeks. The News and Radio Media had announced Sally Evan's husband, Ramsey Evans as being the killer and the suicide, he knew, as bad as it was, it would not be good publicity to have Sally Evans and her family, who would be eventually exposed to the News and Radio Media, to continue working for *The Diamond Club Casino.*

Before he hung up, he got another call and put on hold. He picked up the other line. "Oh, Hi Sally." "Yes, I did hear."

"I am so sorry for you and your son, Sally." "Yes." "Yes." "I understand." "Sally, please call Roberta Wallace in HR at phone number XXX-XXXX, she will be able to help you with your paycheck and other paper work. "It was a pleasure working with you Sally." "You and your son take care."

Ed clicked the other button on the phone and got back to Roberta on the other line. "Yes, Roberta. As a matter of fact, that was Sally Evans on the other line. She has decided to move back east with her sister. Because of the circumstances at hand, she realizes that staying in Las Vegas would eat her and her son alive. So, she gave her resignation starting today. No two-week notice. She will be calling you so we can handle her paycheck and final paperwork. Who? Ed took his pen and wrote down on the notepad in front of him."

"Rose Davis?

"What?"

Roberta continued, "Sally gave you her name and number when she decided to leave before this tragedy happened?

"Yes, Roberta can you please call her today and schedule an interview time for 1:00 p.m. today. We definitely need to hire someone soon.

You have two candidates.

"Okay let's schedule them for today, one at 2:00 p.m. and the Rose Davis at 3:30 p.m. Thank you, Roberta. Have a great day!"

Chapter 39 – Rebecca' Rehearsal – "Dance with Me"

Rebecca came out of Ben's room with Ben's long tailed blue shirt hanging loosely on her and tip toed down the hall to the kitchen for a cup of coffee. Grant looked at Rose. "I think I hear someone in the kitchen." He patted her on the leg and got up from the bed. He wanted to give her some privacy to get dressed. "I'll see you in the kitchen."

Rebecca poured her a cup of coffee and observed the kitchen table with a laptop computer and sheets of paper all over it. Grant came up behind her and sat down at his computer and looked up at her. "Good morning, Rebecca"

Rebecca walked behind the kitchen Island, put her elbows on the counter cupping her coffee and took a sip. Grant looked up at her. She had that Alice in Wonderland Chemise smile. "Good morning, Grant." He looked down at his computer and started typing. "And what, may I ask, is on your agenda today?"

Rebecca took another sip of coffee. "Well, I'm going to go to my first Dance Rehearsal at *The Gala Casino* today." "I have one week of training and then I start the nightly performance." "They are premiering two shows a night Monday through Friday." "One starts at 7:00 p.m., and the other at 9:00 p.m." "They each last one one-half hours each."

Rose walked in dressed, stood behind Rebecca and poured another cup of coffee in her coffee cup. She turned and put her arms up on the Island holding her coffee cup and took a sip. Grant looked up and smiled at her. And then he looked at Rebecca. They looked like two twins, identical twins, purring, smiling and happy.

Rebecca turned and smiled at Rose, "Good morning sunshine!" "I was thinking that you could come with me to the first rehearsal with me and watch in the audience. I am sure they would allow it, if I told them you were my sister."

She winked at Rose. Rose looked at Grant who was suddenly involved in his work, shuffling through the mass of papers scattered on the kitchen table.

Rose took another sip of coffee. "Sure." "Let's do it!" Let's go over there early, find a breakfast place there, have breakfast and then go." Rebecca put her hand in the air and high-fived her. "Let's do it girlfriend!" "Ben's working all day at the car dealership today."

She put her coffee cup down and turned and started walking down the hallway. "I'm going to get dressed." Rose yelled at her. I'll meet you at the elevator in 5." Rose left Grant in his thoughts with work and walked down and grabbed her purse and put her shoes on. She brushed her teeth and gave Grant a quick kiss on the check and headed towards the door. Grant typing like a mad man, yelled. "I'll talk to you later Rose!" "You and Rebecca have a good day!"

Rose closed the door and stood at the elevator waiting for
Rebecca. Rebecca closed the door quietly behind her and
stood next to Rose at the elevator. They both got in and
Rose pushed Casino Floor. She looked at Rebecca. "I am
so excited for your first dance rehearsal." She quickly
hugged her. "I am so happy for you Rebecca!"

They walked *The Gala Casino* and found a food court that
had all kinds of different foods. There was a French
Restaurant in the court. They both ordered an omelet and
some orange juice and sat down and girl chatted and then
headed down the hall to the auditorium. They looked at all
the shops along the long purple, orange, yellow, green, red
colored carpeted hallway with beautiful butterflies and
flowers. Rebecca pointed to a store. It was *Juan Paul's
Fine Jewelry*.

Rebecca grabbed Rose's hand, "let's go in for a minute."
Before she could say "no", they were in the store. Pierre,
Juan-Paul's brother was helping a customer. He glanced
up and smiled and gave a small waive. Rebecca looked
down at the wedding rings. "Look Rose!"

She pointed to a ring that was square with two small
diamonds on each side. Juan-Paul walked out from the
back area, smiled and walked towards them. "And how are
you two beautiful ladies doing today? He extended his
hand out to Rose first. Hesitating, she smiled and gave him
her hand. He bent down, and kissed her hand, all the while
looking up at her green eyes. "It is a pleasure to see you
again." Rose felt herself blush. She withdrew her hand
and looked down at the jewelry case. Then he took
Rebecca's hand and said the same, my pleasure.

Rose held her purse with both hands in front swinging it a little. Rebecca smiled, "we are doing great! Juan-Paul looked at Rose looking down at a ring. "See anything you like pretty ladies?" Rose looked up. Rebecca pointed to the square ring and Juan Paul took his key and opened the case and pulled out the ring and placed it on the glass counter. Rebecca and Rose's eyes grew wide. Juan-Paul took the ring out of its case. "Try it on!" Rebecca grabbed the ring and put it on her left fourth wedding ring finger. "Oh, it's too small."

Rebecca turned to Rose handing her the ring. "Try it on Rose!" "Try it on!" Being a little shy, Rose looked at Juan-Paul and took the ring put it on her left fourth wedding ring. It fit perfectly. She held her hand up in the air and smiled. "It's beautiful." They all looked at the ring on Rose's finger and commented on how beautiful it shined with all the colors of the rainbow.

Rose took it off and handed it back to Juan-Paul. He held the ring looking at it carefully and said softly. "This is an exquisite ring." "It has firestones which are very rare and have a true quality of the all the colors of the rainbow." Rose looked at Juan-Paul. "It's very lovely." "Thank you for showing us." She nudged Rebecca. "Come on, we are going to be late." Rebecca blurted out. "Today's my first dance rehearsal at *The Gala Casino* auditorium for the *"Enchanted Gems"* Performance. Jean Paul watched the girls hurriedly scurry out the door.

Rose took a seat in one of the red chairs nine rows back behind a group of people that where in the front with their note pads. The Dance Instructor stood on stage and looked at all of them. He started surveying each one of them carefully. The pianist went played the tune Dun dun dun da on the keys. The Dance instructor looked at the cast on the stage holding a "My name is Dominic Julius and my assistant here with me Cache' Sabin worked with me for six years now. Before we came to Las Vegas, I "We have the testing done and the final results." "Cache and I worked in Paris together for 13 years.

We are both the Dance Captains for *The Gala Casino* Premier of the performance, *"The Enchanted Gems."* His hands waved up and down in the air. Please, please everyone sit on the stage with your legs crossed and listen.

Let me start with, you will be working, six nights a week, 52 weeks a year, the red velvet main curtain rises promptly at 7:00 p.m. and 9:00 p.m. to present the longest-running Las Vegas stage spectacular, *"The Enchanted Gems"* Performance, which is noted for its over-the-top costumes, enormous sets and special effects. Dancers are expected to learn complicated routines quickly.

You all will be wearing at one time or another or even several times on the stage hundreds of dollars of rhinestones and balancing huge headdresses down endless flights of stairs with the poise and grace that many a supermodel would envy.

 All of you here sitting in front of me have been chosen. We hold auditions twice a year. The first one being in July of which is why you are all here. And the second one in January in Las Vegas, New York, L.A. and several other locations. Once everyone is hired, it takes one month of rehearsals to train the new hires. The cast has 84 performers; 7 principal dancers, 12 principal/chorus singers, 17 male dancers, 23 female dancers and 25 showgirls.

All Las Vegas showgirls must have certain attributes. All female performers must be a height of 5' 8" without shoes. You all were chosen here because you possess a talent for ballet. We start with a series of basic ballet turns and dancers who can't stay on the beat or don't have the basic technique are quickly eliminated.

Dominic walked back and forth on the stage and looked at each of them. You will be expected to learn many complicated routines quickly during the audition, showing your ability in all forms of dance. We're looking for dancers who have strong training in ballet, jazz and contemporary dance – that will give us a balance and line when wearing as much as 19 pounds of costume.
In addition to height, dance technique and high kicks, we are also looking for performers who have something that makes them stand out, weather that's a great smile or a terrific personality.

Finally, after all the dance combinations and all the eliminations, those of you who are left are asked to come back and line up with the current cast for a callback to how everybody fits together. Dominic waved his hands up in the air to rise.

"Okay then! "Chop! "Chop! Everyone up and fall into three even lines. Dominic pointed at Cache'. If you have any questions or any other concerns, Cache' will be happy to help. She will be your Dance Captain, trainer for the first month. I will be observing you individual from the theater audience row up front, watching you closely, making notes. "Okay!" "I want everyone to relax and enjoy." "Not to say it will be tough, but I know you will give it your best! "Good luck to you!" Dominic walked off the stage and Cache' began her instructions.

Chapter 40 – *"Rose's are Red, Violet's are Blue"* – Will you be mine?

Grant got up. He needed a break from sitting. He grabbed a bottle of water out of the refrigerator and walked to the bedroom to get his watch and wallet off the bed table. He thought he would step out and grab something to eat before he went back to the kitchen table. He felt good about his progress on the audit.

He walked down the hall to his bedroom. He opened the curtains and let the sun in. He stretched his arms in the air and yawned and walked over to the bed table. He noticed some cards on the floor and he picked them up. One was Rose's Driver's license and one was some sort of business card. He glanced at it. It said *Juan-Paul's Fine Jewelry* on the front.

Grant flipped it over. It read in small writing. *"It was a pleasure meeting you Rose." "Come by and see me!"* He read it again. Then he flipped the card over again and read the front again, *"Juan -Paul's Fine Jewelry*. His heart skipped a beat. He held it flipping it up and down, his mind was racing. "When did she meet this guy?" "Did she meet him before me?" "She never mentioned this guy." All he knew is he didn't like it.

He took a quick shower and then put the business card and the Driver's license in his wallet. He went and got a quick bite to eat. And then he made his way to *The Gala Casino*. He walked around the shop areas. He found the jewelry store. *Juan-Paul's Fine Jewelry*. He casually walked in and nonchalantly started looking around. Juan Paul came out from the back. "May I help you?" Grant looked at him. Casually seeing what his competition was all about.

"My name is Juan Paul, how can I help you? Juan Paul was very handsome. French accent from the way he talked. Very well dressed and no doubt, very good looking. Grant was not going to pussy-foot around. He wanted to know. "I was wondering if someone came into your jewelry store named Rose." Grant lied. "She would have been looking for a small heart necklace for her Grandma Nana Meme."

Juan-Paul looked at Grant square in the eyes for several minutes. He knew this gentleman was lying. He knew Rose would not be in "his" jewelry shop looking for her grandmother a necklace. His shop was a very high-end shop for people who had money. He knew Rose would probably not have the resources to spend that much money on a necklace for her grandmother. Juan Paul walked to the end of the counter. Grant followed him. "As a matter of fate she was here this morning.

Juan Paul scratched his chin and if he was "really" thinking about if he remembered. He knew very well he would never forget Rose and her beauty that captured him from the moment he saw her at the Italian restaurant with her

338

friend Rebecca. "Mmm, "Yes, she and her friend Rebecca where here."

Juan- Paul looked at Grant again and smiled. Juan-Paul thought he would give Grant a run for his money. Juan-Paul opened the case and put the black box with the three carat firestone diamond with two small diamonds on each side of the ring on the counter.

He looked at Grant and then looked down at the ring on the counter and then looked back up at Grant. "She seemed to like this ring a lot." She put it on her left hand, fourth wedding finger, and it fit her perfectly."

Grant eyed Juan-Paul closely. He also was going to give Juan-Paul a run for his money. He looked at the ring and then looked back up at Juan-Paul, "May I?" Juan-Paul put both of his hands on the counter and looked Grant square in the eyes and said "Sure, be my guest." Juan- Paul told him how the ring was a firestone ring of superb quality and how it displayed all the colors of the rainbow exquisitely.

Grant looked at Juan-Paul and asked to for the Jewelry Loupe. Grant holding the Jewelry Loupe looked at each diamond closely. He looked at Juan-Paul again. "Is this a 10X Loupe? Juan-Paul smiled, "Only the best!" Grant held up the Jewelry Loup and rotated the ring to see each diamond. Juan-Paul watched Grant looking closely at the diamonds. "The ring has FL/IF (Internally) Flawless diamond quality."

Grant was beginning to dislike this guy's perfectly French accent. Grant put the ring back in the black box on the glass

counter.   He looked squarely again in Juan-Paul's eyes.
"How much?" Juan Paul thought, okay here we go." Juan-
Paul looked at Grant studying him closely. "Obviously this
guy knows Rose and knows her well, he thought." He was
going to see how well this gentleman standing on the other
side of the jewelry counter really knew her. *"$10,000
dollars"*

Grant, still looking at him square in the eyes, didn't flinch.
"I'll give you $9,000 cash today." Juan-Paul, still looking
Grant square in the eyes, took a step back. He crossed his
arms against his chest and then asked, "All Cash?" "Grant
looked him square in the eyes again, "Yes!" "Oui!" "All
Cash today!" Juan-Paul put his hand out. "I believe we
have a deal!"

Grant raised his lips slowly in a smile. Grant pulled $300
out of his pocket and handed it to Juan- Paul. Here is a
deposit to hold the ring. Grant started walking towards the
jewelry entrance door, turned back and said, "I'll be back
today with rest of the cash."

"Please wrap three boxes in silver foil for me. "Make two
of them being slightly larger than the ring box. Each one is
with a silver bow." Juan-Paul watched Grant leave,
waiving two fingers over his brow at him, in a "yes", "I got
it fashion." After Grant left, Juan Paul picked up the ring
and looked at it. The ring's exquisite beauty was stunning.
"My beautiful Rose will be wearing my special ring."
"But, just not from me."

Grant walked out of the Jewelry shop. He took Juan Paul's
business card out from his back pocket and looked at it

again. He started laughing and flipped in the trash. "Bye"
Bye" Asshole! **"What plays in Vegas, stays in Vegas!"**
"Rose is my Rose!"

Rose's phone rang and she quickly got up and walked out
the door and push answer on her cell phone. "Yes." "Yes,
this is Rose." Yes, I can be there today at 3:00 p.m. Rose
called Grant. Grant picked his cell phone and answered it.
"Hi Rose." "I didn't want to disturb you but a Roberta
called from HR at *The Diamond Club Casino* and said that
Ed Johnson the General Manager there wanted me to come
in for an interview for an Administrative Assistant position.
Grant sat there holding the cell phone for a moment
deciding what he wanted to say.

"Oh, I forgot to mention that "yes" one of my Clients, Ed
Johnson, is looking for an Administration Assistant and I
gave Sally his secretary your name. Rose shifted the phone
to her other ear.

"Well Roberta Wallace called me from HR and they want
me to come in at 3:00 p.m. today for an interview." "I'm
going to swing by and get a dress out of your closet." "I
promise not to disturb you. "I really hope you get the job
Rose!" "Me too!" "Thanks Grant!" "You know I really
need this job!"

Rose walked *into The Diamond Club Casino* at 2:45 p.m.
She approached a girl sitting at a desk. "Can I help you?
"Yes, my name is Rose Davis." I went to HR and talked
with a Roberta Wallace and she said to come down here to
interview with Ed Johnson for the Administration Assistant
position. The girl looked down at her papers on her desk
and got up. "Yes, yes, right this way. "Mr. Johnson, Rose

Davis is here. Ed stood up. Please come in and take a seat. Ed waived at Jennifer to leave, "Thank you Jennifer." Ed took a seat behind his desk. He looked at Rose. "So, Rose tell me about yourself and your work experience."

Rose looked at Mr. Johnson and began to speak slowly and softly. The only real experience she could really tell him was she took computer classes such as Microsoft word, Excel, as Google certified and typed 98 words per minute in high school and she made all As, in all her all her classes. Ed looked at her. She was pretty and smart. Ed began to tell her about the position. "It is a 9:00 a.m. to 5:00 p.m. position, maybe some 6:00 p.m. days." "Just depends on how busy we are." "Are you good with that?"

Rose pulled her clutch purse tighter with both hands. "Yes sir." "I am very dependable." "I am not married and I don't have any children." Ed continued. "Jennifer at the front desk outside my office is a temp from an agency." She will be training you for two weeks.

"I am looking for someone who is smart." His eyes shifted over his black rimmed glasses. "And from what I hear from you, you are smart." Also, I am looking for someone who is personable, pleasant, and congenial and likes working with lots of people.

"As you can see, there are lots of people who come and go every day from *The Diamond Club Casino*." "I need someone, Rose, that is going to stay and work with me side-by-side long term." Not someone who comes to Las Vegas and then decides they don't want to live in Las Vegas anyone. Rose looked at him square in the eyes. "Yes sir, I understand." Ed sat back in his chair and studied Rose for a moment. She was young, younger than Sally. But he decided he liked her. She was smart and fresh. The other two candidates were not as polished as Rose and they didn't seem to have the working qualities and requirements he was looking for.

Ed knew he had to make a decision. He took off his glasses, put them on his desk and looked at Rose again. He sat forward and entwined his fingers together. "Okay, Rose from what I see and what you have told me." "I like you." "It is your first impression that I like."

Ed stood up and quickly pulled up his trousers putting his hands on his waistline. Rose quickly stood up, dropping her clutch purse of which she bent down and picked it up. Her face beet red, she stood up and quickly put her hand out. "Thank you, Mr. Johnson." "I promise I won't disappoint you."

Ed looked at Rose in with her green eyes flashing, smiled and shook her hand. Ed proceeded out his office door to Jennifer's desk. Jennifer looked up from her computer. "Ms. Rose Davis will be starting on Monday." Please have her fill out all paperwork with, HR Roberta Wallace, before she leaves. "Jennifer you will be training her for two weeks." Jennifer looked at Rose and put her hand out. "Congratulations Ms. Rose Davis!" Welcome to *The Diamond Club Casino.*"

Grant picked up the ring. Juan Paul's brother Pierre was there to help him close the deal. Juan- Paul was nowhere in sight. Grant got home and put the small bag with the three boxes in his bottom dresser drawer. He went to the kitchen table and sat down and put his glasses on and opened his laptop and got right back into his work.

His cell phone rang. He looked at it to see who was calling. "Hello Patsy!" "It's been awhile since I've talked to you. "How are you doing?" "Hi Grant." "Yes, it has been awhile." "First of all, I called to see how you're doing? And second, I wanted to let you know, I am selling Mom's and Dad's house and moving to Florida. I have been offered a Nursing Director position.

Grant sat back listening. "Congratulations Sis!" "I am so proud of you!" Patsy sighed on the phone. "Yaw, it's a big commitment and job." "I will be supervising the nursing staff and overseeing patient care as well as administrative functions such as record keeping and budgeting."

"I wanted to know if you wanted to buy the house back before I officially sold it." She knew and Grant knew also, according to Mom and Dad's Will and Last Testament whomever wanted to keep the house the other child (Grant or Patsy – the only two children) would have to buy the other out with the funds from the Will and Last Testament.

"So, Grant, I was wondering if you have any interest in keeping Mom's and Dad's home?" "You know they lived in it for 29 years and it was paid off before their accident." Grant sat back in the kitchen chair, his mind pondering a moment. "You know, Patsy, I think I am good with you selling it." "Even though there were a lot of good memories growing up, I don't have any real interest in moving back and living there anymore. It would only bring back bad memories of New Years' Day when they both were killed in the automobile accident by a drunk driver."

Not only that, but the two years you and I spent suing the guy that killed them while he was intoxicated over the limit by four times the legal alcohol amount to drive. Patsy, sighed another sigh of relief. "Then we are both good with me selling it?"

"Yes, Patsy, go ahead and sell it!"

"Any of the final proceeds will be split between us."

"Yes, Grant I'm good with that! Yes, any of the final proceeds will be split between us." Grant shifted in his chair.

"I am so happy for you Patsy." Patsy put the phone to the other ear.

"So, is there anyone special in your life?" Grant smiled.

"As a matter of fact, I am glad you asked me that. Yes, there is!" Her name is Rose Davis. Patsy giggled.

"And how did you meet this, Rose Davis?"

Grant could hear Patsy teasing him, her only brother. Of course, she had too. He got up and got a bottle of water out of the refrigerator. He started laughing. "Oh, I see, you want more details!" Well, to be honest with you, I haven't been dating her very long, but I bought her an engagement ring today and I am going to ask the big question, so I guess you can say, "She's the one!" Patsy really started laughing.

 "How casual is that, Grant?" I would say you are "head-over-heels "in love!" "Now, I'm going to tease you, just to see how in love you are. How big is that diamond you bought on that ring? I know you can't judge love by the size of a diamond, but I just want to know how deep you are in? Grant really started laughing.

"Patsy, Patsy, my little sister Patsy!" "Well, I would say three carats deep with two diamonds on each side and the perfect sized ring for her left-hand 4th ring finger." Patsy still giggling said.

"I would say that is pretty deep! Have you asked her yet?"

Grant sat back down in the kitchen chair.

"Well, I plan on taking her out to dinner tonight and asking her." Patsy put the cell phone to the other ear. "I am so happy for you Grant!" "I am looking forward to being an Aunt, or Auntie Patsy."

Grant took a sip of water and almost spit it out from the bottle." In the best John Wayne voice he said, "Whoa, take it easy there, Pilgrim!" "Pasty started laughing." "Okay bro, I will be there at your wedding then." Grant heard a knock at the door. "Hey Sis I hate to cut you short, but someone is at the door!" "Love you, talk to you again soon." "Okay, Grant, love you too!" "Take care!

Grant opened the door. Rose stood there looking at him with a Alice in Wonderland, Chemise smile. "I know you said that you were going to be super busy, but I just wanted to stop by and let you know. "I got the job!" "I got the job at *The Diamond Club Casino* working for Ed Johnson, General Manager, as his Administration Assistant!" "I start on Monday!" Grant picked her up and spun her around. "I am so happy for you Rose!"

Grant put her down and smiled at huge smile. "I think it is time to go celebrate tonight, my dear!" Rose looked at Grant.

"Are you sure?" "I thought you were super busy. Grant cocked his head to the right and looked at Rose.

"I am good Rose. Let's go celebrate! I know you have a dress that is a little more formal for a nice dinner at a nice restaurant in the bedroom closet." Grant looked at Rose. Rose winked at him.

"I am sure I can dig one out of the closet you bought me." Grant looked at her and smiled.

 "I'll take a quick shower, while you decide what you want to wear and grabbed his dark blue jacket out of the closet." "It was his favorite jacket that had several inside jacket pockets."

 Grant took a shower then dressed, while Rose took her shower. He proceeded to the living room and poured himself a drink. He put on a light blue dress shirt with a pair of cuffs his dad would wear. He took the three boxes from the small bag and put something in each one of them. The smallest box had "the engagement ring."

He put the dark blue jacket on. He tucked each of the boxes in the inside pockets and looked in the bedroom closet glass mirror. The jacket looked fine. Nothing was bulging. He heard Rose getting out the shower.

He finished dressing and took the jacket off and went to the living room, draped the jacket over a chair and poured another whiskey and coke. He took a sip and thought about Patsy and her phone call to him. He was happy for his sister. They had been through a lot together and he only wanted the best for her.

He picked up his cell phone and made dinner reservations and then called Ben. Rose came down the hallway wearing a beautiful A-line Princess Sweetheart red velvet long dress with a slit on the left leg up to her lower thigh.

 It had black somewhat big embroidered black roses on the bottom half knee area down of the red velvet dress. Her hair was high up on her head with French curls all over with pearl bobby bins all around it with some falling on her back. She put her leg out of the dress and smiled. She was wearing black velvet sandals with a strap around the ankle holding a black velvet clutch purse with small pearls on it. She looked stunning!

Rose put one hand on her hip, while doing a pivot turn. "You like, Mr. Grant?" Grant stood there with his mouth agape. "Do I like?"

"Wow, you look incredible, Rose!" He stood standing from afar looking at her beauty. He was amazed. He felt a rush of uncontrollable emotion come over him. He knew then at that moment, looking at his Beautiful Rose. She was the one! She was his soul-mate for life.

He walked over, put his hands around her waist and pulled her close so he could look deep within her eyes. His face relaxed and with all his sincerity he said. "I love you Rose." She looked into his eyes and she knew he was sincere and softly said.

"I love you too Grant." Grant smiled and took her hand. Grant bent down and gave her a long French kiss. He looked into her teary eyes and then squeezed her hand.

"Let's go celebrate!"

Grant picked up his dark blue jacket carefully. "I've made reservations at the *"Bonjour Belle Femme Restaurant."* (French for: *"Hello Pretty Lady"*). All the tables in the restaurant had white linen table cloths with white napkins and a small candle and small vase with a red rose in it. Grant knew the restaurant. It was a romantic French restaurant he had had dinner with one of his clients. Grant looked around the restaurant. He had reserved a seat on the patio near an iron gate that circled the patio. It had small white lights around it with four chairs. It was 8:00 p.m. and the sun was setting in Las Vegas.

The Hostess took them both through the restaurant to their seats on the patio. Grant pulled out the chair and then sat

across from Rose. The waiter came by and handed Grant
and Rose a Wine Menu.

Grant looked at the Wine Menu and looked at Rose. "Do
you mind Rose if I make the selection." She smiled at
Grant. As she already knew and Grant did too, she was not
any kind of a wine connoisseur' at all. "Yes, please do."

Grant gave the Wine Menu back to the waiter and said. "I
think we will have the *2014 Duck horn Vineyards – The
Discussion Napa Valley Red Wine*." The waiter wrote
down the Wine order on his tablet and looked at Grant.
"Very well, sir and made a small bow to Rose, "my lady"
and walked off. Rose looked at Grant, got up and said,
excuse me while I use the lady's room.

Grant stood up and watched her go. Then he quickly took
out the boxes from his coat jacket and put them on the left-
hand side of his chair, moving slightly to the right to allow
room for them. He put them in order. The largest box first,
second largest box second and smallest box last.

Rose came back with a fresh red gloss and put her clutch in
her lap. The waiter came, opened the bottle of red win and
poured Grant a small amount of wine for Grant smell and
taste. He looked up at the waiter. "Very good." The
waiter poured the wine. Grant raised his glass and they
both clicked their wine glasses. "To a wonderful evening
with a beautiful lady!" Cheers!

Grant leaned back looking at Rose amusingly. So, tell me
about your interview with Ed Johnson at *The Diamond
Club Casino*. Rose took another sip of wine and began

telling Grant all about the interview. He liked watching her eyes twinkle with excitement. She was so child-like, innocent and enchanting in her own womanly way.

 He loved that about her. When she finished, she asked him how his Audit was going with *The Diamond Club Casino*. Grant took a sip of wine and looked at her. "I see some snags in the financial earning statements, I'll need to discuss with Ed, but really "that's pretty normal" in audits."

Grant felt the three boxes next to his leg on the chair. He picked up the large box and put it on the table. It was silver foiled with a bow on top. "This is for you Rose." She looked at the silver wrapped box and then she looked up at Grant. "Really?"

Rose looked at the box on the table, a present for me?" He smiled and looked at her. "Open it!" Rose took the box and opened it and looked inside. There was a small heart shaped necklace with small diamonds around it on a sterling silver chain.

She held it in her hands, looking at it and then looked at Grant. "It's beautiful!" Grant immediately got up and fastened it around her neck and sat back down across from her.

Grant took a sip of his wine and put the glass back down on the table and looked at Rose. "It was my mothers." It was a present my dad gave to her for their 25th wedding anniversary.

Rose touched the necklace with her hand. "It is beautiful Grant!" Grant felt for the second largest box and put it on the table. Rose looked at him. "No, you didn't." "This is way too much!" Grant took another sip of his wine and looked at her. "Nothing is too much for my beautiful Rose." "Open it!"

Rose took the box and opened it. She looked inside. There were two small heart shaped diamond ear rings. She put her hand to her mouth and gasped! "Oh, Grant this is too much!"

She got up and went over to Grant and gave him a big kiss on the lips and then went back to her chair and sat down. She took out the ear rings she was wearing and put the heart shaped ear rings on. Grant smiled.

"You like?" Rose smiled back. "I love them!" Grant smiled. "They were also my mothers." "My Dad gave them to her on their 25th wedding anniversary." Rose smiled at Grant.

"Thank you, Grant. They are lovely. I guess we never talked about your parents." Rose took a sip of wine and looked at Grant. "What are they doing now?"

There was commotion and loud talking coming towards their table. They both looked up and saw Ben and Rebecca came waltzing casually towards them. Grant felt for the small box and quickly put the box in his left-side pocket. Rose was too busy talking with Rebecca to see what he was doing.

Grant stood up and shook Ben's hand. Rose got up and
took both of Rebecca's hands in hers and gave her a kiss on
both cheeks. Rebecca looked at Rose up and down. "You
look marvelous dear!" Rose smiled, "thank you!"

"And you do too my dear in that fabulous green dress."

Grant pointed to his chair, hey Ben you sit here and
Rebecca you sit on the other side of Ben here." "Rose and I
will sit on the outside".

 "Rose, do you mind?" "No, let's do it."

Ben took the inside chair and Grant took the outside chair.

Rebecca took the inside chair and Rose took the outside
chair. They both were facing the girls across the table.
The waiter came back to the table. Grant got up and looked
at him. "Please bring another bottle of *2014 Duck horn
Vineyards – The Discussion Napa Valley Red Wine."* Grant
got up from his chair and smiled, "Excuse me a moment,
I'll be right back."

The waiter bowed, left and then brought another bottle *of
2014 Duck horn Vineyards – The Discussion Napa Valley
Red Wine*, along with two more wine glasses and poured
each a glass of wine. Grant came back. Standing he took
his wine glass. They all stood up and raised their wine
glasses. "Cheers to Rose and her new job!" Grant then
turned to Rebecca and bowed and said, "To Rebecca and
her new job! Cheers!" They all clinked their wine glasses
together.

As Rose sat down and put her wine glass on the table, she
felt something touch her finger. She looked down around
the stem of the glass. There was something shiny tied with
a small pink ribbon. Grant amusingly looked at Rose who
was studying her wine glass. Ben and Rebecca were
looking at her too with big smiles.

Rose picked up her wine glass and looked at it. There was
something hanging from a small pink ribbon on the stem of
the wine glass.

It was a ring, a beautiful ring, hanging from the stem of her
wine glass. Dangling, sparkling with brilliant colors of the
rainbow hanging around a small pink ribbon from her wine
glass.

Grant stood up. "Here let me help you with that." He took
the wine glass and then took the ring off the small pink
ribbon and knelt down in front of Rose on one knee holding
the ring out to her. "Will you marry me, Rose?" "Will you
marry me Ms. Rose Davis?" Rose put her hands over her
mouth and tears began to roll down her cheeks. Rebecca
looked at Rose and smiled with tears in her eyes.

Ben watched his best friend proposing to Rose on one knee.
Rose wiped her tears away and put her hand out to Grant to
put the ring on.

"Yes!" "Yes! "Of course, I will marry you!"

Grant looked into Roses eyes. He knew. He knew. She
was the one. He took Rose's left hand and put the ring on.
Grant stood up and took her hands in his hands. Rose took

her hand away and stared at the ring on her hand. She thought in the back of her mind.

"Wow! "This looks like just like the ring I tried on today in the jewelry shop?" She looked at more closely. "No, it can't be." She held the ring up again and looked at it one more time. She didn't care! "It was beautiful! Rose put both hands to her heart and then looked at the ring again and then looked at Grant.

"Oh Grant, it is truly beautiful!" Rose put her arms around Grant's neck.   Grant picked Rose up, spun her around and gave her a long French kiss.

Everyone in the restaurant stood up, applauding, shouting *"Fabuleux!" "Fabuleux!"* (French for: Fabulous!). Grant's mind ringed out again, **"What plays in Vegas, stays in Vegas!"** *Grant's heart skipped a beat. He was truly happy. And, his beautiful Rose was his! "All his!"*
Chapter 41– *The Diamond Club Casino* – "What You don't See, You, don't Know!"

Dan arrived early the next morning. He got in the golf cart and made his way around the parking garage structures. He wiped his forehead. It was going to be a hot one! He radioed Jimmy. "Hey Jimmy, where are you? I'm on the golf cart now. I'm coming to pick you up."

 Jimmy radioed back to Dan. "I'm on the sixth level parking garage structure." "I've got to get some cleaning supplies out of the 6th floor garage storage unit." "Come pick me up!" Dan circled the parking structures, "Okay, I'm on my way, over and out!" Jimmy turned on the light. "Dammit Dan!" he thought. The lighting was still low and dim in the storage unit. Dan had not replaced the light bulb. He walked all the way back to the left side of the storage unit. He heard some kind of noise, chirping, in the back. He reached down to pick up some cleaning supplies and felt a pinch on his arm. He looked at the thin small tear on his shirt arm. He walked back and turned off the light and locked the storage unit.

Dan pulled up on the golf cart. "Got everything?" Jimmy looked at him. "Dam light bulb is still not fixed in that storage unit!" "You can barely see in there!" "I snagged my shirt on a nail or something in there!" Dan started laughing.

"Is the boogieman still out to get you?" Jimmy looked at his sleeve again. It had a slight cut in it. Then he looked down at his hand. There was a small trail of blood running down his arm to his hand. He took a rag from the back of the golf cart and wiped the dripping blood on his hand. He looked at his hand again. He didn't see any more blood. He threw the rag in the back of the golf cart.

Jimmy looked at Dan. "Hey, I thought we could go eat a Monster Burger with French Fries today! Dan spun the golf cart around to the lower garage structure level. Dan looked at Jimmy and smiled "I'm in!" He started laughing out loud again and thought, *The boogieman got him again!"* **"What plays in Vegas, stays in Vegas!"**

THE END